FAR FROM HOME

BOOK 1

PAUL BOYCE

authorHOUSE®

AuthorHouse™
1663 Liberty Drive
Bloomington, IN 47403
www.authorhouse.com
Phone: 833-262-8899

Published by AuthorHouse 12/03/2020

ISBN: 978-1-6655-1028-8 (sc)
ISBN: 978-1-6655-1027-1 (hc)
ISBN: 978-1-6655-1035-6 (e)

Library of Congress Control Number: 2020924278

Print information available on the last page.

Also by Paul Boyce:

Black Harlequin   (currently under re-editing)

My sincere thanks and appreciation...

... goes to my lovely wife Jane who has had to tolerate my periods of silence, no doubt glad of it at times, and many late nights while I tap away on my keyboard. Without her encouragement and support I might never have inflicted this publication on an unsuspecting public.

... goes to the team at AuthorHouse publishers who, with their insistence, made me realise that I can achieve what I had considered a challenge too far, in spite of being technologically naïve, increasingly disabled and relatively poor.

... goes to other members of my family: Being a 'very, very old man' (according to Max, my grandson – careful young man, you may find yourself disinherited!) and admitting to being cantankerous and impatient old git when things don't go according to plan, my disability has to live with me, not me with it.

PROLOGUE

"SO, MY FRIEND, ye ask me who is this young elf of whom tales are being told in this peaceful place? If ye buy me a cool mug o' mead for I have a king's thirst upon me on this hot day, we shall sit here awhile and I shall take delight in telling you a little of this most colourful of elves. If the luck of the Lady Neilea, the Lady of Serendipity, is with us then he will be in here shortly. Well, where to begin? For a start, he is young. Barely eighty years of age. Thou hast the face of bewilderment! Does this fact surprise thee? Nay? Nor should it by the great gods! As aforesaid, he is a princeling elf of a high and noble race, from the ancient but troubled realm of Faerhome, the race of High Elves who live long indeed. And him being uncommon tall for all that, having been also blessed by Tambarhal, the Deity of all things considered normal in nature and, by the natural intervention of his parents of course, endowed with a wiry but muscular and athletic physique. There! Look yonder, he enters – aha! And with an entourage of young elves and human lads and of course, the flock of maidens! Look at him! Being broad-shouldered - which is also unusual for an elf – dost thou not agree? Aye, but then many years of swinging blades and shooting arrows will do that to a warrior. Oh, has this been aforementioned by me yet? Nay? Aye indeed; there walks a proud warrior of growing ability and some notoriety already in one so young. A leader of a successful warband at that! And with many an orc ear to his credit! But how might thou recognise him, dear traveller? There - take a look at him again – over there, yonder, by the pillar, surrounded by those panting maidens as usual – hah! Observe his features if thou hast a care to! His typically long elven face is tanned and extraordinarily handsome, thou must surely agree. Aye, that is so! His hair is golden and very long but with those side braids such as a dwarf may be partial to; unlike other elves he doesn't tie his hair back except for when he is hunting goblins and those other despicable creatures of the wooded hills, caverns and valleys. His agility is legendary amongst his peers and many young elves and men aspire to be like him; they emulate him and swagger hither and yon but they do not have his flair and self-assuredness. It is said that his father does not consider him to be the best role-model for the youth, however. Silmar is wont to be flirtatious with the girls and a terrible show-off and it sets his father in a terrible lather at times. There, observe thou? He does juggling tricks with the pretty little dark-haired maiden's bauble! The back of his hand lightly presses her plump breast as he shows his dexterity, and she laughs! Aye, indeed, how they all laugh but she will be bedded before the day wanes. Mark thee my words well. Oh, were I but a score of years younger and my hair not quite so grey..."

Crystelle Brightblade, Travelling Bard
Writer of the "Freemen of Carrick Cliffs"
Town of Refuge in the Home Territories
World of Amaehome
Year of the Brown Bear

PART 1

THE GATHERING

CHAPTER 1

YAZAMA JIUTARÔ (RONIN)

JAPAN IN THE YEAR 1701

I, YAZAMA JIUTARÔ, Samurai warrior in the service of the *daimyo* Lord Asano Takumi no Kami tell this story in the hope that it offers inspiration to you, my students. It tells of hierarchical injustice that resulted in the enforced death of my honourable master. But also of the very patient and calculated revenge by his forty-seven Samurai retainers, of which I am proud to be one, I shall tell later. Be patient for much adventure occurred between these two tales, which I insist are true, and these shall shortly be recounted in the tale to be told by others and no doubt in song. But where?

Know only that the core of this tale is that these forty-seven *ronin* (ah! You ask the meaning of this term? Masterless Samurai - literally meaning *wave men!* That is what we were to become) fully knew that their plan of revenge would certainly result in the deaths of every one of us and at *our* own hands. However, know also that the code of the Samurai revolves around the sense of honour, duty and sacrifice in order to achieve a higher end.

April, the month of late-winter at the Asano *Han* in the town of Ako in the Harima province of Japan was usually cold and windy with knee-deep snow. This year, 1701, was different. Instead of the wintry conditions, there had been two weeks of torrential rain which had washed away the deep blanket of snow that had covered the forests and rice-fields in the area. At this time however, I was too overwhelmed with my duties to be bothered by the weather.

Traditionally at this time the Han's *Ryū*, or training school, took on a batch of students who aspired to be, or rather their fathers aspired them to be, future Samurai warriors. Each year, training was offered to eight boys aged eight years but they would, if found to have the necessary determination to succeed, take eight to ten years to become competent to bear the coveted *Katana*. In reality, only one student, two on a rare occasion, would achieve this remarkable feat. Our captain and principal counsellor, Oishi Kuranosuké, would oversee the progress of the training; it would be two years before the students even placed their hands on the *bokken*, the bamboo practice sword. By this time, the number of students would have diminished to four.

At thirty-four years of age, our esteemed master, Asano of the once influential Naganori family, was young to inherit a *daimyo*, or estate, such as this. The value of a *Han* is measured in *koku*, that is the amount of rice necessary to sustain one man for a year. A *Han* of a very wealthy warlord, such as the revered Tokugawa Shogun, could be as great as half a million *koku*, that of the Asano *Han* was a mere fifty-five thousand. To protect his Han, Asano-san had a retinue including forty-seven Samurai warriors. I, Yazama Jiutarô, am proud to be one of these men. Many of us, though sadly not I, have experience in battle. I am yet to use my sword in the defence of my master. When my time comes I hope to die with honour. I would dearly wish for my master and fellow warriors to speak in the future with pride of my own courage in the face of the enemies of my master.

It was before dawn one Sunday morning that I was summoned to speak with Oishi-san. Further to being our leader, he was the adviser and counsellor to our revered master. I stepped onto his porch and removed my swords from my obi, the large blue sash around my waist, and placed them to the side of the doorway. I removed my dusty sandals then adopted the customary *Za-rei* kneeling position, rapped on the door, announced myself formally and waited. A minute later the door slid to the side and Oishi-San was similarly kneeling on the other side.

We bowed to each other; Oishi-San had a beaming smile this day, one that the students never saw. He had been given a nick-name by students some years earlier - *the man who never smiles*. I think he rather liked that and, to preserve the dignified stern image, he always took care not to show a smile in front of the students.

To look at, he was tall, though a little shorter than I, and broad-shouldered. He carried scars on his face, one from the centre of his left eyebrow to the bottom of his left ear, which gave his face an almost lopsided appearance. I have seen students blanch as his gaze passed across them, just as mine did some years ago when I was a young student. His prowess with the katana was legendary. Unusually for these times, he encouraged the use of the *yumi* asymetrical bow and its arrows with us Samurai. This has proven to be an advantage with me – it may sound like I am boasting but I have, I like to think, a competency with this weapon that has impressed my captain. In no way though, can I begin to match the bow-skill of Oishi-san – I have seen him on horseback, at full gallop, put three arrows into a straw figure at one hundred paces in as much time as it takes to count to ten. I can only achieve this at the canter. I will better myself in time. It is only recently that I discovered the trick of success in this art – to release my bow-string as the horse's hooves are all off the ground; that is when there is a pause in the jolting.

"Yazama-san," he began. "Come in, leave your swords inside my door and make yourself comfortable here. Partake of tea."

An honour indeed and for only the second time. I settled down onto a cushion on the *tatami* mat while Oishi-San sat down on the *futon*. Like me, he was wearing a thick kimono with a dark-blue *obi* about his waist. He carried no weapons when in his own house but I could see they were within arm's reach. No Samurai would have his weapons more than a couple of paces away from him. I had made every effort since achieving my manhood to emulate this man, taking every opportunity to hone my fitness and stamina just as I know he did every single day.

Oishi-San ordered tea from his housemaid. I knew that he would make this a formal occasion.

"You have a rather important day today, young warrior. Have you prepared your presentation?"

"I have, Oishi-San."

"We are pleased that you have volunteered to give the opening demonstration and speech to the new students, I look forward to your katana display in the dojo. Make sure you keep it short enough to whet their appetites."

The '*we*' signified that he had spoken with our master. I sat up straight and squared my shoulders.

"I shall, Oishi-San."

"I have some news that I shall speak to all Samurai about during the morning. As you will be occupied with the introductory presentation, I shall briefly tell you of it now. Our honoured master has been given a special task for the court of the *Mikado*, Tokugawa Tsunayoshi."

I immediately focussed; Tokugawa was the supreme military dictator, a member of the ruling class and a man of high nobility. This could contribute greatly to raising the status at court of our master.

The tea arrived and Oishi-san carried out the formal serving of it.

He continued with his dialogue. "I am sure that you know of Kira Kotsuké no Suké – a warlord of greater seniority than Asano and a man greedy of money and prominence. It is no secret however, that he has a coarse manner at times, but he has the ear of the Dog Shogun at Yedo himself."

I confirmed my knowledge of this man and am sure that my face would have betrayed my dislike of his reputation. For the purpose of etiquette though, I said nothing of it.

"Well, Kira Kotsuké no Suké has been commissioned to entertain envoys of the emperor at the Kyoto court. Our esteemed master has been summoned to assist in order to get instruction from him and thus avoid any errors of etiquette."

"Oishi-San," I said, "with respect, what effect on our duties will this have?"

"I, together with thirty of our Samurai, will accompany our master to Kira-San's mansion and then onto the court of Tokugawa Tsunayoshi. I would like you to come with us. We leave tomorrow. Make your preparations and pack what you need to sustain you for the journey there and back, probably about fifteen to twenty days in all."

I was so happy at this time. If I knew of the events which were to unfold perhaps I would have been better prepared than I was, perhaps we all would have been.

"Yazama-San, I shall detain you no longer, this is an important day for you, I shall be in attendance but please, do not let it affect your presentation."

With that, we gave the formal bow, standing this time. I collected my weapons, bowed again at Oishi-San's door and returned to the *dojo*, the practice hall. I had a nervous feeling in my stomach; this would be the first time that I would stand in front of students and give them formal presentation. I must be firm and assertive – how would Oishi-San do this?

I arrived at the *dojo*. This hall was large, probably measuring forty paces by thirty although I had never measured it. The practice area covered much of the floor of the dojo although there was seating area down one side. In the centre of this seating area was a raised dais with a low seat mounted on top of it – this would be for our captain, the senior teacher. On the practice area, on the opposite side away from the high seat, I had placed a man-sized straw dummy supported on a wooden frame. The students had already arrived and were kneeling in line at one end of the practice area. They were fidgeting, laughing and poking each other.

I dimly remembered my first day as a student.

"Silence!" I roared sharply, just as my teacher had done then. The effect was wonderful, I had total control.

I modulated my voice so they would have to remain quiet in order to hear my words.

"You are not here to play. If you wish to play then return to your homes now, otherwise you will give full attention to your studies. This way, one or two of you may become a Samurai."

I paused to let this information sink in as I took up a formal kneeling position in front of and facing the students.

I called the formal command to bow.

The dojo was now quiet except for a low rustle noise from the end of the hall behind me.

I remembered that I had omitted to introduce myself. "I am Yazama Jiutarô. From this moment you shall address me as *Sensei* but only when invited to speak."

I turned to face the straw dummy. Bringing my right foot forward I leaned forward with my weight onto it and brought my right hand in an exaggerated swing to the grip of my katana. I then swept myself up onto my feet and withdrew my blade. Swinging the sword in the double-slash butterfly stroke, I removed all four limbs from the straw dummy. I then executed the upward left-to-right diagonal with one hand, the swordsman's second most difficult stroke, which sliced the dummy into two pieces from right rib cage to left shoulder. Re-sheathing the sword with a flourish, I returned to the kneeling position. The whole demonstration had taken no more than three heartbeats.

The faces on the students were worth a purse full of gold.

"If you wish to be a Samurai, an elite warrior, you must abandon play and childish behaviour; you must embrace discipline – self discipline. Is that clear?"

The students gave anxious looks to each other. I raised my voice once more. "Is that clear?"

"Hai!" came their anxious response.

"In future, you will answer *Hai, Sensei* to all teachers. Is that clear?"

"Hai, Sensei!" they responded.

"Better," I said, softly again. "You will at all times show respect and courtesy to teachers and all Samurai here at this *han*. Is that clear?"

"Hai, Sensei!"

"At no time shall you make eye contact with the Master of this han, His Excellency Asano Takumi no Kami. You shall bow deeply until he has passed by. Is that clear?"

"Hai, Sensei!"

"It is expected that at all times you will show respect to each other. It takes anyone courage to learn the arts that you will achieve. Petty squabbles and bullying between yourselves and with other students will not be tolerated. Is that clear?"

"Hai, Sensei!"

"You will obey your teachers in every task given to you; it is for your advantage and betterment. Is that clear?"

"Hai, Sensei!"

"Good," I replied. I felt that now they knew where they stood, it was time to ease off slightly.

"Your training will take some years, I am sure you are aware of this. You will be expected to fetch and carry, wash and clean, exercise daily and learn from everything you do. These duties are designed to develop your abilities and attitudes. Do not become disheartened. I was where you are now not so many years ago. Every Samurai here today has been where you are now. Some of these Samurai are heroes who have already proven themselves in war and battle."

I paused for a moment and observed as they gave each other looks then returned their gaze back to me. I could hear a soft noise from the gallery at the end of the dojo but chose to ignore it.

"Do not expect to be wielding swords and other weapons in the near future, you will not be swinging katanas for a long time to come. This will be the last time you step on this practice area for a long time, unless you are wielding a cleaning cloth, so make the most of it. You will be assigned a senior student who will act as counsellor for you. If you have problems of any kind, fears, difficulties, illness or anything else, do not hesitate to speak with him. You will find him a source of inspiration as well as advice. This person will make himself known to you later this morning."

I paused once again as their young faces looked towards me with bewilderment. "I shall speak to you of the *bushido* code," I continued. "Can anyone tell me of the meaning of *bushido?*"

One student nervously raised his hand. I pointed at him to answer.

"S-Sensei, it m-means the w-way of the warrior," he stammered.

"Hai, well answered," I replied. "The way of the warrior commands a man's entire being without concession, it demands *total* loyalty, courage and etiquette, inspires inner dedication and outer composure without equal. You will learn that it is more sentiment than a belief. I can tell you that writings about *bushido* over the last few centuries are found more in poems by countless Samurai than in books of learning. Read these poems, they will all have the same theme: the purpose of a Samurai's life is death – to die properly at the proper time."

The mouths of the students were hanging open, I continued with my speech.

"Having spent his boyhood training to die in the right way, a Samurai will spend his manhood waiting to die at the right moment. Take heed, this is the Samurai spirit – knowing when and how to die. Not only does the Samurai have no fear of death, he considers it his sacred moment of honour. If cheated of the honour of dying for his lord in combat, the he will receive the honour of performing his own death. For him, life and death are not two things but one. And this contradiction is the strength and character of the Samurai."

I could sense that the young students had some difficulty in fully understanding the terminology of what I was explaining but I knew that in time they would come to comprehend and accept the bushido code, provided that they managed to continue with their training. I slowly and reverently withdrew my katana, in its sheath, from my obi. Holding it horizontally in two hands in front of me, I continued with my dialogue.

"I have one or two final things to discuss with you. Understand that the soul of Nippon, our sacred land, is the Samurai and the soul of the Samurai is the katana. To the Samurai, failure only occurs when the swordsman fails the sword, because the sword shall never fail the swordsman. A man's will and a man's act must be one, thus sword and swordsman must be one."

I allowed my rather clever observations, as I thought them to be, to sink into the minds of the students.

"Does anybody have any questions for me?"

A couple of hands were raised. I gestured to one student. "Speak!"

"Sensei, why is the ritual act of suicide carried out on the belly?" This one spoke with self-assuredness.

"This is to release the soul, which followers of Buddhism say resides in the belly. It is said that it is why Buddha has such a large belly!" This brought one or two low chuckles from the students.

"This now concludes my talk with you. *Ja-mata*, I shall see you soon."

I concluded with a formal kneeling bow and left the training area. Yoshida Chiuzayémon, a good friend of mine with a couple of years more experience than I, was ready to take over the teaching from me.

"Good sword-play, my friend," he commented with a grin. "Pity about your ugly face though!"

"This face will make the maidens swoon with delight one day," I replied.

"With pity, more likely." We both laughed.

I stepped out of the dojo into the cold, damp air. Oishi Kuranosuké was there waiting for me. I bowed deeply to him and he returned the compliment.

"I witnessed all of the presentation, including the speech. Don't be so hard on them, they are only young. Well done though Yazama-San, I shall make a teacher of you yet!"

"I am grateful for the opportunity, Oishi-San," I replied.

"Showing off a bit with your sword demonstration, weren't you?" he commented. "Your second stroke was nicely done but I do not approve of showing a single-handed technique to students as young as these. They may be inclined to think that this is the norm."

"My apologies, Oishi-San, but it seemed the most expedient way of finishing off the enemy."

A broad grin appeared on Oishi Yoshio's face. "It was good to see that you continue with your sword practice to such good effect," he answered. "You and I will practice together perhaps this afternoon."

"I shall be honoured, Oishi-San." An honour indeed!

At that, he bowed and strode away, I bowed too.

Early next morning, with our master Asano Takuni no Kami in his carriage and Oishi Kuranosuké riding on his horse beside him, together with the thirty other mounted Samurai closely behind, we rode out through the gates of Ako on the long road to Kyoto. This would be a nine-day ride at least and that was assuming the roads had not been damaged by the inclement weather and that adequate accommodation was available in the wayside inns and taverns on the way. We could see that our master was engrossed in reading scrolls and parchments. Our captain reckoned that he was reading up on etiquette. Although this would be a learning experience for him, he would not want to show his ignorance of these matters to an oaf such as Kira Kotsuké no Suké.

We need not have worried unduly. Our group was large enough to deter any wandering bands of *ronin*, those masterless Samurai who, as criminals, were known to wander the highways and rob travellers of weapons and belongings, sometimes even food and clothing. They kept well out of our way. From time to time, some of us would be sent out into the countryside to track down and put an end to these itinerant bands, I was somewhat disappointed that I had yet to be asked to go.

The weather, although cold, stayed quite dry which was a bonus to us Samurai because the *yoroi* armour we were wearing tended to become uncomfortable in the wet. We eventually arrived at Kyoto and, at the suggestion of Kira Kotsuké no Suké, the Samurai were accommodated in the local militia barracks but, fortunately, our master, together with our captain of Samurai, were allowed to stay in the mansion of Kira-San.

That evening, Kira-San held a reception to welcome his visitor, our esteemed master. A deep embarrassment spread across the face of our master when he realised that he had brought no gifts for his host. This was a grave failure of etiquette on the part of our master who should have shown appreciation for the fact that he was to be given instruction by his host in matters of protocol. Kira was deeply offended and proceeded to pour insults on our master.

We later heard that Kamei Sama, another young Lord receiving instruction from Kira, had also neglected to provide a present. He remarked to his own counsellors at a secret conference "Kotsuké no Suké has insulted Takumi no Kami and myself during our service in attendance on the Imperial envoy. This surely is against all decency and I was tempted to kill him on the spot; but I bethought me that if I did such a deed within the precincts of the castle, not only would my own life be forfeit but my family and vassals would be ruined. So I stayed my hand. Still, the life of such a wretch is a sorrow to the people and tomorrow when I go to Court I shall slay him – my mind is made up and I will listen to no remonstrance."

One of Kamei Sama's counsellors was a man of much perception and when he witnessed his lord's enraged manner that it would be useless to dissuade him, he said "Your lordship's words are law – your servant will make all preparations accordingly. And tomorrow, when your lordship goes to Court, if this Kotsuké no Suké should again be insolent, let him be the one to die the death."

However, the counsellor was deeply disturbed at his master's words and as he reflected on them, it occurred to him that since Kotsuké no Suké had a miserly reputation, he would almost certainly be open to a bribe. It would be better to pay any sum of money, no matter how great, rather than his lord and his house and family be ruined.

He collected all the money that he was able and, with his servants carrying it all, he rode off to Kotsuké no Suké's castle and said to the man's retainers "My master, who is now in attendance upon the Imperial envoy, owes much thanks to my Lord Kotsuké no Suké, who has been at so great pains to teach him the proper ceremonies to be observed during the reception of the Imperial envoy. This is but a shabby present which has been sent by him, but he hopes that his lordship will condescend to accept it and commends himself to his lordship's favour."

With these words, he produced a thousand ounces of silver for Kotsuké no Suké and a hundred ounces to be distributed among his retainers. Thus was Kamei Sama's position strengthened in the eyes of Kotsuké no Suké. The counsellor had saved him, his family and his house from ruin.

It was by unhappy circumstance that Oishi Kuranosuké had not been at his master's side – there was nothing he could do. Kira had dismissed our master Asano-San from his castle. He was fortunate enough to find lodgings in a decent tavern.

The following day, Asano-San returned to the mansion to apologise to Kira and to present him with gifts purchased that morning. Kira however, went so far as to rebuke him in public. Although Takumi no Kami ignored the taunts and ridicule and submitted himself patiently to Kotsuké no Suké's orders, this only made Kira despise him more.

Asano-San had that morning directed Oishi-San to assemble the thirty Samurai in front of the tavern. By this time, Kira had left his mansion without our esteemed master for the castle of the 'Dog Shogun'. When word of this latest insult reached Asano-San, he lost his temper and with his mounted Samurai close behind, strode into the court of Tokugawa's castle.

At last, Kotsuké no Suké said haughtily "Here, my Lord of Takumi, the ribbon of my sock has come untied. Be so good as to tie it up for me."

Although burning with rage and humiliation at the affront, Asano-san realised that he was still on duty and was bound to obey. He bent down and tied the ribbon of the sock.

Then, turning away from him, Kotsuké no Suké petulantly exclaimed in front of the envoy "Why, how clumsy you are! You cannot so much as tie up the ribbon of a sock properly! Anyone can see that you are a boor from the country and know nothing of the manners of Yedo."

Kira laughed scornfully and moved towards an inner room.

Our master, Asano Takumi no Kami, now lost his patience – this last insult was more than he could bear. He called at Kotsuké no Suké to stop, drew his wakizashi, the short-sword, and wounded Kira on the forehead. He lunged again but the blade skittered off a pillar. Kira, his face bleeding from what was really a small cut, screamed out "Close the gates!" and ran away.

Asano Takumi no Kami was restrained by an officer, Kajikawa Yosobei, who having seen the affray allowed Kira Kotsuké no Suké time to make good his escape.

The castle gates quickly swung shut separating our master from his Samurai. The Shogun's Samurai, armed with bows, swarmed to the top of the walls. Oishi Yoshio leapt from his horse and hammered on the gates to no avail.

There was a great uproar and much confusion. It was reported to us that Takumi no Kami was disarmed and arrested and confined in one of the palace apartments under the care of the censors.

A council decided that the prisoner was to be given over to the safeguard of a daimyo called Tamura Ukiyo no Daibu, who kept him in his own house. It was soon after decided that as Takumi no Kami had committed an outrage - even to draw a weapon in the presence of the Shogun was a very serious matter – and had attacked another man within the precincts of the palace, he would perform *hara-kiri*, ritual suicide by the stomach-cut. His *Han*, the lands, property and livestock, were to be confiscated thus making his former retainers masterless Samurai, or *ronin*. We would be masterless and humiliated, but worst of all, our master's family would be destitute.

A proclamation to this effect was immediately made from the top of the walls. Our master would be under lock and key and we, his loyal Samurai, were ordered out of the city. Many of us wanted to fight it out with the occupants of the castle but, wisely, Oishi-San warned us that this would not be an honourable act against the Shogun. Kira was the one for which justice should be brought to bear.

"Ride out, my warriors," he commanded. "We shall stop outside of the city and discuss our next course of action."

We followed the road back out of the city and continued for an hour until, after checking for signs of pursuers, we felt we were safe enough.

Oishi Yoshio gathered us about him. His anger and sadness were etched deep in his face.

"There is nothing we can do about our master; he is doomed to an honourable death. It is fortunate that he is in the hands of the Shogun and not Kira, who would delight in tormenting him further."

"Death awaits Kira Kotsuké no Suké!" cried my friend, Yoshida Chiuzayémon.

"Yoshida-San, you are quite correct, but now is not the time. We have more pressing matters to attend to. The Han of our master is about to be descended on by the forces of Kira Yoshinaka. They will take everything of value and may even kill those who defend it. We must ride now, stop only when the horses can take us no longer; keep to the road night and day."

A roar of approval erupted from all thirty of us Samurai. We remounted our horses and began the long, hard ride home. Many of us were puzzled at the reason for the haste and, at the end of the first day's ride Oishi-San once again gathered us round to explain.

"We have left sixteen Samurai to protect our Han. They may not be enough. But the primary reason for our haste is that the Asano Han, in common with many other such daimyo, has issued currency notes. Typically, the gold held in the Asano treasury will only cover sixty percent of the note issue. We must have the notes converted to gold coins at this rate. It will enable us to recover something before the confiscation order descends and, of course, deprive the Shogun of a sizable sum of money. From this, we can go on to arrange our revenge in slow-time. The bastard Kira will be expecting us to attack and will be preparing for it. Let us scavenge what we can and ensure the safety of our dependants at Ako. Time to ride."

Ever the practical and logical thinker, Oishi Yoshio proved to us that day that *bushido* may have its duty but the abacus is never far behind the sword. We continued on the road and hurried back to the castle in Ako, covering the one hundred and thirty leagues in five days.

As we arrived at our master's Han in the late afternoon of the fifth day, we could see that the place was in turmoil. The gates were locked and barricaded and a large number of Samurai bearing the symbol of Kira Yoshinaka were striding about in the town streets. They did not make any attempt to stop us. Our own Samurai we had left behind to protect the Han were glad to see us.

"Thanks be to the gods you have arrived," panted Kano Kiyomasa, Oishi-San's lieutenant who commanded the rear-party. "A pack of Samurai and debt collectors arrived just two hours ago to say our master was dead and you all were scattered. They demand the contents of this Han and will kill any of us who oppose. We have one hour to comply."

Oishi-San wasted no time. "Collect all that is of value and load it into your saddle packs. Then make ready to ride. Meanwhile, I shall negotiate safe passage of the women, children, non-combatants and students. Kira's men would not dare harm them; he would lose face if anything untoward happened."

At the top of the wall, Oishi Yoshio introduced himself and demanded to see the leader of the group of Samurai who were besieging the gate of the Han. Safe passage was guaranteed. The non-combatants were led out, each one being carefully scrutinised and searched for valuables. Oishi Yoshio noticed that two or three of the refugees, mainly the teenage students, were taken to one side.

"Now you *Ronin* may leave," shouted the leader, emphasising the new epithet intentionally in order to demean us. "Take nothing of value with you."

Oishi dropped to the ground and mounted his horse. All of the Samurai were mounted and ready.

Quietly he commanded "Open the back gates, as silently as you can."

A woman's or boy's scream came from outside the front gates of the Han. Oishi's head whipped round towards the sound.

"The faithless bastards, what are they doing? I shall remember that leader – I *shall* receive his death"

The screaming stopped. The back gate was now open. At once we forty-seven *Ronin* broke into a trot, then a canter and then into a full gallop. Screaming could be heard again. After an hour in the fading light, the group stopped. Oishi-san directed that they ride into the hills, share the coins they had collected and decide on their strategy.

It was the early hours of the morning before we found an ideal stopping place. All currency notes were handed to Oishi. The gold would be sufficient to last each member of the group for a considerable period of time.

"I can convert much of this paper money in a city," he assured us. "With luck, if I am quick enough I shall be able to do it before news of the confiscation of the Han becomes general knowledge. We shall scatter. Discard your armour; it will only point you out for who you are. Take service with other daimyos if necessary, or become merchants, teachers or craftsmen. I suggest we give the matter time to settle down and meet in the very barracks where we stayed, in Kyoto, on mid-winter's day, not this one coming, but next. I shall use the money to install myself in Kyoto, keep a watch on Kira and start collecting the armour and equipment we need to avenge the treachery that led to the death of our master. Once we have completed our task, there shall be only one course of action left to us: to die with dignity and honour, our duty fulfilled. What say you all?"

As one, we all cried our agreement. Oishi Yoshio placed his hand on each of our shoulders in turn and spoke words of encouragement to us all.

To me he said "Yazama-San, you have learned well, you have a potential to be a legendary warrior. Go with words of appreciation from me. *Sayonara.*"

Within an hour, we had all left the stopping place, each of us making for a place of safety, a haven where we could continue with our learning in secret. I decided that I would make for Kyushu, the main island at the southern end of our country. I had a horse, clothing, my precious weapons: katana, wakizashi and tanto, a considerable amount of money in gold coins and most of all, my courage. I would need more equipment and clothing and probably a pack horse. I had a long journey of probably about three months.

After a week riding west, I turned south to ensure that I put plenty of space between myself and Kyoto.

Eight weeks of riding in all weathers took me to the Straights of Shimonoseki, the barrier of sea between the main island of Honshu and that of Kyushu. I paid a boatman the overpriced sum of five yen for him to take me, my two horses and my equipment across the Straits. He was drunk when I loaded the boat. His wife, a formidable woman with a most unpleasant face, forced his head into a bucket of cold water. The payment was indeed a considerable amount of money; I could have bought a boat for that. I lashed my horses to the boat's side-rail. We cast off into the waters and he pointed the boat to the dark cliffs across the straits.

The weather was worsening and the seas were getting rougher. I tethered my riding horse between the two side-rails at the stern of the boat and was about to do the same with my packhorse when a strong gust of wind whipped the sail at the same time as a wave lifted the bow of the boat. My foot slipped on the wet planks and I crashed to the bottom, falling into unconsciousness.

So there you have it. That is the story of how I became *ronin* – a wave man. But I shall return on the day that has been appointed, to the barracks in Kyoto.

CHAPTER 2

SILMAR THE GOLDEN

YEAR OF THE BROWN BEAR

*T*AMBARHAL'S DAWN, as it was termed by the elves, was passing; that trick of the light, as the sun began its climb towards the horizon in the east, giving the impression that dawn was arriving early. True dawn would begin to appear very soon afterwards. This would be the time that the animals and birds of the forest would abandon some of the caution taken to protect them against the predators of the night. Time to drink from the river's bank and graze in the eaves of the forest before the predators of the day began their hunt. The mountains to the west of the trees held a multitude of predators, some 2-legged, others four-legged, many with even more; some flying – although these vicious predatory monsters were rarely seen during these years of relative peace and prosperity.

As the light slowly grew, the snow-covered tops of the mountains just to the west seemed to glow with a rosy hue while the forest was in relative gloom. The first sign of life was from the song of birds from the wood. After a while a number of deer warily and delicately approached the water's edge, the antlers of the young bucks still stubby at this early time of the year but one magnificently antlered buck led the does. Other beasts timidly came into view while others still watched from within the forest's shadows.

From the cover of the trees, one pair of eyes watched every movement by the riverside in silence, the owner making no sound and no movement. Other pairs of eyes close by were shut, their owners taking their last opportunity for a light sleep – they had been on the move all night.

There was a sudden flurry of movement from the forest not fifty paces away. A hail of arrows arced through the air and buried themselves in and around the most magnificent of the bucks. The stricken animal gave a throaty alarm call and took a few steps into the water before falling in a fountain of spray flecked red with its blood. Three does also fell but one struggled to rise again with an arrow protruding from her neck. All the beasts and birds bolted for the cover of the forest and their panicked movement was heard for many moments until it faded to nothing. Then there was stillness. A short distance away, the sleeping eyes had snapped open but the raised arm of the watcher halted any further movement.

Some minutes passed before the hunters appeared from the forest. They were grotesque to look upon, savage-looking bipeds with short legs, thick arms and foul faces. Their dark faces had large lower jaws from which protruded porcine-like tusks. They were well-armed though; four with crossbows took up a defensive position around the other five bow-men. All had short but heavy scimitars although none had sheaths to put them in. They wore thick leather tabards over which an assortment of armour had been hung. Their coarse guttural language betrayed an aggression which often manifested itself, even amongst themselves.

"Damned *tuskers!*" breathed the watcher from the forest. He made a sweeping signal with his arm to instruct his party to move. They quietly dropped down from the tree branches and crept stealthily through the forest.

The goblins were now quiet as they dragged their prey from the water. They quickly set about removing the antlers, this was looked upon as a prize which would perhaps buy them a human slave, and some fighting broke out among them. A vicious bite from one goblin, larger than the others, settled the argument; he took the antlers for himself. The head was removed and cast into the water – there was little of value there.

Unexpectedly, the faces of the goblins looked up in alarm as a new flurry of arrows flew towards them. Four went down immediately and two others gazed in shock at arrows protruding from their own bodies. The five survivors fumbled for their bows and crossbows but had little opportunity to use them as six grey figures rushed the twenty or so paces from the trees towards them. The goblins were no match for the lithe, fast fighters who confronted them. One by one they were killed until the last, which refused to yield, was finally run through with a longsword. Only one of the attackers had sustained a wound, a long gash which bled profusely until the leader, who had been the watcher, tightly bound it with a clean cloth taken from a belt pouch.

"Watch that wound, it may fester. They do not take care of their weapons as we do," he instructed. "Touch nothing here; let them rot where they lie but chop off their right ears; there will be a bounty for them. The bastards have killed the strongest of this little herd – a damned waste. This herd will take a couple of years to recover before one of the young bucks will doubtless make it strong again."

The others nodded in agreement, their faces grim with anger. They took what meat they would need to sustain them on their two-day journey back home; the remains would provide food for other hungry scavengers. The leader also took the antlers and handed it to one of his companions.

These were High Elves, tall and slim though deceptively strong. Their leader was quite young even for High Elves but when measured in the years of humans, he was older than many of the human elders of the town where he lived. The others however, were younger than he. All the elves wore a grey-green cotton tunic over their chain mail and a similarly-coloured hooded cape to enable them to conceal themselves in trees and scrub-land. The only features that distinguished the leader from his companions were the long golden hair worn loose to well below his shoulders, the others wore their hair of a shorter length and tied back for practicality, and the fact he carried two swords, one long and the other a little shorter. They had very few items that would rattle and give away their presence. Only their arrows were white although these were concealed in quivers worn at the waist for speed of withdrawal. The elven band made almost no sound as they moved across the countryside, keeping their profiles below the skyline or in trees to avoid detection.

They were a hunting party; hobgoblins, goblins and trolls were their game. Their tactics were ambush, hit and run; to destroy the enemy and move away before they could themselves be ambushed. There were many such hunting parties during these times. They were necessary to keep the monstrous beasts under control for they were prolific in their breeding. Towns, villages, settlements and farmsteads close to the mountains were always in fear of attack from bands of goblins. Travellers on the roads were generally under threat from ambush by Trolls. Foolish indeed were the travellers and caravan masters who travelled without a well-armed and experienced escort in this area.

The elves were making progress though. For the last ten years attacks were less frequent. The road between Westron Seaport and Northwald City and the area as far east as Gash on the eastern border were safer although travellers were still inclined to attach themselves to caravans for safety. Adventurers were making a small fortune by hiring themselves out as guards to travelling parties.

The bustling, multi-racial little market town of Refuge, on the western fringes of the great but daunting Highforest, nestled close to the eastern foothills of the Spine Wall Mountains. The town straddled a minor route leading north from the Great East Silk Road and into wild lands towards the Highforest. The road through the region was often plagued by troublesome goblins, a few hobgoblins and occasionally ogres, the most ferocious of the monstrous beings. It had been that way for many, many years, in fact. If nothing else, it had provided a valuable training ground for the young elven warriors of the Refuge militia. They had become skilled in the use of a wide variety of weaponry, in ambush and formation attack techniques and in noiseless movement through both mountainous and forested terrain.

High elves were relative newcomers to the region. A turbulent period spanning some decades had followed the collapse of the elven kingdom of Faerhome a few centuries previously. The elves had dispersed and set up communities in many of the lands throughout the Baylea continent generally sharing townships with other races, including human, Halfling and gnome. Dwarven too, but these were rare occasions as dwarves rarely saw eye to eye with elves and Halflings. A large group of High Elves had settled in Refuge and had integrated into the human society, albeit keeping their culture separated from that of what they considered to be disorderly humans.

The protection and safety of Refuge and the area between Spinewall and the peaks to the west had become the responsibility of the highly disciplined elven population. These days, the little-used supply route leading north through by the Highforest and Refuge region was largely safe, with very few incidents from the marauding monstrous goblins, goblins, ogres and trolls. The most difficult times would be during the late summer when goblins came out of the mountains in search of livestock and, if they were lucky, weapons and slaves from poorly guarded wagon trains. At all times though, elven militia from Refuge offered escorted passage, for a fair price, for travellers through the region as well as a safe haven in Refuge itself in times of rare but serious activity from the goblins.

The day had started with light rain during the early hours of morning but the clouds took their heavy load eastwards. The morning was misty but this would soon burn off to leave a bright warm day. A mounted hunting party came in through the town gates and trotted towards the militia muster square. One member handed a fine set of antlers to his leader who proudly held it high.

A collection of young ladies, elven and human, rushed forward, keen to be the recipient of the prize, not necessarily to be the proud owner of the antlers, but more for the attention of the handsome troop leader.

"I shall decide all in good time," laughed the young elf. Cries of disappointment followed from the flock of girls. It was the same every time he returned and they had not really expected anything different this time.

"Hail Silmar!" was the cry of the townsfolk. His return, as well as that of any other leader who returned with all members of his team, was always welcomed on their return to the town. He sent his injured troop member off to the healer's house; the elf's arm was indeed inflamed and had caused him much pain. The Sergeant at Arms strode out from the militia barracks. Silmar handed him the leather bag of goblin ears.

"Good work. Your report in an hour, Silmar Galadhal. Get yourself and your equipment cleaned up, sort yourself out with a meal from the cook and I want you and your squad on parade at noon. *Move!*"

Silmar Galadhal felt at his most comfortable when wearing tightly-fitting deerskin hose which, it must be said, left little to the imagination of the elven and human maidens in Refuge; it was no surprise that they would try to brush past him in the hope of acquiring a light-handed contact with his muscular buttocks or, for the more daring and perhaps hopeful, with something of a more personal nature. A tightly-knit group of young maidens in the town would swap stories; most of them being just tall tales indeed, of the number of times they had manage to 'accidentally' brush past his most private of areas! Some stories were elevated to description of antics in a hayloft and, on more than one occasion, he had been confronted by a would-be suitor of an aforementioned young lady. At one time, the confrontation involved the furious father of a maiden who, eventually and tearfully, admitted the whole thing had been a just a tall tale made to impress her friends!

But hold! This tale digresses and, perhaps to a reader of sensitive disposition, it may not be to the best of good taste!

To return to the description of his garb then, he also favoured a slightly looser-fitting deerskin shirt over which he wore a grey-green tunic. His sword belt was buckled over this tunic along with another belt to which was fitted his pouches and small packs. Soft light-brown leather boots reached up to just below his knees. He clearly cared much for his attire which was kept in a good state of repair. Apart from being warm in the winter and cool in summer, his clothing assisted him in hiding in forest and plains alike.

On his shoulders he carried an old, shabby and battered, but well-loved, pack. It had also been well-repaired over a number of years for it had once belonged to his father. Inside this he carried his spare clothing, a whetstone, a blanket and his close-woven, waxed, woollen cloak which afforded protection from the wet and cold. Taking up most of the space in his pack and adding much to the weight of it, however, was a corselet of fine chain mail that he liked to wear beneath his tunic when the prospect of battle was likely. Twenty arrows were carefully wrapped in a linen bag and strapped to the outside of the pack. His small pouches carried items of more value; coins, flint and steel, a spoon and knife for eating and an expensive rarity, a bottle of bathing oil, carried on the off-chance that the opportunity for him to bathe (or be bathed!) might arise; in this activity he could be quite fastidious but then he hoped the young maidens might appreciate it! Each of these items was also carefully wrapped in rags to avoid them rattling together when in hiding or waiting in ambush.

Although this young elf gave the impression of a playful and, at times, immature attitude to his learning and fighting skills practice, he actually demonstrated a number of skills which would be of future benefit to him. His rapid progress within the ranks of the militia was in part due to his proficiency with weapons, in particular a double-sword skill which he had learnt over many years from his less-than-patient father and from the militia he had joined when he came of age at his sixtieth birthday. His father never envisaged that the day would come when *he* would be bested in swordplay by the one he considered to be his rather wayward son. It hadn't happened yet but that time was not far away. Skill with blade and bow alone are not sufficient to ensure the value of a warrior. That rapid progress also owed much to his leadership qualities, his knowledge of tactics and his ability to plan a campaign. He treated his team with respect and trained and looked after them well.

As an elfling, Silmar and his friends had dreamt of the day when they would become part of the Refuge militia, the elite fighting force that was sent out into the hills to cull the goblin, troll and ogre numbers. Human warriors were also accepted into the militia ranks and they did indeed make very effective fighters but the elves had qualities of agility, dexterity and acute senses that couldn't be matched by the humans. Men were generally happier when assigned to protect the little town. Once again, Silmar had honed his skills with some other elf-children by practising escape, evasion and creeping up to 'invade' one of their homes. Wooden sticks were their makeshift weapons and bruises and scraped knuckles were their 'battle-wounds'. Furthermore, elves had that advantage of sharp vision in very faint light, an innate ability which developed as they matured. Once he became old enough to train with his father, Silmar quickly developed his incredible agility and his ability to climb rocks, trees and buildings and to hide in trees and undergrowth, moving in silence and, when using his newly-acquired ability to see in almost total darkness. This was one aspect which pleased his father.

"He could climb a fifty-foot mirror!" he would proudly boast. "And with a bow, he cannot be bested by anyone in this town. Why, I have seen him on a bare horseback, at the canter, loose off arrows and hit a pumpkin at forty paces three times out of five!"

Other skills however, displeased his father. Silmar could be a practical joker and a trickster. He had the dexterity to perform sleight-of-hand tricks, he would hide coins and make them reappear, do balancing acts, turn somersaults and juggle apples. He had a rather good singing voice too and would sing and play a reed pipe, often imitating bird calls, mostly for the purpose of entertaining the young ladies – of course! These skills had often gotten him into, and out of, trouble on occasions beyond count.

But, the Baylea realms change, people change too and Silmar was beginning to show signs that maturity was at last setting in. He was never happier than when he was on a patrol leading his hunting party. Everything else he did was just to alleviate the boredom he felt when being back in Refuge. At times, the little market town seemed to be getting smaller, too small and at times constricting, and sometimes he would walk alone into the hills nearby although often with friends or perhaps with a young maiden. The outside world seemed to be beckoning to him. Traders, travellers and adventurers passed through with tales of battles, heroism, fame and riches galore. They spoke of Westron Seaport, the famed City of Magnificence; it wasn't that far off, perhaps a tenday-week on foot, but he had never been there. Many stories he took with a pinch of salt, but some were also of hunger, pain, injury, death of comrades, of wild animals, undead and long, cold and wet nights under trees. These interested him as much as tales of treasure and fame. But then, Refuge was still the centre of his life and he couldn't, or wouldn't, envisage a time when he would leave. He was still tied to the militia and there were words being hinted to him that promotion was possible.

His father watched him closely though and considered his future.

Silmar Galadhal had spent three decades of his youth as a militia cadet developing his skills by tracking and hunting marauders on the mountainous borders of his homeland. The more experienced warriors of the militia would administer the final kill to a troll or orc, the larger of the goblin species. After completing his cadet training, and in the last few years before finally venturing out from his homeland, Silmar gained much experience as a militia member, under instruction, of the town defence. Many years passed before he earned the honour of becoming a member of the hunting party, still more before he earned the distinction of leading one.

At first, his ability in this area was considered by his father, Faramar, as 'disappointing'.

"Teamwork, teamwork, teamwork!" he yelled. "This is essential if the troop is to work together. This is *not* a game! You are *not* a one-man band, Silmar. You will *not* survive on your own, dammit!"

Meanwhile, Silmar had imagined a life of travel, although not necessarily of warfare and battle, of death and destruction. It wasn't that he couldn't use fighting and weapon skills. He was an accomplished swordsman and a more than reasonable bowman. Unusually, he favoured a two-weapon style in hand-to-hand combat having gained expertise through practising hour after hour, day after day and year after year with a longsword in one hand and shortsword in the other. He could hurl a dagger with some accuracy. His ability to move quietly and blend into the shadows was the envy of other young elves. He was very agile, much taken to hiding in ambush within the branches of trees and he coached his party likewise. After all, he had had a good teacher in his father. He had a habit of leading his team much further afield than was advised by his father.

Referred to by the townsfolk of Refuge as *Silmar the Golden* because of his flowing yellow hair, it was his strong, wiry physique and his ice blue eyes that acted as a magnet to young elven maidens, human girls too, who all turned their heads in admiration. His love of poetry and music and his penchant for showing off to these young ladies of the town, was not considered by his father as being in the correct place in Silmar's list of priorities. Faramar was stern at one particular liaison in which Silmar became more than friendly with a young human lady.

"You must *never* become involved with a human woman," he yelled, "not only because they are sometimes unworthy of an elf; I will always consider them inferior as should you. You will no doubt love her and she will love you. She will grow old but you will not. You will see her die while you are still young. You will see your children die of old age before you reach your middle years. And their children too. You will have a life of misery. Similarly, it will be a life of sadness for the woman who will become old and see her husband in the prime of his life. That cannot be fair on you or the woman. Think, damn you! There will be no happiness, only despair. You mark my words well, Silmar." This would be a lesson he would remember for a long time, in the time measured in the years of elves.

His enjoyment of entertainment though, was further enhanced by his ability to demonstrate his sleight-of-hand and to pick pockets or pouches. This also had resulted, more than once, in an irate townsman reporting him to the militia sergeant-at-arms and once being brought before the elven Tribunal of Venerables. On this occasion his exasperated father had used his influence to bail him out of difficulty with payment of restitution and guarantees of good behaviour.

Faramar Galadhal was habitually stern when dealing with his son's indiscretions. He was, after all, a very proud Elven Principal descended from the original House of Galadhal, one of the six minor noble Houses of Faerhome.

"Damn you boy," his father Faramar would shout. "Your tricks will get you into serious trouble one day. You lack self-discipline. When I was your age I was leading my own company of warriors – dammit, I've got the battle scars to prove it!" This was one of a series of oft-repeated phrases, which Silmar had learnt and mouthed in surreptitious synchronisation with his father.

As usual, Silmar's mother tutted and nodded her head in agreement with Faramar. Silmar would listen with rapt attention to the tales from long ago of the beautiful city state of Faerhome, how the gods had warred among themselves in the cataclysmic god-war and the city-state had fallen in the resulting earthquakes. Faerhome was now a ruin inhabited by creatures of foul nature said to have emerged from the depths of the Void. But elves from other places were beginning to turn things around.

Faramar placed his arm around his son's shoulder. "You have achieved much over the years and have made me very proud. But our family status will one day require you to take your place on the Elven Council for the defence of the Refuge region, and beyond."

His father continued. "Before you can be trusted with the responsibility for the lives not only of fellow warriors, you will first need to reprioritise your life, discover your own senses of responsibility and duty and further broaden your experience of life. In short, my boy, you need to grow up!"

Silmar could feel a feeling of uncertainty creeping through him.

Faramar sat down on an exquisitely-carved chair and beckoned Silmar to do the same, but on a small, padded stool. "My son, you need to spread your wings and get some experience of the world around us. There is an old friend of mine, a dwarf, Ralmon the One-Sided, who was once an adventurer and who now runs a Tavern in Westron Seaport. He's got two visitors staying with him. It seems that they seek adventure and are looking either to join a party or for people to join them."

Silmar's jaw dropped and his heart lurched. He now knew what was coming next. His mother's hand went to her mouth and her eyes opened wide in shock and fear for her son.

"Husband!" she gasped. "He is still very young and –"

Silmar meanwhile, could hardly contain his excitement. He leapt to his feet sending the little stool tumbling across the floor. "Father, I didn't think you would ever approve of me leaving the town, let alone leaving you, Mother and the home."

"My son, you've never been able to keep secret your longing to travel. Speak to this Ralmon and these people, but if you do decide to travel with them, ensure they are honourable and of good heart. *Tambarhal* will guide your future decisions providing that you speak to Him at times. Do not go off on your travels without first saying goodbye to your mother and me. I'm afraid you cannot take the weapons and equipment that you train with and bear with you on your patrols; those belong to the militia. I do, though, have something for you that will start you on your journey."

"A dwarf, father?" Silmar asked through his excitement and bewilderment. "When did you become friendly with dwarves?"

"He is no ordinary dwarf," his father explained. "We campaigned together and fought side by side many times."

"Any why One-Sided?" gasped Silmar. "What sort of name is –"

"You will understand when you meet him."

Silmar left his home with mixed emotions. The house now seemed both a sanctuary and a cage. Maldor, an old friend, was distraught when he heard the news.

"My father thinks I am immature and need self-discipline," Silmar told him. "He tells me that the caravan of wagons over there leaves for Westron Seaport within the hour and I'm to be on it."

"No room for another to go with you, I suppose?" The request was half-hearted; Maldor would never leave the town on such a hare-brained scheme, as he was to put it later to other friends.

The young elves clasped forearms. "Travel well Silmar, my dear friend, may *Tambarhal* guide and care for you." The final remark, customary for one who was about to embark on a journey, was very comforting for Silmar.

He left his friend standing in the middle of the street. The sun dial in the square showed the time a half an hour before noon.

"By the gods!" he exclaimed! "My report!"

He rushed to the Barracks and swiftly wrote out his report, a reasonable tally but which would do little to earn him praise. His team was already lined up on the square when he strode out. He positioned himself in front of his patrol and brought them to order.

The Sergeant at Arms marched out of the barracks and up to within one double-pace distance from Silmar.

"To order!" he barked. "Absence will not be tolerated, do you hear me?" Silmar was confused, what was all this about? He had not been tardy.

"Leaving your place of duty without application for leave of absence is a court martial offence," the Sergeant at Arms continued at the team in general. "You can be flogged for less!"

Silmar felt beads of sweat starting to run down his face. All of his team were present; no-one was missing.

"I understand you are about to desert your place of duty, young Galadhal." The Sergeant at Arms was now smiling, a rare sight indeed.

"Under orders from my father, Sergeant," gasped Silmar. The relief he felt was overpowering.

"Sorry to see you go, young 'un. Guess you didn't think anyone else knew about you leaving us but your father spoke to me of this, and the reasons why, the day before yesterday. Can't help but agree with him on that decision. Should make a mature elf of you. And, well, we got together this collection and bought you this."

He brought out a fine dagger from behind his back, removed it from its well-crafted sheath and handed it, hilt first, to Silmar.

The elf took it with trembling hands and tested its weight and balance. The steel of the blade was of very high quality indeed and its hilt was made from ivory; a pea-sized ruby was set into the pommel of the hilt. The dagger, in its engraved leather scabbard, must have cost a lot of money.

He looked from the Sergeant to his patrol. "Sergeant! I can't thank you all as I should. This is beautiful and I shall treasure it for always. It will remind me of my friends that I leave behind when I have times of trouble and loneliness."

"Fall Out!" the Sergeant at Arms commanded. He warmly shook Silmar by the hand and said "I meant it lad, I *will* be sorry to see you go. Over the last year or few you've built yourself up a good team spirit with your squad and they've benefited from it. I'm getting a bit old for this now and my retirement is only a couple of years away; you would have been in line for promotion you know."

"That's not what my father says," moaned Silmar. "He thinks I need self-discipline and experience."

"That's nothing to do with your job, that's your social habits, young 'un. Good luck, travel well and return to us all the better for it. May *Tambarhal* guide and care for you."

Silmar bade his farewells and strolled about the town centre saying more farewells to other friends and more than a few young maidens. He soon ended up in the Tavern by the market square. Being a market day, it was busy inside with many traders and travellers sitting at the tables or standing at the bar. The atmosphere was stifling even though the day was not particularly hot. His eyes smarted at the thick smoke of the pipe-leaf. The noise was loud and somebody was trying to sing in a corner although few were paying much attention. Silmar ordered himself a quart tankard of ale and looked around the taproom at the variety of people. A few curious and analytical eyes looked his way too. He needn't have tried too hard, his bearing and a few small battle scars were testimony to his active life.

After a while, Silmar returned home. He was breathless and excited. "Father, I am now resolved to travel. I have spoken with the wagon master. We leave soon."

"My son, I am already regretting having mentioned the idea to you. Your mother is in tears in the next room. Our blessings go with you but first, take this." He handed his son a small bag.

Silmar opened the bag, surprisingly heavy, to find a large number of gold coins. He had never held in his hand so much money in his life. Also in the bag was a copper disk on a leather thong. He recognised the design on the disk as the symbol of his father's House of Galadhal.

"One hundred and twenty gold crowns and a few silver." He said. "Take this, when you get to your destination, give Ralmon the *One-Sided* my compliments, he will advise you as to which trader will provide you with clothing, weapons, armour and other bits and pieces for you. Choose wisely and listen closely to his advice. Wear the medallion and think of your mother and me from time to time." He then handed his son a sword in a battered scabbard.

"I can't let you go into the world without a sword, Silmar. Take this but when you get to the great city, purchase yourself something better and just sell this in a market. It is an old blade from the militia armoury."

Silmar was unable to speak, being elated and overcome all at the same time.

Faramar hugged his son and continued. "See your mother before you go. Travel well; come back to us safely, my son. May *Tambarhal* guide you and care for you. Send word of your whereabouts when you can."

Half an hour later, with no possessions other than the clothes he stood up in, a few items in his pack and belt-pouch, his precious dagger, sword, coins and his medallion, Silmar left his home and his family.

CHAPTER 3

"*I* *MUST ADMIT, contrary to all our original opinions, she ends her twelve years here as the best new acolyte Priestess of Neilea that I have ever seen. Observe now her confident manner. Others want to be with her, to be like her. The young trainee men follow her rather than those other new priestesses who are possessed with greater beauty. See how she swings her quarterstaff with an effortless grace and a confident efficiency that will afford her great protection in the years to come. She has warmth about her but she has strength of character too. And what dedication! She puts me in mind of another young girl five decades ago; but I did not have her confidence then. And aye, hahaha! Was I not one for the boys, as were you too Helania, as I remember aright? Did I not also carry out the very same experiment? To this day, she is not aware that we know of it! We shall doubtless hear more of her in the years to come if Our Lady of Kismet protects her – as I have no doubt she will. I would pray that she will return here one day. There was little more we could teach her and always she wanted to learn more. I perceive that she will achieve great things and will be powerful one day. Go, our Daughter of Neilea, with the shining protection of Our Lady of Serendipity. You carry Our Lady's favour; I can sense its strength dwelling within her.*"

Simenine Tarathtelle,
Matriarchal High Priestess of the
Temple of Neilea
Year of the Plentiful Harvest

FOR MANY years now, in fact from the age of five years, Taura Windwalker had been studying in the hope of becoming a novitiate priestess of Neilea – the Arcane Scientist, the Goddess of Magical Knowledge and Destiny. It had been hard for Taura and a wrench for her parents too, for her to be given over to the Temple by her family on the insistent say-so of the local Priestesses who claimed to have seen a potential in the little dark-haired girl. Life had been hard for the family. Taura's mother had also been a Priestess of Neilea until a disease had left her partially blind. The offer of their daughter to be brought up and taught at the Temple would ensure that she wouldn't share in the times of hardship and even starvation that constantly threatened.

The weeks of journeying in wet, windy and cold weather from Lopastor to the Temple of Arcane and Divine Learning in Karne were now only a faint memory. The years that followed had been tough at first but they eased noticeably as she grew older and as younger girls, and on the rare occasion boys too, came in as little students to fill the space as older students moved on. She had cried herself to sleep every night for two years. Now, at last, she was trained sufficiently to serve the lands of Baylea in the name of her beloved Goddess.

Apart from her mother, her family were virtually illiterate and had kept progressively less contact with her until it eventually stopped altogether. There was no explanation for it ceasing and they were too far away for her to travel to see them. Having lived near to coastal city of Casparsport in the country of Lopastor, a lawless land of continual upheaval and disquiet, there were any number of reasons why she no longer heard from them. She had vague memories of an ocean and a high rocky promontory upon which stood a tall stone tower that was surrounded by a high stone wall. It was not her family home, she knew, but it was quite close by, but something about the memory disturbed her. Perhaps one day, once her learning was at an end, she would try to find her mother, father and two younger brothers. This mystery of their disappearance from her life plagued her mind for some years until she lost the memories of what they looked like. But now, after lying dormant for so long, the memories, such as they were, resurfaced and became significant once again.

Taura was quite short in stature and, when dressed in a travelling cloak, tended to appear slightly plump. When her cloak was cast off though, her true build was plainer to see. She was stocky and had clearly spent much time in physical exercise. She boasted that she had been able to outrun every other novitiate in the Temple of Learning over a measured mile. Her quarterstaff skills could not be matched by other students either. By the time she was fourteen years of age, she was participating in the town games and was besting the boys of her age with quarterstaff and at wrestling. In fact, by the time she completed her twelve years of studies, she had developed her muscular stature to a point unexpected of a young woman. The senior lecturers had hoped to encourage her to stay on after her studies so that she could teach fitness and the use of a quarterstaff to the newer students. It was not to be, however. She had promised herself that she would travel through the realms of Baylea.

She was not considered particularly beautiful. She didn't even consider herself attractive in any way but to others, she was. Her large brown eyes shone and sparkled, particularly when she smiled and even more so when she laughed. She had full lips and dark eyebrows that only enhanced her appearance. The day before leaving the Temple, she cut short her luxuriant long black hair so that it now barely reached her shoulders; she didn't miss it one bit. Her slightly tanned skin and her nose just a little wide, were not the product of time spent in sunlight and accidents when wrestling. Her lineage could be traced to Qoratt, the *Land of the Burning Sand,* far to the south, where the peoples were of a darker complexion. When a smile broke out on her oval face though, she looked very attractive; she did smile often and laugh at the least excuse. She was not in the least proud of her figure, considering herself to be too wide at the waist and thick in the legs – *apple stampers* she called them, much to the protestations of her friends. She also disliked her breasts; she thought them too large although her male friends insisted that that was a matter of opinion and that to complain about them was like slapping their beloved deity, Neilea, in the face!

In one aspect though, she had excelled. She had worked extremely hard at her studies over the last three years after having shown the signs at an early age that she would one day make a very proficient Priestess of Neilea. She certainly had the favour of The Lady of Serendipity because a promising destiny followed her throughout her years at the Temple. She had been popular with her peer group mainly because of her zest for life and sense of fun.

There had been two instances though, which had got her into trouble and each time they had involved dalliances with young boys in the village. "You have more to lose than they have, you foolish girl!" thundered the Matriarchal High Priestess. "Do you realise that the longer you retain your virginity then the more potent will be your gift of divine magic and prayer spells from Her Gracious Lady!" She bowed her head in reverence at mentioning one of the many titles bestowed on the Goddess of Destiny, Neilea. "All they lose is a spoonful of bodily fluid! You will lose infinitely more! You may be called upon to protect others and heal them. You will be hampered if you lose that other gift. Cogitate on this in your cell until the morning feast."

Try as she might, she couldn't shake the image of a spoon of fluid out of her mind!

Even on that day, Taura had doubts that her magic potency would be depleted were she to lose her virginity, certainly not by a significant measure. She discovered, at the age of fourteen, that a couple of the very few trainee male priests of Neilea had not appeared to lose their powers after she and a few other young novitiate priestesses, at her instigation, had witnessed them shed their seed the evening before – all in the name of research of course, as they convinced each other! As her reward to the boys for taking part in the experiment, she had allowed one of them, tall and handsome but rather spotty, to explore the parts of her upper body beneath her tunic. She had also conducted a little exploration of her own and he gasped as she touched him. She watched with curiosity and then laughed lightly as her hand caused him to shed his seed for his second time! This was her first tactile experience and although exciting, the young man had nervously fumbled and one of his fingernails had scratched her breast next to a sensitive and delicate point – that ended the fortunate lad's reward!

The next couple of incidents were to result in those severe warnings from the Matriarchal High Priestess. She had been accused of having scant regard for the authority of her tutors. Chastened, she dived headlong into her studies and completed her training without further incident - or *without being caught* she would boast but she refused to elaborate and the rest was sheer speculation!

Her studies had taken on a new importance at this stage but as the last days of learning approached, she knew she wanted more. She was not averse to asking questions of her tutors. But she would learn little more here, not now; perhaps later. Certainly not while the breadth and depth of her study would be restricted by the controls imposed by the hierarchy at the Temple.

Now, finally, she would soon be free to pursue her destiny. She decided she would travel west to the great city of Westron Seaport on the Landsdrop Coast.

Perhaps the great libraries here, or those of Norovir in the far-off eastern realm of Cascant, would enable her to peruse the great tomes, scrolls and books of divine magic. But at what price? She had very little money and may need to find work. Meanwhile a wide world continued to beckon her. And she was more than ready to heed its call. But on the morrow, after early prayers and a celebratory dawn feast, she would be presented with her silver holy symbol; she only wished her family could be there to witness the occasion – would they have been proud? She cried herself to sleep that night for the first time in almost ten years.

CHAPTER 4

S ILMAR CAUGHT his breath as the caravan crossed over the high pass on the brow of the hills to the east of the city of Westron Seaport; an amazing sight lay before him. The massive city was spread below but even the description 'massive' seemed inadequate to Silmar. Not even in his wildest imaginations could he ever have visualised the city with the great sea glinting beyond. The caravan master, who had seen all this before, grinned at the expression on the elf's face.

"Impressed, young 'un?"

"By the gods!" Silmar gasped. "How can this enormity support itself? And the ocean! Look – I can see the sea!"

Everyone within earshot laughed at his look of wonderment.

"You wait until you get inside those walls, kid. You've seen sod all yet!"

What walls they were. As far as Silmar could make out, because of a mist, the city was in the shape of slightly more than a semi-circle, with its flat side facing the sea. The sandstone walls were very high with watch-towers topped with wooden turrets at regular intervals. The road before them stretched to the city where it led through a great arched gateway. Even from this distance of maybe two leagues or more, the elf, with his keen eyesight, could only just see that the gates were open and that traffic was entering and leaving through it. Within the city he could see towers, minarets, domes and palaces. Some of the domes were painted, he assumed, in gold and these shone brightly in the misty sunlight.

A huge ditch encircled the walls and the elf was certain that it contained water. A great wooden bridge spanned the moat.

The wagoneer confirmed his thoughts. "Aye, it does that but you wouldn't be wantin' ter fall in cos yer wouldn't drown; it's too thick. Gods know what diseases yer would be gettin' b'cos it's full've shit an' dead things.

Don't be askin' me what dead things b'cos it ain't jus' animals an' stuff, iff'n yer know what I means."

Another sight grabbed his attention. The walls had been built long ago but the city had continued to grow in size since then. It had been only a matter of time before there was no room left to build inside the walls. Many buildings had been erected slightly beyond the moat at first, then spreading outwards further and wider until the city almost doubled in size.

There were sheep pens, pig pens and corrals with cattle, horses and camels outside the city that were, in the main, run by honest dealers, according to the wagon master. Also, there were grain stores and warehouses built of both timber and stone.

"A thousand of your puny towns could hide in this city and still leave room for the gentry to become rich on the pickings," said the wagon master. In his wisdom, he had warned Silmar not to stray too far from centres of activity, not to enter establishments promising the excitement of ladies of ill repute and to get himself properly armed straight away. He warned that a rough sort frequented the dock area, always on the lookout for easy prey, but the city watchmen were generally patrolling.

"City watchmen? Even their watch-dogs move 'round fully armed," the wagoneer japed.

"I have lived not a tenday week's travel from this city and in more than a century of my life I have not seen this – this – oh, this wondrous sight!"

"A century? So you're just a kid, young elf, eh?"

"Aye, but we elves can live up to four hundred and fifty, even five hundred years. I didn't come of age until I was sixty. My father thought I was very immature and sent me to join the militia. I was hunting goblins by the time I was eighty and have been a hunting party leader since I was eighty-five. And he still thinks I'm immature!"

"Ye gods!" cried a wagoneer. "Hey men, we've been travelling with my grandfather!"

Good-natured laughter erupted from the wagon teams. Even Silmar couldn't help but chuckle. But respect was clearly evident on their faces, particularly as they had seen him practising with his weapons on many occasions.

While heading westwards, they had passed many other caravans travelling in an easterly direction, each of them heavily laden with cargoes.

So this was where they had all been travelling from. The caravan continued on its journey and in less than two hours they were approaching the gates. It would soon be evident that many of those living outside the walls did not enjoy the privileges and standards of living of those on the inside. There was much deprivation and squalor among the hovels; beggars lined the road leading towards the gates. The sight of wagoneers wielding whips was enough to keep child beggars from crawling all over the wagons.

The sight and smell of cooking fires, manure, human waste and the squalor around the huts and hovels was an assault on the senses of Silmar, as well as those of the teamsters.

There were other sights however, that were even more distasteful. An area to the right hand side of the road, up against the city wall, had been set aside for criminals to be hung on gibbets and in small, metal cages. There they stayed until long after death and their flesh had been picked clean by carrion birds, only then were the remains removed and cast into the sea. Silmar was appalled at what, to him, seemed like an act of barbarism. Six bodies, one of whom was still alive and appealing for water to children gathered close by, were hanging from beams or in cages. The wagon master observed Silmar's revulsion and explained the reality of the situation.

"You must understand, young Silmar, that these are not just thieves and burglars. These are murderers, rapists, spies, arsonists, child molesters and persistent criminals. There is no room for these bastards in this society. It is not fair on any society to expect them to spend money to keep these criminals in a prison cell and, to be quite frank, their crimes are too severe for them to be trusted to be, er, enlisted into the militia. And this does act as a deterrent to visitors to the city to encourage them to be on their best behaviour. You'll find other areas like this at the North and South gates. And near the quayside, there are gibbets from which hang many pirates and buccaneers. Don't feel sympathy for these pieces of shit, they're not worth it."

Although he could appreciate the Master's point of view, Silmar knew that he would never approve of the practice. The wagons continued to the gates where, after a brief discussion with the gate watch, they made their way into the city. Thus began Silmar's introduction to the life within the mighty city of Westron Seaport.

The road surface inside the city gate was paved or cobbled and very smooth. Here, they encountered a different type of beggar; these were offering trinkets, flowers, fruit and other wares for copper coins.

"Ignore them, boy," gruffly warned the wagon master as he observed Silmar reaching for his money bag. "Encourage one and the other shits will swarm all over us like locusts!"

Silmar's hand dropped away and the stern face of the wagon master and teamsters' whips were sufficient to deter the beggars.

The wagons skirted around an open area with lawns and flowerbeds. Well-dressed couples, families and children were leisurely walking through the park. It seemed to Silmar to be an incongruous sight so close to the poverty outside the gates. He looked about him, at the buildings, homes and palaces and realised that this was indeed a very rich and opulent district of the city. Carriages, with well-dressed passengers attended by liveried servants, being drawn by well cared-for ponies and horses, were becoming a common sight in this area of the city.

After a long while the caravan turned to the left and continued past shops, store houses, inns, taverns, livery stables and blacksmiths, and even a great amphitheatre. The wagon master explained that these arenas were in common use for the enjoyment of the public with displays of martial arts, battle re-enactments, archery, swordsmanship and spear-throwing skills, and of horse-racing.

He went on to explain further. "There are also amphitheatres for the arts such as music, theatrical plays, poetry and comedy. You can watch juggling, sleight of hand and gymnastic skills. They got a few places like that in the city. For a silver piece, you can watch a variety of entertainment all day. Have to watch out for cutpurses and pickpockets though. Get lots of them in the crowds at the arena or amphitheatre."

They eventually arrived at an open square and it was evident that the rich houses and palaces had been left behind and the business classes of peoples were now more commonplace. Broad paved or cobbled streets, with raised walkways at the sides, had been evident in the more opulent centres; they were now trundling along rutted dirt roads strewn with litter, gung, or worse, and seemed to be the best that could be found in these poorer districts. The wagon master had said that the streets around the docks area would mainly be cobbled because these would have to carry the weight of loaded wagons to and from the warehouses of the quays. There were not so many beggars to be seen but street tinkers had boxes of wares for sale; their voices cried out to attract attention.

A woman approached the lead wagon and, baring her chest, called to Silmar. "A silver piece, 'andsome elf, and you'll 'ave a memory of me to treasure for ever!" She erupted into a screeching laugh but backed away as the wagon master raised his whip.

"Your loss, then," she retorted with a sour face, covering herself up again.

"What was all that about?" enquired a confused and embarrassed Silmar. "Why did she do that?"

"Eh? Are you serious?" answered the wagon master. "She's what you might call a lady of horizontal pleasure!"

Silmar's expression showed he was still confused.

"Er, well, a street walker!" the man persisted.

Silmar was still confused.

The wagoneer turned back and looked at Silmar with a toothless grin. "Look, she gives sexual favours then takes all your money and runs for it while you're pulling your hose up!"

"Oh, by the gods, I see!" replied a flustered Silmar. "That's not allowed in Refuge."

"There are places in this city called brothels, bordellos and bawdy houses, lots of 'em in the dockyard district. Watch out there 'cos you'll come away with a lot more than you went in with if you're not careful!"

Silmar was still confused.

"Pox, crabs, knob-rot! – Gods save us! You don't know much for an elf of your age, do you?"

Silmar gave a shy grin; he was learning the ways of the city very quickly indeed.

They passed down a broad street where rows of shops and dealer's establishments lined each side. Some dealers immediately caught Silmar's eye. These were selling weapons, from inexpensive, poorly-made to those of the highest quality, said to be imbued with magical or even god-given properties, if that could be believed. Many different types of armour were also displayed, much of which had seen action and some of which were new, exotic and, occasionally, impractical or even useless! Burly toughs stood outside the establishments to discourage thieves and looters.

In between some of the shop-fronts were eating houses serving food

PAUL BOYCE

and drink from many countries. The strong smell of spices and cooking reminded Silmar that he had not eaten a meal for a few hours. He didn't particularly care; there was so much to see here in this busy, bustling city that it took his mind off his growling stomach. There were inns and taverns with well cared-for fronts and stables for horses and wagons. Again, the smells of food and ale from these were very inviting. Silmar was quite partial to a quart of ale from time to time; more than one if he was in the mood! Other buildings with signs showing coins and playing-tiles were described to the elf as establishments for games and gambling.

"Keep away from them young 'un," advised the wagon master. "They'll take your money off you and leave you destitute in minutes."

Silmar didn't bother explaining that he was renowned as the canniest gambler in Refuge. But then this was a vast city and perhaps he would find himself out of his depth.

The wagon master reminded him that the inns and taverns close to the dockyard district would be more basic, in fact somewhat rougher, than these in the city centre.

Silmar was filled with a sense of foreboding but as his father had recommended *The Ship's Prow* and its owner, a dwarf called Ralmon the One-Sided, it must be of a very high standard indeed.

They passed by a large building that had a sign outside it showing two water jugs, one of which was tilting and water was pictured pouring from it into a large tub.

"What's that?" the elf enquired.

"It's a bath house!" replied the wagon master. "People go there to, well, er. Bath houses are where men can relax for cleansing, massages or to meet their mistresses or whores."

Silmar now understood these descriptions although he had until now thought that the term *mistress* merely meant a woman of high status or a female employer. He was soon put right. He had noticed temples in every district in the city. He already knew that these were dedicated to a wide variety of gods from the Pantheon. They offered solace, rest, prayer, healing and counselling.

The caravan now turned right down a long curving street, somewhat narrower than the others they had travelled down before. It soon opened into a large square and they slowly skirted the biggest market that Silmar had ever seen. There were hundreds of stalls selling cloths, spices, wines, cheeses, meats, fruits and vegetables, leathers, weapons of all sorts, boots and sandals, clothing, tools for farming and for craftsmanship, horses and ponies, dogs, cattle and sheep, reptiles, hawks, falcons and parrots, exotic fish and medicines and healers' accessories. The elf even noticed stalls providing services, at a price, from alchemists, mages and priests.

Silmar resolved to visit the market very soon, if time allowed.

Beggars were, once again, everywhere. Many of them were ex-soldiers or sailors carrying scars or with missing limbs from countless battles, children born with deformities or disease and ageing whores unable to scrape a living with their bodies but still trying to ensnare the desperate or poor into parting with a couple of copper coins. One of them, a particularly unkempt hag with missing teeth and a black eye, offered to use her hand to provide some 'relief' to Silmar for a copper coin. While the others chortled, he almost gagged.

Another turn down to the left brought the wagons outside the front of a large inn. It looked somewhat dilapidated, needing replacement of boards and a coat of paint. The bow of a small boat was attached, albeit precariously, to the front of the building and the sign swinging gently from a small beam read "Shippes Prowe".

"Your destination, friend Silmar," shouted the wagon master. He jumped down from the wagon and Silmar leapt down to join him. "I've enjoyed your company, young elf. Look, you take care in this city. It's a hard place and this district is about the most worsest part and you gotta take care. I'll be back in Refuge in three weeks and I'll tell your pappy that you got here safely."

The other wagoneers gathered round and shook Silmar by the arm. The elf was quite moved and thanked them profusely for having looked after him and he handed over a written message for his father. Silmar had actually written this some days before. He would be back one day, he had promised, and forwarded his love to his mother.

Sailors, mercenaries and adventurers from every corner of the Baylean continent wandered about, individually and in small groups. Silmar turned and noticed that the street had its name scrawled in charcoal on the corner of a wooden building – *Odd Strete*.

The buildings along this street were in slightly better condition than most of those close to the waterfront and docks. A few paces down the street a board hanging on the front of one building, showing a symbol of a stick-man in a large water-tub with a pitcher of water being poured by a semi-naked woman, clearly indicated its function – a bath-house. This was archetypal in city areas such as this because very few people outside of the mercantile and opulent city areas were able to read and write and what written signs existed were poorly scribed and badly spelt.

The wagons trundled off and Silmar was left in front of the inn with just his weapons and back-pack of belongings. As he turned towards the door to the inn, it crashed open and a large human flew out head first.

"And choddin' stay out!" shouted a gruff, booming voice. Framed in the doorway was a dwarf who paused briefly to observe Silmar suspiciously and then went back inside pulling the door shut behind him. The large human slowly picked himself up from the cobbles and staggered to a hitching rail. Bending over, he vomited, straightened up, wiped his mouth on his sleeve, farted wetly and staggered off.

Silmar picked up his pack, took a deep breath and went inside.

As his eyes swiftly adjusted to the gloomy light and smoky atmosphere, he noted that the interior of the tavern was divided into two areas. The bar, little more than a narrow board across three barrels, with a scullery beyond, was on the upper floor area on the left-hand side. The tables on the lower level were merely rough-hewn wooden planks nailed across upturned barrels. Wooden benches were arranged either side. Each table had a thick, greasy candle stub that was mounted on an ever-growing mound of old wax but during the day, with the window shutters open, the candles were not lit. A number of battered metal spoons were attached on each table by an arm's-length piece of chain. In common with many other lower-class ale-houses, it would be the responsibility of the user to wipe the spoon clean before use. Silmar shuddered at the sight of it. The floor was grubby and strewn with spilt beer, dropped food, vomit, spots of dried blood and pipe-leaf.

A flight of stairs led from the right-hand side of the bar up to the next floor. Up here, he assumed, were the bedchambers.

Four steps led to the upper level which was divided into booths, each being separated by four foot-high wooden partitions. Each booth had a round wooden table on which were similarly-mounted candle stubs. Individual chairs and stools were placed about the tables. This was obviously the area set aside for the more discerning clientele or those who required a little privacy.

Both the lower and upper levels were lit by a dozen or so spluttering candles arranged, on dripping mounds of greasy wax, around wagon wheels suspended from the ceiling. These two wheels would be raised and lowered by chains hooked on the taproom walls.

An overpowering smell of stale ale, vomit and pipe-weed assailed Silmar's nostrils as he took in the sight. He had been in better places than this. No doubt though, there were far worse places too.

A small number of people were seated around the lower taproom. The place did not appear well looked after by any means, surprisingly, but then it was quite early in the day. A one-armed, heavily-bearded man stood behind the bar; but Silmar had been told to expect a one-armed dwarf. The barman came out around the bar with a cloth, obviously to clean the tables, and dropped down three low steps. So he was the dwarf after all and one that had been standing on a ramp behind his bar.

"You layabouts get to cleaning this place up!" he bellowed at two pot-boys who were engaged in chatting to a scantily-clad woman at the end of the bar. "An' you can 'elp as well, ya strumpet!" he added. "I was outa here for a couple've hours an' I comes back to a shit-heap! I wants this place clean an' gleamin', the shutters wide open and this place smellin' like a tart's bedchamber! Get to it!"

Noticing Silmar's gape, the dwarf's expression became suspicious again. "Ah, what's this in mah tavern? An elf!" he cried. "Watchta want? Don't see many of your sort 'ere! What yer gawpin' at, eh? Ah, me platform?"

Silmar nodded.

"If you don't fit the world, you have to make the world fit you!" explained the dwarf. "Well, ya best come in iffen ya got silver to spend, elf stranger. So what can I do for you? Oh, I s'pose I better tell you, yer lucky I don't usually mind pointy-ears like you in mah place! They don't stay long 'ere. Not that I get many."

It was midday; Silmar had worked up a mighty thirst on his dusty journey and was more than a little hungry.

"Um, ale, if you please," he asked somewhat weakly. He felt, rather than heard, his stomach rumble. "And may I trouble you for a meal?"

"Aye. Not seen yer in 'ere afore. I'm Ralmon Cleaverblade. They calls me *Ralmon the One-Sided* – can't think why. You'll get yer ale an' some food then you can go." He stopped dead and scratched his head. "Er, just who're you?"

"I am Silmar, of the house of Galadhal in Refuge. My father sends his compliments and hopes that you are well and that business is good."

"What? Who? Hah! Well, bugger me with a toasting fork! You'll be Faramar's lad then" laughed Ralmon, reaching across the bar with his hand. "Hahaha, it's been many years since I campaigned with him, the old bushwhacker. Hey, I can provide you with a pottage, that's a vegetable stew, a chunk of bread – mah own bread mind you, none of the bakery rubbish that's only good for a doorstop! Needin' a bed?"

Silmar replied that pottage would be fine and a bedchamber would very much be needed. He cast his gaze around the taproom. A young, dark-haired woman, probably a cleric – Silmar couldn't see the holy symbol – sat at a table in a corner, her slightly well used quarterstaff leaning against the table beside her. A gnome sat chatting to her from the other side of the table but his gaze repeatedly took in Silmar. Four other drinkers sat at another table, smoking pipes and deep in quiet conversation. The rings of ale on their table from the bottom of their tankards suggested they had been there for some time although they didn't seem the worst for wear from much drinking. Occasional raucous laughter erupted from their table as they recounted lewd tales. The daringly-clad young woman sat at one end of the bar eyeing up the young elf. After a while, one of Ralmon's pot-boys sidled over to her and started talking to her while ogling her breasts.

"Get to cleaning, I tol' ye!" roared Ralmon.

Later on, once he had finished his meal, Silmar engaged Ralmon in conversation while drinking his ale. The grizzled dwarf was keen to relive some old experiences and Silmar was an enthusiastic listener.

"Lost this arm in a skirmish when I was with yer pappy in Lopastor. An uprising by some damned religious sect. We was underground. Would 'ave lost the other bugger had yer dad not waded in an' kept the bastards off me. Well, that was the end o' me as an adventurer, I can tell ye. But I 'ad gotten meself enough of a fortune in me adventures to set up this 'ere business. Still 'ave a bit put by for when I retire; plan on going to Refuge in a few years an' live out the last o' me days with me memories an' a glass or five of elven fire-wine with your old pappy."

Silmar asked if Ralmon could suggest a reputable, but not too costly, dealer for weapons and clothing. "I need a cloak, another pair of boots and a good pair of swords."

"Just a few doors away from 'ere, turn right outside the door an' it's up a little way on the right. Can't miss it, choddin' great big stuffed bear in the window. Tell Jaspar I sent yeh an' he won't overcharge yeh." He looked at the barman. "Hey! Get to work yous! I don't hire you to chat to, er, an' touch up the whores!" This latest outburst was directed at the pot-boy who was still talking to the woman; his hand was inside the top of her blouse and they were both laughing. "And you, yer strumpet, put them teats away an' get some drawers on an' make yerself useful! Else yer out of here!"

"Frack you!" she retorted but went out into the kitchen.

"You already done that an' yer couldn't walk proper for days, yer hussy!" His reply brought a laugh from her and from everyone else in the taproom.

Ralmon was quite accurate in his description of Jaspar's shop. Almost 60 gold crowns later, Silmar had a rapier, a shortsword and a hunting knife, as well as boots, a couple of leather belt-pouches, a spare deerskin tunic and hose, a new whetstone, flint and steel and some miscellaneous items.

One requested item though, raised an eyebrow of Jaspar, "You won't buy something like that over the counter of any shop," he gasped. "Shove me! Thieve's lock-picks aren't really legal, you know. Seein' as you're acquainted wiv me pal Ralmon we'll say no more about it. Shove me back'ards! Now then, a friendly word of advice, if you want something like that then Ralmon's the one to ask, he's had a use for that sort of thing in his past, see? I don't want to get involved with that. Shove me! If the watchmen catch you wiv 'em they'll lock you up! Keep quiet about it, don't want nobody getting' the wrong idea, right?" He shook his head. "Shove me!" he exclaimed again.

Silmar agreed, paid the account and strapped on his weapons. He carried his equipment back to the Ship's Prow. It was beginning to get dark outside. Lamplighters were lighting small braziers that hung from metal lamp posts up and down *Odd Strete*.

On his return, he went up the stairs to the bedchamber allocated to him by Ralmon and dropped off his sack of equipment and swords. He decided to leave his knives strapped onto his belt – to get used to wearing them, naturally! A celebratory quart tankard of ale seemed an attractive proposition.

Although it was early evening, it was late in the day and the inn was still unusually quiet. The elf presumed people would still be working. Two of the four drinkers had gone but the cleric and gnome were still there. Two well-to-do men, most likely traders, were just settling themselves in one of the booths on the upper taproom floor. All of the patrons turned their heads to watch Silmar as he sauntered over and stood once again by the bar. Ralmon was busy changing a barrel and teasing in the tap with a mattock.

Silmar was more than halfway through his ale at the bar when the gnome came up beside him and plonked his tankard down on the surface. "'Nother two, Ralmon, and one for this here Goodman Elf, that;s if he don' mind drinking with a gnome."

"Glad to, Goodman Gnome, if you will allow me to buy the next" said Silmar. The response was the standard interchange between two strangers at a bar that were striking up a new conversation.

The gnome chuckled. He stood about four and a half feet in height and although a little thick around the waist he looked unusually muscular. His skin colouring was a pale orange, although tanned and leathery beneath his long red hair, and was typical of his race. He was dressed in an opulent dark-blue, hooded, silken gown that dropped to just below his knees. A beautifully-crafted belt, on which a large number of small packs and a pair of daggers were hung, was buckled around his middle. Also unusually for a gnome, he wore a well-cared-for pair of travelling boots of the highest quality rather than the normally-favoured sandals.

"Aye, young 'un, that sounds good to me but I suspects that the young lady over there would argue that I've 'ad enough, but sod it, a couple more can't do someone no harm, can it? Allow me to introduce meself. Called by some as Billit, on account that humans can't get their mouth round my proper name, at your service."

"Silmar Galadhal, at yours," he replied, offering his arm for the clasp and being given a firm shake of the wrist. "And I am no human, as you know."

"O' course you aren't. Over 'ere," indicated Billit with an extravagant wave of his arm, "is one of Neilea's finest, name of Taura Windwalker." He dropped his voice to a whisper. "She would probably be considered quite lovely by humans but for the life of me I can't see it meself! Good talker though; she don't shuddup sometimes!"

Surprisingly, the Priestess of Neilea offered an even firmer clasp of wrists. Taura was much tanned, quite stocky, with short dark hair and dressed almost entirely in the light blue travelling clothes of her faith. A slightly darker-blue travelling cape was draped over an adjacent chair and she wore dark brown riding boots. Silmar couldn't help but notice that she was buxom and quite attractive, for a human of course.

"Well met, Silmar," she purred with a voice like honey. "Sit yourself on the bench over here next to me. What brings you to Westron Seaport?" Her silver holy symbol dangled from a chain around her neck; it featured two spinning coins, one the obverse face with the eagle-head representation of the Father God, Amae, and the other the reverse face with the representation of the Goddess of Kismet and Magical Knowledge, Neilea.

"Ah, well," he started, settling onto one of the adapted barrels serving as a seat at Taura's table. "My father thinks I need to travel, get experience of the world. He seems to think I'll be important one day. I can't think what as though. What about you two?"

Ralmon brought over a tray holding four tankards of ale, no mean feat for a halfling with one arm. "Mind if I join yer all? Couldn't 'elp but overhear, these first ones is on the 'ouse 'cos I wanna hear yer stories."

The ales were starting to go to Silmar's head already. Rarely had he had more than two or three ales at any one time; they always seemed to go straight to his head and then starting to affect his speech and actions soon after. He knew it would soon go to his bladder too. He wasn't sure if he could manage another – it would be rude to refuse though!

Billit scratched his head as if working out what to say so Taura spoke first. "I've spent some years in my clerical training," she began, "and it's now time for me to start spreading the word and doctrine of Neilea, my Lady of Kismet, Magic and Serendipity, referred to by some as the *Arcane Scientist*." She bowed her head slightly as she spoke her deity's name.

"Well, me now, I've been under trainin' too," said Billit conspiratorially while looking surreptitiously from side to side. He spoke quietly. "Between you, me an' these tankards of ale, I've learned skills to enable me to travel too, and this is what I intend to do. A user of the powers gifted to us by your Lady Neilea through the sun's power am I, just starting out, you may say. Don't let on to too many people though, there seems to be a sort of mistrust of mages and wizards in this city, can't think why!"

"Where do you travel, then?" asked Silmar. "Do you have any plans?" He sensed an opportunity here.

"None as such!" replied Taura. "Looking for a cause perhaps."

"Sounds good!" answered Billit just as Taura was about to speak.

She took her chance now though. "Look, Silmar, Billit and I arrived here together some three months back. We spoke with Ralmon to ask his advice on adventuring. After a while he said he had an idea but it would take a couple of tenday-weeks to arrange. So we waited wondering what would happen and you turned up. When you went out to buy your gear, Ralmon said you might be ideal to travel with us. We have no real plans. What about you?"

"Well, nor me!" replied Silmar, answering his own question. "My father hinted that there were people here who were hoping to strike out as adventurers and that I should offer my assistance. Obviously he was referring to you two."

"Aye, it was them," Ralmon responded before either of the other two could get a word in. "I sent a message to yer pappy near on a month back."

"Does that mean you have been waiting here all this time then?" Silmar asked incredulously.

"Aye, we 'ave," answered the gnome, "an' it don't seem a day over six months!" He winked at the elf.

"Cheeky chod!" retorted Ralmon. "Bin lookin' after yous both fer two months an' all I get is yer cheek. Well, now that you met, I feel a deep, meaningful an' profound plan comin' on. Done some adventurin' o' me own, as you know. Like I was saying to Faramar's little lad 'ere, that's 'ow I lost this!" He raised the stump of his missing arm. "In fact, when I were a youngling, in addition to choppin' lumps off the bad sorts, me own skills was more in line wi' somebody who might be tempted to remove things from their original owner, if you is understandin' my meaning, but o' course, only to make sure they didn't fall into the wrong 'ands."

Silmar put his ale onto the table. "Ah, I've done a small bit of that myself you know, but only in jest. I must admit to getting myself into one or two difficult scrapes when people took me too seriously."

"Oh, right, er, aye. Well, I never took nothin' from them what didn't deserve it, an' *never* from the poor, o' course," growled Ralmon, none to convincingly. "But o' the future, we must now parley."

The conversation paused for a few seconds as if everybody was trying to work out how to say what was forming in his or her mind.

"We could travel together, mebbe," said Billit, changing the subject and the sombre mood that had descended onto the party. "Sort of see how things go?"

After a few minutes of ideas being passed across the table, but no clear objective being suggested, Ralmon interrupted.

"Yer all goin' round in circles with no clear plan. Look, I got me an idea," he said excitedly. "It's like this. I need a job doing. M' brother, Jasper, he's got an inn up north, called the Wagon Wheel, town of Nor'wald City. It's way, way up north, and this time o' year I always sends 'im up some goods in a wagon. It's choddin' expensive hirin' a wagoneer to take my wagon, and all. Gotta pay for a two-way journey, see, an' a couple o' outriders for protection. If you can do this for me I'll pay yous an' it'll give yous an intro into some *real* adventuring. What do yer think? Can yer do it? Eh, eh?"

His enthusiasm must have seemed infectious. Taura, Billit and Silmar readily agreed without even having heard how much he was to pay them.

Billit soon asked the question though. "Hey, wait a bit! How much will you pay?"

"I'll give you twenty five gold. How's that?"

Everybody nodded, delighted happy, after all, this was more money than many hard-working labourers would earn in a year.

"Which of you can drive a wagon?" he continued.

They looked at each other hopefully. Silmar shrugged. Billit studied his ale pot.

The dwarf sighed. "Ooh! Thought things was goin' too good fer a minute," he grumbled, scratching at his beard. "Look, if yous meet outside the city south gates, not tomorrow but the nex' day, at 'bout an hour after sun-up, there'll be someone waitin' outside with a wagon and a couple 'v 'orses. Don't be late, that's when the gates open an' because the wagon's gotta be on the road later in the day. Drover's name is Harald. Oh aye, seein' as yer working fer me now, dinner and rooms are on the 'ouse 'til you go. Hope it's soon!" He rose to his feet and stomped off towards the bar, berating his pot-boy for his laziness.

This was good news indeed. "Another round of drinks then" said Taura.

"Yer can pay for that yerselves!" called Ralmon gruffly. "I'll 'ave no choddin' freeloaders!"

Soon after, Silmar wandered over to Ralmon and asked, "I'm after a special item which I can't buy from a dealer and wondered if you could give me some advice on where to get it."

"Tell me what it is and I'll see what I can arrange, provided it won't get you, or more importantly, *me*, into any trouble."

"It's a set of lockpicks," whispered Silmar.

"What? Shit, elfling! What yer needin' them for? You get caught wi' them on yer an' you can say farewell to yer freedom for a year or so."

"I need them just in case!"

"Ahhh! Right. Look, I might be able to call in a favour from an ole pal. Leave it to me an' I'll see you 'bout it tomorrow. These might cost ya anythin' up to thirty gold crowns. Er, at a rough guess, o' course, not that I knows anythin' about such things, yer understand. But I might be able to get 'em a bit cheaper for yuh. I'll get back to yer."

CHAPTER 5

A STONE'S THROW from the harbourmaster's post stood a large, pitch-blackened, wooden building. Its walls and roof were completely given to tar which gave the structure its blackness protecting it and its contents against the ravages from the occasional storms which plagued the Landsdrop Coast. No sign adorned the building, not even by the double doors which indicated the building as being a warehouse. Although the city was at its busiest time of the day, no movement showed that the building was occupied. Meanwhile, from the grimy, cracked window of another partly-derelict building opposite, a pair of eyes watched the black warehouse. The owner of those eyes had been in hiding there for two days having arrived undetected during the dead of night.

The afternoon became evening as the sun dipped below the horizon across the sea. As darkness fell and the general hustle and bustle died down, figures approached the building through a side door in an alleyway. Each figure was observed by the patient watcher who took in every detail: race and weaponry particularly.

As darkness fell, the watcher moved away from the window and silently roused other figures.

The merchant was of middle-years but his mighty girth made him appear much older. His waddling gait suggested that he resisted any need to exercise but not the need to eat. He was lavishly dressed and had a white silk turban upon his head. A red conical adornment, almost a hand's length in height, sprouted from the centre of the turban at the top and upon the front there glistened a ruby the size of a pigeon's egg that was set into a gold filigree mount. A wide sash of gold silken cloth, into which was tucked an ornate curved dagger in a golden sheath, was wrapped about his enormous belly. He breathed with some difficulty as he walked into his room in the black warehouse and carefully lowered himself onto his sofa. His bulk caused the furniture to emit creaks and groans of protest, hence the necessity for him to sit carefully. A recent incident that had caused him to descend hard onto a sofa had reduced it little more than firewood under his considerable bulk. Without doubt the overpriced piece of furniture had been poorly manufactured.

He reached across a small, gilt inlaid table to a crystal pitcher of elven blood-wine and poured himself a generous measure into a silver goblet. *Ah, to relax after a particularly gruelling day,* he thought to himself. An opportunity for an acquisition of almost unbelievable importance was presenting itself. He just needed to separate the item from its owner; he had retainers who would take care of that part of the business. He reached back across the table to replace the pitcher and carefully placed it on the table. As he drew his hand away, a long, slim and powerful dark-skinned hand grabbed his wrist firmly. It had appeared suddenly, silently and out of nowhere.

"Wha – what?" the merchant exclaimed. His gaze rose up the arm and shoulder and came to rest on the ebony face of a Darkling! "No! You!"

Darkling, known as shadow-elves or black-elves, were the dreaded and evil elves from places hidden deep below ground. Small, wiry but immensely strong, they were the cause of nightmares and of stories told to unruly children in order to encourage good behaviour. "Do as you are told or the Darkling will steal you in the night," the children would hear.

One Darkling stood before him, still gripping his wrist in a vice-like hold. Behind, in the shadows, stood three others; two armed warriors and the third that was tall, unarmed, hooded and menacingly silent – *a priest or mage?* The figures exuded a sharp, acrid, unclean odour.

With an impassive expression, the Darkling said "We have business, human!" His voice sounded thin and reedy but the threat from it was palpable. His breath was foul. The way he said the word *human* clearly marked his contempt for the merchant's race.

"Business? What business?" the merchant whined. "We always have business. I have paid you in alchemical substances and weapons for the opportunities you have given me and I have similarly given you information for your profit." He was sweating freely and the Darkling released his wrist.

"You humans disgust me," he spat, wiping his hand on the merchant's sofa. "How I despise you all." He raised his hand to his nose. "Yeesh! You stink like auroch dung." The two Darkling warriors laughed quietly but humourlessly; the fourth Darkling remained silent.

The hooded Darkling spoke with a coarse whisper. "You are about to enter into the business of, shall we say, procuring an artefact from a traveller. Do not insult my intelligence with denial, this much we know. Speak, merchant!"

The merchant wiped his brow with his sleeve and then winced as pain shot up his arm from his aching wrist. "There are many who come this way with artefacts religious, magical and regal. I negotiate to purchase them, of course. How many times have I invited you to make me an offer on some of the items that come my way? Your patronage has been profitable at times for us both but I continue to be successful with or without it."

The first Darkling leaned forward until his grey eyes were but inches from those of the terrified merchant. "Some? Some? You tub of goose fat! You pick at the cream of your crop and offer us those items for which you have little use. Not this time. I will have you know that without our patronage you would *have* nothing, you would *be* nothing! I enabled you to build this business and I can cause it to fall!"

Hearing a commotion in the passage outside his room, the merchant found a morsel of courage deeply buried within him. He rose to his feet and towered over the Darkling.

"Do not presume that you can threaten me – one shout will bring the host of armed men at my command to my aid."

Stepping forward, the cloaked Darkling pulled back the hood – *a woman!*

Her smile was cold and without emotion. Her hands moved in a complex, circular motion and then her right hand closed like a fist around empty air; her thin, cruel lips formed a single word, barely audible.

With a gasp, the merchant felt his chest tighten such that he was unable to breathe or even speak. The pain in his lungs was excruciating. He desperately needed to bring his forearms across his chest in the manner of protection but he could not; his arms were pinioned at his side by an unseen force. He couldn't lift his foot and was unable even to turn his head or move his jaw. A hammering came from the door to the room accompanied by shouts of *"Master, master!"* He hadn't locked the door; the Darkling had not even been by it! *Was that also held immobile by force of magic?*

The first Darkling speaker withdrew a slim dagger and idly used it to pick at his black fingernails. "My companion can have you held thus and then I could slit your throat. You will not even be able to cry out. Do not dare to offer threats to Darkling. Not now, not ever."

The mage spoke. "Where is the priest?" Her voice was dry and threatening. Although she might have been a strikingly beautiful woman, her face was granite-hard. She moved one hand and uttered another word. As if a puppet with the strings cut from above, the merchant slumped to the floor released from the magical bonds that had held him immobile. His lungs wheezed as he gasped deeply for air.

"Answer the question, human!" urged the first Darkling.

The merchant held his hands imploringly in front of him and the words tumbled from his lips. "He comes tonight an hour before midnight to meet with me in the Street of The Moon in an alleyway between the rope-maker and the cattle-shed on the right-hand side. Bring him to me and I shall give you a fair price for it."

The hammering and shouting at the door continued but the Darkling elves were ignoring it, showing no concern whatsoever.

This time it was the female Darkling who spoke. "It is *I* that shall determine what is to be done with the artefact. You can thank whatever of your inferior gods you waste words with that you yet live. But, human, if you lie, you die! Lay on your belly on the floor, fat worm, *now!*" The snarling woman was clearly the leader and not the first warrior as the merchant had construed.

With stained wheezing and grunting, the merchant turned himself from his side to his front as instructed. The room was in silence except for the continued hammering at the door. With a crash, the door burst open and the merchant's retainers and guards burst in. They were astounded to see their master struggling to his knees. Apart from him there was no other person in the room.

"Fools!" screamed the merchant, his belly and jowls quivering with rage and with sweat dripping from his face. "There were Darkling elves here, only four of them but I beat them off!" He was now almost apoplectic with rage and fright. "Where were you? Where were you? Why do I pay you?

Get me on my feet! Do I have to do everything myself?" He climbed with immense effort up onto his knees. "Two of you – yes, you and you – stay here. The rest of you get about your business. Begone!"

Sweat continued to run down his face and he staggered towards a stout, padded chair. He collapsed into the cushions but despite the solidity of the chair, it groaned under his corpulent obesity. It was many moments before his composure started to return and his breathing slowed down.

"Post guards outside the building; I want them there all night. Bring me food, blood-wine and, ah yes, one of those dusky maidens from Gorador. No, no! Bring me both of them. I want them stripped when you get them in here! Move, toads!"

CHAPTER 6

THE GROUP RELAXED in the Ship's Prow tavern and were enjoying themselves and getting increasingly merry as one drink followed another. Except, that is, for Silmar who generally took pleasure in a quart tankard or two, was happy just to watch his companions deteriorating as they consumed more ale. He took perverse pleasure in observing his new friends losing their self-control. There was so much to see in this City of Magnificence that was new and exciting to him and there was so much more that he wanted to see during the short time he would be here. He decided he would take a walk around the neighbourhood, perhaps down towards the docks.

He made his excuses amidst calls of warnings from his comrades. Assuring them that he would be cautious, remain aware and be armed with his precious dagger and his new shortsword, he quietly left the inn through the side door. Even though it was now approaching midnight, the road outside was full of people. Many were drunk; some were even throwing up in the gutters or pissing in passages to either side of the street. Beggars were still about and pleading for coppers from revellers and late-night traders.

The street was filthy with horse and cattle dung, and worse, litter and assorted rubbish strewn everywhere. Silmar could not believe that children ran about and played among it all.

Silmar's senses were at their highest state of alert. He sensed, rather than felt, a hand at his money-pouch on his belt. With lightning reflexes, his hand whipped to his side and caught the wrist of a girl, probably of no more than fourteen or so years of age. She winced with pain as his hand twisted her wrist and locked her arm behind her. She had a mane of long dark hair and was extraordinarily pretty.

"Be off, child" he growled and released her. She spat an obscenity, ran off into the crowd and was gone from sight in seconds. A shout of alarm was soon raised however, and he could hear calls of *"Stop thief!"* Perhaps she had relieved somebody from the burden of carrying a money-bag as she ran through the throng. He smiled grimly. This was a good opportunity for him to untie his money-bag from his belt and tuck it deeply inside his vest and jerkin. He continued along *Odd Strete*, making his way through the crowds. He did not rise to calls of 'pointy-eared git!' and similar from drunken dwarves – he had been warned about this before leaving the Ship's Prow.

The crowds were thinning out as he wandered onwards towards the docks. He decided to take a turn to the left. There were a number of store fronts here, all closed, which sold mainly work clothes, tools and fishing accessories. There were one or two weapons dealers but the standard of swords looked to him to be mediocre at best. This street was virtually deserted and soon he was passing by sheds and small warehouses on the left and approaching a stockyard full of large, long-horned cattle on the right. The cattle had not been well cared for and the smell was quite overpowering. There were some decrepit residential buildings and a few people were drinking from jugs and smoking pipes on doorsteps. They looked at him with suspicion as he strode by. He continued on but decided that he would soon turn back. It was very dark down here and he was beginning to feel vulnerable on his own.

He passed by the stockyard and its adjoining shed on his right-hand side. The passage between the shed and the next building was dark but his keen eyesight caught some movement a few yards down. He heard a gasp followed by the sound of a struggle. His elven night-vision came into use and clearly showed a standing, darkly-clad figure looming over another that seemed to be on its knees. The reflection of starlight on a blade forced Silmar to act and he stood in the shadow beneath the eaves of the cattle shed.

"Ho there!" he cried.

There was a blur of movement and Silmar moved slightly away from the building. A short dagger thudded into the woodwork where his chest had been a second before. Silmar drew his sword and, with a yell, he launched himself at the assailant. The dark figure straightened up and drew a short scimitar – a typical assassin's blade, short enough to enable mobility but heavy enough to kill with a single strike if wielded well. The dark one stepped forward to meet Silmar head-on and with the grace and poise of a dancer, easily parried Silmar's first attack.

Now that he was up close to the swordsman, Silmar tried to look into the eyes of the assailant but could see nothing. The dark figure was dressed fully in black, it seemed. Boots, hose and hooded tunic were all in black and the face, which must surely have been veiled, was black too.

Silmar regained his own poise and, bringing his own training to the fore, circled about with the dark figure. His enemy made a slashing, downward, oblique cut from Silmar's left shoulder to his right hip but the young elf easily stepped back with his right foot. As the scimitar's blade whistled past him, he stepped forward again and executed an upwards slash from the dark one's left hip to right ribcage. Silmar was more fortunate in that he opened the black tunic and felt the little bit of resistance that came with inflicting a light flesh wound.

No sound came from the dark figure; instead he kicked with his right boot catching Silmar's left knee. The young elf staggered back, barely managing to retain his balance, and he crashed against the warehouse to his left. By the time he had regained his balance, the dark figure had nimbly swung up the side of the cattle shed and was disappearing into the dark. All was now still but the elf could hear the laboured breathing coming from the victim now lying on the ground.

Silmar put away his blade and crouched down next to the figure. "Are you wounded?" he asked.

"He has killed me! I am dying," replied the figure amid coughs and splutters. "Stabbed … chest! Aaahhh!" *Cough!*

Silmar was taken aback. In the dark, he still had his elven night-sight and could see the spreading stain of blood beneath the man's cloak. He screwed up a ball of the cloak and pressed it to the stab-wound. The man cried out in pain but Silmar still held it there.

"Are you –" *Cough!* "– a man of good –" *Cough!* "– good heart?"

"I am an elf; I am Silmar, known as *The Golden*, son of Faramar Galadhal of Refuge."

The figure's hand clutched at Silmar's jerkin. "Oh, by the Gods!" *Cough, cough!* "– I am to die! Aaiii! The Lord Clamberhan help me –" *Cough!*

"No, I shall fetch help!"

"Listen elf." *Cough!* "Beware the Darkling! He wants this –" *Cough, cough!* "– Aaahh! Take it, guard it –" *Cough!*

Darkling! That was a word very familiar to Silmar. Was that his attacker? The young elf could now see frothy blood appearing on the lips of the dying man. As the stricken man reached inside his leather jerkin, a polished wooden medallion on a metal chain swung into view. It looked to Silmar like a divine badge of office, a holy symbol, but not one that he was familiar with. The end of a wrapped package appeared too but the man's hand fell away. He reached for it once more.

"Take it –" *Cough!* "– please take this – *aaahh!* Feel cold!" The poor man was stricken in pain but he continued to grip the package tightly.

"What must I do with it? Who can I take it to?"

"Take –" *Cough!* "– take to Carrick Cliffs, east to Kam –" *Cough!* "– Kamambia –" *Cough!*

"Do not fear, it shall be done, I swear it. What is your name?"

"No matter –" *Cough!* "– give to Gallan – *aaahh!* – Gallan Arran –" *Cough!* "– Priest –" *Cough, cough!* "– vital stop evil. Ohh Clamberhan, I failed you! I come to you –" *Cough!* "– in shame!"

There, that name again. Clamberhan! It sounded familiar. Of course – He is the God of Learning and Knowledge. "No! No! You go to him with honour and courage! Gallan Arran at Carrick Cliffs, I shall not let you down, I swear it!"

The man's body stiffened and a stream of hot blood issued from his mouth onto Silmar's left sleeve. He was dead; his hand fell away from the package. The elf reached inside the man's tunic and grasped it. Immediately, pain flashed behind his eyes and a wave of nausea coursed through him; he was close to bringing up the contents of his stomach. He released the package and the feeling passed. There was no other choice left to him except to take the package and bear the discomfort. As he did so the feeling appeared once more. Gritting his teeth, he thrust the package inside his tunic and rose to his feet.

He whispered a few words to his own God, Tambarhal, over the body, asking Him to beseech the dead man's own god, Clamberhan, to watch for the spirit of his subject. The feeling of nausea reduced a little. *Hmm, that is interesting* he thought. He also removed the wooden priestly symbol that hung from a chain around the dead man's neck; although it may help identify the dead man to the City Watch but he didn't want to leave it for the assassin to remove should he return.

As he turned to make his way back he heard a creaking sound from above and, once again, ducked just in time as a throwing star embedded itself in the woodwork behind him. He saw the dark shape of the assassin on the roof as it turned to dart away.

Hah! I'm going to follow that piece of shit!

The young elf relied on his dexterity to easily swing easily up onto the roof. Thanks to his elven dark-sight he easily spotted the figure as it leapt across from the cattle shed roof to another shed behind the stockyard. The assassin was moving fast and, probably because he was not expecting to be pursued, took little or no notice behind him. Silmar followed silently, years of hunting goblins in the forests and mountains serving him well. The pursuit carried on from rooftop to rooftop and finally the figure dropped down to street level. Noiselessly, Silmar turned to the right and dropped down to an adjacent street. He moved towards the corner of the building and carefully peered down the alleyway. He recognised that he was only a few hundred yards away from *Odd Strete*; there were still a lot of people about, he could hear them in the distance, laughing, singing, carousing, shouting, blissfully unaware of the death and danger only a few streets away.

There he is!

The figure had rapped on the doorway of a black warehouse and the door opened allowing light to pour out. The brightness almost blinded Silmar and he realised he was still using his night-vision. He turned his head to one side and blinked his eyes, reverted back to normal sight and looked once again down the alley.

Although he could see the killer more clearly in the light and he could also see a man in the doorway, there were boxes and barrels in the way that were making it difficult to see properly. He crept around the corner and silently edged over towards the warehouse, keeping the boxes and barrels in between himself and the figures.

"Do you have it?" the figure in the doorway asked. He was obviously wealthy; he had a cape edged in white fur and a turban of white cloth with a conical projection at the top on his head. Similarly, he wore a wide sash of gold silken cloth about his huge belly. The man was immensely fat and huge jowls hung from his fat face.

"The priest was there waiting as you said he would be. I killed him; I was interrupted before I could find and take the artefact. A damned fool white-elf. He was armed and almost as good with a blade as I. I had to get out of there. I think he now has the artefact."

Silmar edged forward further.

"Damn. *She* will not be pleased, you know that. I suggest that you get it back. I shall send out the lads and see if we can spot him. Describe him to me."

The dark one hesitated. "He was tall, golden-haired."

"Hmmph! Most elves are and many humans."

Silmar moved again but this time his foot caught a pebble and it rattled against a barrel.

"*Have a care, we are seen!*" the fat man exclaimed in a shrill voice.

The assassin whirled around. "There! It's him! He's mine!"

Silmar looked up. There was a gantry above him from which hung a rope through a pulley. By it was an opening into the building. He leapt up and started to climb just as another throwing star thudded into the building where he had been standing. He swung in through the opening and pulled the rope in behind him. Running through the hayloft, he found he was inside a stable. He didn't wait, however, but ran through the building and out through an opening onto another roof. He kept running over three more buildings, leapt across a narrow passageway and carried on until he was able to hide behind a small structure. He could see no sign of a follower but to be sure, he waited for many moments. He could hear the busy streets below him and eventually he decided to move.

Keeping low, he crept to the edge of a roof he looked about him for signs of the assassin. Nothing! He swung down and made his way to the main street – he was on Odd Strete once more!

He looked for large groups of people and tucked himself inside them. Eventually he arrived back at the Ship's Prow. Entering in through the side door he stepped into the bar-room. He waited and glanced about him. There were now very few drinkers in the inn. Of his new companions, there was no sign.

One of Ralmon's pot-boys looked across at him as he entered, breathless, nauseous and bloodstained, and then bent down to whisper in Ralmon's ear. The dwarf looked across at Silmar and hurried over.

"Ye Gods!" he exclaimed. "What has happened to you? Look at that blood! Are you badly wounded?"

"No, not at all, I think," the elf answered. "Not mine."

"Get yerself out back into me kitchen and sit down! Come down to my height, you pointy-eared elf! What's that?" Ralmon indicated the package that Silmar carried.

"Don't touch it," the elf warned. "It has a curse on it or something. It is making me feel quite ill. Can you call my friends down?"

"They're all pissed an' sleepin'! Best leave 'em there an' we'll sort 'em out tomorrow. Tell me what 'appened, all of it mind!"

Silmar recounted the events and took out the wooden medallion. He repeated the names he had heard and then laid the package onto the table. Once again, the influence he had felt while carrying the package passed from him and he sighed with relief. Ralmon took up the medallion and studied the symbol engraved upon it.

"This is the 'oly symbol o' the God Clamberhan, look, it's a bound book with a hammer on the cover," he said. "This is the god o' wisdom an' learnin'. Thought you would've known that, elf. The dead man must've been 'is priest. Didn't you say that the assassin said somethin' about killing the priest?"

Silmar nodded.

Ralmon laid his hand upon the package, his face paled and he withdrew quickly. "Eugh! Now I understand," he gasped. "I'm gonna call the local Watch Commander in. You 'ad better tell this to 'im, I think. But for now, leave out the bit about the package. An' don't open it, neither. I'm gonna call in another old friend o' mine first thing in the morning. Stay 'ere, I'll be back in a short while. Clean yourself up else they'll think you did the murder!"

The dwarf went out into the taproom and Silmar removed his tunic. The blood washed off easily in a bucket of cold water and he hung it over the ovens to dry. Ralmon came back in after a while and stated that he had sent one of his pot-boys off to find the Watch Commander. He had a canvas bag into which Silmar could put the package.

"Wanna eat somethin'?" he asked. "Parsnip stew's gone cold now."

He offered Silmar a chunk of bread, some cheese and a quart of ale. By the time the elf had finished these, his tunic was dry enough to put back on. At that moment, one of the pot-boys came into the kitchen to tell them that the Watch Commander and a couple of his men were in the taproom.

Strangely, or perhaps not, the taproom cleared of drinkers within a few moments of the City Watch entering. It was just as well because Ralmon did not want all and sundry listening in to the conversations. The Commander, looking and acting very imperiously in his smart uniform, demanded to know what he had been called in for. Silmar gave him the full details of what had occurred while omitting the references to the package and the names: Gallan Arran and Carrick Cliffs. *This business may be better left to Ralmon's friend, whoever he is*, he thought.

The Commander sent his two men out to search for the body and to look at the area where the murder had occurred. "Right then, um, Silmar is it? I want you to tell me again what happened, but slowly so that I can write it down."

Silmar dictated clearly and slowly and after a while completed his tale. One of the watchmen came back into the inn and whispered into his commander's ear.

"My thanks, Tasken," he responded. "The body is still there, just as you said, Silmar. I suggest you stay around here for the next day or two. I may need your evidence again but if you don't hear from me by tomorrow evening then you can consider your part in the matter as closed."

The Commander gave Silmar his appreciation and Ralmon led him and his men out of the inn door. When the dwarf returned, he told Silmar that he would be happy to put his belongings in another, bigger, oh yes, and more comfortable room with Taura and Billit and hoped the elf wouldn't mind. Silmar shook his head saying that he preferred to sleep on his own and that, generally, he slept in his blanket on the floor.

"A cot is too soft and I wake up with aches," the elf added.

When Silmar went to his chamber he bumped into Billit at a door opposite. The gnome beckoned him in. "Come in 'ere, Silmar. Where in the seven hells of the Void have you been? I was worried you had been killed dead."

"I nearly was, Billit," replied Silmar. "But I'm fine. I'll tell you all about it in the morning."

"Is it morning?" murmured a sleepy-eyed Taura as she propped herself up in her cot. The blanket had fallen away to reveal more of her than she might have intended.

"Not for hours yet, and cover yourself up, yuh hussy!" replied a flushed Billit. "Not very shy, is she?"

Taura huffed. "You are such a prude, Billit. Have you not seen breasts before?"

"Er, um, aye, I did once. Just not yours, lassie!"

Silmar chuckled, shook his head and stepped out into the passageway and into his bedchamber. He closed his door, propped a chair behind it and checked the window was secure, having been advised as being the normal action that would be carried out by anyone staying in inns in the rougher or remote parts. Within minutes he was asleep on the floor.

CHAPTER 7

D AWN WAS an hour away when the companions woke up. Silmar had been awake for ages with the names echoing around his head: Clamberhan the God of Learning, Gallan Arran the priest from Carrick Cliffs. Names he must not forget. The Darkling. What Darkling? He knew that these were the evil shadow elves of the deep, ancient mines of the Dragon's Teeth Mountains to the north of Northwald City.

He was now very curious as questions echoed around his head. *Was the assassin a Darkling?* The killer seemed to think that he, Silmar, was a good swordsman. *Was that a compliment from a man or a Darkling?* The poise and grace of the assassin was an indication of a very fine swordsman indeed; Silmar considered himself to be accomplished with a sword but there were many elves in Refuge who were far better than he. The killer was someone who spoke the *universal* language but the voice sounded sharp somehow. *Do the Darklings speak their own language, or universal or both?* He did not know. *Ralmon may know.*

He stood up from his blankets on the floor beside the cot and stepped over to the window. The shutter was closed so he opened it. Other thoughts came to him and he crossed back over to his bed. *Who is the fat man? He seemed very rich from the way he was dressed. Who was Ralmon's mysterious friend who was going to meet him this morning?* These thoughts had kept sleep at bay for ages but Silmar was too excited to be curious.

A hammering at the doors brought all of them to their senses. Silmar could hear movement in the adjacent bedchamber.

"Get up you lazy chods," yelled Ralmon.

Silmar pulled back the chair from his door and opened it to find Ralmon standing outside.

"Good morning, elf, or it was when I got up," the one-armed dwarf said.

"Got a visitor comin' to chat to you in 'alf an hour an' I got a morning feast laid out on the table downstairs."

"Thanks Ralmon, we're on our way," called Billit from behind a partly open door. "Madame girlie priestess ain't up yet an' she tells me I 'ave to avert me eyes so I can't see. She weren't so shy last night, was she, showin' 'er wobblies? You best come in an' make sure you don't look."

Taura groaned and covered her head with a pillow. Billit pulled it back off and told her to get up and drink a quart of water.

"I'll bring it up again," moaned Taura. "Gods, my head!"

"Then drink some more!" the gnome insisted.

They made their way downstairs, Silmar with his package in the canvas bag; it was the only way he could carry it without feeling too ill. Bread, eggs, cheese and fruit were laid out on a table. Flagons of water and tankards were lined up behind the food. The companions and Ralmon tucked in. A hammering at the door was answered by a young scullery maid aged barely sixteen years of age. Silmar rose half-way from his chair – she blushed when she saw him and dropped her head downwards; she was the very girl who had attempted to lift his money pouch the previous evening. After a moment she looked up at him again. The elf winked at her and put his finger to his lips to signify silence.

She smiled, dipped a curtsey, blushed again and opened the door.

A man stepped in.

He was tall with closely-cropped, dark brown, curly hair. He was dressed in a cowl of grey and purple beneath his travelling cloak with a sword belt around his middle and wearing a medallion around his neck. His cloak was long and white and he carried weapons of quality the like of which they had not seen. A large morning-star hung across his back on a large loop of leather. A smaller but very ornate mace was tucked into a beautifully-crafted leather sheath on his belt. A similarly ornate but very functional longsword hung from a fine-looking scabbard, also at his belt. These weapons had seen action, nonetheless. A number of pouches were attached to his belt too. He moved with athletic grace and the width of his shoulders bespoke a great physical strength.

But it was the man's eyes that took their attention. Apart from the pupils, they were completely black. Was he blind? He seemed to be able to move between the tables and chairs effortlessly. He looked at them all in turn and smiled, with a slight bow, when he looked towards Taura. She flushed immediately and dropped her gaze; the effects of her hangover did not seem so significant now. Billit nudged Silmar who tried not to laugh.

The new arrival warmly shook hands with Ralmon and they embraced each other.

"Let me introduce you to each other," Ralmon smiled. "Taura Windwalker, the Priestess of Neilea. Niebillettin, a Chthonic gnome mage, and this is Silmar, son of Faramar Galadhal of Refuge. This is Halorun Tann, High Knight Commander, Priest of Tarne the Just God."

Halorun Tann bowed to Taura again and said, "Blessings, dear lady, from the House of Tarne be upon you." He reached for her hand and kissed the back of her fingers.

"Oh, my!" she whispered. "And, er, oh, aye, b-blessings be upon you, dear sir, f-from the House of Neilea." She bowed in return. She was now scarlet and her heart hammered.

Oh, he is so *handsome,* she thought, *and those eyes – he can see right through me, I am certain!*

"My eyes as you see them, dear lady, are a gift from my God," he said, as if he had read Taura's mind. "I see in the near-dark as you do, Master Galadhal. And that is also a gift from my very own God; a story for another time, perhaps."

Halorun warmly shook the arms of Billit and Silmar and bade them all to sit around a table. He removed his cloak, hanging it across a nearby chair, and sat down.

"I believe that you, Silmar, have much to discuss with me," he continued. "I have met your father on more than one occasion and respect him greatly, counting him as a friend. I am honoured to meet the son of the leader from one of the great houses of the old elven Kingdom of Faerhome. Tell me what occurred last night and what you have to show me."

Silmar once again recounted his story. Everyone, except for Ralmon, was surprised to hear what had happened with the elf during the night. This time he told the whole story and included the parts of it that he had omitted when he was interviewed by the Watch Commander the previous evening.

"An evening walk crowded with incident," said Halorun. "The time has come for me to be shown the content of this package that you carry, and also that medallion that you took from the murdered man. Bring them forth, Silmar, so we may all see them."

The elf reached for the canvas sack and upturned it onto the table. The package rolled out and thumped onto the tabletop. It was about two feet in length and the thickness of a man's upper arm. The object, whatever it was, had been wrapped in a rough cloth and then tied with cord.

"It is not pleasant to hold," murmured Silmar. "It made me feel very nauseated and my head ached severely."

Billit reached across and put his hand around the middle of the package, and promptly threw up over the floor. "Ye Gods!" he exclaimed. "I enjoyed that morning feast too! Suppose I had better wipe that up then!"

The Dwark shook his head. "I'll get the scullery maid onto it; she's used to doing that. *Sheena!*" he yelled.

The young scullery maid came out of the kitchen and Ralmon told her what was wanted. She appeared with a wooden bucket and rags and, flashing a nervous look towards Silmar, proceeded to clear up the mess. Once finished, she glanced again at Silmar, who smiled and winked back, and disappeared back into the kitchen.

The elf reached for the package and, with a shudder, untied the strings and peeled back the wrappings. He was feeling the effect of the package quite badly now and it was all he could do to avoid emptying the contents of *his* stomach. Finally, the artefact was uncovered. The group seated around the table looked on wide-eyed.

Here, laid before them, was the most ornate dagger any of them had ever seen.

The hilt, guard and blade were crafted entirely of a rich gold. Rubies, diamonds, amethysts and a multitude of other precious stones were set into the hilt and blade. One ruby, the size of pigeon's egg, was set into the pommel of the hilt. The cross-guard was beautifully and exquisitely crafted in a filigree design and set with clear crystals. Beautiful designs were etched into the blade but one had been quite crudely erased, similarly on the reverse side of the blade. A new design had been etched, also quite crudely, of a scorpion. However, the beauty of the dagger took everybody's breath away. There was no sheath for the dagger; it had never been intended for use as a weapon to be carried into battle for its edge was quite dull. This artefact was special, perhaps ceremonial.

"I have seen this before!" exclaimed Halorun. "But not as we see it now." The companions were silent; even Ralmon was lost for words. But everybody could feel the influence emanating from the dagger.

Taura gasped "Is it cursed?"

"That I'm not sure but I can find out; it can wait for a little while though. You see that scorpion design?" They all nodded. "That is an emblem of the Scorpion Queen, Adelenis. She is worshipped by the Darkling elves and by assassins! Adelenis had brought scorpions into the world long ago. I understand that she enslaved elves, poisoned them and corrupted them so they themselves became Darklings. There, embittered, they shunned the light. This was many, many thousands of years ago.

"She lurks in hiding in the darkness of the Void and of late her followers appear to be collecting powerful magical and divine artefacts of which this may be one. Perhaps she has aspirations of becoming a greater god than the mere demigod that she is and may be using artefacts to develop greater powers and strength."

The group gathered around the table were in a state of silence. They looked at each other and down at the dagger.

Taura was the first to speak. "You said that you have seen this dagger before. Where? When?"

Halorun leaned back, clasped his hands behind his head and his gaze seemed to become lost as if far away, merely emphasising what might have been construed by others as blindness. "I was once a member of an adventuring party," he began. "We were like you, new to campaigning. We travelled north through Cascant into Kamambia and came to the small town of Carrick Cliffs. This town was overrun by Hoshite troops who had set up a garrison there. The townsfolk were very much oppressed and the churches and temples were sacked and looted. Those priests who were not able to escape in time were killed. A suit of armour said to have once been worn by the god Tarne himself had been stolen by the half-human, half-hobgoblin renegade Rolv Hebbern, had been taken to Carrick Cliffs as a gift to Adelenis. I was ordered by my Temple to recapture the armour and execute Hebbern. We organised the towns-folk and drove out the Hoshites."

At this, both Silmar and Billit sat up straight and their jaws dropped.

"But this is the story of the song of the *Freemen of Carrick Cliffs*!" cried Silmar. "Does this mean..?"

"Yes, I am one of those adventurers, one of the *Freemen of Carrick Cliffs!* I carried out my mission successfully and recaptured the precious armour. To this day, I believe, the town of Carrick Cliffs is free of oppression. I hope so anyway but seeing this dagger here puts me in grave doubt."

"But, Halorun, what of this dagger?" cried Taura. "What are we to do with it?"

"This is, I mean was, the ceremonial dagger which is precious to the Church of Clamberhan. This is of unique religious significance. I last saw it when we re-established Clamberhan's church in the town. The Temple is a centre of learning and wisdom and boasts a great library. The wooden medallion is that of a Cleric of Clamberhan. The murdered man will have been a Clamberhan Cleric himself, of that there is little doubt. I did not recognise his face when I investigated the scene of the murder early this morning and looked at the body. He had been stabbed twice through the lungs by a very narrow blade, a typical assassin's blade."

"So what is to be done now?" asked Ralmon. "We 'ave this dagger and there is a tale of horror behind it. Will the assassin be looking for it?"

As if to emphasise his next words, Halorun leaned forward in his chair and placed his hands on the table. "Oh yes, he will want it. I know the identity of the fat man; he is Menahim Begim-Bey. He is a trader from the southern land of Qoratt and will be involved somehow with this plot. It is suspected that he is implicated in kidnapping and slavery as well as the collecting of magical and religious artefacts for sale to the highest bidder. It is also suspected that he has links with people from extremely low places. What he is doing in supporting Adelenis I have yet to find out but if he is then Darkling may be involved too. But he will have some profitable reason for doing so, I have no doubt whatsoever. He seems to have gone to ground but I shall find him, sooner or later."

Taura's hand flew to her mouth. "But the assassin has seen you, Silmar," she cried, "and will surely be looking for you."

Silmar nodded slowly. "Aye, and if that dagger is of some importance, he will not stop looking for me either," he replied. "But the odd thing is, he seems to find it necessary to hide his features. I wonder if he is Darkling! All indications point to him being so because he was small in stature but moved like a cat. He may not be alone either."

The companions gasped. This was terrible news and it would doubtlessly put Silmar, perhaps all of them, in danger. Halorun sensed their concern and gave words of comfort and advice.

"He will not risk being seen during the day. Assuming he is Darkling, he cannot afford to be recognised and wearing a face mask will arouse suspicion. He will hide up during daylight and will hunt during the night."

"I must leave, and alone," gasped Silmar. "I cannot risk the lives of my new friends in this. I shall return to Refuge straight away."

In one voice, each of the friends rejected this and vowed that they would face this hazard together.

"Well, we was talking about campaigning, wasn't we?" Billit asked. "A bit of adventuring? Well then, this is the ideal start for us. What d'yer think?" The little Gnome mage gave a wide grin across his rugged features.

"Aye, your friends are right, Silmar," responded Ralmon. "They are, aren't they, Halorun?"

"I would say so," the Priest of Tarne confirmed. "For one thing, if you are considering riding back to Refuge, he may come on you in the dark of the night. He *will* be looking for you, Silmar. Although it was dark when you fought him, he will have been able to see your features, so you will need to disguise them."

"What should I do?" enquired the elf.

"Nothing drastic. Colour your hair and tie it back. Wear a large cap or a hood that will cover your hair and ears. Darken your skin a little with a skin dye, just enough to last for a few days. I think Ralmon will help you with all that."

The dwarf nodded in agreement. "Aye, I done this sort o' thing afore. You 'ave no idea 'ow difficult it can be to make a dwarf look taller! But yer tall enough already so it ain't a problem!" The group laughed.

Halorun leaned back in his chair. "The time has come for me to find out what this power is that binds the dagger. To do this I need to be left alone with it for a while. Ralmon will see to your disguise and the rest of you can help him. I shall call you when I am finished."

The companions rose up from the table and Ralmon led them into the kitchen. Sheena, the scullery maid, looked embarrassed when they entered. She had tied back her long hair and her grey blouse sleeves were rolled up. Silmar took her arm and led her aside.

"I shall say nothing," he said softly, "providing that you thieve no more.

And if you behave, I shall bring you back a gift on my return. What do you say?"

"I mean no harm to anyone, sir," she replied timidly, clutching at his arm. "I looked after my brother 'til he died last month and all my money, five coppers a day, goes on giving me shelter in a shed behind the blacksmith's shop. There's just me now and this work does not pay enough for anything better. My mother died to give birth to him and my father is in gaol. I only work in the mornings and I am lucky enough to have this. I can't survive on such little money and I refuse to sell my body for more. The blacksmith's boy keeps trying to have his way with me, too. What is to be done?"

Silmar scratched his head. "How old are you girl?"

"About sixteen I think."

"Many girls are wed at your age, with children of their own. Look, leave it to me, Sheena. I shall ask Ralmon for a favour and see if he can help in some way. No promises though."

Together, Taura, Billit and Sheena applied colouring to Silmar's hair, face and hands. Ralmon provided a large woollen cap that would cover the elf's head and ears. With different clothing he would be almost unrecognisable. As an elf, Silmar had no facial hair so he would be unable to grow a beard. Elven features were quite distinctive compared to those of humans and would be difficult to alter.

Taura observed Sheena watching Silmar's transformation with interest. The young scullery maid giggled bashfully as Silmar stripped to the waist. Eventually, Billit and Taura went back out into the taproom. Silmar spoke quietly with Ralmon by the door. At first the dwarf shook his head vigorously but soon he shrugged his shoulders and was nodding in agreement.

The elf rejoined his companions and they stood back to watch Halorun Tann as he continued with his examination of the dagger. The Priest of Tarne was sweating heavily and chanting softly. While his body was gently rocking back and forth, his hands weaved a complex series of movements over the artefact. The words being chanted seemed muffled and distorted, as though the companions were being deliberately prevented from understanding the divine spell or prayer that Halorun was uttering. Only Taura, being a priestess, could see the faint blue glow that surrounded the dagger and Halorun's hands. The chanting finished with a sudden shout and gesture and the Priest of Tarne slumped back in his chair. His face was drenched in sweat but he had a calm and triumphant look to his face.

Halorun used the corner of his cloak to wipe the perspiration from his face. "I had to invoke all of my powers and strength of will to establish the nature of the artefact and with help from Tarne I have established what it is that it has been imbued with. It is not a curse; that I now know. It is, however, altogether evil and I believe it has been used to murder or execute a victim, probably as a sacrifice and most likely a priest of Clamberhan. It was never intended for this purpose. The use of it in this way, together with the foul symbol being etched upon it, has imbued it with the evil that we can all feel."

Silence descended on the taproom.

"I did ask earlier what we should do with it," stated Taura, "and you did not answer."

Halorun had by now regained his composure. "Then this is my answer," he replied. "It must either be destroyed or preferably, have the evil it contains removed by the High Abbot of the Temple of Clamberhan, Gallan Arran, if he still lives. The murdered priest seems certain the High Abbot still lives so he may be in hiding somewhere. He must be located and brought to Carrick Cliffs to meet with you and the dagger. This really must occur at the place at which the atrocity happened. It would be a great advantage if the one who carried out the execution, could be brought along with it. I know it sounds very hard to bear but proving the guilt of a killer and then his execution will go a long way to removing that evil."

"Will you not be able to travel with us, Halorun?" enquired Billit. "Your experience would be of such benefit to us."

"Unfortunately, no," he replied. "I have some trials to conduct and then investigations to carry out relating to this plot. I have to try to find this Menahim Begim-Bey, then try to find others who may be able to help. I then have some trials to give judgement on in the Barony of Bocaster. Oh, I also have a particularly nasty criminal to apprehend in Grappina. I shall, hopefully, be able to meet you though, before you arrive at Carrick Cliffs. I may have some support with me, too, all going well."

"You mean *we* are to travel to Carrick Cliffs?" gasped Silmar. "We hoped you would take this dagger with you today. But we are so inexperienced and new to this. What are we to do?"

Halorun laughed. "You, Silmar, son of Faramar, have experience in battle; look at your scars. You have the beginnings of a team and I predict your team will grow as you travel onwards. Don't ask me how I know, I just feel this. Together, you will have the strength both of will and for this campaign. Take the dagger, guard it well and tell nobody of its existence from the time you leave this inn. Keep it a secret and keep it hidden well away. I can help you with that. First though, I must have some water, I have such a thirst."

Billit shouted for Ralmon, who was still in the kitchen. He appeared with a very tearful Sheena in tow. As Billit asked the dwarf for water, Sheena threw her arms around Silmar's neck and burst into tears. A few eyebrows raised and questions were hovering on everybody's lips. There was a story to be told too, but that would wait its turn.

"Get us some water, girl," called Ralmon, and out she ran. "She's got a new job with me, thanks to your pointy-eared, choddin' elf pokin' 'is nose into other people's choddin' business!"

"Looks like you have a very pretty new friend, Silmar," laughed Taura.

"It rather does, it seems," he replied. "Perhaps she likes my new hair colour."

"I think it is your muscular hairless chest," she replied with a chuckle.

Silmar posed by puffing out his chest and flexing his arms.

Halorun cleared his throat to get their attention. "I would recommend you travel north out of this city and head for Northwald City, a full seventy leagues but it is a very good road and very busy. That will take you seven or eight days by horseback but double that if you have a wagon. The roads to the east of here will more than likely be watched as this would be the logical route for the bearers of the artefact to take. Once at Northwald, you could take a path from the East Gate, following the road eastwards round the mountains and find your way back towards Gash, perhaps a twenty-day ride." Halorun smiled at this point even though he admitted that the road, although minor, was good providing the weather stayed dry but the mountains were treacherous and alive with goblins and trolls.

"Oh how wonderful!" exclaimed Taura. "Goblins and trolls, my favourite!"

Silmar shook his head. "There are very few of them these days. They just have small hunting parties of half a dozen. You can smell them before you see them. If we pick up a merchant's caravan we shall be quite safe."

"You will pick up the Great East Silk Road below Gash that will eventually would lead eastwards through the Shordrun capital city of Nasteed and the pass through the Dragon's Teeth Mountains and into Polduman. The road swings down; make sure you follow it and not the old road. You will eventually reach the coast. Take the ferry to The Wildings, a lawless region. Be on your guard there. Make for south Cascant and the city of Norovir. Your journey will then take you eastwards though the Brash Mountains and into Kamambia. The road north will then take you to Carrick Cliffs. I estimate that your journey is about seven to eight hundred leagues which, all going well, would take forty to fifty days, perhaps more."

"How shall we remember all that?" enquired Billit. "I shall need to pen it 'cos we'll not remember that."

"Fear not," laughed Halorun. "I shall draw a nice picture for you."

When Silmar asked how they would meet up with Halorun, he simply replied that he would know where and when.

"I can help you solve the difficult burden of carrying the dagger too," he explained. "I'll need a box that will take the dagger."

"I 'as the very thing," cried Ralmon and he rushed over to his bar. He returned with an oaken box with a hinged lid and metal clasp. "This is a box used fer bottles o' dwarf liquor," he announced. "Don't need it no more, I drunk the liquor! Choddin' nice!"

The group laughed. Dwarf liquor was very strong and few were the elves and men who were able to drink it.

"I will want some sort of lead powder or grains, or thin lead sheeting, for the dagger to be bedded into or wrapped in," the priest continued. "Perhaps a window-fitter can provide that."

Ralmon nodded. "I knows jus' the man; 'e drinks in 'ere all the time. I'll haul 'is arse outa 'is cot." He walked out of the door of the inn. Sheena had reappeared with water and gave Silmar a huge smile and returned to the kitchen.

"I just helped her out, that's all!" he protested as all eyes turned to him.

Taura laughed. "I think she wants your body next to hers since she saw you with your top clothes off!" she said.

They drank some water and helped themselves to some of the dawn meal that was still laid out on the table. Halorun told them a couple of tales from his adventuring days and told them a little about the other members of the Freemen of Carrick Cliffs. Most of them were still in the local area and now had businesses of their own. He spoke of his wife, Sharness, and they were astounded to hear that she was a Darkling. She was surprisingly a Priestess of Tambarhal, the god worshipped by surface elves, but not of course, by the Darkling themselves. Although she lived with Halorun and their son, Halness, at the new Temple of Tarne-In-The-West, she spent weeks at a time spreading the word of her own god and giving aid to travellers of all races. She had long become accustomed to living on the surface and was well-known and trusted across the Home Territories.

An hour after he left, Ralmon returned with a heavy sack over his shoulder. He opened the sack and folded the edges down so they could see its contents. It was full of lead – powder, small pieces and thin sheets.

"Perfect!" said Halorun.

"Cost me a choddin' fortune," Ralmon mumbled.

Halorun part-filled the casket with the lead fragments and he laid a small, thin sheet of it on the table. Silmar took a deep breath and lifted the dreadful artefact. He winced as pain shot across his temples. With a gasp, he lowered it onto the sheet. Placing another sheet over the top of it, Halorun tightly wrapped the artefact without coming into contact with it. He placed the package on top of the bed of lead granules and then loaded the casket with more until it was full. The priest closed the box and fastened the clasp.

Silmar picked up the box and could barely feel any evil influence at all. "It's very heavy," he observed.

Halorun continued, "I have just one more task to fulfil." He placed his hands over the casket and mumbled a chant. The companions could not understand any of the words except for *Tarne* a couple of times. When he finished Taura could see a faint blue glow around the box.

"I have placed upon it the blessing of Tarne," he said. "And you, my dear Lady of Neilea, can do the same when the burden on Silmar becomes too much to bear. Offer the blessing of the Lady of Kismet." He bowed with each mention of the Goddess, Neilea. It was always a matter of etiquette amongst the priests of various deities when they speak to another. Taura bowed in return and was lost for words, even more so when Halorun stepped close and kissed her on the cheek. He clasped arms with each companion and lastly with Ralmon. He bade a final farewell and went to the door. They all followed him into the street and marvelled at his great white warhorse. A junior Cleric of Tarne had been outside tending to his own and Halorun's mounts all the while. The pair rode off and the group returned inside the inn.

"Well, there we 'ave it," sighed Billit. "We have a quest, a mission."

"I was hoping we would be able to start with something straightforward, a bit easier, like saving a damsel in distress from an evil knight, or something," said Silmar. "Now it seems we have to take on the Darkling! Maybe more than one."

"Perhaps not," replied Taura. "All we have to do is get the thing back to its original home. We have to avoid being found but we do have skills. We have another advantage in that your appearance has changed, Silmar. He may not now recognise you. It is a pity you would not let us cut your hair. He also does not know that you now travel with friends. We will protect each other and you can rely on us to be there for you."

Billit nodded in agreement. "Halorun predicted we would find other companions, too. We gotta take care though. You never know who it is who'll offer to join us."

"How does he know?" asked Taura.

"Some sort o' scrying, prob'ly," answered Ralmon. He had been listening to their conversation. "I got some advice 'bout adventuring, so listen close. I'm pleased ter 'ear you're using yer common sense. You're all startin' to think like profesh'nial adventurers. You must all feel free ter talk 'bout yer ideas or problems with each other. All ideas must be listened to an' considered, no matter 'ow good, or bad, they may be. One idea will spawn another. No idea must be ridiculed. Trust each other but beware of all outsiders. Halorun was right; keep all knowledge of this, um, *burden* that Silmar carries a secret 'tween the three of yer only. Never mention it by name and never mention where you are going an' why. Keep to yerselves the name of the person you seek in the far-east. Other people won't be able to tell yer secrets and pass on information. And remember to keep yer disguise, Silmar. You can darken yer 'air an' skin with berry juices like you saw me doin' earlier. You 'ave a couple o' days now to prepare an' ask me questions. Remember, any questions yer like. I'll 'elp an' advise yer where I can."

The companions looked at each other in silence and all of them took a deep breath. Silmar suddenly realised that this was a world away from goblin-hunting that had been his life before. He now felt as if he were an amateur which perhaps, it could be argued, he was. He had confidence in his weapon skills even though he knew there were many who were better than he. This Darkling assassin, he considered, was probably a better swordsman. If he was in fact a Darkling, then he may well have the same, or better, dark-sight ability; he would, after all, be living in the darkness of the underground cities – miles of tunnels and mines. The female dark elves were the most vicious and powerful with their magical skills given to them by their Scorpion Queen goddess, Adelenis. Normally, only the male warriors ever climbed to the surface to spread the evil and mischief of the Darkling. This knowledge was commonly taught amongst the elven race in Refuge and probably other communities too. Silmar shared his knowledge with his companions and saw real concern on their faces.

It was now time for lessons in driving a wagon.

The sun was still quite low in the morning sky and the shadows were long as the gates of the city were opening just as Silmar, Taura and Billit arrived on foot. They found a surly, hard-looking wagoneer standing by a wagon with a pair of horses that had obviously seen better days. The man was tall with broad shoulders and a long, bushy, brown beard. He carried a coiled whip tucked into his belt.

He looked at them with disdain and shook his head slowly. "Is yous all Ralmon's victims, er, I mean wagoneers?" he said with a wry grin. He should not have displayed his teeth – they were badly stained, some missing and others broken.

Taura admitted they were the candidates for the training in wagon-driving.

The man's mouth worked its way around Taura's words and then he nodded. "I'm Harald. You're late; bad start. Right then. Who's the wagon driver? Who's done it afore?"

"None of us," replied Billit.

"By the dancin' gods, looks like I got me a right bunch of amateurs. One girlie, one gnome and, what are you? An elf?"

"Some elvish blood," replied Silmar. His woollen cap covered his long, newly darkened hair and, thankfully, his ears. Obviously, his facial features still marked him as elf-kin.

Although none of them responded to the wagoneer's last jibe, their expression said they were all new to wagoneering.

"Well, which of you sorry specimens is first then?"

The day went on and Harald seemed to be enjoying the struggling of the trainee wagoneers. Silmar showed absolutely no aptitude for wagon driving at all. Billit demonstrated some promise but it was Taura, having never tried before in her life, who took to it as if she had been doing it for years.

"You've been havin' me on, young lady. You've done this before. Don't piss me about or you'll feel the end of my whip."

Taura straightened up, looked him in the eye and glared at him with a ferocious expression. "Do not try it, Harald!" she warned. "I haven't, if you must know, but it's hardly difficult is it? I mean, if a man can do it, well, for the love of the gods, anyone can."

The wagoneer had a face like thunder for the rest of the morning.

They returned to the inn for a hearty lunch and more ale. Driving a wagon was dusty, thirsty work and Ralmon's ale was sufficiently good, providing he served them with that which had not been watered down. The one-armed dwarf had apparently heard of the difficulties and couldn't resist the occasional leg-pull. The trio decided to take a walk down to the docks, more for Silmar's benefit because he had not seen the sea before, and the large ships would be an interesting diversion to take their minds off their forthcoming journey.

He kept his cap pulled well down.

CHAPTER 8

D READFUL DREAMS echoed inside his head. This was nothing unusual but this time his dreams were accompanied by a severe headache. The screams of the dying man back at the *Han* in the Harima province town of Ako gradually turned into the shrieks of seagulls circling and swooping overhead.

Oh how my head aches! Jiutarô slowly returned to consciousness in his boat. He pulled himself up onto the rail. *It is daylight; no clouds. The storm must have passed.*

He shook his head to clear the fuzziness and immediately regretted it. There was a sharp ache in his fingers. He looked down and saw that the little finger of his left hand was in agony – broken. It was bent backwards, grotesquely, at the second knuckle. He plunged the hand over the side of the boat into the sea to cool it down; he was surprised that the sea was warm. *Never is it warm in the Straits of Shimonoseki.*

Gritting his teeth, he closed his right hand around the broken finger and yanked it back into place. Pain coursed through his hand and a wave of nausea rose in his throat; he grimaced but uttered no sound; the nausea passed quickly. He put his right hand onto the left side of his forehead, it came away bloodied but some dryness showed that the wound, the size of a one-yen gold coin, was already scabbing over.

The sail was badly torn and hung partly in tatters from the broken spar. The drunken, bad-tempered boatman was gone, presumably washed overboard during the storm. *He has probably managed to swim ashore; either that or his body will be washed up somewhere.*

His riding-horse remained tethered between both side-rails at the stern and seemed unharmed but of his pack-pony there was no sign. The remains of its harness lay in the scuppers. His horse must have been panicking during the storm; many of the deck planks were damaged and there were cuts and scratches on its front legs. His precious weapons and armour were all in the bottom of the boat, thank the stars! *Damn, my food and most of my spare clothing were on that pony!*

He looked for the familiar landmarks of the Straits, the black rocky cliffs topped by clumps of dark forest – nothing! He could see land no more than a mile off. The low skyline in front of him showed cliffs but not as high as would have been expected at the Straits. The sun was at his back and was quite high in the sky. *It must be past midday but the sun should not be that high, it is winter; it is far too warm, damn, it's hot! The storm must have carried me far to the south but this looks like nothing in my home country, as far as I know.*

A huge walled city stood a little back from the shoreline. Not even Edo was that big. The walls were of stone of a light brown colour, as if made of a particular type of sandstone. They must have been sixty or even eighty feet high. There were towers, domes and minarets, the like of which he had never seen before. A long harbour, with many large ships moored, filled much of the shoreline to the right-hand half of the city walls and, even from this distance, Jiutarô could clearly see movement and bustle on the dockside.

Not knowing where he was concerned him deeply. He retrieved his weapons, he may have need of them particularly if he had drifted somewhere off the coast of Korea. Nippon and Korea had been at war on and off for decades, if not centuries. He had heard tales of Korea from battle-scarred warrior veterans who had been garrisoned there. The people there were primitive, cruel, with no culture. He did not know where Korea was or what it looked like, but he was sure that this did not resemble a primitive land.

There was enough sail left on his little craft to catch some wind and, using the single oar and what scant knowledge he had of sailing a craft, he slowly but steadily made for what appeared to be the quieter right-hand end of the docks. The sea was very calm, thankfully, but he was not happy, nor confident, on water, particularly when alone. His horse was skittish and its chaotic movements caused the boat to rock unpredictably.

Gulls shrieked and wheeled around his boat but soon lost interest and flew off, some of them swooping at prey on, or just below, the surface of the sea. He slowly, and awkwardly, sailed closer to the docks.

It was a while before anybody on the jetty noticed the little craft arrive at the docks. Probably forty paces in length, the wooden jetty stretched out from the wharf. It was untidily covered in barrels, sacks, ropes, buckets, and seagulls. Panishak, the taskmaster, led his team of four labourers along the platform and started them on clearing up the mess. The harbourmaster, a bossy, nosey and meddlesome bastard, had castigated him in front of his team and to put it bluntly, he was many shades of pissed off particularly when they sniggered behind their hands. *I'll work 'em, work 'em hard!* he thought. He'd had his share of warfare, it seemed. He was once broad and very muscular but much of this was turning to fat. He was still mighty, however, swarthy with deeply tanned and leathery skin from years on the ocean. Many of his teeth were missing and those that he still had were turning bad and painful; perhaps this partly explained his own generally unpleasant temper. He wore a greasy black silk scarf tied around his pock-marked head; a long and heavy dagger hung in a battered leather scabbard at his belt. The bottom half of his right ear was torn, or cut, away but in his other was a large gold-coloured earring. Whatever had taken that piece of ear had also left a vicious scar on his right cheek. He liked to boast that the earring was gold and would challenge any man to take it from him. Nobody had ever succeeded in nearly twenty years. A successful challenger would have been disappointed, it was brass! To keep up the pretence, he regularly removed it an gave it a rub, buffing it until it gleamed. The metal was wearing thin after the years; he would replace it soon.

One of his workhands, a small half-goblin with short, bowed legs, a jutting chin and skin as dark as coal, gave a frantic shout. "Mashter, come quickly!"

The taskmaster was standing a barrel up onto its end. It looked and smelled like a rum barrel and it felt full. And it was now his! He looked up from the barrel to see the hand hopping from one foot to another and pointing out into the harbour. "Wadya want, pig-face?" he growled.

"A boat comesh, mashter," came the reply. Snot filled one nostril and the hand wiped it on the back of his forearm.

"It's a piggin' harbour, you thick git!" bellowed Panishak, clearly becoming very annoyed. "It's a tossing boat park!" He was deep in thought on figuring out how he was going to get the barrel from the jetty up to his meagre home. The pained look of anguish on the face of the half-goblin led to laughter from the other human workhands prompting Panishak to berate them for being lazy bastards.

"Mashter," pleaded the labourer. "Come and look, pleashe mashter!"

Panishak gave an expletive, of the sort rarely used in higher society or even in some of the lower sort. He lowered the barrel and strode over, a face like thunder. The hand pointed. "Shee mashter! A boat."

The taskmaster saw the battered craft, a small fabric-covered shelter and the tattered remnants of a triangular sail indicating that it had come through some fierce weather. He considered the vessel. *Strange looking boat, not seen nothin' like that 'round here. Odd, look at the state of it, there ain't been a storm on these waters for soddin' months.* A figure stood in the bow, holding a length of rope to tie up the craft as it moored at the jetty. He had a sword and matching dagger tucked into his sash around his waist and he had an unusual-looking longbow propped up against the shelter. A fine large horse stood in the stern. Panishak's mind was thinking in gold crowns now.

"Listen you," called Panishak in an aggressive and officious tone, his hands on his hips. "Tie up here and state your name and business. You 'ave to pay to tie up here, a silver piece! To me." He looked over to his group of men and winked. They laughed, that would be ale for each one of them in the tavern.

There was no reply from the figure in the boat, just a blank uncomprehending expression. The strange looking man was dressed in loose-fitting grey leggings over which a black and grey silk gown was wrapped. Across the wide collar were unusual symbols embroidered in gold thread. A broad, blue, silk sash was coiled around the man's waist and knotted at his right hip. Apart from the beautiful black scabbard of a long sword was its shorter matching pair. His features were also strange to Panishak. The man's skin colour was pale and his eyes narrow, like almond-shaped slits. The front of his head had been shaven but his remaining hair was well oiled and formed into a tail which was folded forward on the head, then back again, and tied in place. The man seemed young, probably no more than twenty-five summers.

"I said, tie up and state your name and business here," he shouted, even louder. Obviously, the louder he shouted the more likely the figure would be to understand.

Again, there was no reply from the strange occupant.

"Gods, he's a piggin' outlander!" grumbled the task master. "Gannack, take his rope and tie the bastard's boat to the jetty."

The little labourer gingerly strode to the edge of the jetty. The virtually expressionless face of the sailor had just a hint of a confident and menacing look. Gannack nervously motioned for the rope and the figure tossed it over, all the while staring at him in a puzzled manner. The half-goblin tied the craft securely to the mooring post. Panishak used a hand signal to beckon the figure from the craft. "Out you! Come on, move it!!"

Again, there was neither reply nor reaction.

The taskmaster tried once more, emphasising each word with a corresponding hand signal. "Out – of – the – boat – now, erm, and – on – to – the - jetty!" No reaction. "Oh gods, he's as thick as crap!"

"Careful mashter, he hash weaponsh," whined Gannack. Panishak wasn't worried about this small newcomer. He liked the look of the black and shiny sword scabbard though and imagined it hanging from his own belt.

The figure suddenly stepped from the craft and stood confidently on the jetty with his legs slightly apart and arms loosely crossed in front of him. Panishak was not going to be humiliated by this calm-looking slanty-eyed outlander. "I'm taking you to the harbour's watch patrol," he said, again loudly. He moved forward to pin the figure's arms.

"Take his weapons men!" he ordered. As he moved in towards the foreigner, there was a blur of movement and Panishak suddenly found that his right wrist had been forced up between his shoulder blades, the small *wakisashi* short-sword had been whipped from the scabbard in the sash and was now positioned across his throat. The foreigner was behind him and Panishak couldn't, in fact did not dare, move. A small trickle of blood indicated to all those who were starting to congregate around the scene that it would take the smallest movement for Panishak to be sent to meet his forefathers. Nobody had ever seen Panishak bested in an altercation, particularly not in this manner and so quickly.

Everything went quiet. Nobody moved a muscle. The foreigner's dark eyes took in the complete scene but there was no expression of fear or concern on his face. A trickle of blood ran down the left side of the foreigner's face from a reopened wound on his head.

Jiutarô was, in fact *very* concerned. He would not show it. He was not afraid because he knew that if fear rose within him then his mind would be numbed. His years of training were serving him well. To him, these people were indeed primitive. The one who had taken the rope from him was the ugliest human being he had ever seen. It had *tusks* and smelt foul; its faeces encrusted the backs of its legs. *Ughh!!* This huge human smelt foul, too. *This place must be what the Jesuits called hell.* He looked from side to side. The city walls were behind him and he could see the harbour bay to his front. His horse waited patiently on the deck of the boat.

A shout came from the dock to Jiutarô's right. The sound of marching feet approached and a growing number of onlookers gave way to allow more room for the newcomers. The six men wore a uniform, of sorts; black hose, a red tunic and armoured breastplates. They wore small helms upon their heads. Their weapons were varied but each had a shortsword. The leader, Jiutarô assumed, of this militia had a dark tanned face with a short, pointed beard. Jiutarô had seen similar before, the Portuguese Jesuit missionaries were everywhere in Nippon these days, spreading their creed and becoming a nuisance, and they all seemed to favour these little beards. Perhaps he was in *their* country, not in *hell* after all; he hadn't heard rumour of tusked men though. *Perhaps this is really just a bad dream; maybe I am still unconscious in the boat.* He shook his head to clear the fuzziness.

Words were being said by the militia leader; Jiutarô did not understand and did not respond. This officer was getting more and more agitated and an apprehensive expression briefly appeared on his face as he took in the weaponry carried by the stranger. The man barked a command; all six of militia drew their short-swords and circled around Jiutarô and his prisoner who, by this time, was in tears.

Jiutarô was convinced the pathetic man had just pissed himself.

He used his training well. Hooking his right leg about that of his prisoner, he gave a firm push and sent the hapless man sprawling on top of the militia leader. Both fell to the ground in a tangled heap. With a controlled sweeping motion, Jiutarô withdrew his *katana* long-sword with his right hand, disarmed one attacker and cut straight through the short-swords of three others. One man only was left with his sword intact in his hand but he had no intention of fighting; the point of Jiutarô's *wakisashi*, now held in his left hand, was at the man's throat. Jiutarô's complete action had taken less time than it took to breathe in and out once. As before, his face was impassive as he once again took in the scene around him. Not one person had been hurt in the fight, except perhaps for the militia leader who had the full weight of Panishak on top of him.

The militia was in fact a detachment of the Westron Seaport City Watch. Harmon, its leader, was no fool. As he pulled himself out from underneath Panishak, a foul, stinking wretch, he knew immediately that the stranger could easily have killed them all. He had never in his life seen swordplay like it. The ability to pin the huge Panishak's arm while remaining so calm indicated a fighter with uncanny ability. A different approach was needed here.

"Panishak," he instructed. "Get your men out of here. Squad, put what remains of your swords away and form up over there, two ranks, smart now!" He pointed to an area near to the jetty. He looked over to the newly-arrived figure and gave a slight smile. "My man, if you please."

The stranger seemed to comprehend. He took the blade away from the man's neck and gently shoved him forwards.

Panishak and his men sloped off, although he did continue to look longingly at that barrel. The Watch had formed two ranks and stood easy. Panishak couldn't get close enough to the barrel to pick it up. *Soddit!* He hoped it would still be there later. A small group of people, adventurers by the look of them, stood close by; a tall, athletic fighter wearing a woollen hat, a young female priestess and a gnomish monk by his garb. One could never tell with gnomes.

The stranger remained with his blades at the ready but Harmon gave him a signal that he should put his weapon back into its scabbard. The stranger did not respond.

"Oh shit!" said Harmon.

"May we be of help here?" came a call from the small group of adventurers. The female priestess strode confidently over with a smile.

"He's an outlander, can't get him to understand me," replied the Watch leader. "You can have a go if you like."

"Alright, let's try it!" She stepped over to the stranger and offered her arm in greeting. He looked down and slowly lowered his katana and wakisashi but didn't return the greeting. The blades were the most beautiful she had ever seen. She had noticed, as had her companions, how the blade had cut right though the weapons of three Watch Men in one sweep.

She placed her hand upon her chest and said "Taura!"

The stranger raised his eyebrows and gave a look of comprehension. "Yazama Jiutarô," he replied with a small bow of his head. His countenance remained stern notwithstanding her kindliness. He eyed her from head to toe which she felt a little unsettling; she blushed and beckoned her companions over one at a time. The tall athletic figure strode over with confidence.

"Silmar," said Taura. "He calls himself Yazaa Juto, or something."

"Yazama Jiutarô" repeated the stranger as he cast a curious gaze over the elf's features.

The gnome stepped over and Jiutarô's gaze was one of complete amazement at the short but muscular figure with orange skin.

"And this is Billit," she introduced with a chuckle as she observed the stranger's expression.

The gnome growled "Not bloody funny, girly! Hey, is this outlander taking the pi-"

"I gather that you are going to take control of this stranger then," interrupted Harmon. He hoped she would accept; it was quite possible that this stranger could cause problems. He was fortunate because she replied with a nod. "Make sure he behaves himself or we'll have to run him in – if we can!" He strode over to his squad, brought them to the alert and marched them off.

"He'd better bring plenty of guards then!" sighed Silmar. "After all that, it looks like we have another companion, even if we can't talk with him!"

"That might be to our advantage," replied a sullen Billit. The other two laughed. "Let's get his kit off the boat then."

Jiutarô collected his weapons, armour and his belongings that remained on the little craft and put them on his magnificent horse. With gentle persuasion, they all managed to move the nervous horse off the boat and onto the jetty.

Silmar glanced at the horse as it stepped onto the jetty and immediately noticed the wounds on its forelegs. "They'll go bad if we don't clean them up" he recommended. "Can you do anything about them Taura?" Although priests were generally well-trained in healing people, regardless of their race, it was often a different matter when attending to animals.

"Well, I'll try," she replied. "Don't expect too much from me, I'm not very experienced." She rummaged inside a bag hanging on her belt. From it she took a small bottle of fluid that looked as if it contained water.

"What's that?" asked Billit.

"It is water! Very clean water with a plant extract to help wounds heal better. I'm going use some on Jeti, J—er, Juto's face too."

Using a cloth and the fluid, she cleaned up the horse's leg wounds and expertly bandaged the worst cut. Jiutarô looked on appreciatively. Taura then turned to Jiutarô himself who, after a brief refusal, reluctantly allowed her to treat the wound on his head. She started to quietly chant words while placing her hand over, but not touching, the injury. After a few moments, Jiutarô felt a warm glow followed by a tingling sensation on the side of his face. This went on for some minutes then she said "You'll live, Yazza Juto!"

"Yazama Jiutarô!" corrected Jiutarô, again. He put his hand to the side of his head and was surprised to feel that it no longer bled copiously. He looked at his fingertips, no wet blood, only dried scab.

"Aii!" he called. "Domo! Domo Arrigato!" gives a faint smile and gives a slight bow to Taura.

"Don't they do that in his land then? Hey, what's in that barrel?" asked Billit. "Have a look, young elf."

"Shhh! I'm not an elf, remember?" Silmar stepped over to inspect the barrel, turning it and sniffing around the bung.

"It's *rumm*!" he announced with a whoop.

They lifted it up onto the horse and he tied it securely, covering it with a cloak.

Five minutes later, as they rounded the corner of a small timber shed, they almost bumped into the taskmaster and his group of workhands. Panishak took a step towards Jiutarô with a face full of fury. "Now, look!" he yelled, "You got my –"

Jiutarô withdrew his curved *katana* and, with a cry of "Kii-ai", swept it in a perfect circle and replaced it back into its scabbard, all in a heartbeat. A wisp of the taskmaster's hair floated to the ground.

Panishak shrank back and called, "Back to the jetty men".

They were gone in a trice. The little group of adventurers gasped at the incredible, hitherto unseen, display of swordsmanship.

"I know what the fat slob is after!" laughed Billit. They all laughed, even Jiutarô chuckled. His hand was still going up to his now completely closed wound; just the scabbed-over red swelling that still irritated him.

Twenty minutes later, it was late afternoon and they were back in the Tavern. Ralmon was laughing too; he was now the proud owner of a barrel of rumm, a rare and expensive commodity in these lands towards the north of Baylea. Not only were the adventurers now staying at the inn at no cost but they seemed to be consuming endless ale, mead or wine. Now there was a fourth member of their group. The rumm however, more than covered his losses.

Jiutarô was devouring a mutton stew and his second quart tankard of ale. His weapons, the strange, colourful armour and his belongings, such as they were, were neatly stacked beside his table. The group looked at the bow and armour with curiosity.

"Ale!" called Jiutarô, in the *universal* language, as he slammed the empty pot down onto the table.

"He's learnin' choddin' fast, that one," grumbled Ralmon. There was more laughter from the group as an impolite belch burst from a nonchalant Yazama Jiutarô.

"I do believe we now number four," murmured Silmar to nobody in particular.

During the evening, Jiutarô was quite drunk and Billit wasn't far behind him. Ralmon beckoned Silmar over to the bar and glanced about the taproom furtively.

"'Ere, elf," he murmured, "take these." He passed Silmar three items.

"First, young elf," he said. "This is your pay in advance for getting' me wagon up the road to Nor'wald. Go on, open it up."

Silmar took hold of a small leather pouch and pulled on the drawstring. Inside a large number of gold crowns glistened!

"Five an' twenny!" whispered the one-armed dwarf. That was a considerable sum. "Right, now," he continued. "This is a map o' your journey up to Nor'wald City. I'll come over an' speak with you all when I'm not so busy. Also, Halorun Tann got one of 'is acolyte priests to leave you a list and a rough map so you knows where you is goin' when you turns east."

Silmar looked at it and was surprised at the detail. There was much writing on the map but he couldn't read it in the dim light of the tavern. Ralmon then handed him a package rolled in cloth. The elf was about to unroll it when Ralmon slapped his hand over the top.

"Gods, boy!" he gasped in a coarse whisper. "Keep this 'idden away, young 'un. It's that special thing you asked for. If yer gets caught with it on yer person, you didn't get it off 've me."

"I'll give you something for these now," said Silmar, reaching into his pouch to give Ralmon the payment.

"No, ain't necess'ry," said Ralmon. "They ain't new; the feller I got 'em from 'as adapted 'em for some of them modern locks that are comin' out o' Cascant these days. As I said, I called in a favour. No charge, just tuck 'em away inside your tunic, lad, quick now!"

"I cannot thank you enough, Ralmon. Well, in that case, quarts of ales for us all and one for yourself as well."

"Done!" The dwarf scratched at his thick beard for a moment. "Hey, 'ang on – you ain't payin' for 'em, anyways!"

Silmar sat down with the quart pots.

"Ale!" cried Jiutarô once again. "Domo!" The others laughed.

"I suppose *domo* means thanks in his speak," observed Billit. "I'm gonna try to educate him in speaking proper."

"You and Ralmon were deep in conversation," said Taura. "Anything for us?"

"Aye," said Silmar, brandishing the moneybag and map. "Five and twenty gold for our payment and a couple of maps. He's coming over later to chat about our road north."

"Don't like the look of this area here," said Taura with a worried frown. "It is a symbol of a grinning skull. On a map, a symbol like that which is drawn by a temple, it usually means that there is undead in that area."

"Well," replied Billit, "it's clearly not a new map. Mebbe it's not a dangerous area now. Mebbe Ralmon can explain the route. Mebbe it's guarded. Mebbe –"

"Maybe there's liches, zombies or skeletons!" suggested a pessimistic Taura. "Or all of them – ugh!"

"Maybe you won't be going on your journey alone," said Ralmon. They all jumped as he crept up behind Silmar from behind a wide pillar. "Heehee. Heh heh!"

"Very amusin'," muttered Billit. "Didn't think dwarves were renowned for moving with stealth."

"The road will be fairly busy," warned Ralmon. "I've 'ad a word with a caravan master. His name's Kassall and 'is wagons leave from outside the North Gate an hour after sunup tomorrow. There's a couple of things to remember though."

He leaned forward as if they were discussing a conspiracy. "Although they are travelling as a caravan, you can't travel as part of it 'cos if you do then he has to take responsibility fer you an' that could cost 'im extra in tolls and stuff. Keep fairly close an' they'll 'elp look after you. At night, camp close to 'em but not as part of 'em an' they'll give you what protection they can. If trouble comes to 'em though, you'll be expected to 'elp. Any questions?"

The friends all shook their head, it all seemed perfectly clear.

"I'll be out back in mah courtyard after yer dawn meal tomorrer; I'll provide you with plenty o' food, water, some blankets an' stuff, an' two ponies. Just make sure that my bruvver Jasper 'as it all when you get there. Best yer get an early night; I'll be callin' yous for yer morning feast an hour afore dawn."

On that, the four went up to their rooms and settled down for the night. Silmar was just about to settle onto his bed when there was a knock at his door. Ralmon stood there with a backpack in his hand.

"Look, young elf. I got this huge debt o' gratitude for yer pappy; like I told yer, 'e saved me life once or twice durin' our days together. There was no judgement fer me bein' a dwarf an' all. I'd be 'onoured if you'd take this 'ere ol' backpack o' mine. Couldn't help but notice all yer gear in that sack earlier. Well, that's no choddin' good is it? Put yer bundle in this. It's well worn in and you 'ardly feel its weight when the waist strap is tightly done up. I'll be 'appy knowing it's back in use again by the son of an old campaigning partner. Go on."

Silmar took it with gratitude, saying he hoped to return it sometime in the future when the world was a safer place, if it ever would be. Ralmon bade him goodnight and left.

Silmar closed the door and propped a chair up behind it, for security as always, and settled down to sleep. Some moments later there was another knock on his door but lighter this time. He climbed up off the floor, sighed, removed the chair and opened the door. The caller was invited in and remained there for the rest of the night.

Although he recalled his father's words of warning, in this instance he gave them scant regard.

CHAPTER 9

T HE DÖKKÁLFR, or Darkling, slayer of the Priest of Clamberhan in
that lightless passage off the Street of the Moon in Westron Seaport,
now lurked in a disused shed behind a stockyard. His skin was as black
as pitch but his hair as grey and colourless as the slate-rock on the sides
of the mountains. He could never show himself to the people who lived
on the surface; he was safer underground. Not that he couldn't protect
himself though, he was a weapons-master without equal in Myrkheim, the
Dökkálfar subterranean city complex, the Darkling city of the deep below
the western end of the Dragon's Teeth Mountains. The hue and cry that
would result, however, would seriously jeopardise the mission on which he
and his warband had been sent. He moved only at night, kept clear of the
highways but always keeping them within sight.

He had a troop of comrades waiting for him in a cavern at the north of
the Spinewall Mountains. He preferred being alone; a group of riders were
more noticeable, but he was not given the option this time. *She* saw to that.

During the day he shunned the light, covering his head in a sheer dark
brown cloth through which he could see but not be seen or recognised. His
clothing was of a blue so dark as to be almost black; this would make him
almost invisible in the night, wherever he was. A hood attached to his tunic
could be pulled so far forward as to hide his head and face, covered or no.

This servant of the Goddess Adelenis sect and the High-Mage cabal
was furious. The foolish *Ljósálfar* elf, as the Dökkálfar referred to the
surface-dwelling pale elves, had interfered with his mission and taken the
very artefact that was much desired by his mistress, the soceress – *she*
who thrived on killing and torture. He dare not fail. He would hunt for
that *Ljósálfar,* the so-called *high elf* that may have been able to identify
him, who may yet alert the single-minded tenacious Tarne priesthood to

his existence, the one who carried the prize. The white elf would feel the full power of the dagger; he would then need guidance from a priest with power and knowledge – hah! Perhaps the infamous meddlesome Halorun Tann himself.

The Darkling knew of the dogged determination of the Priesthood of Tarne and that one in particular, Halorun Tann, was the most feared and resolute warrior-priest of them all. Tann, of the black eyes, who was said to be able to see into the very soul of a man, Darkling, white elf or dwarf. He both founded, and presided over, the newest and largest temple on the West Coast yet to have been dedicated to the God of Justice, the head of the Pantheon of the Greater Gods. Tarne it was, so it is said, who intended to dispense justice to Adelenis, the Scorpion Queen, after a trial in her absence which left her a fugitive in hiding. Her surface-bound devotees and her most loyal of followers, the Hoshites, had been confused and leaderless for some centuries but with clandestine guidance from the Darklings, they rallied and were slowly beginning to spread westwards from the far side of the East Brash mountain range.

The assassin considered the most likely course of action that the surface-dwellers would take. The precious dagger would be taken away by Tann's lackeys, that was clear. Tann, or perhaps even the city's Magelords, would not tolerate the *thing* remaining in the city, let alone his own temple. It would surely be moved on the road but which way? West? No, not to the sea. South to the land of the burning sand? Unlikely. East through Shordrun and Polduman towards the Kamambia from whence it came? Very possible indeed; logical too. North towards Northwald City or even further to Icedge? That was also very possible, albeit unlikely.

Where to wait then? East by the Great East Silk Road to watch the travellers, pick them off those that seemed to be the likely ones. Give him two days, maybe three, and if the white elf did not appear, he would ride north and overtake him in the night. Yes, watch for that elf then take both his life and the dagger. Or *with* the dagger; hah, a fitting use for it!

Yes, the Scorpion Queen, mused the Darkling. *A fanatical but naïve Goddess too big for her boots! But the priestess-sorceress, the Cabal's fanatical emissary from Myrkheim, an impatient fool but* nasty. Adelenis and the Cabal should be more careful whom they choose as their agent. The Darkling female mage-priest chosen specifically by the Scorpion Queen, it was said, was devious and calculating. The Cabal and the Adelenis priesthood would continue to send out Hoshite agents and spies, hatch plots and collect more artefacts of power. They would bide their time and when they had amassed sufficient power and resources, their armies of Dökkálfar would strike swiftly and simultaneously at the very hearts of the power bases of the Landsdrop Coast, Shordrun, Cascant, Kamambia and other countries on the continent of Baylea. But she couldn't do this alone; she needed allies. Who better than those of the *Shadow World* beneath the Dragon's Teeth mountains? The mighty Dökkálfar would gather and lead the vicious Grullien Shade Dwarves and the expendable kobolds and goblinoids. The Hoshites, though, would need to be paid and would never accept the majesty of the Scorpion Queen.

But the Great Adelenis would lead and in the end even the Hoshites were expendable.

He smiled as he pictured the face of his God, her spiteful and bitter beauty; the pure whiteness of her face, although she had been Darkling once; Her bulbous, round crustacean-like body with its long thin barbed tail; her desire to feed on living flesh, human or even better, elven – but not Dökkálfar. A Priest of Tarne was said to be her favourite delicacy. Hmm, a pity he could not feed her Halorun Tann! Perhaps one day.

Meanwhile there was that stupid bastard of a yellow-haired elf to find. And kill. Slowly.

CHAPTER 10

*T*HIS IS NOT *real! Perhaps I am dead and in one of those absurd Jesuit hells. Perhaps it is a nightmare. Am I still unconscious in the bottom of the boat? Shall I awaken and find myself back in the boat with my two horses and that drunken boatman? I hope so, this place is bizarre! I have seen a bestial man with tusks, an orange-skinned, red-haired midget, a one-armed long-bearded dwarf and many other strange beings. I am in a city where chaos reigns. This cannot be real therefore I am not really here. Is a god, Buddha perhaps, punishing me for my past transgression by putting me in this nightmare? It cannot be real therefore I refuse to believe it. If it is not real I cannot die. I shall awaken sometime and all will be well. It is strange that the pain in my hand did not wake me up. My destiny is to die beside my forty-six comrades after having avenged my dead master. I must be there. I cannot let them down. My face wound was healed with a touch and a whispered prayer or mantra – surely this cannot happen; it does not happen; it is not real. These people have been kind to me, they have offered friendship. I shall remain with them while I am in this nightmare and, if necessary, fight alongside them provided they are just in their actions. I have my weapons, my yoroi armour and my skills. I shall follow the stream as it flows; although its course constantly changes, it always reaches its destination. Then I am sure I shall awaken. It will all have been a bad dream. It cannot be real.*
    I refuse to believe it.

It was still dark when Ralmon banged on their doors, typically showing little respect for his other slumbering guests. Silmar had slept in his separate bedchamber; accepting the offer to share with his new companions the previous night would not been conducive to a good night's sleep. Well, that was the excuse he had given them the previous evening! However, they weren't fooled.

The dawn meal was good once again and afterwards, they collected their equipment and met with Ralmon in the courtyard. A fully loaded wagon, with the same two tired-looking horses they had seen the previous day, waited for them. A fit-looking pony and Jiutarô's horse were tethered to the rear of the wagon.

"Don't look so worried," the grizzled innkeeper said. "Them cart 'orses may look like plodders but they're strong enough an' will go all day. Make sure that you're 'appy with the wagon. There's barrels o' mead an' wine aboard look, but this small one 'ere," he said pointing to a smaller barrel tucked in a front corner of the wagon, "contains a special brew, elven blood-wine."

Silmar's eyebrows shot up, this was a valuable cargo indeed. "But this is worth a small fortune!" he exclaimed excitedly.

"Just make sure that Jasper gets it *all*. He gets special clients, see! Right then, Kassall is waiting for yer outside the gates, yer need to be there in an 'alf-hour." He pointed to their supplies and blankets and continued. "Yer all lookin' like folks who can look after yerselves but may the gods protect you on the journey. When yer gets to the town of Nor'wald City, get yerselves some warm clothing, furs and the like. It gets cold up north."

There was a cry and Sheena ran out into the courtyard. She glanced around until her gaze locked on Silmar. Then she rushed across and flung her arms around his neck and kissed him full on the lips. He made no effort to resist. Then, in tears but without another sound, she turned and rushed back inside.

Taura chuckled and made a face at Silmar who stood there with a bewildered expression. "Is she the reason you slept in your own bedchamber last night? She is very pretty and I'm *so* jealous of her figure! You did, didn't you? None of us were fooled you know and she wasn't all that discrete during the night."

Silmar didn't reply immediately but beneath the dark facial colouring his cheeks flushed and he looked down at his feet. "Look," he began. "I only –"

"What are you up to with mah new cook?" demanded Ralmon. "She's 'alf asleep this mornin' an' I got lots of work for 'er to do."

Silmar took the dwarf to one side. "You will look after her for me, won't you?"

"Aye, I will, elf. But think well about this and the implications. You knows what I mean, doesn't you?"

Silmar knew what he meant. His father had nagged him for years over this. Unions between elves and humans were generally doomed because of the long lives of elves compared to those of humans. The tragedy came when an elf would outlive his or her spouse, children and grandchildren. But, although these unions were not common, there was often happiness and success but these were tinged with tragedy.

While the strange swordsman, Jiutarô, made ready his horse, Taura checked the tackle but stepped back with a frown. "This isn't done up the same as it was yesterday."

Billit came over to the wagon. "What's different, girlie?"

"Well, the yoke traces are the other way round and this buckle's joined up to that strap instead of this one." She indicated the differences.

The others looked on uncomprehendingly.

"Can you still drive the horses with the different way it's strapped up?" asked Silmar. "It may not be important."

She looked at the traces and rubbed the back of her head. "Well, aye, I think I can. It may be done that way to help the horses pull up hills better. I'll have to see. If there's a problem, I'll have to see if I can retackle the ponies."

Silmar and Billit nodded knowingly, while barely understanding a word of what she was saying, but also impressed with her newly found knowledge of the terminology.

Billit, being too short in stature to ride in a saddle, climbed up onto the wagon's seat. Silmar indicated to Jiutarô that they were about to ride off and they both climbed onto their mounts.

With final farewells from Ralmon, they rode out of the courtyard and on through the city to the North Gate. After a while they passed out of the still, quiet city through a large gate and spotted the caravan in an area by the left-hand side of the road.

Kassall was waiting for them. He introduced himself. "We're off in a few moments," he explained. "Keep close, by all means but if anyone asks, you're not part of my caravan."

Taura nodded to indicate that they understood the terms. Soon, the caravan pulled out and Taura positioned the wagon at the rear, although a good fifty yards back. Silmar rode in silence with his wide, woollen cap pulled low over his face, his watchful eyes hiding the fact that he was deep in the thoughts of his night with little sleep.

As the journey progressed the group found that they were beginning to lag behind. The road surface was good and there were few slopes. By midday however, they were almost a mile behind. Although the horses did not appear to be labouring, it was clear that they were not able to go at a faster speed than they were already travelling.

"We must stop to give the horses a break," advised Silmar. The others readily agreed. The horses were given water and food and the trio fed on some of the food that Ralmon had provided.

"P'raps it's the way the nags are strapped up," ventured Billit.

"I think not," answered Taura, "but I'll look at the straps later when we stop for the evening."

The journey was resumed after a half-hour and the caravan was spotted about a mile ahead. At this distance, the friends could see that outriders from the caravan were halting to observe their progress.

Although having no understanding of the language, Jiutarô had settled into the journey well, having ridden out on the flank or in front to keep an eye on the safety of the little group. When he did ride close in, he listened avidly to the exchanges of conversation between Billit and Taura. The gnome spent much of the journey speaking words and phrases which the Samurai echoed back.

Finally, evening came and the concerns of the trio were growing. "We'll have to stop soon," Taura advised. They all agreed.

"Let's go on awhile," said Billit. "P'raps we'll catch 'em."

As darkness descended further, the glow of cooking fires could be seen in the distance.

"That's probably no more than a mile ahead," Silmar called from thirty yards up the road. "It shouldn't take that long to get there."

He was right, fifteen minutes later they arrived at the edge of the caravan's camping area.

Kassall strode over with a relieved expression. "We were worried about you!" he exclaimed. "Thank the gods you're here safely. I was about to despatch one of my riders to see where you were."

"We are grateful for your concern, Goodman Kassall," replied Taura. "Are you happy that we take this spot for our camp?"

"Aye, this is fine. We'll be mounting a guard but I suggest you do the same. Unlikely to be any trouble in these parts but you don't always know what's come out of the mountains to the north."

"We're here if you need us," offered Silmar.

"Likewise. G'night," said Kassall.

The companions tended to their ponies and horses and lit a small fire. Billit cooked a meal of three rabbits from the six that Ralmon had thoughtfully provided. Being a mage required Billit to take as much sleep as he could during the night but he took the first watch regardless. He woke Jiutarô soon after midnight and, using sign language of sorts, indicated that the man should take over the watch.

Silmar volunteered to take the *graveyard watch*; that being the period leading up to dawn when everything appeared grey until the sun's first light shone over the horizon. It had taken a long time for him to get to sleep before that. The previous night, Sheena had come to his room soon after everybody had retired to their quarters. The elf had opened his door when he heard the light tap and when she had reached to touch his hand; he took hold of hers and had gently led her into his room. She had stayed there with him all night and they were still wrapped up together when Ralmon had knocked loudly on the door in the morning.

Happily, there were no incidents during the night and the friends had a reasonable night's sleep. They awoke at dawn and finished off the cold rabbit with some bread. The sun's first light did not appear as bright this morning as it had the previous day. In fact, the heavy clouds threatened rain. The caravan was still preparing to move off by the time the friends had hitched the horses to the wagon and mounted their ponies.

The ride continued although the countryside was now more undulating than before. The snow-capped summits of the mountains some leagues to the east were blanketed in heavy clouds but seemed a little closer than they had appeared the day before. Fortuitously, the rain passed them by to the south. Within a couple of hours, the caravan was once again a good half-mile ahead. Billit and Silmar agreed that, with Jiutarô, they should all act as scouts to ensure the safekeeping of themselves and the wagon.

"Don't get out of sight of each other, or the wagon," suggested Taura. Billit tried to explain to Jiutarô. They nodded their agreement.

The sound of horses galloping towards them caught their attention soon afterwards. Their hands hovered very close to their weapons. Two riders from the caravan approached.

"Kassall sent us," one rider explained. "We're some way ahead now and it will be difficult for us to lend you our protection, but we have these whistles. They are very loud. If you need us, use these."

With that, they turned and spurred their horses away, eager to be back to provide, as well as to receive, the safety and protection of their caravan.

"Thank–" called Silmar towards their rapidly disappearing backs. The little group gained little measure of comfort knowing although they had to rely on their own they at least had a means by which help could be summoned if necessity arose.

An hour later, a sudden, piercing yell like a war cry emitted from beyond a low hill to their right. Silmar immediately reined in his mount, turned it about and galloped back to the wagon, much to Taura's relief. A moment later Jiutarô's horse, with him upon it wielding his unusual bow over his head, thundered over a low rise. Without slowing his horse's pace, his right hand flashed over his shoulder and drew an arrow. He turned in his saddle to release the arrow behind him. He yelled something unintelligible as he approached the wagon.

CHAPTER 11

A MASSIVE FIGURE abruptly appeared over the low rise from which Jiutarô had ridden. It rushed straight towards them though it was still some way off. Silmar recognised it immediately although it was the first that he had ever seen.

Jiutarô watched with an incredulous expression, another arrow at the ready which he then released at the figure just as his horse reared. He thought the arrow passed between the thing's legs. He yelled something in his own tongue.

"An ogre! An ogre, by the gods!" Silmar screamed. "Arm yourselves, make ready."

He leapt down from his horse and hitched it to the rear of the wagon. He drew both of his swords for the first time.

Jiutarô threw his bow to the grass and dropped from his saddle, leaving the reins trailing. He slid his katana from its scabbard and stood with both hands on the hilt.

Billit remained on the wagon, to give himself the advantage of extra height. He began to chant in a singsong voice and his hands weaved an intricate pattern before him.

They were all unmistakably nervous at what could be their first encounter.

The ogre was huge, fully eight feet in height, probably more. It had an animal-skin cloth stretched across its bulbous midriff. Its muscle-bound body was covered in short, dark hair but the head was completely hairless. It was obviously male. It was unarmed but its muscular physique, long arms and great, clawed hands made weapons seem pointless. The ogre roared as it ran towards them, its arms flailing. Then, unexpectedly, it turned away to their right in a direction that took it away from them.

Suddenly, there was another call, a war cry, but this time not from the ogre. Immediately, two monstrous beasts rushed out at high speed from around the base of the same hill. None of them, not even Silmar who seemed knowledgeable on beasts and monstrosities, had seen creatures of this kind before. They could only be described as crab-like but with the head of a humanoid – bulbous and bald but with elongated canine teeth. These were huge monstrosities beyond belief, being twice the height of a man. They scuttled partly upright on six legs and had two large pincers.

They were heading directly for the wagon and the group.

Taura's horses stamped and reared in panic. With Taura struggling, the traces and reins barely held them under control. The wagon rocked back and forth as she fought for control.

Once again, Jiutarô watched the monstrosities in disbelief and horror. His mouth hung open but then his own horse began to rear in panic. He stepped over and grabbed the reins with a free hand and fought to pacify the terrified beast. He dropped the reins and stamped his foot on the trailing ends. He swiftly sheathed his sword and grabbed at his bow once again.

"Taura!" yelled Silmar. "Get the wagon away, fast!"

Amongst the sound of thrashing reins were yells of rage from Taura as she continued her fight to control the wagon and horses and to get them moving. Billit slumped down onto the seat as the wagon lurched forwards, grabbing hold of the backboard as his attempted spell dissipated into nothingness. Silmar took out the whistle and blew hard, repeatedly. Its sound reverberated around the hills.

"Help will surely soon be on its way," he cried, his voice high-pitched from both anxiety and excitement. In the past he'd had the protection of many other elves, all of whom he knew and trusted, in a potential battle situation; now, he had his own wits together with the unknown capabilities of his three new comrades – their first real test.

Jiutarô loosed off an arrow at one of the crab-like abominations but it flew harmlessly between its gangling limbs. It seemed not to notice.

The two beasts suddenly veered to follow the ogre, whether as a result of Billit's spell or because the ogre was in reality their quarry they couldn't tell. But soon it became clear that the two beasts were now chasing after the ogre.

The battle-cry sounded once more but it was not from the crab-like abominations. Another figure, this time on horseback, burst out at full gallop from around the hill. A man, bare-chested and with long, straw-coloured, flowing hair, chased out after the two monstrous beasts and proved to be the originator of the battle cry. He carried a long, wooden javelin in the manner of a lance.

By now, Taura and the wagon, with Billit hanging on for his life, were fifty yards along the road with Jiutarô, back on his horse, riding alongside in defence. His bow was over his shoulder and his katana was in his hand. He shouted something at Taura but she didn't understand. Billit rose to his feet again and commenced his chanting. Silmar took up a defensive position but neither the galloping horseman, the crab-like humanoid figures or the ogre appeared to be taking any interest in them.

Billit's chanting fell to a whisper while confusion as to what was going on set in. Silmar's sword arms dropped a little.

Taura slowed the wagon and, with Jiutarô helping by tugging the bridle of one of the horses, started to bring it about to return to the point where Silmar was positioned; she was not going to be left out of the action!

The *crab-men* were onto the ogre in an instant; one of them chopped its front limb at the ogre's legs and it went down with a roar of pain and terror. Their crab-like pincers held its arms and their mouths hovered just inches away from its head and upper body.

The horseman, a barbarian of some kind, was large and quite pale of skin although he was tanned by prolonged exposure to the sun. He was dressed only in a loincloth and what appeared to be goatskin boots. He reined in a few paces from the *crab-men* and climbed out of the saddle. He signalled to them, with his hand, to eat. The monsters continued to wait, though.

The look of terror on the face of the ogre raised some sympathy from Silmar despite the fact that ogres would show no mercy whatsoever with their captives. He shuddered inwardly as he thought of what would inevitably occur soon. He could hear the *crab-men* chattering to each other.

With Billit on the seat beside her and Jiutarô riding close by, Taura pulled the wagon up alongside the elf. "Wasn't going off to let you have all the fun," she called. Her face became grim as she looked across at the crab-men and their prey.

The barbarian strode slowly towards them. He was at least seven-feet tall and very muscular. They raised their weapons. He looked at the weapons seemingly with little concern. They noticed that as he walked forward his horse followed him less than a pace behind. The barbarian did not make any threatening gestures.

He stopped five paces from the companions.

"Are you the master of these beasts?" asked Silmar.

The barbarian didn't answer but continued to look at them with a quizzical expression.

"Are the beasts yours?" repeated Silmar.

"Perhaps he don't understand," offered Billit. The barbarian continued to look at them without speaking.

Billit placed his hand on his chest and said "I am Niebellittin, er, Billit."

The barbarian echoed "Billit, a gnome." He placed his hand on his own chest and replied "Makkadan, man-name Falcon. I do understand."

Silmar pointed to himself and said "I'm Silmar."

Falcon echoed "Silmar, an elf," and then added "I am Makkadan, man-name Falcon, a goblin-slayer. From the north." He pointed to the wagon.

"She is Taura, er, and Juto," answered Billit.

"Jiutarô!" corrected Jiutarô. "Ji – u – tar - ower!"

Falcon again echoed the names.

By the god's, thought Billit, *this is 'ard work, just like getting Juto to understand me the other day!*

The monsters chittered again. Silmar jerked his head up; he was certain he could make out the word *Hunger!*

"Eat all!" exclaimed Falcon. "The beasts are not mine. We shared my meat and then I brought them to this hunting ground. They eat ogre, goblin and troll. They will leave soon. They will eat the ogre first but they waited to see if I wished to share. I did not."

Immediately, the *crab-men* set about their prey, rending the ogre limb from limb and feeding as if they were starving. To the group, the sight was gruesome but Falcon seemed unmoved by the sight and sound of the carnage. Jiutarô grimaced and turned his head away from the grisly scene.

"Oh, damn it!" cried Silmar. "I called for help from the caravan. Somebody will be here in a moment." He rode off up the road and reined in after about a hundred yards or so. He could hear the approach of horses already. They were probably only a moment away.

Meanwhile, the *crab-men* were chittering excitedly. Falcon answered back in a manner that was difficult for the others to follow – a combination of words and hand signals.

Jiutarô looked at Billit and fought to find the word. "Aii, um, bad," he said. He raised an eyebrow triumphantly.

Billit nodded. "Aye, bad," he agreed.

"They shall go now," explained Falcon. The *crab-men* scuttled away in the direction from which they had appeared, leaving behind them the detritus of their meal.

Up the road, Silmar welcomed the four riders from the caravan with a look of some embarrassment and explained the situation. The riders could clearly see the two *crab-men* in the distance heading away from the road but, on the insistence of Silmar, made no attempt to follow.

"What in the hells of the Void were those things?" asked one of them.

"I have no idea," he responded and then went on to describe the last few moments.

They were somewhat amused by Silmar's explanation although they fully understood the difficulty the group had thought they were in. With a cheery wave, the riders rode off towards the caravan. Silmar returned to the others.

Taura advised the group that they continue their journey. "We're miles behind them now," she warned.

Falcon was invited to travel with them awhile. He shrugged and looked about the hills but then nodded.

The midday rest came and went and their journey progressed. Rare were the times now when the group spotted the caravan. It was probably more than two miles ahead of them, by now far out of range of the sound of the whistle were the need to arise. Falcon spoke the Universal language haltingly but as time progressed during the afternoon he showed his willingness to learn from them all.

The afternoon passed quietly and once again thoughts turned towards catching up with the caravan by nightfall. The glow from the campfires was spotted while the group was still some distance away and it was fully dark by the time that they came within sight of the caravan camp. The guards patrolling the perimeter of the camp showed obvious relief once again. Kassell was relieved to see them and mentioned that there was an abundance of rabbit in the area and that with the half-moon it was not too dark to hunt.

"We have one coney left," Taura told them, holding the rabbit before her. "Not nearly enough for us all tonight."

"Then I shall hunt," replied Falcon.

"I would like to join you," Silmar stated. "I can use a bow, but I have never seen one such as yours."

The barbarian's bow was unusual. It was short, probably no longer than four feet from tip to tip. The bow appeared to be made of wood, horn and sinew and looked very powerful, albeit ungainly.

"You may come," answered Falcon, with his impassive expression.

Do you ever smile? Taura thought. "We'll get a cooking fire going and keep watch then, shall we?" she asked with more than a hint of sarcasm in her voice. "Then you boys can go out playing!"

"We guard," said Billit to Jiutarô, while tapping his dagger and pointing to his eyes.

"*Hai*, guard," replied Jiutarô. He strode off to the periphery of their campsite, watching Silmar and Falcon as they walked off over the nearest hill. He slowly strode around the edge of their camp, listening and looking intently.

Silmar and Falcon searched for sign and soon found a rabbit run. Droppings were scattered everywhere. In the darkness the rabbits had come out of their burrows and were grazing out in the open, well within an arrow's distance. Falcon withdrew a pair of flint-tipped arrows, held one in his teeth, readied the other and fired at the group of rabbits. He hit one but the others scattered before he could make ready his second arrow. Retrieving the rabbit, and the arrow, he made a signal for them to move on.

"You move quietly, it is good!" the Barbarian quietly pronounced to Silmar.

The elf was pleased with the compliment and explained that he had some experience in this kind of movement. "As do you. I have also hunted goblins near the lands of my kinsmen," he stated.

Now fully dark, Silmar used his dark-vision, an ability of all elves to see a short distance in almost total darkness. Dwarves had the gift too, evidently, although Silmar had in the past cared little for these beings despite the fact that his hometown had a very small and reclusive dwarven community. This attitude had changed somewhat since meeting Ralmon in the Ship's Prow tavern. "I see well in the dark," he explained.

"I know this," answered Falcon. He obviously had some knowledge of elves but he offered no further explanation.

Falcon offered Silmar his bow and an arrow, similarly flint tipped. He pointed out a rabbit less than fifty yards away and Silmar took aim and fired but the arrow went wide by inches. The weapon felt heavy and unbalanced in his hands. Falcon seemed impressed though. Once again, the rabbits scattered. They waited patiently and quietly but it was quite a while before the rabbits reappeared. Shooting their arrows simultaneously, they brought down two more, and a third from an arrow that Silmar swiftly let fly. It was time to return to the campsite.

The first rabbit was already prepared and stewed by the time the pair returned and Falcon, Silmar and Jiutarô went to work preparing the other three.

The group followed the caravan this way for another five days. Each evening they arrived at the caravan's camp an hour or so after sundown. Billit would sit beside Jiutarô for a couple of hours each evening teaching him some of the Universal language – the *Samurai*, as he referred to himself, picked some of the phrases up quite quickly. Taura spent time doing the same with Falcon.

On the sixth day they were too far behind the caravan to even consider catching up with it at the end of the day. Kassall sent a pair of his outriders to them to say that the caravan would not expect them to catch up and that he could no longer wait. He had wished them a safe journey. The riders waved and rode away. They were on their own, and unprotected.

CHAPTER 12

A MOTHER SOBBED over the loss of her son who had died from a disease a week ago; influenza, the wise woman had informed her. Why, oh why, had she not taken advantage of opportunities to leave this village behind and journey with her son either north to the city of Northwald or south to the huge city of Westron Seaport? Either city might have given her opportunities for work. She was still young, only in her mid-twenties as far as she could reckon. She was very intelligent and extremely nimble with her fingers. Her husband had been dead these last six years and she had scratched out a living on the little plot of land. It provided her with enough money to keep her hut clean, her son and herself clothed and fed; but precious little else. The opportunities didn't seem to come these days; was she losing her looks? Her hair was long, dark and, when cared for, lustrous, and her figure was one to be proud of; she needn't have been concerned about that. Her hands were roughened from hard work but when cared-for they looked better. The trouble was that there was nobody there to tell her that; only the occasional traveller on the road.

She heard the sound of hoof-beats and looked out of the window. It was a man, or so it appeared, sitting on a small black horse. The hazy sunshine seemed to make the rider's costume look a deep blue; so deep as to almost make it appear black although road dust had made it scruffy. It was always a hazy sunshine here; something to do with the nearby saltwater swamp, the village men said. She couldn't see the rider's face; the hood was pulled so far forward that the face remained hidden. He carried very little baggage on his horse except for whatever may have been rolled up in his dark-grey blanket, but she did notice a black sheath as he wheeled his horse to look about him. She suddenly felt uncomfortable and an ice-cold shiver went down her spine.

The dark rider had stopped his horse to address an elderly man who was sitting, with a smoke-weed pipe in his hand, on the porch of his little hut. "I seek a traveller, an elf," the rider rasped in a thin, reedy voice. "Long golden hair. A friend. He travels this way. He may be with others. When did he ride through?"

The old man coughed on his smoke and spat onto the road. "Nay. Not seen no-one like that, not today," came the response.

"Yesterday, the day before, or before that?"

"Nah. Not in a ten-day week."

The rider was becoming impatient. "You see every traveller who comes through?"

"Got nuttin' else to do," the old man wheezed.

"If you lie, I shall be back," growled the rider. He spurred his horse and galloped through the village, pausing for a moment at the little square to replenish his waterskin while his horse drank from the stone trough. He considered his options and then rode eastwards along a little-used road towards the small mountains to the east.

The old man puffed on his pipe, shrugged his shoulders and shook his head.

The woman, still watching from her window, held her hand to her thumping chest. *He seeks that young man that rode through here yester-eve with his friends, I'll be bound. Silmar was his name but there was something elvish about him.* That rider did not seem to be one that Silmar would call his *friend*. She would have to warn him when, or if, he came back. She sat on her wicker chair and rocked back and forth clutching a piece of her son's clothing, crying softly.

Two hours later, a heavily-laden wagon pulled by two massive, long-horned oxen slowly creaked its way into the village. Two men sat on its high board and an armed rider followed closely behind. The drover jumped down and called to the old man. "Is there a priest in this village?"

"In Nor'wald City, why?"

"My son has been murdered in the night. He did nothing wrong, he was only fourteen summers." The man's face was tear-streaked. "A rider in black came into our camp, next thing we know he's riding out again. There was my son lying dead on the ground. Is there a provost or thief-taker here?"

The old man shuffled over and pulled back the blanket. The boy's neck had been slashed. His long blond hair was matted with blood.

The grieving mother had stepped out of her hut and now rushed to the wagon and what she saw made her gasp with horror, her hand flying up to her mouth. The elderly villager replaced the blanket and shuffled away puffing on his pipe. He sat on his porch and shook his head sombrely.

The woman immediately took the initiative. "My name is Janna," she declared. "Send your outrider onwards. A wagon with two on the board and three riders will be no more than half a day ahead. Speak with them. They have a cleric with them. Tell them a rider in a black cloak is looking for them. They may know what to do."

The wagon, in fact, was no more than half a league along the road. They had stopped at the little community of Dange Marsh the previous evening but, because of the lack of a tavern, they had camped in the little square. They left at dawn but within the hour one of their wagon-horses had thrown a shoe. Although Taura had swopped the horse with Jiutarô's mount, it was a far from adequate solution – the horses were badly-mismatched and Jiutarô's mount was resistant. They decided to return to the little village. Taura still drove the wagon but Jiutarô had to coax his horse into performing a task to which it was unsuited and unfamiliar.

"This is gonna take ages," complained Billit. "We'll never catch up with Kassall now, will we? We're on our own an' we got that scary undead area to ride through sometime, ain't we?"

They had barely travelled a mile when Silmar alerted them. "Rider coming up fast from the village," he warned them. "Keep your weapons handy."

The rider was upon them within moments. He reined in thirty yards or so from them and leapt down from the saddle. He kept his hands well clear of his shortsword, as was the custom when approaching other travellers on the road.

"Greetings," he hailed. "I seek holy assistance for my master back in the village. I am informed by the village woman, Janna, you have a cleric among you. But I expected you to be travelling northwards, not south. Are you those that I seek?"

Silmar eased his horse forwards while constantly scanning their surroundings. "Aye," he replied. "You have found us. One of the horses pulling our wagon has thrown a shoe. We are returning to the village to see if they have a smithy. What is the problem that makes you require our cleric so urgently?"

The rider looked more intently at Silmar. "Murder, Goodsir. My master's son was cruelly killed in the night. Am I right? Would your cleric provide comfort for the bereaved family and speed the boy's soul on its final journey?"

"Boy?" Taura called. "Lead us on." She exchanged a glance with Silmar who, despite the fading colour from his face, looked shocked.

It was an hour later, just after midday, when the wagon trundled into the hamlet of Dange Marsh with Silmar, Jiutarô and the gigantic Falcon in the lead. The guard spurred his horse and galloped into the village ahead of them. The group had been on the road for only five hours but Taura was already tired from the strain of coping with mismatched horses. They drew up in the little square and were immediately met by Janna.

"Come with me, all of you," she beckoned as she turned towards the heavy wagon and the small group that stood by it.

"There was a murder on the road in the night," she gasped. "A young boy had his throat slashed ear to ear by a rider in a long, black cloak. The boy was just fourteen years old and had long, blond hair. Oh, I had better warn you that there has been a rider here this morning wearing a black cloak and I think he is looking for an elf with blond hair, long like yours but not so dark," she indicated to Silmar. "The man was small though; not as tall as you, I would guess."

"Døkkálfr!" exclaimed Silmar.

"Whassat?" Billit replied.

"Døkkálfr," he repeated under his breath. "Darkling!"

The adventurers looked at each other. Taura gives a deep sigh. "It's him, isn't it?" she whispered. "That confirms it. You *are* being hunted, Silmar."

"No doubt about it, I think," mumbled Billit. "But a Darklin' though, up on the surface and on a killing spree?"

"Darkling? Oh, may the gods save us!" Janna wailed. "We are in mortal danger!" She turned and walked over to the merchant with Taura close behind.

The group tactfully watched from a distance as Taura sang *Neilea's Lament for the Dead* by the wagon. They could see that the body was covered in a blood-soaked sheet of canvas. The merchant and his two companions stood beside Taura as she ended the lament and chanted verses to which they gave short responses.

Silmar led their wagon-horse to the edge of the village and requested the blacksmith to reshoe the horse.

"I'll have a look at your other nag, if you want," he offered. "Be best if I do, you never know." The man was heavily muscled and barrel-chested. Although his head was bald, it was more than adequately compensated by his great brown beard.

Silmar accepted. It was just as well that he did.

"Your nags would have lost a couple more shoes if I hadn't checked," the smith advised in his deep, booming voice.

"We had better be on our way," Silmar called an hour later. He leaned against the side of the wagon and rubbed his forehead with his left hand.

Janna had provided them all with a meagre meal but the merchant declared that he was staying in the village an extra day while the body of his son was laid to rest close by. Janna had watched him closely as he fought back his emotions.

"You feelin' tired, elf?" enquired Billit. "You look it." He had seen Silmar swaying and gripping the side of the wagon.

"Aye, I think so. I can still faintly feel the influence of that damned ceremonial knife in my backpack even though it is cased in lead and wrapped up in the bottom of my pack. Its weight chafes my shoulders."

Jiutarô was beginning to get a fairly good understanding of some words of the *Universal* tongue and Taura slowly explained to him what had occurred.

The Samurai squared up, tapped the hilt of the katana tucked into his *obi*, the sash and, with effort, said "We, um, to fight! Hai?"

"Hai!" they all said in unison; the *Samurai's* word for *Yes* was now in occasional use by all in the party. With grim faces, though, they hitched the horses to the wagon, under Taura's direction, and prepared to leave. Out of habit, they checked their weapons, marvelling once again at the beauty and quality of the matching blades carried by Jiutarô.

Despite the language limitations, he was gradually becoming an important and valuable member of the group. His fighting skills were extraordinary; his swordplay when practising was fearsome and without equal, his bow-skill was awe-inspiring and far excelled that of Silmar. He referred to himself as a *Samurai* and they could only surmise that this was his term for a soldier or warrior. He had recently demonstrated his bow-skill and horsemanship by putting three arrows into a tree-stump at a slow gallop. He had throwing stars that he called *shuriken* and could hurl these with uncanny accuracy, even while running at full speed. He had two matching blades which he kept in black lacquered scabbards, the long-sword he called a *katana* and a short-sword he called a *wakizashi*. There was a third dagger-like knife, a *tanto*, also in matching scabbard, in the pack on his horse. He cared for these lovingly and with total respect, often chanting a verse in his obscure language, as he cleaned and oiled the blades. Taura wondered if he was intoning a magic spell. All members of the group would eventually see how the katana could cut cleanly through not only the sword-blades of those he fought, but also straight through the body of a foe as though it were made of straw.

The Samurai's armour was the most unusual that any of them had ever seen. The helmet, with its curved cheek-pieces, high crown and its neck guard, looked heavy and cumbersome. But they had all donned the helmet during the early part of the journey and found it easy to wear, padded on the inside, light and surprisingly comfortable. The burly Samurai was using more and more words in the *Universal* tongue, with encouragement from Billit. He seemed to be a quick learner.

Together, they discussed the new precautions they would need to take on their journey in light of the potential threat from the Darkling. Silmar had called him a Døkkálfr, explaining that was the proper term for the Darkling. The party still had some way to go before they reached Northwald City, perhaps a seven-day short week or even a ten-day full week; the map was not accurate.

With a wave, the band of adventurers slowly rode out of the village. Janna went back towards her cabin. On a little table, near to where the gnome Billit had been standing earlier, were twenty silver coins. *So much money!* She rushed out of the hut and stood on the road but the wagon and riders had gone. This money would keep her in food for months. Once more, she cried.

The merchant found her a moment later and placed a comforting arm around her shaking shoulders. She looked up and saw his sad but kindly face and put her head on his chest.

The Døkkálfr spurred his horse to a quicker pace. Killing the boy had achieved nothing, except to soften his frustration at not having discovered his prey. It was a mistake that could draw attention both to himself and his mission. Somewhere up ahead was his intended victim and the sacred dagger that he bore. He dare not return to Adelenis' High Priestess without the artefact but perhaps there was another way. If he couldn't find the elf, whose name he did not know, then perhaps he could cause the elf to find him. He would have to rely on the fact that the elf would *want* to find him, would *need* to find him. A plan was forming.

It took six days for the Døkkálfr to reach the gates of Northwald City. He arrived just as dusk descended. Fully cloaked and hooded, as if against the cold, he was not challenged as he entered through the city gates, people rarely were during these peaceful days. Only at night, after dark, were the gates closed. Within an hour of entering the city, he had found a stable, paying the stable-boy enough money to enable him to care for his horse without questions being asked. He did not look particularly out of place with his cloak wrapped around him; most people were dressed that way as protection against the bitter cold winds this far north; colder still as the sun sank below the horizon. He watched the city gate from a safe distance and started carrying out his plan.

CHAPTER 13

TEN DAYS AFTER leaving the village Dange Marsh, the party arrived at Northwald City. Their fears of riding close to an area reputed to be plagued with undead came to nothing, much to their relief.

Strangely, to the concern of the regular visitors, all people both leaving and entering were now being challenged. In truth, the city was little more than a large town. It boasted a large market square, a little more than a few minute's ride from the gate, around which were almost a dozen inns and taverns as well as a few gambling establishments and whorehouses. Just inside the city gates, however, was an array of stockyards, animal pens and livery stables. This was clearly a market town that dealt in livestock.

This was not the first thing that focused their attention though.

A major hue and cry was evident. City watchmen, aided by the local militia, were everywhere. They patrolled overtly in small groups. Visitors to the city were constantly observed by sharp-eyed, uniformed pairs of guards that were stationed on virtually every street corner.

Taura called over a youngster who was sitting astride a corral fence. "What has happened here?" she asked.

The lad looked at her suspiciously until she tossed him a copper coin.

"A kid, well, a bit more'n a boy really, 'ad been viciously done to death, mistress," he replied. "Throat was cut. I think he was 'bout fifteen years of age and was of the northern barbarian tribes."

"What did he look like?" asked Silmar. "Was he short with black hair?"

"Nah, 'e wasn't," replied the youngster. "You wasn't list'ning to me, was yer? Northern tribes, 'e was. A barbarian. That means tall with long blond hair."

A shiver ran down Silmar's back as he asked for more information. Falcon gave a grunt and shifted uneasily in his saddle. This could cause an incident by enraging the tribesmen that were camped outside the city walls.

They were there for the annual horse fair and had several fine, sturdy horses for sale. The city watch was trying to calm the situation down and allocating much of their resources to hunt the killer.

All the companions exchanged worried looks.

Taura pulled the brake lever on the wagon and leaned over towards Silmar. Her face was stern as she whispered, "It's him again, isn't it? That gods-damned Darkling. He's looking for you and that wretched dagger, isn't he? He's probably here in the city still and may even be watching us right now. He may even know you have changed your hair colour by now, Silmar. What in the name of the gods have you got us into?"

"There ain't no point in gettin' angry with the elf, missy," replied Billit. "We knew what we were letting ourselves in fer when we took up this challenge, so instead of layin' the blame. Let's see what we're gonna do to sort this out. An' there's no call fer you to be apologisin' fer it, young elf!"

Falcon eased his great horse over to them. "The Darkling?" he asked. "That one you told me about, huh? He is here?"

"We do not know," answered Silmar. "He may be. I have to be vigilant. We have to be vigilant."

"Us watch!" said Jiutarô. Due to his limited knowledge of the *Universal* tongue, he spoke rarely. "Um, Darkling, hai?" He patted the hilt of his beautiful sword.

"We had better find Jasper's tavern, the Wagon Wheel, and speak to him about it," the elf mumbled with a worried frown. "You are right, Jiutarô," he added, indicating his eyes. "We will all have to be extra vigilant now. Keep together, everything we do."

"Watch, um, tavern, night, just one, hai?" Jiutarô struggled.

"Good speaking, Jiutarô," said Billit with a rare smile. "Hai?"

"Hai!" they all responded in agreement, smiling and taking heart from the *Samurai's* confident manner. His proficiency with his *yumi* longbow, a very unusual weapon that had a short lower limb and a much longer upper limb, was almost supernatural. The arrows were longer than normal but Jiutarô would draw one back so that its flights were adjacent to his right ear. They though it very bizarre.

Their enquiries soon led them to the Wagon Wheel tavern and on entering they found the dwarf behind the bar cleaning the jugs and tankards. The dwarf blanched momentarily when he saw the elf standing at his bar but almost immediately recovered his composure. He had immediately recognised Silmar for what he was despite the disguise.

Taura introduced herself and then the others to Jasper and he shook their arms warmly although he eyed the elf with some distrust.

"Yous is friends o' me brother?" Jasper boomed. "Haha! How is the old chod? Must be goin' soft in the head if he is friends with an elf."

"He fares well and he sends you his warmest regards," replied an indignant Silmar. "He was friends with my father, Faramar Galadhal, many years ago."

"Ah, I knows that name an' the one who bears it. An elf, but a damned good 'un. Hey, what is that giant with the big beard holdin' on 'is shoulder?"

Jasper went out into his corral and looked into the wagon. He was delighted to receive the barrels of mead and wine from his brother, even more delighted with the little barrel of elven blood-wine, and asked many questions about his brother, Ralmon, the City of Westron Seaport and the road to Northwald City.

"I knows o' the murder o' the barbarian kid but what was all that I 'eard o'the killing o' the other young boy on the north road? Sounds like someone 'as a hatred of young kids with long 'air."

He looked around the bar as if to check he wasn't being watched and opened a small trapdoor on the floor behind the bar. Beneath it he placed the little barrel of the elven blood-wine. He closed the trapdoor and wiped his hands on his leather jerkin.

"I can offer yous all one room but that's all I got," he said. "It's got six cots in it an' a stack o' blankets. They all got straw bolsters fer yer 'eads too, 'cos I know how soft you humans an' elfs are, heh heh! No disrespect to the gnome intended, o' course! Oh, fer now, you can stow yer equipment 'ere in my taproom."

Falcon towered above every other person in the taproom. People skittered nervously out of his way when he passed by. But it was the Samurai who attracted most of the interest for a while because of his arrogant demeanour and his strange appearance. However, by keeping quiet and sitting together in a dimly lit corner, the companions eventually became almost unnoticed.

The tavern was very busy and as the evening wore on the revellers became more and more boisterous. Two scantily-clad whores were walking around the tap-room and attracted much lewd behaviour from many men. At one point, this started to spiral out of control and one or two fights occurred. Jasper waded in with a wooden mallet and put a stop to one of the fights, but one disruption was too much for even him. He was laid out cold by a punch from a tattooed muscle-bound fighter and he crashed to the floor stunned.

"Hey, we got trouble!" Billit cried.

The party rose to their feet immediately and went to the dwarf's aid. Jiutarô was a blur of movement. He took a leg from a broken table and, using it with phenomenal skill, managed to clear a space around the hapless bartender. The tattooed fighter was unconscious on the floor so quickly that nobody was sure how it happened.

Meanwhile, Silmar was tackled from behind by two assailants, one of whom had his arm around the elf's neck and the other was lifting him up by the legs. Despite his struggles, he was being unceremoniously carried towards the door. Suddenly, all three of them collapsed to the floor and were completely still.

Taura was using her staff to restore the peace with some success and Billit was standing on a chair in a corner with his hands weaving a complicated series of movements.

The trouble stopped as quickly as it began and some of the people wisely left the tavern before the City Watch arrived. Others sat down and resumed their drinking as if nothing had happened. Jasper was sitting on the floor nursing a swollen forehead. Falcon was holding one man aloft by a single leg while the man swung a spittoon at him. The barbarian strode through the tavern door and then returned without the man.

Billit stepped off the chair and rushed over to Silmar and his two attackers; they were all still unconscious. The gnome seemed very pleased with himself.

Taura strode over. "What has happened here?" she enquired.

"Silmar was being carried out by these two," the little mage explained. "The best I could think of was a spell to knock 'em all out." He gave a sardonic grin. "They'll all wake up in a minute or two."

Jasper stepped across to them with a wet cloth held against his head. "What in the hells of the Void was all this about?" he gasped.

Jiutarô haltingly answered. "Wait, Silmar wake, um, mans gone."

"Nearly time to shut the place anyway," he mumbled then yelled at the top of his voice. "Sod off, you lot! Time to go to yer choddin' hovels an' give the wife somethin' she'll remember for an hour or so, if yous can raise yer wherewithal!" Then he raised a hand to his head and regretted having shouted. He looked about him at the unconscious bodies and damaged furniture.

"Right then," he stated, a little quieter. "Let's get these two chods out into the street afore they wakes up."

With the help of a few revellers, they dropped Silmar's two attackers outside without ceremony. By the time they all re-entered the tavern, Silmar was coming to.

The spittoon that Falcon's assailant had used on him had rolled under a table. Falcon picked it up and replaced it next to the bar. "I likes a good fight in bar," he laughed, "but I never ends up on me floor! Never!"

"What happened to me?" Silmar asked with a look of puzzlement on his face. "I remember being carried out of the tavern by a pair of toughs and then I woke up."

Taura explained about the fight and Billit admitted how he was the one to cause Silmar to become unconscious, along with the two attackers. "I put a slumber spell on you and those buggers." The little gnome looked very guilty, but this expression lifted when Silmar burst into laughter.

"We 'ad better talk," said Jasper. "What's goin' on? I needs ter know. This fight weren't right. Some chod organised it."

The tap-room was soon cleared and Jasper locked the front and back doors and secured the window shutters. Two of Jasper's pot-boys, one a human and the other a dwarf, both having also taken an active part in the fight, were clearing the tables and the debris. Jasper assured the companions that his pot-boys were totally trustworthy. They sat round a table, each with a leather tankard of ale, and Silmar described the events starting with their experiences in Westron Seaport, the journey on the North Road and their arrival in Northwald City.

"I think it's clear what happened 'ere tonight," the dwarf explained. "This fight was planned to take attention away from yer young elf while 'e was bein' carried off. You'd better check your baggage in the back o' me tap-room."

Taura and Silmar rushed over and were relieved to discover Silmar's pack had been undisturbed. The *burden*, as he had started referring to it, was still there; they recoiled at the sensation that emitted from it. The overwhelming feeling of nausea still ran through the elf as his hand closed on the casket containing the dagger. It felt ice cold! He removed his hand as though it had been stung.

They returned to the table. Silmar sighed. *"He* knows we're here now and may attempt to take the artefact during the night."

"Take all yer gear up to the bedchamber," instructed Jasper. "We'll mount a watch during the night. One o' you on watch upstairs at all times an' me an' my men will take turns down 'ere."

They agreed to Jasper's proposal. After ten days and nights of continuous watch out on the road, they were extremely tired.

They all remained vigilant during the next three days, not venturing out into the city at all, and each taking turns to watch at night; two of them at a time, one upstairs and one in the tap-room. Billit spent hour after hour teaching Jiutarô the Universal tongue and the ways and customs of the various realms.

They were sitting in a corner of the taproom at the end of the night's revelries. Jasper came out from behind the bar with six quart-mugs of ale.

"This reminds me o' the old days when I was campaignin' with me brother, an' yer pappy, young elf," stated the dwarf. "Aye, I remembers 'im well. A tough un, yer dad. Saved me brother's life a couple o' times. In fact, I remembers me brother savin' *'is* life once, too. That was underground durin' the Goblin Wars in far-off Cascant."

Although Silmar wanted to stay and listen, the others had made it clear that they needed some sleep. Suddenly, there was a knocking at the tavern door. Jasper went to the door and, without opening it, asked who it was at this late hour.

"Janniff, City Watch," came the reply. "Need to talk to you, Innkeeper."

The others in the party stood by, fully alerted. Billit, meanwhile, had rushed over to their equipment and tossed each of the party their main weapons. Jasper opened the door a little, checked the visitor was who he said he was, and then let him in.

"We're questioning all the tavern landlords," said Janniff. "Want to check your visitors, Good-dwarf Jasper. May I come in? I have two men with me."

"Aye, Cityman Janniff. Bring yerselves in." Jasper opened the door wide and three uniformed watchmen marched in. Jasper offered the men a mulled wine to ward off the night's chill but Janniff declined.

"There have been two more killings this evening," Janniff began. "An elf this time. His throat was slashed from ear to ear. Then a rider, in black, forced one of the city gate-wardens at sword-point to open one of the gates to let him out. The bastard killed the gate-man too, for no reason. He's got a family, poor man. One of my men saw it happen but was too far away to raise the alarm. I need to know if your visitors know anything about this or have had any dealings with someone dressed in black."

Predictably, they all shook their heads, each one knowing that if they owned up to being involved in the dealings of this Darkling killer, they would all be forced to answer questions and bring attention to the artefact. It would also impose delays that they could ill afford.

"We shall be collecting some monies for the gate-warden's family," Janniff stated. "May we ask for a donation from your tavern?"

"Aye. Aye, o' course," answered Jasper. "Return on the morrow. I'll get some coins out o' my regulars."

Janniff was satisfied, bade them a good night and left.

"The Døkkálfr is taunting us now with these killings," said Silmar. "He knows where I am. He's trying to draw me out."

"Let's do it then, let's find him," said Taura.

"If we leave this place, the Darkling will follow," suggested Falcon.

"Hai, kill Darkling in wild place," said Jiutarô. "Hai?"

All the others agreed. They decided to leave in the morning. The watches were mounted and the night passed without incident.

CHAPTER 14

T HEY WERE roused just before dawn by one of Jasper's pot-boys. Yawning and with bleary eyes, they took their baggage and weapons down into the taproom. Jasper had laid on a dawn meal of cold mutton, bread, cheese, eggs and fruit. He pointed over to another pile of baggage and weapons next to the bar.

In response to Taura's quizzical stare he beamed. "That's mine, I'd like to come with yer all."

Despite their reservations, he waved them aside and explained. "Look, mah boys can run this place. I'm tough, I ain't old yet an' I got all me faculties. I got lots o' experience with this sort o' thing which I reckons will be sort've 'andy fer yez. Me weapons are in good order an' I've cared for 'em over the years. See this battleaxe?"

They looked at the blade; it had a high quality and a wondrous shimmer.

"Well," he continued. "It's got these qualities what makes it special, see. Almost sort o' magical, you might say."

He was beginning to win them over by now, so he offered his best argument. "'E's Darkling, right?"

They nodded.

"Where will 'e feel most at 'ome if 'e wants a confrontation?"

They looked vague.

Jasper pointed downwards. "Under the ground, right? The Shadow World! Said by some to be in the west parts o' the Dragon's Teeth Mountains."

Silmar and Taura paled; Billit gasped. Jiutarô shook his head and shrugged his shoulders, not understanding the implications. Falcon sighed and looked downwards.

"Anyway, me, bein' a dwarf in case yer didn't yet notice," he grinned.

"Well, I'm at 'ome underground an', if I ain't mistaken, elf, we both can see in the dark, can't we?"

Silmar nodded.

Billit said "I can too, but just a few paces."

"Well, I've bin in the Shadow World," continued Jasper. "'Undreds o' years ago, dwarves an' gnomes mined deep fer gold, silver an' precious stones. You prob'ly know 'bout this too, Billit. They mined fer coal too. An' when the mines run dry they closed 'em down. But other bein's moved in. Black Elves, what we know as Darkling, or Døkkálfar, an' Grey Dwarves – nasty bastards. Then there's spiteful Deep Gnomes, Grullien, who kill yer an' eat yer. They file their teeth into points. It's terrifying. But not all them what live there are evil. Aye, there are creatures who will want ter eat you! There's creatures that *you* will need to eat to survive. There's water, if you knows how an' where to find it, but not all water is drinkable. There's other food sources too. I can 'elp with all o' this. And I'm a choddin' good fighter! Well, I was once. Aye, I know I got knocked on the breadbasket last night but 'e was a chodding great big muscled chunk o' beef an' 'e crept up behind me, unexpected like!"

They all laughed but somewhat half-heartedly. Billit patiently explained to Jiutarô what was being discussed. The Samurai looked very concerned.

"Now, look at these. I'll be takin' these leather tubes too – they're kinda special!" He refused to say any more about them. Each of the leather tubes resembled a narrow scroll case, sealed at one end, and each had a leather cap to close the other end.

The group was quiet for a moment and they looked at each other.

Silmar broke the silence. "Aye, join us. You'll be more than welcome if everyone else agrees," he stated. "But where do we go?"

"I think I may know the answer to that one," offered Jasper.

The road from the North Gate of Northwald City was not as busy as that of the South. The long road led northwards, inland a few leagues from the coast, to the town of Icedge, aptly named for the sea ice would approach the north coast during the depths of winter. The climate there was generally cold, even during the summer months, but it was bitterly cold during the long winter. Nevertheless, snow was a rarity on the lower ground. The proximity of mountains to the north and east of the town and the direction of the prevailing wind off the sea, gave almost total protection from the winter snowstorms.

The Døkkálfr travelled on a route parallel to this road. He no longer had a need to hunt; he knew now that he was the prey. This suited him perfectly. He would be waiting. He would be completely at home in the *Shadow World*. He had his dark-vision. That gave him, and all of his kind, the Døkkálfar, the ability to use his eyes to see in virtually total darkness; he believed it was far more effective than that of the Ljósálfar, the surface elves. Their's was inferior and relied upon there being a vestige of light that could be enhanced. Admittedly, there was occasionally some light down there, mostly that given off by the mould growing on the walls, for instance. It was the Døkkálfr's ability to see differences in temperature of whatever was down there and thus make out shapes that made his keen dark-vision so much the superior. As far as he was aware, the white-eye elves had lost this ability because they did not live under the ground. He did know that dwarves and gnomes had a limited ability but the bastard elf did not have a dwarf in his party. The race of men was pathetically weak, poor at swordsmanship and no capability to see in the darkness. They would need to carry light to travel through the Shadow World but the use of flaming torches was cumbersome and only lasted an hour or so. They would need to carry scores of torches to see where they were going and these were often slow to light and difficult extinguish.

I will be invulnerable in the Shadow World, the domain of the Døkkálfar. Hah! I positively relish a confrontation.

They had a human priest – what god she worshipped he couldn't tell - and a gnomish mage. Both were young and would be inexperienced. The large Barbarian was the greatest threat and would have to be the first to be taken down.

The white-eye elf will be the last to die, his ragtag band of misfits will be no match for me and I shall pick them off one at a time if necessary. Eventually, there would just be the white-eyed elf and myself – a Døkkálfr. The sacred ceremonial dagger would then be mine.

CHAPTER 15

"**W**HAT DO YOU MEAN by saying that you can help with where we go next?" asked Silmar.

"I think I knows where the Darkling wants yer to go. 'E'll leave a trail o' dead bodies for us to follow 'til we gets to the very entrance to the Shadow World. Y'know? Like breadcrumbs."

The party listened carefully, hanging on every word spoken by the Dwarf.

"'E prob'ly assumes that none o' you knows where this entrance is," continued the dwarf.

"He's right there," answered Taura. "We haven't a clue where it is."

"Aye, but 'ere's the rub – I does," said Jasper, the look of triumph crossing his face partly obscured by his bushy brown beard. "I been down there with yer dad, young elf."

"What?" exclaimed a shocked Silmar. "My father never told me about the Shadow World or said that he had been there. By the Gods!"

"Aye, lad. Scary as shit, eh? Believe me, it is. But *I'll* go there again with you. Don't make the mistake o' thinking we'll all get out, though. That's where me brother lost 'is arm."

The group exchanged apprehensive looks with each other amid murmurings. Taura fidgeted with the end of the cord around he gown.

Jasper continued. "Now, pin back yer ears. There's many rules that we gotta consider when we are down there." He spoke slowly and carefully making sure that Jiutarô understood and that each point was driven home with each of them.

"It will be totally an' completely dark down there. Silmar, me an' Billit can see a little in the dark, the elf best of all, sod yer, but there 'as to be some source o' light down there. If you shine a light or light a torch then we will be blinded for quite a few moments, an' it 'urts. An' so will the Darklin', don't forget. 'E will almost totally rely on 'is dark-seeing but 'e don't need no light down there to 'elp 'im. Oh no! If a torch needs to be lit then we must use a codeword or give a warnin' or somethin'. Or if you're gonna shine a light you gotta give a warnin' with that codeword. A codeword is best 'cos the Darklin' won't know what yer talking about. Does yer know whay I mean?"

Apart from Jiutarô, they all nodded with understanding.

"Good. Now, this is important. We gotta stay together," Jasper emphasised. "Even when we needs to relieve ourselves! No-one can be left behind, 'less they're dead an' the survivors *all* agrees on it. Taura 'as got wonderful 'ealing abilities, so I'm told, and I got a couple of potions that relieve pain an' 'elps recovery. Use it all but use 'em careful, partic'ly the potions, them's gotta be the last resort. Don't touch anythin' that you don't recognise, it may try to do you 'arm. If in doubt, ask me. There will be deep pits and crev – crevasses an' in some places, we'll 'ave to jump some wide gaps. I suggest we ropes ourselves together to do that."

"What about other races or peoples down there?" enquired Billit. "Are they all out to kill us?"

"Surprisingly, there's quite a variety," answered Jasper. "Døkkálfar, one of 'em is called Døkkálfr, ain't very common an' they tend to stay within the confines of their cities like Myrkheim. That's way off. But there's the Grey Dwarves, nasty bastards who roam about in small war-bands lookin' for surface folk who wander down there to do mining. These are the sworn enemies o' my peoples and are 'ard, spiteful fighters. I came up on them down there all those years ago. There are hundreds of them and they still mine for silver. Then there's the Bucca, or Kobolts as they are called by northern tribesmen, are known to be there somewhere; these are sort of small, dog-like little buggers who go about on two legs an' carry barbed javelins. They are small but fight in big groups to overwhelm their enemy. Aye, they fights 'ard 'cos of their large numbers but aren't all that good at fighting individually and a couple o' dozen of 'em will run at the sight of a few humans, elves an' dwarves. They don't 'ave no armour. If their javelin gets stuck inside you the only way to get it out is to cut it out or push it straight through. Nasty little buggers, they are! Yappers, us dwarves used to call 'em, on account o' the noises they makes. Nasty!"

They all shuddered at the thought.

"Aye, the Bucca. They are totally ruthless little shits," Jasper continued.

"They talk with a barkin' sort o' language with our words scattered in it. I seem to remember that their god is the same one that the Darklin's worship - Adelenis!" He whispered the last word. The group shuddered at the mention of that name. "Worse of all though, are the Grullien, the Shade Gnomes. Nasty, 'ard an' full o' spite. They 'ates the Grey Dwarves with a passion, yer might say. They wander around with war-bands too. Might find 'em near to the end o' the mines."

"What about friendly races?" asked Billit, hoping to hear something encouraging. "Are there any?"

"Funny it should be *you* to ask that o' me," replied Jasper. "There's a couple o' colonies of Gnomes, not much diff'rent to you, Billit. They've learned the art of evading detection an' concealin' their whereabouts now for cent'ries. They mine for precious stones, mainly rubies, sapphires an' emeralds which, I think, are only found beneath the western Dragon's Teeth Mountains. They are the only race of the Shadow World who comes up to the surface to trade. I think they 'ave their own entrances down to the Shadow World tho' I don't know 'em. The Grey Dwarves though, they trade *their* silver with some o' the criminal human gangs on the surface."

By this time it was approaching mid-morning and they were all ready to travel. Jasper suggested they should ride their horses and ponies to the hamlet of Burrak, about a seven-day week's ride northwards. There they would leave their mounts and continue their journey on foot. Jasper looked uneasy and was scratching his chin and looking unusually worried.

"What is it?" enquired Taura. "What worries you so?"

The dwarf turned away from her and cleared his throat. He then slowly turned back to face her. "Well, it's sorta like this," he said softly. "The people of Burrak locks their doors an' secures their shutters at night. It's only a little village, prob'ly only twenty or so dwellings, an' a trading post that doubles as an inn. Bin there afore, many years ago, an' just rode straight through. Oh, they was scared o' somethin' an' din't like to talk about it. Somethin' or someone takes a victim from their village. Usually at night, always after dark. Not often but occasionally."

"Wait, I know something about this!" Silmar exclaimed. "There have been rumours like this for years."

"Best avoid this area, I reckon," said Falcon, his deep voice sounding strangely calming in the tense atmosphere.

"Best it, um, avoid we!" added Jiutarô. He had been listening attentively and was picking up some of the details as the others spoke slowly. They nodded in agreement. "Hai, we strong!" He patted his blades. "We show we fight well."

These were probably the most heartening words that the Samurai had strung together since they had known him. However, nervous glances continued to be exchanged from one to another.

"Aye, listen well to him. We are powerful," Falcon emphasised. "You make magic. We can all fight? We are strong, not weak and afraid!"

"Aye," answered Silmar. "Mayhap you are right. Look, we are all about to go into the Shadow World, right? We are putting our lives at risk to bring a killer to justice. Perhaps there is a lunatic or monster at large near Burrak. If there is something we can do to help, well, it's what we do, right?"

Laughter erupted from Jasper. "That's yer dad talking. By the gods, Silmar, yer is just like 'im. But, tread carefully, all o' you. You don't know what yer gonna meet. Whatever's out there 'as been around fer ages and we're prob'ly not the first to go lookin' fer it. Let's 'ope we don't have to."

"Aye, but we must fight to help others," stated Falcon. "That is the honourable way. So it is with my peoples."

"Ye gods!" muttered Jasper. "What 'ave I got meself into? A right bunch o' idiots who wanna save the world!"

The party set out from the little corral behind the Wagon Wheel an hour before dawn. Northwald City was already bustling with people pushing handcarts, herding geese, goats or sheep, and setting up stalls in preparation for another day's trading. They passed through the East Gate as soon as it opened and rode in a north-easterly direction towards the village of Burrack. The weather was overcast and the ground very frosty. After a while however, the sun shone for an hour or two and the frost had disappeared. Now that they no longer had the wagon, they were able to move much faster.

The track was well-defined and clearly well-travelled although they met few other travellers in either direction during their ride.

They continued for six days; each rider remained very quiet, lost in their own thoughts of the challenges that lay ahead but constantly remaining vigilant. A couple of hours after dawn on the seventh day, the group reined in by a junction in the tracks. They could see a small wagon ahead but with no horses or oxen. Three people, one of them a boy, were huddled around a little fire. The sounds of a woman wailing could clearly be heard. As they drew close, they dismounted and showed their hands to prove they had not drawn their weapons.

A man came over cautiously towards them. He looked distraught, almost panic-stricken. He started to babble incoherently and Taura handed her horse's reins to Falcon. She took the man by the shoulders, looked him in the eye and calmed him down.

"Now start again," she said softly. "I am Taura Windwalker, a Priestess of Neilea." She gave her customary light bow at the mention of her deity's name.

"I am Tor Angle," he wailed. "Someone came into our camp in the night. We were sleeping. When we woke up we could not move. He, or they, drove off our two horses that were hitched up to the tree just there, he took our lovely daughter, Tassie, an' made off with her into the night."

Taura took him gently by the shoulders once again. "Tor, you said *they*, now you say *he*. What was it?"

"It was probably just one. We saw only one but it didn't walk properly – it sort of floated down among us then floated of with our Tassie." He began to weep again.

Taura and Silmar exchanged a glance. Both had noticed the man said *it* and not just *he* or *him*.

"Describe him to me."

"He was dressed in dark with a black cape and hood. Expensive clothes like a lord or baron or someone. Dark hair, white skin – very white. A pointed beard. A very unhappy face almost like he regretted it all. Our horses were terrified. He used a sort of magic to make us keep still."

Silmar quietly whispered in Taura's ear. "Not Døkkálfr then."

She shook her head imperceptibly. "Where were you going, Tor?"

"We were leaving Burrak. Look, it's become too dangerous to stay with people going missing for so long. Oh, not many; not often, but we are always wondering when the next one will go. Now our pride and joy has been taken from us, not three hours ago. Oh my Tassie! We should have stayed, but all I wanted was a better life, a safer life, for my family. We left too late in the day. The wagon and horses were too slow, we didn't get away far enough!"

Taura called over Falcon and Jiutarô. "See if you can find the horses, would you?"

After looking about for tracks they galloped off, following the sign on the ground.

Tor Angle was visibly frightened and shaking violently.

Taura continued. "What is it that does this? You know, don't you?" She had her own suspicions.

"Oh, do not ask me, mistress! I cannot say. It is too terrible."

"Tell me, perhaps we can help but you must tell me."

"Very well, but you will not believe me, nobody ever believes us villagers. We have suspected for years but people from the outside laugh at us. Look now, we're serious about this. We think it's a *vampyre*, or some sort of horror! Oh, gods preserve us!"

The friends glanced at each other with doubt and misgiving etched on their faces, apart from Taura who was eager to know more.

"What makes you think that?" she questioned.

Tor trembled with fear and despair. "Many years ago," he explained, "before we suspected what lay behind this, people were being attacked in their own homes. Their throats were torn out and an unholy mess was made. We thought some attackers were bringing dogs with them but we neither heard nor saw any other sign of these. Then the little temple of Clamberhan here was broken into and the priest was killed. He was tied up on his own altar and his neck was cruelly ripped out. His temple was desecrated and much of it was destroyed by fire. We sent a rider to Nor'wald City to find a priest, any priest of any god, to come and advise us. As luck would have it a Priest of Tarne was visiting, a young lad name of Halorun Tann, and he recognised the signs of a vampyre immediately. He made a search of the local area but found no trace and it all went quiet for a few years. We thought he had chased the monster away. Now the troubles are on us again but – but it's only occasionally. Oh gods, my poor Tassie, my lovely daughter. Gone from us for ever!"

"I am convinced that you are correct, Tor Angle," murmured Taura. "It is a vampyre indeed."

She turned aside from Tor, an immensely distressed man, and spoke quietly to her comrades. "I studied the characteristics of undead during my years of training and this seems to be typical of a vampyre. I must say though, that vampyres generally feed off their victim's blood and although most of the poor people die horribly, every so often one victim is selected by the *master* to become a vampyre too. This does not at the moment seem to be the case here. Well, as far as I know."

"What do we do now then?" asked Billit. He looked ashen-faced, the idea of something as foul as this monster, a vampyre, having its place on this world being absurd to him.

Jiutarô appeared blissfully unaware of their predicament.

"We could end this once and for all," replied Silmar. "We heard rumours of something terrible in my hometown of Refuge, which is way across those mountains there but this horror was never defined as a vampyre. We have heard vague reports of a fiend of some sort that lurks this end of the mountains. It was long intended that sometime in the future my father would send out a party to investigate this. With so much activity from goblins, hobgoblins, ogres and trolls in the mountains, we never got around to it. I was hoping that my father would let me lead the expedition but he was going to let it be the last mission of our Master-at-Arms before he retired."

"So, let me get this aright, you seriously think that there is something in all this then?" asked Billit.

"I do," replied Taura. "We now have a good idea of what is out there and it needs to be ended, as you say Silmar. Turning back to the man, she asked "Do you know where this vampyre lives, Tor?"

"No. No, well, um–"

"You do, or you think you do," persisted Taura. "Out with it, man, if only for the sake of your daughter!"

"Look, in the mountains there's an old track that leads down through the peaks. If you were to follow it all the way it would eventually take you towards the town of Refuge."

"Aye, I know of it," responded Silmar. "It is many, many leagues."

"Ah, well, we used to trade with them during the summer months, years ago when I was a lad. That all stopped with this vampyre. The way to the track leads from near to Burrak, our village. It will be rough and poorly maintained by now because we have had no need to use it. It's about three or four hours by horse from there, I believe, most likely six or so on foot. Well, up the track a way and then turning left up a paved roadway, so I was told way back in my youth, there's this old stone keep, on a grassy plateau. The keep was built long ago by a noble who is long forgotten, to protect this side of the mountains from attacks by war-bands of hobgoblins and goblins. Old rumour says that it's in there where you'll find it, the monster."

A few minutes later Jiutarô and Falcon returned with two horses in tow.

"See to your family, Tor," Silmar advised, "Let's get you all back to the village. We shall see if we can get your daughter back for you. What say you all?"

Without exception, they all agreed, albeit with much apprehension.

Tor scattered the embers of his little fire and loaded his wailing wife and son onto the wagon. A few moments later the wagon was ready to move out, this time with Taura at the reins. It was an hour before midday when the party arrived at the village. The gates were opened but manned by ill-equipped guards, little more than farm workers holding the tools of their trade. Silmar and Jiutarô shook their heads at the inadequacy of their defences.

Silmar suggested they waste no time in the village but get on their way immediately. "It is past noon and it gets dark early in these mountains," he explained. "And it may take a while to get there because we shall be going on foot."

"Why no horse?" Jiutarô asked. The others voiced in their support of him.

Taura answered. "Because we may not be able to get the horses close enough to the vampyre's keep if they sense that there is something nasty lurking there. They can be very sensitive to threats like that and they may bolt. We must waste no time and get on our way immediately."

One of the gate guards offered to guide them to the start of the track but would go no further; he turned about and rushed back to the village as fast as his legs would take him.

The track was quite steep and was clearly not in regular use but there were some signs that it had been recently used. Scratch marks from a horse's hoof on a rock here, a tiny piece of tattered and faded torn cloth on a thorn there. There was hard frost on the grass and bushes, giving an almost ghostly effect which did little to maintain courage amongst the group, and as they climbed higher there were signs of recent snowfall. It took them almost six hours before they arrived at a junction in the track. The path to the left wound up a steep hill where they could just see the crenellations of a stone tower through the dark coniferous treetops. With trepidation gnawing at their hearts, they bunched together and took the path, walking softly through the powdery snow until the steep path flattened onto a lightly snow-covered grassy plateau. The grass had not been attended to for a long, long time, being tall and full of weeds. They all nervously fingered their weapons.

The keep was built almost up against a rocky cliff face and was partly encircled by a defensive wall. Each end of the wall butted up against the cliff face and in the centre of it was a pair of entry gates mounted between two gate-towers. In the shadow of the tall cliff, the keep looked dark and foreboding. The gloomy effect was augmented by the late afternoon sun dipping below the hills.

Without a word, they simultaneously withdrew their weapons, even Taura held her staff in her right. From under her robe, she withdrew her precious holy symbol. It dangled on a stout silver chain. She then reached for her dagger which she grasped tightly in her left hand. Their approach to the keep was extremely tense and they all felt fear rise inside them. A Darkling was one danger that they understood, to a point, but undead, a vampyre, was an unknown foe that was completely different.

"Taura, how do we kill it?" asked Silmar. The burden in his pack was weighing more heavily on his shoulders and an ache was growing in intensity behind his eyes. He felt that it wouldn't take much for him to throw up the dried meat that they had gnawed on the walk up the mountain path.

"A strong fire will burn it," she answered. "A wooden stake through its heart or cutting off its head will destroy it too. Choose any one but try them all! Chopping the bastard to bits will work too! It looks like there's only one way into the keep, and there it is, the main door."

Darkness was descending very quickly now, and every nerve was jangling. The walk to the keep's door was interminably slow and every sound only served to increase their fear. The sound of a calling vixen from the trees behind them put the fear of the gods into every one of them, Taura almost dropped her staff.

The door opened with a push from Falcon's bow. He stepped in, closely followed by the others.

Unexpectedly, burning torches were mounted in sconces on the walls. The comrades spread out and looked towards the flight of curving stairs at the back of the entrance hall. It was bitterly cold in the hall and their breath was clouding in front of their faces. Their boots made clicking sounds on the exquisite marble-tiled floor. Great tapestries hung on the walls and they seemed to be in immaculate condition, depicting hunting and mountain scenes. There were some pieces of elaborate furniture about the hall: chairs and tables, padded sofas and gilded cabinets. On tables and cabinets were items of great value including ornaments made of the finest porcelain and even silver and gold candelabras, plates, ewers and bowls.

"Welcome!"

A resonant, pleasant-sounding, baritone voice spoke from above. "I expect you have come here in the vain expectation of destroying me. You are on a fool's errand. It has been tried before and no doubt will be attempted again in the future. It has, and will always, end in failure."

On a gallery, some way up the rear wall of the hall, they saw the dark figure of a man, tall and distinguished. The facial features were hidden in the shadow of the gallery balustrade.

"Do not be so sure of yourself," replied Taura. "You have taken someone we want back. Someone of value to those who love her."

"Ah yes, the pretty young girl, Tassie. I make no apology when I say that you will have to return without her, if I deign to let you, or some of you, survive. She will stay here, but I promise to bury her remains with care and dignity. I – always do." His voice was seductive, smooth and compelling and completely void of emotion.

"Very touching," Taura chuckled, "but we are prepared to take her from you by force and destroy you in the meantime."

"You are a very cock-sure young lady. Ahh, a Priestess of Neilea, I see. With a gnome mage, an elf warrior, a dwarf, a barbarian fighter and, what's this? Another warrior, but I do not recognise your origin. Full of confidence, each of you. Have you fought anything yet? Are you ready for me? Hah, I doubt it very much. The last threat to me was a young Priest of Tarne. I played with his mind and clouded it from seeing this place. But *he* arrived in the night when I was at my strongest. Fortunately for him I let him live; there was a certain strength about him that I greatly admired and I felt it would have been wasted otherwise."

Silmar motioned to Falcon, Jasper and Billit and together, they rushed up the staircase.

The figure on the gallery vanished from sight in an instant.

Slowly and quietly, Jiutarô and Taura climbed the stairs. The priestess was in deep concentration while chanting a prayer-spell and her hands were weaving a complex pattern of movements. Jiutarô brandished his katana in front of him, his dark eyes flashing up and down, from side to side.

At the top of the first flight of stairs, Falcon, closely followed by Silmar, Jasper and then Billit, rushed into a large chamber through a partly-open door. They were immediately overcome by a wave of total immobility. They slumped onto the floor, completely oblivious to their surroundings.

Jiutarô entered the chamber and also immediately succumbed. Taura stood at the doorway a few moments after. Her heart thumped as the dark figure stepped over to the five inert bodies and bent forward to look at them.

"There is great evil on this one," he murmured, with his eyes on Silmar.

Taura's voice sounded out to him. "So, you think you have them at your mercy?"

The vampyre whipped round but the Priestess was not there. *Clever, using her god-magic!* For once, he felt vulnerable. He took a sharp intake of breath as his head turned from side to side searching for her.

"Where are you, priestess?" called the vampyre. "Come out so I can see you."

"I can already see *you*," she answered confidently, "and as foul a creature to behold I have never seen, not even in the filthiest gutters or swamps."

"I can appreciate how you feel about me, young priestess," he responded. "Many decades ago I would have felt the same abhorrence. Know that I did *not* choose to become what I am but it happened to me nonetheless. I loved the sun and the feel of warmth on my skin. Now, it would destroy me." He paused as if for dramatic effect. "And we really cannot have that now, can we?"

Taura had quietly moved while he had been talking. She had studied his face and features. He was tall and slim. His hair was a rich dark brown, almost black, but his skin was a deathly white. His hair was cut and perfectly arranged and his beard was trimmed to a point. Unusually, as if from a style that had been popular decades in the past, his moustaches were long and drooping well below his jawline. His clothing had been made for a man of great wealth and rank and was of the best silks and linen. He wore black breeches which came to just below his knees and here they were tied with black silk tapes. He had white stockings and the shoes were of soft, black leather with a large buckle atop them. His white shirt was also silk with a wide ruffled collar and loose in the arm. To look at, his face had a distinguished appearance. His eyes did not reflect this persona, however. They looked extremely sad, as if the troubles of the world weighed down upon him. A normal man with this almost fastidious appearance would be considered very handsome. His voice however, had a richness to it which, together with his refined speech, was pleasurable to hear.

Notwithstanding this, the odour of ancient death and decay hung in the air. Taura almost retched and just managed to stifle a cough.

"I consider that to be an ideal option," she replied after a slow, silent breath.

Once again, he whipped around to face the direction from which her voice now came.

"Don't play games with me, young lady. So, you are invisible; a clever conjuring trick for which I compliment you. Your elven friend carries an item of immense power; I shall take it and study it at my leisure once you and your companions are dead."

"You think so, do you? Tell me, how did you become a vampyre?" Her voice came from behind his ear and he jumped forward, turning again. He reached out for her but his fingers touched only the cold air of the keep. "Do not for one moment begin to consider that this is an existence that is pleasurable to me, mistress priest! I was once mortal; I still have human feelings and emotions, when I allow them during my countless hours of solace in the night. These things do not change with undeath. I feel loneliness and have the propensity to hate but never to love. I did love once – and she made me like this. She started me on the wave of destruction and killings for that was the only way we could survive. When she attacked the village temple of Clamberhan, she killed the cleric so violently and desecrated the temple so wantonly, I could stand it no more and I destroyed her on the mountain path. But as a parting gift, she cursed me. Yes! Even a vampyre can feel revulsion."

Taura paused. "I don't believe you, vampyre. You seek to escape just retribution of your destruction with a tale of heroism."

"NO, priestess!" he barked. "I was made thus by her; I shall forever be thus. I am dead but I am destined to live an undead existence for eternity. I am destined to feed on the blood of humanoid men, women, children, and sometimes worse, for eternity with a constant and unbearable hunger. Eternity is a long time, I can assure you of this."

"So end it, step into the sunlight in the morning dawn. I shall accompany you."

Taura was thinking at a furious pace now. At the far end of the room to the door, she became visible. She had used a *Conceal from Undead* prayer-spell, the most potent spell she had ever used. It had worked perfectly but had exhausted her; she would offer prayers of sincere gratitude to Neilea if she was to survive the night.

"Do you think I could if I wanted to?" His voice had risen almost to shouting and its echo reverberated from the stone walls around them. "I am cursed to continue like this. I am cursed to forever protect myself from intentional destruction. I do not have the will to end my own non-life. Therefore I have to protect my miserable existence by feeding off what I can. If I am able to feed from the animal world then I do so otherwise I have no other option than to take men, elves and dwarves, usually whatever comes within my reach. If I was able to, I would feed from the goblins and orcs that infest these hills but their blood is tainted with an unsuitable foulness – believe me, I have tried on numerous occasions when the need is great. I shall be forced to take your lives too now that you have blundered your way into my home."

"Wait!" she exclaimed. An idea began to form in her mind. "You live in misery? Explain!"

His voice became calm now. "Have I not already explained this? For more than a century I have hunted to survive and survived to hunt. I am cursed to this existence and cannot wilfully end it. There is no future other than to hunt and be hunted. There will be no restful peace for me."

"Cursed? But what if we were to end this misery for you? An honourable ending with the curse lifted; an opportunity for you to live at peace in death."

"You can do this? You would do this? Ah, a stupid question; of course you would."

"I can lift the curse but it will tax me to the limit. Your end will be swift and without discomfort. It would be honourable and the gods, in their understanding, wisdom and compassion, may offer you a life after death particularly if you atone for your misdeeds."

The vampyre stood at the top of the curving stairs. "I cannot deny that I desire this ending," he stated after pausing for a few moments. He paused once again as he paced from side to side wringing his hands. "Dear mistress, I am tempted now to accept although the words do not pass my lips with ease. When it is done, search my keep, and yes, it was always mine from the days before I became thus. Very well, an end to this permanent nightmare is desirous. If you can do this then my atonement will benefit those whom my life has shattered. You will find many treasures and wonders. I leave them to the community, to you and your friends. Use it to give the village down there some comfort. They have lost much at my hands. Give me this ending and everything shall be yours. Burn and bury my remains. Say a prayer to your god, Neilea, that She may judge me favourably. You shall also find, in the chamber yonder, the young lady you seek. She is unharmed but I have left a trauma upon her that she will find it hard to recover from promptly. It is fortunate I was not hungry; I had just feasted on foul goblin blood. That is not a pleasant dish but I could not feed constantly on the villagers. There are not enough of them, you understand! One of your comrades, the mysterious warrior, is awakening. The others shall soon."

Taura wanted to vomit and it took considerable willpower to avoid doing so. Jiutarô shuffled unsteadily to his feet and stood there, now inside the door to the room and leaning on the doorframe, with an impassive face and with his katana at the ready. The others were all still comatose.

"Shall we proceed?" she asked.

The vampyre dropped to one knee. "Yes, do so. Please dear lady. But first, I would like to know your name."

"I am Taura Windwalker, Priestess of Neilea."

"I was once the Baron Armid Harcuthnut. May my own blood wash away my terrible misdeeds, Taura Windwalker, Priestess of Neilea."

She quietly tried to explain to Jiutarô what she wanted of him and motioned for him to take up position. He had been able, just, to keep up with the conversation and understood what would be required of him.

She explained slowly. "Jiutarô, I shall give you a sign when you are to, er! You know?"

"Hai, I know this."

"Please kneel; I shall too," she instructed the vampyre. As he dropped his other knee to the floor, she asked him, "Do you regret and atone for the terrible transgressions of the past in and trust fully to the judgement of the godly Pantheon?"

He bowed his head and in a quiet voice, said, "Mistress Taura Windwalker, I do indeed."

Taura's chanting began and her voice rose in intensity. She had not performed a *Curse Reversal* prayer-spell before and, although she knew the routine and wording, she understood that it would be difficult to perform due to her inexperience, and she was already drained. Many moments passed and she was getting drenched in he own sweat. Jiutarô watched her intently, waiting for the sign. Taura's shoulders became hunched and fatigue was clearly evident upon her. With a sudden gesture to the Samurai, she fell forward onto her face away from the dreadful Baron Harcuthnut and Jiutarô swung his katana. The vampyre Baron's head was cleaved from his shoulders and the body fell forward to the floor. No blood flowed to soak the richly-patterned carpet. All went quiet.

The four members of the party who, for so long had been immobile slowly regained their consciousness and looked around themselves in surprise.

At that moment, a slightly warmer draught of air moved through the keep, tainted slightly by the smell of flowers and mild spices. The remains of the vampyre aged before them. A sound of whispered laughter, which had probably not been heard in the keep for many, many decades, rose and then fell again to silence. Taura was exhausted. Falcon helped her to a sitting position and she smiled at her friends.

"It is over," she sighed. "He agreed his own destruction, I reversed his curse and Jiutarô destroyed him. It all seemed very much civilised but also a little sad, I think. He endured misery and sadness at his plight for so many decades and was forced by a curse to exist as he did. He tried to make it more bearable by attacking the goblins in the mountains and what animals he could snare to avoid too much destruction to the villagers and travellers. But there were times he must have been desperate and had no choice. He has gone but we must burn and then bury the remains with dignity – it was his final request but his remains are now harmless. Tassie is in that chamber over there."

The atmosphere in the keep had changed. A little warmth gradually filled the hallway; not the warmth of a fire, or of hot food on a cold day. This was the notion of warmth that had for decades been rejected by the evil.

"By the Gods! I no longer feel the weight and influence of the burden now," gasped Silmar. "It has passed but, oh, my head did ache. Let's find the young girl."

They entered the adjoining room and found the young girl huddled in a ball on the bed. Her eyes were wild with fright and she was shivering violently. She was otherwise unharmed. Billit took a blanket from the bottom of the bed and gently wrapped it around her.

The gnome gave words of comfort. "Come, little one, you have had such a difficult time. Let us go back to your family. They are waiting for you." Silmar was surprised to hear words with so much compassion from the Gnome. This was a side of Billit that had not been seen before.

"Who's the little one that he's referring to?" whispered Silmar with a broad grim.

"Sod off, fool of an elf!" retorted Jasper.

With Falcon's help Taura was back on her feet. She held Tassie's arm and took over the care of the girl.

Jasper suggested that they look around the keep and collect what valuables were around and lock them away. It took most of the night with each of them taking it in turns to sleep, eat, drink and work. Fires were lit and the keep gradually regained physical warmth. By the morning, the group were staggered at the wealth of furnishings, money, gems, jewellery, weapons and armour that were in the keep.

Silmar gathered the others around him. "I would suggest that this keep belongs to us now," he stated. "I say we can use it for the good and benefit of the village and for our futures. What say you all?"

"What can we do with it?" asked Falcon. "We travel."

Taura answered before Silmar took the opportunity. "We have the vast majority of the goods now locked in a cellar chamber. Perhaps a chest-full of coins can be set aside to rebuild the village and bring prosperity to its people, if they would be prepared to take it."

"I think they will," Silmar replied, "especially if we tell them the story of the last occupant of the keep and the sadness that went with it. A new temple to Clamberhan, and perhaps one to Trangath too, for this is a farming community. A new trading post in the village may bring people and trade here. There is so much good this money can do. There is much set aside for our own futures too, I would say."

The keys to the keep were found in a drawer of an ornate desk and as the party, with Tassie, made ready to leave, Silmar locked the great door to the keep and placed the key in a side pocket of his pack.

Many hours later, the party entered the village through the gate. Tassie was greeted among tears and laughter and the companions were welcomed and treated as heroes.

"What of the vampyre?" a village elder asked them.

"Destroyed!" replied Jasper. "For all time!"

There were massive cheers and people clasped each other amid tears and laughter. For them, this was unexpected but wonderful news, nonetheless. The people in of Burrak had only ever known life under the threat of the horror lurking in the mountains. Now the threat, and with it the constant danger, would become history and eventually a distant memory.

"Can we gather the village elders together?" requested Silmar. "We have something of importance to discuss."

By early afternoon, the small trading post, which doubled as the village inn, filled with people, more than just the village elders. The adventurers stood together and the noise soon hushed.

The story was told of the vampyre, once the Baron Armid Harcuthnut, and how it existed in despair up until its destruction the previous evening. Taura explained that the keep was now the property of theselves but they had brought down a treasure to help the village to recover and rebuild its community. It would give the village an opportunity for growth, trade and prosperity for everyone.

"How can we take this treasure? It has the blood of our people on it!" called one villager.

Another voice raised the same objections but many more were raised to agree that the money should be used, not for any one individual or family, but as a business investment for the good of the whole village.

"We can build a new wall, higher and stronger, with larger and heavier gates. We can build it out from the village to allow room for us to grow larger."

"Aye, and temples with new clerics and for the success of our wellbeing, our farms, our produce and tools."

"And store sheds for our produce."

"Aye, and a new trading post, well stocked. And a new tavern."

"Aye, also well stocked!" shouted a villager. Much laughter erupted.

"And set up our old trading agreements with Refuge, Gash and Westron Seaport. We can buy new wagons and horses, and farm tools. And perhaps the gnomes from the mines will trade here with their opals and rubies. Does anyone remember when they were last here? Many years ago now. Why, I were just a lad!"

"We must give our thanks and praise to our new friends! Our saviours!"

Suddenly, everyone in the village wanted to embrace and shake the forearms of their new heroes. The inn's tap-room was opened and ale flowed as if it were water, while it lasted. People offered their beds to the party members for the night. They were fed and looked after and their horses were well cared for. They did not make any mention of it to the villagers, but very soon they would be entering the Shadow World.

But tonight, they might get a little drunk.

That night they got very drunk indeed. Jasper and Billit consumed ale, lots of it. Each tried to out-drink the other and both eventually collapsed onto the floor. They were left where they lay. Only Taura kept her drinking under control. Oh, how she would make them all suffer in the morning.

Jiutarô sang songs from his own land, unintelligible to those around him because of his strange language; even if he had been able to sing in the *Universal* tongue, the songs would still have been unintelligible. Then he stopped singing and swayed forward until his head landed on the table, and he fell asleep.

Falcon seemed totally immune from the effects of the ale and his drinking continued well into the night. Finally, some time after midnight, he was the last one drinking. He finished his quart tankard, stood up, and fell flat onto the floor.

Silmar didn't even attempt to get into heavy drinking. He found a quiet corner and, with his quart pot of ale and his pack with the burden buried deep inside it, settled down to relax. He was given a second, and a third, quart of ale and proceeded to drink these too, albeit slowly.

The crash of chairs! The scrape of tables! The clatter of weapons, armour and baggage.

The yell of "Wake up! Wake up you lazy goats!"

Taura had found a whistle that she blew and blew. She laughed until her sides ached. Five very tired and hung-over adventurers groaned and complained and cursed. Five villagers, each with a pitcher of water, emptied the contents over each of the recumbent forms simultaneously. Then they ran!

Jasper did not react well and, rolling to his feet with a chair in his hand, looked for the cowardly enemy who had tried to drown him. He did calm down when he spied Taura laughing loudly. The rest of them clambered to their feet with groans and grunts. There were some really serious headaches amongst them.

"Good morning, my friends," she cooed. "You've had a wash and the kind villagers have left you some dawn meal – although the dawn was a couple of hours ago. You'd better eat it all up like good little boys because Momma is taking you all for a nice walk into some mines soon, mayhap today if we are fortunate!"

"Momma going to get her arse slapped inna moment!" moaned Falcon and made as if to leap at her. Taura squealed and jumped back.

The best any of the rest of them could reply was with a grunt although Silmar was sitting on a chair laughing. The dawn meal disappeared as if it were a carcass being devoured by a pack of ravenous hyenas, with the same sort of noise too.

Within an hour the companions had eaten, drunk a lot of water and began preparations for the next part of their journey. Jasper called the companions together and they sat round a large table to talk about what was to come.

"There ain't much else I can say right now," the dwarf said. "We just 'ave to get on with it an' work together. We'll be fine if we take care an' take no risks at all. I knows I made it sound terrifying and there's a lot of evil down there but there is some good too. You'll see."

"It may not mean much," responded Silmar. "But I feel the effects of the burden when we get near something evil. You know, the headaches and nausea. It acts as a warning and goes when the evil has gone. It was very strong in the presence of the vampyre. I could feel it even before we entered the keep. It lifted when he was destroyed."

"That's understandable," answered Taura. "Vampyres are evil because they are created by evil to be evil. Simple really."

"So I should feel its effect when we get close to the Dökkálfar, then."

"You no sick on me, hai?" ventured Jiutarô.

"Hai!" answered Silmar with a face simulating throwing up in Jiutarô's direction.

"You're like choddin' children!" groaned Jasper. "I have an idea where the entrance to the Shadow World is, just takes a bit o' searchin' for, that's all. Time to get goin'. Let's load up and go. It's a few hours away, we'll be getting there on foot. Like I said, there ain't no point in taking the 'orses so we'll 'ave to carry everythin' we need. From 'ere we should get there by midday I reckon."

Fifty gold coins ensured their horses and some of their belongings would be taken to the Ship's Prow in Westron Seaport. A few villagers clamoured to be the ones selected to take them.

With sombre faces, the companions strode out of the village. A small crowd of people waved them out, knowing nothing of where they were going.

The weather had turned very dismal and a cold rain had been steadily falling but the leaden skies showed that much heavier rain threatened. By the time that the downpour arrived, Jasper had led them into a shallow cave. For him, it was routine that caves, and similar places, were checked for undesirable occupants. Fortunately, in this case, there were none. That they were here at all was most unfortunate indeed.

PART 2
SHADOW WORLD

CHAPTER 16

JASPER INDICATED a rocky rise. "It's up there," he said gruffly. The rocks were huge blocks that looked as if they had been cemented together by rough grass and heather.

Jiutarô muttered in his own language. "I see nothing," he grunted as he followed behind the dwarf.

Jasper pointed up the steep slope. "Yer will in a minute."

Falcon reached to grab Taura's arm as she stumbled among the stones, almost dropping her staff. Although, from a distance, the entrance to the cavern was completely concealed among tall pillars of rock, the faintest of animal tracks made by those rare visitors to the tunnel indicated its presence only to a skilled tracker with a keen eye. Moreover, it only became noticeable to the group the closer they approached the entrance. Passing through a narrow defile, they entered an even narrower fissure warily and, even though the day was very cloudy and dismal, it took their eyes a few moments to adjust to the darkness of a cavern. A doorway, deep within the cave, was almost concealed between two natural columns of stone. It was constructed from very heavy oak and reinforced with four rusting iron bands. It was framed in a stone archway with ancient runes and symbols engraved around the entrance.

The door was closed. Falcon stepped over to open it but Jasper stopped him with a stocky restraining arm across the mighty Barbarian's midriff.

"Wait, laddie!" the dwarf commanded with a gravelly voice. "The door may be warded. Well, it may not be but if it is, you might be the unlucky bastard 'it by a powerful magic spell or somethink. 'Ear me well, all of yous, and mark my words wi' care. I 'ave been 'ere before, an' other fell places too. Girlie, what can you find out for us?"

Taura was irked and was not slow in showing it. "Girlie?" she retorted.

"That's the second time you've called me that, you cheeky bastard!" Looking at the others she asked, "Who made *him* king, anyway? If it is a magical warding, Billit is the one to ask, surely."

"That is not a very pious way of speaking with your bestest friends now, is it?" grunted the dwarf.

"Move aside, let me see," mumbled Billit peered at the door.

A few inches shorter than the dwarf, Billit pushed himself through nonetheless, stood back from the doorway and started a soft chanting. None of the group could understand his words; as always when he was voicing a spell, they all felt as if they could not focus their hearing onto his chanting. He waved his hands in a wide arc and a very faint blue glow that only he could see illuminated the doorway. He slowly dropped his hands, relaxed and reached into his pouch. He scattered some powder that looked like shiny sand over the doorway with a smile on his face. Beads of perspiration lined his forehead. "Well, there's no magical ward apparent 'ere," he stated with confidence. "Wasted my shiny sand though. Don't have much so we'll have to try somethin' different when I run out."

"Well, there may still be a booby-trap o' some kind," persisted Jasper as he peered around the doorway. "Think about where we are. These doorways ain't meant to be easy for just anyone to enter, you know. An' I don't trust that nasty darkling; 'e wouldn't miss an opportunity to do us some damage. Can *you* check to see if 'e laid a trap for us, Silmar? Your eyes is good in the dark."

The dour elf replied that it really was not something he was well suited for and cautiously stepped over towards the door. As he placed a foot down, there was a *click!*

"Oh shit!" breathed Silmar. "It's under my right foot, whatever it is!"

A hush descended.

After a few heartbeats, Jasper rubbed his face with his right hand. "Um, aye. Oh right, don't lift yer foot, yer dumb elf, keep it there. Nothin's happened yet but it may do when you lift yer foot off. Now take care all o' you, watch where you put yer own feet. Clumsy choddin' elf! I'm gonna show you what these leather tubes are for. Need yer 'elp, Billit, nothin' hard, just a magic spell."

The dwarf took a gold coin out of his money pouch and handed it to Billit.

"That's very nice o' you, Jasper, but you don't have to pay me for a spell," gasped the gnome as he flashed a nervous glance across to Silmar.

The dwarf was about to stomp in frustration but, glancing down at the floor, he suddenly froze on the spot. "Aye, funny choddin' gnome, ha, ha, choddin' ha! I want you to put a *Glow* spell on it so it shines real bright in the dark. Can yer do it? Iannus, my old associate, she could do it. She was a wizard, choddin' good 'un, too. Dead now. Shame really, she 'ad a lovely chest!" He let out a sigh tinged with sadness.

Taura tutted but said nothing.

"Aye, I can do this, but if you want one for everybody then I can't; magic *is* a bit taxing 'specially when I've not eaten for a couple of hours, you know!"

Jasper glowered at him.

Billit held out his two hands in front of him, his staff leaning against his shoulder. "Steady on, I'm just fooling Jasper," Billit chuckled. "Heh heh! Serious though, I can do one now and then a couple more in a few hours. To use a spell, I have to practice the words first; don't wanna get the spell wrong an' the gold coin turns to dust or somethin'. It can 'appen if a wizard is under pressure, you know. You didn't tell me you wanted this spell so I need to think 'ow it goes."

The dwarf was growing impatient. He glowered at Billit. "Well, GET ON WITH IT THEN!" he roared.

Billit hopped backwards but regained his balance and composure. He flexed his voice to produce the required, almost musical, intonation. He placed the coin in his left hand and moved his right hand in a circular motion above it. As he began uttering some words in a tongue unintelligible to the others, the coin started emitting a red, then pink which grew progressively brighter until a white glow between his fingers. It continued to became brighter and brighter until its light became almost too bright to look at directly.

"Done!" the gnome muttered. "That shine, it won't wear out for weeks." He handed the brightened coin back to the dwarf.

Jasper replied "I 'ear that it don't work so well on a silver coin an' 'ardly at all on a copper one, does it?"

"'S right," the gnome mage agreed. "You wanna see what it does to a diamond though; it looks like the sun!"

"Ain't givin' you no choddin' diamond," the dwarf grumbled as he pushed the coin deep inside the leather tube and pointed it at the door. A beam of light shone out and the door was bathed in a white light while all other parts of the cave remained in the gloom. "An' when I wanna cover the light, I do this," he said and put the leather cover over the end of the tube. The light was gone – completely.

"Ha, not bad for an old dwarf, eh?" Jasper said. "I've got five o' these tubes with covers an' with the 'elp of the gnome most of us should get one. Event'ally."

He removed the cover again and handed the light tube to Silmar. "See what the trap might be, elf."

"At last," Silmar sighed. "I thought you had forgotten me. My leg is beginning to tremble."

There was total silence from the companions. Silmar slowly moved the beam over the door and the archway. "Nothing to see," he whispered. He started looking around the walls of the cave adjacent to the doorway. He took his time; after all, he was the one at risk of something terrible happening. His right leg was now aching and a small tremble was building up in his knee. "Oh Gods, I really do want to move my leg!" he whispered.

"Don't you choddin' dare!" growled Jasper. "We could all be burned to ashes or somethin'"

Jiutarô, Taura and Falcon quietly stood out of the way, apprehensively looking on.

"Wait, what's that over there?" Silmar pointed to what appeared at first to be a narrowl fissure in the cave wall about three feet up from the floor. Jiutarô was the closest and he started to move towards the wall.

"Jiutarô, take this light thing," Silmar instructed. He was sweating profusely. "Check the floor before you go over, there may be more traps."

The Samurai dropped to his knees and started to examine the floor, moving slowly closer to the wall. He stood and pointed the light tube at the crack in the wall. "Hole! Stick, look at you," he warned Silmar. "Give rock, Falcon."

Falcon lifted what for him was a fist-sized rock from the ground and passed it to Jiutarô who held it over the hole but at an angle which would deflect the apparent missile out of harm's way.

"Foot up, Silmar," instructed the Samurai.

Silamr did so.

Another click sounded and immediately there was a loud *crack* as the missile struck the boulder. A dart, the length of a man's forearm and the thickness of a thumb, clattered off the cave roof and dropped down onto the ground.

"Feelin' like wiping yer arse now, elf?" asked Jasper. Everyone laughed this time, including Silmar, who thought it best not to admit that Jasper was not that far from the truth with that question. He sat on the ground and rubbed his thigh.

The dwarf looked down at the mechanism that Silmar had stepped on and called Billit across. "Take a look at this, gnome. How do you think it works?"

Gnomes were renowned for their natural aptitude with mechanical devices and Billit often showed curiosity with locks and unusual objects. "A floor plate, with a length of cord connected to it, by the looks of it. Aye, the line's buried under the dust and rubble but it looks like a very recent addition. Clean as your mother's bonnet, this cord! It goes up behind this rock pillar and, ahhh, hmmm." He studied the rock face near to the doorway. "Aye! Ahhh, right, aye!"

"What, yer choddin' midget?" yelled Jasper. "What? Tell me!" He was hopping from one foot to another in frustration.

Billit huffed in indignation. "Simple. It goes through this gap and connects up to this little lever. When Silmar stepped off the plate, the lever released the spring retainer and shoots the dart out. Simple really! I could make a few improvements here."

"Not now, gnome!" laughed Silmar.

For once, the dwarf agreed with him. "Yer don't wanna improve it, yer wants ter bust it!"

"Right, er, no, then. Another time p'raps. Lovely bit of cord this, feels like silk. I'm keepin' this." He pulled on the cord and it came free with the lever assembly attached. He cut the device off with his small knife and coiled the cord around his hand.

Meanwhile, Silmar picked up the dart. It seemed to be made of bone. He looked at the point and noticed a slight discolouration. "I think this is a poison or venom on here," he warned. He sniffed it and grimaced.

Jiutarô struggled to find the words. "Wet dirt, to safe," he suggested and he took it from Silmar. He was back in a few moments and the company turned as one towards the door.

"By the way, where did you find wet dirt, Jiutarô?" Taura asked him, although she had a feeling she knew what his answer would be.

"I piss!"

She would have chuckled but a tenseness was growing among the group. They drew a collective breath knowing it was time to enter the Shadow

World. All of them were anxious about entering, some more so than others. Jasper was the least apprehensive of all of them and even he was edgy. What waited for them in the darkness the other side of that door? Would they all make it through the ancient mines and back out safely? Would Jasper's skills in the ancient mines be sufficient to keep them all alive or would his age and memory let them down? His new friends were all amateurs but together, their fighting and magical skills were awe-inspiring. Yet they trusted him completely. They had no choice, after all.

The ageing dwarf looked at each of them in turn, perhaps in an attempt to gauge their feelings but also to offer some encouragement and comfort. Taura was the most visibly nervous and he put an arm around her waist – he could barely reach her shoulders! "Fear not, m'lady, we shall care fer one another an' protect each other down there, eh?"

She nodded, feeling a little encouraged by his words and noticing how his demeanour had softened now they were about to step through the doorway.

Jiutarô handed him back the light tube and the dwarf replaced the cover.

"I think I need to relieve meself afore we enter," mumbled Billit.

"Oh gods! Best yer have yer crap out 'ere," grunted Jasper. "The stink will warn all the beasties that we're on our way!"

"It's a stand up, not a sit down, ya fool of a dwarf!"

"Just tryin' to cheer us up, that's all. You feelin' alright now, missy?"

The Priestess of Neilea nodded and gave a half-hearted smile. "I'll be fine," she replied, but she was still trembling. This time she didn't mind the dwarf's nickname for her.

The barbarian, however, looked quite comfortable but his knuckles were white with his grip on the handle of his warhammer. Jasper glanced up at him.

"Watch yer 'ead down there, yer big lummox!" the dwarf advised sombrely. "The tunnel roof can be very 'igh one minute and barely 'igh enough even for me the next." He patted his weapons and with a deep breath. "Keep yer 'ands close to yer weaponry, all've yez. Are we ready?" he asked.

"Aye!" they all replied.

"Hai!" replied Jiutarô softly. "Ready."

"Hmmm, try it once more with a bit more feelin' all've yers? Oh, nay, p'raps not. Let's do it then!"

He placed his shoulder against the door and pushed hard. He needn't have, the door opened easily.

But loudly, the hinges hadn't ever been oiled, it seemed.

"Shit, sod it, bugger it!" Jasper could be coarse, even for a dwarf! He earned a *Shush!* from Taura.

The echoes of the door being opened came back at them for many heartbeats.

And they were heard by other ears.

The Dökkálfr had waited impatiently for too long. Their first test would be the trap by the doorway. He had known it was there, of course. There had been other traps laid there by the ancients but time had ruined most of them. He had repaired the one that looked the most promising. The chain linkage from the floorplate to the firing spring had rusted and he had carried out a repair with the silken cord that he carried. He was loath to part with such a valuable length of twine but perhaps the followers wouldn't spot the trap in the gloom of the cave and they would lose one of their number.

Two days, he'd estimated. *That's how long I have waited for these weaklings.* Being much more at home in the darkness of the ancient mines, he, like others of his race, had developed an accurate body clock although it failed him up on the surface. The headaches plagued him constantly during the daylight hours. *Oh those damnable headaches!* He muttered angrily to himself, now suffering the pain despite the precautions he had taken to protect himself from the daylight's glare and the heat. He felt some relief already now that he was in the ancient mine's tunnel and could concentrate on the passing of time. It was said that subtle changes in the rock were felt with the rotation of the sun and moon around the world of Amæus and this effect was felt in the bodies of Dökkálfar, so it was alleged by the sages of the surface world. This knowledge was now claimed by the depraved female Dökkálfar mages and the priesthood, who rigidly governed the Dökkálfar race, as their own.

He carried a small bow barely two and a half feet in length. Not particularly powerful, nevertheless, it was ideal for the narrow confines of the Shadow World. His arrows were short such that he was unable to draw the bowstring back to his chin; it did not matter, he wouldn't need a long range down here. It was more usual for *Shadow Elves* to be armed with a light crossbow. Although very light and unlikely to cause much damage, a crossbow bolt's point would be coated in a powerful and fast acting venom milked, predictably, from scorpions. Unless treated, death would come quickly and excruciatingly. He did not favour the crossbow – it was cumbersome, unpredictable and inaccurate – he favoured the short bow.

Now his mind wandered while he waited for the arrival of the fools from the surface. He reflected on the society he had left behind. Their female mages, those spiteful *volvas* who practised their *galdr*, song magic, and the clerics chose chaos and trickery for their oft inexplicable causes. The clerics wielded an awesome and terrible arcane power in the name of Adelenis, the evil Scorpion Queen goddess; *She* with *Her* foul army of *adelonnes*, the huge white scorpions that they farmed, fed, trained and milked. Even the Dökkálfar mages and warriors feared and despised them!

Ah yes! The *adelonnes*! He had seen one in Myrkheim, the grand Shadow World city of the Dökkálfar that he had left behind on this challenging errand to recover the artefact, a ceremonial dagger that had been touched by the very hand of Adelenis, so it was said by the Esteemed Volva who had sent him and a troop of warriors on the mission. He quietly harboured doubts; to express them would have meant death as a heretic because it was rumoured that Adelenis was in hiding from the god, Tarne, He that meted out justice, usually at a sword's tip. Her hiding was temporarily, of course.

His subterranean home city was far to the north-east, deep beneath the Dragon's Teeth Mountains. The *Adelonnes* were hated and feared by most Dökkálfar who regarded them as an aberration. The priestesses venerated them, however. These beasts were fearsome, bloodthirsty creatures created by Adelenis herself, so her priestesses lectured, from male Dökkálfar agents and warriors who had failed to complete the sacred tasks set by Her, through her priestesses and volvas, of course. Yes, loathsome they were to look upon, the body and tail of a gigantic, white scorpion. The one he had seen, long ago, was caged and tormented. It had eventually broken out from its cage and had been slaughtered in the main marketplace, but not before it had killed some Dökkálfar and even more Dwarven slaves, worthless surface scum that they were. The full length of the carcass was estimated at eighteen feet, ten of these being the barbed tail.

It was said that Adelenis Herself took the form of a great, white scorpion but with a Dökkálfar head, startlingly beautiful in its appearance. It was also said that she was not dark at all but white-skinned like the surface elves. She was normally illustrated in the temples as a beautiful, dark-skinned woman, resplendent in her nakedness, bipedal with a typical scorpion tail with its huge poison sac and barb at its tip. Priestesses taught that She did not yet inhabit the Outer Planes, where resided the Pantheon of the Gods, as did the other senior gods of evil persuasion, including Killik and Terene. Rather, She had *chosen* to remain closer to her followers from whom She took her powers and Her strength; so it was said.

It was also said, albeit quietly, that She did not have the strength to rise to the greatness accorded to those older and greater gods in the Outer Planes because She was in hiding and too weak at this time. It was being said that She needed these artefacts of power to develop the power so that She could emerge to face Her nemesis, Tarne, and match Him strength for strength, and to oppose Him with His moralistic and judgemental attitudes; that so-called *superior* god with his benevolent countenance and whose name he, the Dökkálfr in the service of his *Exalted Mistress*, the Esteemed Volva from Myrkheim, dared not utter.

And then his thoughts were broken. There came to his ears the sound of the door being opened. The sound was faint because of the distance, but not too faint for his keen ears to perceive. This was the sound he had waited for. *Two gods-damned days!* Those hinges called out their warning that the fools were on their way. Then he heard a strange hooting sound.

He sniggered quietly to himself and shook his head. *Amateurs. Hah!* One at a time, he would pick them off. *But not yet, let those other aberrations that inhabit the Shadow World have their fun first.*

He rose to his feet and slowly strode away.

CHAPTER 17

I T WAS WITH fear and trepidation that they entered this place of
dread, the unknown realm of the Shadow World. A place rumoured to
be swarming with foul, bloodthirsty creatures, and possibly with undead
too. Parents in villages on the surface would tell stories of creatures from
the Shadow World to scare their children into behaving or to ensure that
they returned home well before dark. Children would suffer nightmares,
some adults would too. Unexplained occurrences were often attributed to
the terrors from the Shadow World. People went missing; for sacrifices it
was rumoured because they never returned.

The Shadow World – that cold, damp place crawling not only with
the rats and great spiders but with the very beasts and devils of the abyss.

"Better shut the door, I guess!" grunted Jasper. He signalled for Jiutarô
to close the door but as the Samurai turned, the door noisily swung itself
shut with a faint *boom* and the group was in total pitch-black darkness. It
wasn't just darkness; it was the total absence of light.

A cold chill had crawled up Jiutarô's spine. "I touch not," he gasped.
"It close."

"Spooky, huh?" whispered Billit. And louder he cried "Whoo-ooo!"

"Idiot!" cried Taura. She swung her staff towards the sound and was
rewarded as she caught the gnome on his leg. He let out a yelp.

It was now quiet. There was very little sound of their breathing –
almost all of them were holding their breath. One of them was panting –
Taura, was it?

Silmar listened to the beating of his heart; he was certain that his
companions could hear it above the sound of their own. He was fearful that
his dark-vision had let him down until he realised he had not enabled it. He

did so now but it did little to aid him; he saw the faintest of outlines of his companions but little else.

"Quite warm down here, ain't it," whispered Billit after what seemed an age. His eyes flitted from side to side, and from roof to floor. He saw very little with his own dark vision.

"Dark too," replied Falcon. He could see nothing and felt totally disoriented as the sounds of their voices echoed back.

"A quart of foaming ale in a lively tavern would be far better, right now," said Silmar softly. Even then, his words seemed as a bellow. His dark-vision, although generally very good on the surface above, was limited because he needed a little light in order to magnify it. Down here, there was little of it, usually none.

"And a nice comfortable bed in the Ship's Prow Inn in Westron Seaport," responded Taura, her voice quivering with fear. Falcon had his massive arm around her shoulder and she felt comforted and somewhat safer. Truth be told, he felt vulnerable too but would never admit to it, particularly in front of Taura.

"Behave all've yous!" hissed Jasper. "I think I'll risk a little light 'ere." Although a whisper, it seemed incredibly loud in the darkness. "Got me the light tube; shield your eyes. Ready? Three, two, one. On!"

Unsure of what was going on with the light-torch, Jiutarô was briefly blinded by the light being uncovered. He gasped an oath in his own language.

They all gasped as a beam of light shot up towards the roof of the tunnel. It was a very uneven rock ceiling that loomed above them. It was high enough for Falcon to stand fully upright. The dwarf shone the beam to either side. The group had enough room in the tunnel to walk side-by-side in pairs. They could clearly see the deep scores on the walls where they had been worked by miners long ago. The tunnel stretched out in front of them far beyond the reach of the light beam. The floor was generally flat and even and few obstacles littered the path, although in places there were signs of loose rocks and boulders scattered on the floor from roof falls. Decayed remnants of lanterns, shovels and picks were stacked to one side.

Niblit's voice, confident compared to those of the others, except perhaps for Jasper, sounded startlingly loud. "I reckon we should keep light on, or light some torches," he said. "That will put anything, or any creature, at a disadvantage, don't you think?"

"Sounds good," Silmar agreed slowly. "We only have a few torches, though, and will need to use them sparingly."

"Hey now, we should limit our talking to just whispers," advised the dwarf. "We'll keep the light tube on but it may make us a target for the dark 'un. Let's go."

They started forward, very slowly at first as they became accustomed to their environment. The sound of Jasper's whispers echoed from the walls but the sound itself seemed dead, as if it was being absorbed by the tunnel about them. Because of the echoing, the members of the group were able to speak to each other only in hushed voices. This was to the best advantage because they would not want their voices to carry along the tunnel.

They had been expecting a rank smell of damp and decay. But the atmosphere was quite fresh, not unpleasant, at all. Nor was the air as stale as would have been expected; they occasionally discerned a faint movement of air on their faces or in their hair. The tunnel was surprisingly dry; from time to time though, they could hear the dripping of water. Here and there were some muddy areas as trickles of water found their way into the dust and rubble on the floor. As they marched on, slowly and cautiously, they passed by a few puddles and occasional pools, some of which seemed very deep. In the larger pools the water was always extremely cold. Jasper explained that the pools would often provide a good source of drinking water but it was advisable to check it first.

"Yer don't know it somethin's pissed in it so smell it first," he advised. "Then put a bit on yer lips, then on yer tongue an' spit it out an' then try a mouthful an' spit that out."

As time crawled on, the mine changed from a low and narrow tunnel to massive, wide, cathedral-like chambers where the roof disappeared from even the reach of the beam of Jasper's light tube. There were times that the bright beam from the light tube could not even find the width of the tunnel. Their path was always clearly defined however, but the mine tunnel became narrower the further they progressed. Stalactites hung down from the ceiling in many places, often in ones and twos but occasionally in clusters. Generally, stalagmites reached up from the floor towards them. Some stalactites and stalagmites met to produce a pillar. The smell of dampness filled the still air.

Time had no way of being measured when there was no light from the sun, the moon and stars. There was no change in the level of darkness, no change of temperature.

At the very start, Jasper had said "We eats when we're 'ungry, we sleeps when we're tired, otherwise we walk quiet-like an' we 'unt Darkling. An' most of all we stays alive."

The party quickly realised the benefits of Jasper coming with them. His knowledge and advice were priceless. They already felt that they had been walking for some hours and some of the group felt they were in need of a rest with some food and water. They passed many side-tunnels and resisted the urge to explore them. The pathway was now becoming narrower with steps rising or falling and slopes here and there which were sometimes quite steep. An order of march was discussed by Silmar and Jasper.

Silmar leaned forward to whisper to the dwarf. "Look Jasper, you are comfortable down here, I am not. You have dark-vision, do you not?"

The dwarf nodded. "Aye, 'bout ten, mebbe fifteen paces or so. Not as good as it was when I was a young 'un. Why?"

"So it makes sense for you to lead the party. I'll take up position at the back of the group so I can protect our rear. Taura is terrified but she is taking much comfort from Falcon. He really is looking after her but he is very much afraid of being here. He doesn't show it but I can hear it when his voice wavers. I think he takes as much comfort by being with Taura as she does with him. They should be in the centre of the group with Jiutarô."

Jasper whispered his agreement and took over the discussion. "Billit is quite 'appy here, 'e is reasonably confident in tunnels. 'E says 'is limited dark-vision allows 'im to make out shapes an' heat-sources up to about twenty paces away. 'Is cheerful manner encourages us all, me included. 'E could take up position next to you, mebbe. Jiutarô is a strange one though, don't yer think? He's picked up the Universal tongue so quickly, ain't 'e? 'E seems 'fraid of nothin' an' you say that 'e told you that this is not real for 'im? Like it's a dream. It's real enough fer me, I can tell you. I'd like 'im behind me with that strange bow of 'is or 'is sword. I can't believe that 'e can loose off three arrows in as many heartbeats and each one can take the eye out of a rabbit at a 'undred paces! I never seen nothing like it."

"Aye, I agree, and it's the same with that sword of his," mused Silmar. "He calls it a *dai-katana* and handles it both one and two-handed. It's so fast that he can take it out of his scabbard, swing it once and replace it again. And in that time two people are dead. It is truly awesome. And that blade cuts through all other swords. I would love one like it. He truly is a weapons-master."

"What say you about our order o' march then, elf?"

Silmar nodded his head in full agreement. "Aye, 'tis good. Let's let everyone know." He gathered the party around him and Jasper, and explained their plan for the march.

"Aye, well," murmured Billit. "I gotta sort out some more o' them light tubes, I s'pose. Taura is givin' me a hard time 'bout 'em. I need a couple o' gold crowns though. Ain't usin' me own!"

Silmar flipped him two coins, the gnome mage sat on the ground and began chanting over one of the coins, making circular motions with his hand above the coin. Many moments passed before a very bright white light emanated from it. Billit had cast a *Glow* spell on the coin. Jasper thrust the coin deep inside another of the leather tubes and placed the cover on it. He passed it to Taura.

"There, girlie," he grunted. "That is for you." She nodded her thanks.

Billit repeated the process for the second coin and passed it to Silmar. The mage was bathed in sweat and laid down to recover.

The dwarf nodded to the little mage. "Choddin' 'ard work, that was, Billit. Good though. Got two more tubes but I guess you can't really do another one yet."

Billit sat up again. "Give me some water, somebody. I spitting dust 'ere! Hey, you wanna see the light that comes when I do it on a gemstone. Awesome!"

"Lookit now," Jasper advised. "We 'ave three o' these light tubes, we must 'ave a spoken code word that could be called by any one of us if the need arises, to both cover the beams an' to open 'em. If me, Billit or Silmar are using our dark-vision an' one o' these light tubes is uncovered, we'll be blinded fer ages an' won't be able to see to fight if we need to."

"What do you suggest?" asked Falcon.

A couple of suggestions came from the others but Jasper held up his hands and shook his head.

"Keep it simple," advised Jasper. "I suggest we use the words '*lightson*' an' '*lightsout*'. If for some reason it ain't convenient for the lights to be covered up or uncovered, then someone 'as to call '*nochange*'. Or something like that. What say you all to that?"

Silmar recommended that they all try to get used to relying on the three members of the party who had dark-sight and move in darkness through the tunnel. "The advantage is that if we come across something down here, or someone, who is used to being in total darkness, if we uncover our light tubes on a *'lightson'* word, they'll be more blinded that us."

"He's not just a handsome face," remarked Taura.

"He's a choddin' elf, so he's not *even* a handsome face!" drawled Jasper. "Time to move on. Let's try it in darkness."

Both Silmar and Jasper had noticed that Taura and Falcon had been sitting together hand-in-hand and the dwarf winked. Silmar raised an eyebrow and smiled. Billit produced the silken cord that he had recently acquired. It was decided that this would be useful in keeping Jiutarô, Taura and Falcon together. The others wouldn't need it.

Progress was extremely slow for a long time and almost every pebble, rock or uneven surface on the tunnel floor seemed to become a significant obstacle. The path turned and twisted, climbed and fell. Sometimes they had to climb up slopes on all fours or slide down other slopes. As time went on, Jasper was able to whisper warnings and progress became slightly faster. After some hours their speed was almost the same as it had been when they had the light tube uncovered. To Jasper, signs of ancient mine workings were everywhere. To each side were narrow openings with piles of detritus and ancient remains of mining tools. He whispered to them of what he could see, despite being only dim in his dark-vision.

"What did the old mine workers do with all the rock they dug out?" asked Taura.

Jasper shrugged his shoulders but it was an action that went unseen by Taura, Jiutarô and Jasper. Realising this, he whispered, "I would reckon it got took up to the surface," he surmised. "Never thought 'bout it really. If it ain't down 'ere it must be up there."

A very unusual and unexpected thing happened to Taura, Jiutarô and Falcon after a while. They found they could see, very faintly, the walls of the tunnel and its floor. An indistinct yellow-green glow seemed to emanate from the rocks. Jasper stopped the party and they all took the opportunity to sit down.

He whispered, "I wondered who would notice it first. It's got somethin' to do with the mould that grows down 'ere on the walls in the Shadow

World. It glows an' you can see a little. Sometimes it's lots brighter than this. This could go on for ages now. Shut yer eyes, ev'ryone. *Lightson!* I wanna see the mould."

The party began to rise to their feet. As Jasper stepped off, he tripped and fell to the floor. There was a swishing sound as an arrow flew into the group. Two more followed almost immediately. Jiutarô gave a cry and staggered to the floor, an arrow protruded from his upper left thigh. Falcon raised his left arm; an arrow had embedded itself just above his wrist. Both of them were groaning with the pain. A third arrow had passed harmlessly through Jiutarô's loose-fitting hose.

"Another trap, an' I didn't see it!" hissed Jasper. "I'm a choddin' idiot." His foot had become caught up in a thin chain which led to a pile of rocks a few paces in front of them and luckily for him, he had fallen to the ground. "Choddin' Darkling been up to 'is mischief again, huh?"

Jiutarô was in considerable pain and was mumbling in his own obscure language. Billit was attending to him and had his hand on the shaft of the arrow. The gnome slapped the Samurai's face hard with his other hand and then, in one movement, pulled the arrow free. Jiutarô gasped out in surprise and agony.

"Why did yer slap him?" asked Jasper.

"To distract 'im from me pulling the arrow out, o' course. Good idea, ain't it?"

"So how do you know it wasn't barbed?" asked Silmar.

"'Cos the arrow that's sticking through Falcon's arm isn't!"

"Ah, aye. I see. The Darkling may have used venom though so take care."

"Let us hope not," gasped Taura. "I can help to heal. As you know, The Lady Neilea has given me some healer's skills. I shall stop the bleeding and then ask Her if She will help with the healing."

She knelt on the ground beside Jiutarô and pulled out a small bag from her pack. She set some of the contents on the ground. She took a bandage from the scattered contents and picked out a glass jar which she opened. She scooped a little of the jar's glutinous contents and smeared it across a bandage which she folded and then tightly wrapped around Jiutarô's shoulder wound. Then placing her hands, without touching, over Jiutarô's wound, she chanted words which, in her sing-song voice, became impossible for the others to understand. It took about three or four minutes before she finished her incantations. Although the bandage was bloodstained, the wound no longer appeared to be bleeding heavily.

Jiutarô was astounded. "How do this?" he asked. "Magic? Aiii, strange."

"You have magic in your world, don't you?" asked Billit. "Your priests and mages do healing and stuff?"

Jiutarô shook his head. "No magic. See none, never." He flexed his shoulder and winced as dull pain shot through it.

"What was that you put on the bandage?" Silmar asked.

"A rare and precious concoction produced by nature," she replied. "It takes one creature all of its life to make just a small drop."

"Really?" he asked. "Ah, it is honey, is it not?"

She smiled and nodded as she gathered up her paraphernalia, replaced it in her bag and attended to Falcon next. He had pulled the arrow out himself by quickly cutting off the flight end with his hunting knife and removing the remaining portion by tugging it out. They hadn't even been aware of him doing it. He grimaced at Taura as she sat next to him with her bag.

His wound was bleeding but not profusely. He was using his other hand to press against the wound on either side of his wrist to stop the bleeding. His wrist and the fingers of both hands were blood-soaked, nonetheless. Without using a bandage, Taura started her chant to her deity, Neilea, once again. A long while passed before the wound no longer bled. She used her substance on a bandage once again and wrapped it tightly around Falcon's wrist.

Falcon raised his hand to Taura's cheek and looked onto her eyes. She leaned over and kissed him on the mouth, hard. It was a few minutes before anybody interrupted.

"Time to sort ourselves out, I think," Jasper said softly. "Come along my little lovebirds! What did yer say that stuff was yer put on the bandage? Somethin' holy?"

"Very much so," replied Taura. "Very holy indeed. It was honey. Just honey. It helps cure many ills and wounds and prevents infection. It's good to use and I can get more of it almost anywhere."

Jasper and Silmar had looked around to check for any other unwanted distractions. They had found none. They studied the trap. It did not appear to have been freshly set; clearly their quarry may not even have noticed the existence of it because there were no fresh signs around it.

Silmar breathed a sigh of relief. "I thought the Døkkálfr had left us another hazard in the hope of reducing our number. We were most fortunate that he had not set it himself for he would surely have used venom. Will the next trap take its first victim? We must try to be careful."

Jasper was quiet but then he spoke, uncharacteristically softly. "I feel so choddin' stupid, elf. I think it's better that you lead fer a while. That trap may 'ave killed one of us an' I didn't even see it there. With the glow from the mould, you may stand a better chance o' spotting somethin' as we go on. I'll take up the rear position with Jiutarô and Billit will 'elp me. A gnome bein' of a minin' tribe will be very 'elpful to me. Falcon an' Taura can stay in the middle – holdin' 'ands."

"You're just jealous," whispered Taura and stuck out her tongue at him.

"Why would he want to hold Falcon's hand?" answered Silmar. They all laughed but once again, they earned a *shush* from Taura.

Billit had puffed out his chest at being told he would be of value in the group. It was generally in the nature of gnomes that they were ignored, being small of stature and easily forgotten.

Silmar emphasised that they all keep as quiet as possible from now so that he could concentrate better. "And we don't want to let the Døkkálfr know that we are behind him."

Once again, the group resumed their march. Silmar felt the weight of responsibility heavily on his shoulders. What if *he* failed to spot the next one? If one of his friends were to die, it would be his own fault. Would they blame him? Traps were designed and made so as not to be seen, obviously. Progress would be a little slower now because the elf would be checking to each side and ahead. The faint light from the tunnel walls seemed to increase a little although there were places where it gave out completely. Their eyes were growing accustomed to its faint glow and it did help Silmar with his dark-vision. The dripping of water through the mines was incessant and annoying, with the dampness giving sustenance to the mould and encouraging its growth. Within the silence, they occasionally heard the sounds of tiny skittering feet, probably rodents or similar, rushing away as they passed.

There were still a number of little caverns and openings in the walls of the tunnels. Often, they passed these with care and silence. Now, at times, they entered them to find nothing, except perhaps the putrid or desiccated remains of a raw meal eaten by some sort of animal. Once, the remains appeared to be human, certainly not dwarf, gnome or elf. It was not recent however; scraps of clothing fell to shreds as Billit pulled upon it to investigate. There was a coin, probably silver, in the dust on the floor though; the symbols upon it were unknown. The gnome put it in one of his pouches.

For many hours, it seemed, they had been on the march. They were all hungry, thirsty and very tired. Jasper finally ordered for them to halt. They went into a little cavern which, except for some dry droppings, appeared uninhabited. Small droppings were not unusual here in the Shadow World; they weren't everywhere but they were noticeable from time to time.

"How long walk?" asked Jiutarô.

"'Alf a day and then some," replied Jasper. "'Bout two leagues I would say."

They lit no fire, having agreed that they wouldn't be needed and, of course, it would affect the dark-vision of those that had it. They ate whatever they had brought with them, mainly dried meat, nuts and dried fruit. A little of this would provide enough energy to march for many hours and there seemed a plentiful supply of water from pools in the tunnels.

Taura, Jiutarô and Falcon were not expected to stand guard during the rest periods. There was no point; they didn't have the dark-vision and the heightened senses of the dwarf, elf and gnome. Billit would need to practice the words of the spells he thought he might need and then get enough sleep to be able to use his concentration to cast them. Similarly, Taura would need to sleep to be able to beseech Neilea for her aid through prayer-spells.

Billit was quietly intoning arcane words when there was a sudden flash of searing light and a *whoosh* of power.

The party were instantly on their alert as they leapt to their feet with weapons in their hands.

"What was that?" cried Silmar, more loudly than he should have considering the risks.

A cry of protest and an oath from Jasper was followed by a sincere apology from the gnome. "It – it was me! I should've stopped before a certain phrase. Shit!"

"I can't see a choddin' thing, you – you chod!" the dwarf groaned.

"What in the seven hells of the Void did you do?" He sat rocking back and forth while rubbing his eyes with his hands.

Although he had been dozing, Silmar's eyes, too, were badly affected although not as much as those of the dwarf.

"I 'adn't done this spell afore," the gnome whined. "It was a, er, an *Energy Blast* spell I was practising the words for but, er, it worked too well."

Indeed, out through the doorway of their chamber and across the tunnel, the beam from Taura's light tube showed a darkened, smoking patch on the wall.

"Put your magic tricks away for now, Billit," she hissed. "Let's all get some sleep while we may."

Billit wilted under the withering glares from his companions. No further words were necessary.

"Make me shit!" exclaimed Jiutarô, lightening the tension. "Dark elf hear, huh?"

He had voiced everybody else's fears.

CHAPTER 18

*T*HEY MOVE LIKE *a herd of aurochs*, the Døkkálfr thought. He was appalled by their careless attitudes when navigating the mines, and at the same time amused at their ineptness. *So, they have light. Their need for it emphasises their human weakness. I must be wary in the event they use it while I am relying on my dark-sight.*

He reflected momentarily on the flash he had seen earlier. There had been a slight *whoomph* sound from its source back along the tunnel in the direction of the white-skinned surface elf and his accomplices.

Magic surely! So, they must have a mage with them; a human with formidable power. I must be wary, and devious in fact.

He considered revising his plan. Perhaps a strike and run tactic. Take one of them out and run while the rest of them are confused and frightened in the darkness. An arrow here, a trap there, although it seemed they had been alerted by another trap that he, fortuitously, had missed; they were now cautious. The arrow-trap some hours ago had taken casualties, he was certain.

He had used the last of his phial of scorpion venom on the trap by the entrance but without success. This had angered him because his *Exalted Mistress* had provided little of what amounted to a very valuable resource and it was wasted.

She expected success. She would not tolerate failure.

He rose off the gravel floor, hefted his pack, grabbed his weapons and sauntered quietly along the tunnel.

They resumed their march but were forced to rely on their light tubes because the dim light from the fungus had waned. It was just as well they had their own light sources because they almost immediately began to find crevasses across the floor of the mine tunnels. The majority of these were no more than a foot or two in width but others made it necessary for them to leap across. These had once had wooden bridges across them but over the long years these had disintegrated or were too fragile to trust. All fissures appeared bottomless but they couldn't be certain.

"I wonder how deep these are," murmured Silmar.

"Deep! Choddin' deep!" gasped Jasper in an irritated manner. "It don't choddin' matter, elf! Don't drop anything down there; you don't know if it is in'abited by somethin' shitty that will come and get us."

At length, they came to a point where the path seemed to end. A vast chasm, many yards across, barred their way. As they approached, it was evident that sometime in the distant past, an ancient civilisation had carved a ledge around the left side of the chasm; the marks of picks and chisels were clearly evident. It was barely wide enough for them to pass and a lot of care would have to be taken if they were to get to the other side. There were also remnants of a bridge. Two short pillars, approximately three feet in height and a foot in girth, stood a couple of paces back from the lip of the fissure. Rusted remnants of an old chain hung from the top of one of the pillars. The drop appeared interminably deep; the beam from the light tube did not show the bottom of the pit.

Although the majority of the party, being quite small in stature, easily managed to find their way along the ledge, two of them had serious difficulties. Jasper was the first to cross and, being wide of girth as were most dwarves, it was a challenge for him to get to the other side. At one point, when he was about halfway across, he had to drop to his hands and knees to avoid the certainty of falling to his death.

Silmar crossed with ease but as he sat down to wait for the others a small ache lanced through his head. *Probably tiredness*, he thought.

He should have recognised the warning sign.

The mighty Falcon did not fare quite so well. Billit had to take himself and his own equipment across and then return twice to take across the barbarian's weapons and equipment. Once the great barbarian started to cross, it was obvious that he was terrified. At one point he froze and could not move. He began, "Go without –"

At that moment, an arrow whistled over Silmar's head and clattered off the rock an inch away from Falcon's head. The great man's right foot slipped from the ledge and he stumbled. His flailing leg found nothing to support it and he began to slip.

"No!" Taura screamed. "Hold on, Falcon!"

Silmar turned and, with his bow readied, searched for the one that had sent the arrow. Jiutarô had already loosed an arrow across the chasm and he pointed and called "There! Arrow hit, I know it!" He readied another arrow.

The elf focussed his dark-vision and saw a dark shape dart from behind cover, disappearing into the distance. He did not pursue it.

Billit shuffled back along the ledge to where Falcon was hanging on for dear life by his arms and one leg and helped him back up onto the ledge. A weeping Taura was already shuffling along the ledge to give her help as best she could and, together, she and the gnome encouraged the barbarian to the far side.

"That sneaky bastard Døkkálfr again!" growled Silmar. "I felt this sharp headache but thought I was tired. It must have been the dagger reacting to that evil piece of shit."

Falcon sat on the floor, shaking like a leaf, and Taura was hugging him tightly and showering him with kisses.

"Not happy in this place," he moaned. "Kill that damned Darkling and get us out of here!"

"Enough. I give Darkling, er, sword teach, hai?" replied Jiutarô, with a ferocious expression of fury that none of them had seen before. He was always impassive and even when under the pressure of seeing monstrous creatures for the first time, he showed little of the anger that they witnessed now.

"I think we'll queue up to cut bits off 'im," snarled Billit. "Oh, a very brave bastard to attack from a place of ambush!" He had yelled the last comment. "Too frightened to face us, eh?"

"No point in trying to keep quiet now," Silmar pondered. "He is probably fully aware of where we are. What worries me is that he may be watching us or lying in wait again. We must remain constantly vigilant."

"Aye," agreed Jasper, "an' 'e is wounded, 'opefully, with Juto's arrow. Hey, 'e might also be dyin' down 'ere." He then added, loudly, "But we don't use poisons. That is for cowards!" He then calmed down. "Bah, what's the choddin' use?"

They continued once again and, fortunately, there were no other wide chasms and no further sign of the Døkkálfr. They marched, albeit slowly, for an hour or so. The tunnel once again widened into a mighty cavern and they agreed to risk using their light tubes to look about them.

"Ready?" whispered Jasper. "Three; two; one; lightson."

The light tubes were uncovered in unison. By habit, they crouched low or behind what scant cover was available, expecting at any moment the whoosh of an arrow.

Their light beams showed where ancient miners had engraved characters on a number of tall stone pillars that supported the cavern roof. Some of them showed runes and symbols but these were not recognised by any of the comrades.

This vast hall showed no suggestion that it had recently been used. They carried out a quick search with some surprising results. Signs indicated that this area of the mines had once been a city occupied by ancient civilisations. Apart from the pillars, there were arches, doorways and stone stairways leading both upwards and down. There were also remnants of ancient battles with scattered bones and heavily rusted remains of weapons and armour. There was nothing that could be salvaged and the group decided there was little reason to remain.

"We should rest," suggested Jasper. He was clearly fatigued. "Forgotten 'ow unused to campaigning I've become. I'm choddin' tired."

Silmar shrugged his shoulders. "I really don't think it would be a good idea rest here," he said. "It is too difficult to defend."

Silmar followed the path through the great hall and led the group through to the far end and back into the mine tunnel. The floor was very uneven now and sharp-edged rocks and fissures made progress extremely difficult. After a couple of hours, however, the path once again became easier to navigate. As before, there were a few caverns to either side of the tunnel. The group halted to eat and sleep. A sentry schedule was set once again and the party settled down to sleep hoping it wouldn't be their last.

Not very far ahead, along the passage, the Darkling attended to his wound. That unusual warrior, the one with the strange shining sword and the extraordinary bow, had sent an arrow quicker than sight. It had unerringly found its target – entering the side of his stomach just above his hip but fortune decreed it hadn't punctured his intestines or any organs. *Ach, the pain though!* This warrior would be one to reckon with. This was twice now that he had received an injury while down in the Shadow World. He had twisted his knee in a poor landing from having leapt across a chasm with inadequate care. It was not supposed to be like this.

Although he was always confident in his ability to survive in hostile environments, he fully expected to feel invulnerable in the Shadow World. He was beginning to recognise the fact that he had vulnerabilities after all. He felt exhausted. Being alone meant that he could only semi-sleep for short periods. There were races down here that would be happy to tear apart the group that followed him, limb by limb. Some of these races would also tear him apart too, given the opportunity. He probably had as many potential enemies down here as did the surface-rats behind him. They might even have friends. But not him.

An idea had occurred to him while he tended the injury. He would lead them towards the *City of Shade* and let *them* deal with the fools. He would be there to collect the artefact from the elf's dead body. Then the *Grullien* should be satisfied with any gold or precious stones they could get from the bodies.

The *Grullien!* The ancient race of *Shade Gnomes* that inhabited an area of the Shadow World that they guarded with a viciousness bordering on frenzy. The Døkkálfr thought about what he knew of this malicious race. He knew that they would give him some aid but only if they could profit from it. They were still some distance away and would rarely venture far from their holes. Their shamans had some basic magical powers granted to them although they would be no match for a wizard and a cleric from the surface world. The Grullien were fierce and relentless warriors but they were armed just with basic weapons such as metal darts, simple spear blades and throwing nets; but they were still fearsome, nonetheless. They had a deep hatred for the races of peoples that lived on the surface. *Well, we have something in common there then, don't we?* he thought. They also had a fear and hatred of the sunlight, their skin and eyes being too sensitive to endure it. Their fanatical devotion to their Rock Mother goddess, Grull, made them a target for derision among other races of the Shadow World. It was debatable whether Grull actually existed.

Let the Grullien have the fools, he considered. *Hah, they might even use, or sell, the surviving surface rats for slavery.* A faint smile briefly showed on his dark, bitter, face.

Once more his mind wandered off as he attended to his wound. This would undoubtedly slow him down for a while. There were Grey Dwarves down here too, but it was rumoured that some were renegades who shunned the ways of the Shadow Dwarves of the Shadow World and their god, *Killik was it?* and embraced the more traditional surface-Dwarven pantheon. These renegades were outcasts, tattooed and treated as criminals by the Shadow Dwarves and would almost certainly be killed if they were to return to the depths. He was in as much danger from them as from the Grey Dwarves.

There were renegade Døkkálfar too, particularly to the east – they were generally nomadic surface-dwellers in The Wildings, the lawless lands in between the Dragon's Back peaks and Cascant far to the east. They also honoured the gods of the surface world and as a reward found that they were able to bear the ravages of the sunshine.

My mind wanders; I must focus.

CHAPTER 19

T HANKFULLY, THEIR break passed without danger and they were all roused by Silmar. They were weary, having slept poorly under the threat of attack by the Darkling. Once again, their long, slow trek resumed. They marched for many hours without incident although they didn't relax their vigilance for a moment. This itself was incredibly taxing and they paused often. The nature of the tunnel changed constantly; they walked along long straight galleries and climbed up long slopes, all of which showed grooves made by the wheels of wagons in millennia past. Old rock-falls were commonplace with heaps of boulders, rubble and dust littering the tunnel floor. Everywhere they looked they could clearly see, or feel, the ancient marks of picks and shovels. They came to a very long flight of steps which climbed hundreds of feet upwards. Alongside it was a slope where the old wagons would have been winched up or down.

They moved as quietly as they were able and spoke rarely. Progress was interminably slow while they risked using their light tubes only occasionally.

Once again, a dim glow began to come from mould-growth on the tunnel walls and eventually, the damp mould provided sufficient light for them not to have to rely on their light tubes.

"How far have we marched?" Taura asked during one of their short breaks.

Jasper paused for a few moments while he rubbed at his hairy chin. "I reckon it's been three days now," he pondered quietly. "That'd be about six leagues. We need to be extra watchful from now, not just 'cos of the Darkling but we might run into other, er, undesirables."

"Like what?" queried Falcon.

"What I told yer about. Like Grey Dwarves, the choddin' bastards, or them Grullien Gnomes. Whatever; watch yer arses. If I remember aright, we're more than 'alfway through by now. Time to walk, not to talk. Keep quiet now."

For a roughly-estimated half a day they trudged on. Jasper had the strangest feeling they were being watched at times, but then he knew there was much down here that was alive, and dead. He did mention it to his friends, however. Surprisingly, Silmar quietly admitted to having the same feelings of being observed, saying he could feel the gaze of many eyes. They kept silent and moved as noiselessly as they were able. No more traps had been set for them, as far as they were aware, and there were no dangerous encounters.

Their fortune was about to change though.

Food was running critically low. Drinkable water had never be a problem down here; much of the water they discovered was not fit to drink but some of it was, provided it was flowing. Jasper had warned them there were very few food sources in the Shadow World. Surprisingly, fish was occasionally plentiful in some of the deep pools but not all were easy to catch or good to eat. There were many different kinds of beast in the tunnels and some of these, if they could be caught, would be a providential source of food. The first problem was that anything that they hunted would swiftly turn tail and flee before they had a chance to catch or kill it. Their other problem was that this source of food would have needed to be cooked and there was very little material available to light a fire with. Jasper identified edible fungus, some of which would have provided an accompaniment to other food but alone, it would not be very nourishing.

"Yer use up more energy lookin' fer it an' tryin' ter find a way of cookin' an' eatin' it than you would get from the eatin' of it," he advised. "It ain't worth the trouble unless yer starvin'. Right now we got 'nuff food fer a day or two so don't fret 'bout it too much."

Without warning, Silmar staggered to the wall of the tunnel, leaned against it and retched onto the ground. Some of them recognised the symptom immediately.

"It your burden, isn't it," whispered Taura.

"Aye, Taura, it is I am sure of it. Urghh! But it usually only happens when we are in the proximity of something evil. Oh, my head!"

Then they heard a piercing scream of terror.

Silmar straightened up, all thoughts of his discomfort put to one side. He raised a hand and hissed a *shhh*.

The scream sounded again but this time accompanied by much shouting. It seemed to derive from a passage off to the left-hand side, a narrow opening in the tunnel wall.

They froze in their tracks. Silmar motioned with his hand and they moved to stand in two groups; one each side of the tunnel entrance. They all slowly and quietly withdrew their weapons and listened for further clues as to what it may have been that made that terrible scream. Once again, the scream came but this time it was muffled as if the person making the sound had been gagged.

"Is woman," whispered Jiutarô. "We go?"

Jasper stepped forward. "Aye," he agreed with a nod. "I'm not 'avin' none o' that, even if she's an elf woman!"

Taura glared at him but he merely winked back.

They cautiously eased forwards along the narrow tunnel. Jasper led with Silmar and Jiutarô close behind. Billit followed with Taura and Falcon a few paces behind but stopped at a signal from Silmar. The leading three moved onwards. It had not been easy for any of them because their way was partially blocked by various items of ancient mining detritus scattered among boulders that had accumulated there for a long time. A bright glow from ahead gave them sufficient light for them not to need their light tubes and even to make dark-vision unnecessary.

The screams had now subsided into pitiful sobbing. Quietly, they eased forward. The leading trio cautiously made their way around a bend and about twenty yards in front of them was the entrance into a chamber that was brightly lit by flaming torches which cast dancing shadows even on the walls of the tunnel. Silmar again motioned to the others to keep back while he, Jasper and Jiutarô used what cover there was to get as close to the chamber as possible.

The noise was quite loud now. One voice seemed to rise above the others but it was in a language that Silmar did not recognise. A single word was clearly repeated though – "Kalanisha! Kalanisha!"

The trio stood slightly back from the entry into the chamber and Silmar risked a cautious look inside. The sight that greeted him was horrific. He signalled Jiutarô to look and the expression on the Samurai's face was pure rage.

A group of six men dressed in the hooded, black and scarlet robes typical of clerics, together with about a dozen worshippers of an unknown cult, were in a state of some sort of frantic trance; they swayed and held their hands above their head. There was no music which may have explained this rhythmic movement, but merely the chanting of "Kalanisha! Kalanisha!" This was occasionally interrupted by shouts from a man who seemed to be a High Priest or shaman. The whole area was lit by flaming torches held in sconces on the cave walls. There was an overpowering stench, Silmar recognised it immediately – stale blood!

The High Priest stood next to a large stone altar. On this alter was bound a naked female human, she was conscious and struggling against the bonds that held her. A wad of grey cloth had been stuffed into her mouth. Her hair was jet black and very long. She seemed pretty although blood ran from the side of her face.

Silmar and Jiutarô backed away from the cavern. "Get the others! Quickly!" said the elf. Jiutarô quietly left.

"Kalanisha! Kalanisha!"

The others carefully made their way forwards to where Silmar and Jasper watched the cavern. They all moved to a position where they could take in the details of the scene. A crudely drawn symbol of a skull with a dagger embedded in the top of it adorned a rock wall. The Altar was heavily stained with, Silmar assumed, old blood. It appeared that it was either used for sacrifices or as a place for butchering animal carcasses, or both.

"Kalanisha! Kalanisha!"

A large metal cage stood in a corner of the temple, inside was a beast of some kind. The High Priest and his attendants were grouped at one side of the altar. The leader removed his hood. His hair was matted in dry blood, so it appeared, and his hair was spiked to give him a grotesque appearance. His face was covered in swirling tattoos. The other priests were bald but their heads were similarly covered in the thick dark blood. The leader started a rhythmic chanting, interspersed with the word *Kalanisha* again.

Silmar's companions were now standing behind him. Jiutarô grunted "We go in?" His face was grim.

Silmar replied "Ready?"

They all nodded.

The elf turned back to the scene before him just as the high priest removed his robe and stood naked by the feet of the female tied to the altar. In his hand was a large stone dagger. The terror on the woman's face was palpable as her wide eyes flicked from side to side. A part of the High Priest's anatomy made his first intentions quite obvious. An assistant passed a large iron chalice to him and he swallowed a mouthful of the dark liquid inside. It seemed to have an immediate effect. Passing it to one of the worshippers, he became almost manic, as did the worshippers as they drank, each of them going into a frenzied gyration. He was just about to climb up onto the altar when a yell came from the tunnel.

"Charge!" Silmar yelled. "Stop their madness!"

With yells and war-cries, the companions rushed together into the cavern. They had the benefit of total surprise and the cultists were immediately thrown into a state of confusion, fuelled by whe frenzy brought about by their consumption of the concoction. Jiutarô tried to make his way directly to the High Priest but he lost his footing on a pool of the liquid from the chalice. Silmar also tried to get to the altar before the High Priest had a chance to slay his victim. The elf was too late; the naked priest plunged the stone dagger through her chest. She was most certainly dead.

Silmar became embroiled in a battle with the assistant priests and although he was far better armed, there were many of them. Jiutarô, having recovered his balance leapt around the altar and with a mighty two-handed swing of his katana, cut through the panic-stricken High Priest from right shoulder to left hip. The two parts of the body separated and fell to the floor. The Samurai's cry of pain, from his previous shoulder injury, was obscured in the melee and he almost dropped his katana; he recovered and leapt to Silmar's aid. The elf was bleeding from a slash to his right thigh as he was almost engulfed by the priests.

Meanwhile, the other members of the party were engaging the worshippers. Once again, these were poorly armed, having short blades and staves, mainly. With a short arcane word, Billit fired a flurry of magical fire-darts with great effect; these were bright points of flame that crackled as they left his hand. Falcon's war-hammer felled two with a single mighty stroke.

None of the cultists escaped. Billit blocked an exit from the cavern with a magical wall of energy but received a brutal blow from a priest's staff. This man's head was crushed with a blow from Jasper's battleaxe.

Eventually, every cultist was killed, not one escaped such was the fury of the companions' attack. The battle ended and silence fell. Taura rushed over to Billit but the gnome bade her see to Silmar first. The elf was now slumped onto the floor and there was quite a lot of his blood pooling beneath him. She immediately went to his aid. With Jiutarô pressing a wad of cloth from a cultist's cloak to the elf's wound, she began the sing-song chanting to enlist Neilea's divine aid in giving healing to the wound. It seemed to work because the bleeding slowed and then, after a while, stopped.

"How did that happen?" she asked Silmar.

"I kicked the man in his tender place and the bastard stabbed me with his dagger as he pitched forwards. You should have seen what I did to him!"

"Well, you are fortunate because your injury looks worse than it really is. You will be dancing with your young lady again in no time!"

"I hope so," the elf replied. His wound was still painful and Taura predicted he would probably have a limp for a few days.

Billit's injury was not serious and Taura liked to believe that another prayer to Neilea had helped with the gnome's healing. The injury was trivial enough for the little mage to not be too encumbered by it.

As the last cultist had died, Silmar had felt the nausea and head pain start to dissipate. It did not fade away altogether though. Taura explained that it was probably the residual evil of the temple itself. The bodies of the fallen cultists were everywhere. Jiutarô used the discarded robe of the high priest to cover up the body of the victim. He removed the filthy wad of cloth that was still stuffed in her mouth. She hadn't been very old; probably no more than about sixteen years of age.

"Break here; destroy here," called Jiutarô, still showing the anger he had felt at first seeing this scene. He now held a large chunk of rock in his hand.

Both Falcon and Billit leapt to their feet and started to smash the wooden benches that were arranged in rows in front of the altar. Jiutarô placed his chunk of rock on the altar, carefully lifted the body of the young girl from it and laid her down on the ground next to the passage opposite to the one by which they had entered. He then returned to the altar, picked up the rock and started to beat it down onto the surface. Falcon joined him and used his massive warhammer with more success. Within five minutes the altar slab was broken into pieces which were scattered about. Then they looked in wonder. The altar mount was hollow! Inside were ornate and plain weapons, gold and silver ornaments and candelabra, and a vast amount of coins.

"Look here," called Falcon. "Treasure!"

They were all on their feet now and came over to peer inside.

"A fortune!" gasped Jasper. "Some of these coins are old, look. These gold pieces haven't been in use for a century. These are from Cascant. There is a likeness of King Dar-Cascan the First."

Silmar was shocked. "Looks like these bastards were collecting and stashing away a fortune for years and years. Perhaps we can put much of this to some good. I'm going into that passage to see where it goes. Looks like some stairs there and, if I'm not mistaken, there is some mud and grass at the bottom. It may be a way back up and out of here!"

"We've still got a Darkling killer to find, don't forget," Taura reminded them.

"And finish off," added Billit. "We 'ad best form an orderly queue when we get to him! In the meantime, let's destroy that symbol on the wall there. Anyone recognise it?"

Nobody did. Taura considered it was just a symbol used as an excuse for a killing spree, raping and sacrificing some poor victims and amassing a fortune. Falcon made short work of smashing the engraved symbol.

Jiutarô stepped over and around the bodies to make his way over to the cage. By it were some large barrels of oil or pitch. These were used to dip the burning torches so they would stay lit for some time.

Help?

Jiutarô spun around and held his hands up to his temples. He faced the cage.

It was made of iron and was partly covered in a sheet of canvas but he could distinctly hear movement from within. It wasn't a spoken word; it was almost as if it had been implanted in his mind.

Free? There once again, an unspoken thought in his head. He lifted up the canvas and stood back.

Inside the cage was a beast that resembled a miniature dragon and it looked Jiutarô straight in the eye. The Samurai was so astounded that he staggered back a couple of paces, dropping the canvas over the cage. He shook his head as if to clear away the subliminal thoughts and cautiously moved back to the cage. He lifted the canvas once more.

A creature surely born of myth, known to him only in tales and theatrical performances in his own home country, his own world, had sprung into the reality of this new and strange land.

Free? Nuts? Drink?

Again, there were no audible words spoken but Jiutarô instinctively knew the beast had communicated with him. In fact, the messages seemed to be more like an idea or notion implanted into his consciousness rather than a word of any kind. Its light red-brown body was about the size of a medium-sized dog but it had bat-like wings and a very long tail that had a large curved barb on the tip.

Silmar stepped across. "What is this? A fire-drake? If so, beware!" He leaned forward to get a better look at the creature. "Oh no!" he exclaimed. "A *Cleret-wing dragon!* If one gets to like you, they can be a lot of trouble. Deadly in a fight though!"

"It attack?" the Samurai asked. "It talk here!" He indicated his head.

Friend! Free?

"It talks to you?" Silmar explained. "Then you are indeed privileged, friend Jiutarô! I have heard many tales that should one bond with an elf or a human then it will be a faithful companion and would be able to talk through the mind. You would see what it can see and it can see through your eyes. Should be fine! Let it out but it may just fly like mad for the passage up there."

"So it be free."

Jiutarô opened the cage door and the beast cautiously came out. It sniffed Jiutarô's outstretched hand and leapt up onto the top of the cage. It stretched its wings and arched its back.

Friend! Nuts?

"Friend!" answered Jiutarô. The cleret-wing dragon climbed off the cage and onto his shoulder. There was a strangled cry from Taura who was standing by the altar.

Kill! Immediately, the cleret-wing dragon leapt off and flew across towards her.

"No!" called Silmar. "It's going for Taura!"

But Taura was struggling against another attacker. One of the priests that they assumed had been killed had risen up behind her and was trying to strangle her with a cord. His face was covered in blood and he had a malicious expression of hatred and pain on his face.

The cleret-wing dragon flew round behind the priest and there was a cracking sound as it whipped its tail and caught the priest on the side of the neck. He was dying before he hit the ground, his hands clawing at his neck as poison coursed through his veins.

Taura slumped to the ground next to the dying priest who was choking and gasping for breath. Then he stopped and slumped against the remains of the altar. The cleret-wing dragon returned and lightly landed on Jiutarô's shoulder. Silmar went over to the body and inspected the neck-wound.

"Your little beast has poisoned him with its tail. By the gods, the poison worked fast! I didn't think they were able to kill a human that quickly."

Jasper looked at the dead priest. "The barb went straight through the priest's skin into his neck artery, pumping the venom into the brain! Ughh! Not a nice way to go. Tough shit on the bastard!"

"It's earned its keep already," said a smiling Billit.

Jiutarô reached for his pack and pulled out a canvas bag of nuts and dried fruit. He emptied a pile into his hand and offered it to the cleret-wing dragon. It was soon eaten, as were the next three handfuls. He took off his light helmet and poured some water from his water-skin into it. The cleret-wing dragon drank greedily until it was all gone.

"You have name?" asked the Samurai as he lifted his pack up onto his shoulders.

Name? echoed the cleret-wing dragon into Jiutarô's mind.

"Ah, you are Sushi! Friend!"

The little dragon-like creature responded to Jiutarô with subliminal word-like thoughts. *Sushi. Friend Sushi.* It glided to the floor, chattered and playfully skipped around his feet and then flew up and curled itself around his shoulders once again. The Samurai stroked its neck and Sushi purred like a cat. It was surprisingly light.

Jasper was deep in thought. "Lookit," he said. "We gotta get out o' here but we can't take all the gold an' stuff. We should bury it someplace safe. Just take what we can. An' we still gotta destroy this place so it can't be used again. An' we oughta get that dead girl back up to the surface. Mebbe she got family."

Together, they piled the wood from the broken benches by the altar.

With time and effort they piled the dead bodies on top. Using a couple of blood-stained robes from the priests, they loaded all of the treasure into them. The hundreds of precious and semi-precious stones and about two hundred gold pieces they divided between them. This was more treasure than any of them had ever imagined, let alone seen.

Falcon carried the dead body of the girl in his arms and Jasper emptied all of the barrels of oil over the pile of dead bodies. Silmar picked up one of the sacks of treasure and, with difficulty because of his new and recent injuries, started to climb the stairs. He counted more than sixty before he emerged exhausted into a cave. There was no door, just a pile of boulders to conceal the passage. He whistled and all of the others, except for Billit, came up to the top.

Jasper called down a signal to Billit and they all stepped back from the passage entrance. They heard the pattering feet of Billit running up the stairs and then there was a flash and a *whoomph* from down the stairway. They were all concerned for Billit and called down to the gnome.

A moment later, his smiling face emerged through the smoke at the entrance. His sparse hair was smouldering, he was covered from head to foot in ash and dust; otherwise he seemed unharmed.

"That was a bit bigger than I expected," he gasped. "Must've been the barrels of oil. It did go up well, didn't it? Can I have some water?"

The entrance to the stairway was many paces away from the entrance to the cave. They looked out but there was only the darkness of the night sky.

Falcon reverently placed the wrapped body of the girl on the ground. His left forearm continued to ache badly from his injury.

"I wonder where we are," said Taura.

"We been walking eastwards and a little south since we was in the mine tunnel," stated a confident Billit.

"More like due east," corrected Jasper, just as confident.

"About four days?" asked Taura.

"Five and a half," replied Jasper and Billit together.

"Oh, aye! That is about right!" Taura answered with an air of confidence. Nobody was convinced.

"I reckon that we are somewhere north-west of Gash then," suggested Silmar. "The foothills near the market town of Dalcutta Trading Post. A lawless place if there ever was one. Full of miners! And dwarves!"

Jasper was irritated by Silmar's barbed jibe. "Got a problem with that, have yer? Pointy-eared elves too high and mighty fer Dalcutta, are they?"

"Leave each other alone or I'll bang your heads together," growled Taura. The pair had been annoying and jibing each other on and off since they had first entered the Shadow World.

"You'll have to cut 'im off at the knees first," muttered the dwarf.

Silmar wisely ignored the barbed comment.

Now that their eyes were growing accustomed once again to the darkness, they could see some mountains and hills. To their right was a long valley which they could just discern when the clouds passed and the moon shone.

"Lights!" called Jiutarô. "Village? Far away." Sushi could sense the Samurai's anticipation of civilisation and stretched her head to improve her view.

Sure enough, they could see the tiny twinkling of lights in the distance and decided to make their way down at first light. They slept in the cave that night, some of them taking turns once again to guard their position.

The next morning they awoke to a brightening dawn. After days in the Shadow World they were cheered to hear birdsong and to see the oncoming daylight. Sushi had curled up next to Jiutarô and when she awoke she played around the Samurai's feet until he also awoke and petted her. She seemed to like a lot of that.

"What do with Sushi?" Jiutarô asked Silmar. He still struggled to find the right words; intensive coaching in the Universal tongue by Billit was paying off but the Samurai followed conversation between the companions with great effort.

"You have taken a lot of responsibility there," explained the elf slowly.

The Samurai frowned. "Not know talk," he replied.

"These are hard work to look after," Silmar explained slowly. "Let me tell you about them." He proceeded to tell the Samurai all he knew about cleret-wing-dragon. There was much to know.

These miniature reddish-brown dragons were playful and benign. They were said to have simple magical powers although this might be a myth. If it chose a humanoid companion, as was the case with *Sushi* and Jiutarô, the cleret-wing dragon could communicate thoughts by telepathy, transmitting an image of what it saw and heard over short distances. It could blend in with its surroundings by using a chameleon-like ability and had dark-sight which enabled it to see quite long distances.

The cleret-wing dragon liked to be perched on top of its human companion's head or curled around the shoulders and upper back. It liked to be well fed and would eat almost anything. It would love to be pampered and groomed and to receive lots of attention and, in this, it would be very demanding. If it was made to feel very important, then it would perform well for its companion. It would not tolerate mistreatment, neglect or cruelty by its companion nor would it tolerate a human who would rather be a master to it than a companion. In combat, it could deliver a vicious bite with its small dragon-like jaws and would rake its claws to tear the clothing or flesh of its adversary. But its main weapon was its barbed tail which carried a powerful poison. It could whip its tail with astonishing speed which could render the victim unconscious for many days. It could, if angry, inject sufficient poison to cause the victim to die slowly or even immediately, although it was not in the nature of claret-wing dragons to inflict this except in times of need. In addition to its telepathic communication, it could vocalise animal noises such as a rasping purr for pleasure, a feline hiss for an unpleasant surprise, a birdlike chirp for desire or a canine growl to show anger.

"So you will have a good friend but never an obedient pet. You must care for it and it will also care for you. It will be a friend to us all in time but your friend first."

Although he had some difficulty in understanding everything that Silmar told him, Jiutarô made sure that the elf repeated or rephrased anything he had trouble with. He felt content that he had found a creature such as this. In his home country, Nippon, there were myths and old stories regarding dragons of all sorts; some of them bad and troublesome and others that were wise and benevolent. Now one had adopted him as a friend; he felt a sense of honour in having been selected.

Jasper paced over to Billit and asked him why there had been such a huge explosion in the temple below.

"Ah, well, er. Aye, it's like this. There was oil everywhere and I thought it might not catch properly if I tossed a torch on it so I went up a few steps and blasted off a small *fire-blast* spell. Well, you see, it's only a small temple and even a fire-blast is quite big and it blasted me upwards about ten steps and burnt my backside. Have ya seen what it's done to me 'air? Look!" His curly red hair was noticeably singed shorter in some places but his skin did not appear damaged.

It took about ten minutes before the group could stop laughing! They were still chuckling as they started their march down towards the village. Even Sushi was chirruping with happiness; it was as if she understood. Alone, Falcon remained sombre. He carried the body of the young girl, struggling at times over the uneven ground. It took over two hours for them to reach the village and its gates were still closed when they got there. Taura used her staff to bang on the gates. Eventually one was opened by a worried-looking villager. He looked even more concerned when he saw the heavily armed strangers standing there.

"What's your business here this early in the morning?"

"I am named Lord Silmar the Golden, son of Faramar Galadhal, warband leader, troll-hunter, and Prince of the town and district of Refuge, on the edge of the Highforest by the eastern foothills of the Spine Wall Mountains in the Home Territories. I have come by perilous ways from the Landsdrop Coast with my companions to speak with a village leader here. It is a matter of immense importance. We are peaceful and bring with us no trouble, but we have left trouble behind us. Bring a village leader swiftly. We have much to speak of that is of urgency and our time presses upon us."

The companions looked open-mouthed at each other at the way by which the elf introduced himself. There would be much for them to speak of later.

A tall, middle-aged man with long, greying hair and an eye-patch on his right eye arrived at the gate and Silmar repeated his introduction. The man introduced himself as Finnucchi, the leader of the village.

"Finn?" cried Jasper from the back of the group. "Is that you, you old bushwhacker?"

"Jasper! It cannot be, after all these years. You old rascal! Come here so I can see you!"

They clasped wrists and it was clear they were old friends from long ago.

"We campaigned together fer many years, *Lord* Silmar," explained Jasper. "We was with yer dad in the Shadow World, were we not Finn?"

"Silmar, son of my old friend Faramar Galadhal, once of Faerhome?"

The man clasped the young elf's hand and cried "Well met. Welcome to Dalcutta. You have your father's features but your hair is darker!"

"That is because I had to colour it. We hunt a Døkkálfr, a Darkling, that is hunting us, or me really! I darkened my hair to change my features but it has not seemed to work. He knows we hunt him. He kills time and time again to lure me in."

"Now we hunt him in the Shadow World," continued Taura.

Finn shuddered. "Never again! That's where I lost my eye and it was the end of my campaigning. That's how I ended up here after Faramar and Jasper got me out of that place and left me here. I recovered and have a family and a small farm, and I am now the village leader. Come with me to the village meeting hall. So, Faramar's son, eh? Lord Silmar the Golden you are called? A grand soubriquet indeed. We shall prepare a meal and somewhere for you to sleep a proper night's rest. You all look like you need it. The village shall look after you tonight."

"I saw very little farm-land here," said Silmar. "What is it you do for trade in the village?"

Finn lifted the bottom of his eye patch and scratched beneath it. "Ah, we trade in lamp-oil and pitch. We have a well not far from here that was made for us by the Chthonic gnomes."

At this, Billit's head spun round and he gave his full attention to Finn's account.

"We pump the well and bring up oil. It is thick and black when it comes up but we have a process which allows us to filter and refine it and make a lamp oil that we sell to towns and villages in the Home Territories and Lopastor. We have stores within the walls but they are kept away from the houses in case of fire – these wouldn't just burn, they would explode in a huge ball of flame! We buy special flasks from Icedge and we fill these with the oil. Tell me, what is it your big friend carries?"

Jasper explained about the cultists and the death of a captive. He spoke of how the cultists were all destroyed along with their evil temple.

"The Kalanisha cult?" asked an astonished Finn. "You've killed them all? But we have wanted to do that for years. We have never found out where they hide to do their evil deeds. That is good! But let me see the body."

He stepped over to Falcon and lifted the robe to see the girl's face.

His face paled as he looked at the body. "Oh, no! By the gods!" he exclaimed. "It's Junkett's daughter. She didn't return home from the farm two nights past. We hoped she would be with friends but she must have been taken as she was on her way back. We started a search yesterday but found nothing. The village folk are out again shortly. I shall have to be off to inform her family. She was to be wed soon." He shook his head and strode off into the village.

The gateman led the group to the meeting hall and they sat around a large table. The body of the girl was reverently laid on one end of the table and Taura carefully adjusted the robe. A while later, Finn arrived closely followed by a tall, lean man and stout woman. The woman held a pinafore to her face and the man wrung his hands; the couple were in tears. They went to the body and the man tentatively lifted the end of the robe.

"It's her, our Kattia," the man whispered. Louder he demanded "Who did this?"

"The cultists," answered Finn.

"Kalanisha! Those blood-soaked, murdering bastards!"

"Goodman Junkett, they have all been destroyed by this group of adventurers," stated Finn as he placed a hand on the farmer's shoulder.

"Every one? Then may the gods bless you, visitors. Anything in my house is yours." He placed his arm around the shoulder of his sobbing wife. "We shall take our daughter and prepare her for her final journey. I would be grateful if your lady priestess would give my wife some words of comfort." He carefully picked up the body of their daughter and made his way out of the hall followed by his wailing wife.

The group sat quietly for a a few moments while Finn busied himself with a sheaf of parchments.

"Finn, what can you tell us about this cult?" Taura asked.

He sighed and shook his head. "There is little known of them but what we do know is of a brutal and violent gang of cutthroats. Many of the villages, farms and even towns in this area have lost men, women and children to this Kalanisha. Wagon trains have been raided in the night and many people slain. Survivors talk of a black-skinned giant who leads a group they call the *Blade Riders*. It is said that they are mainly deserters from the militia or escaped convicts. The giant is a cruel man to his victims and even cruel to his men. Y'see, there is no law in the region like you have on the Landsdrop Coast. We make our own laws here and generally there is peace in Shordrun, but not here in the west of the country. But perhaps now there will be, at last, and we have you to thank for it my friends. How many did you kill? Was one of them a huge man with black skin?"

"We slew 'bout fifteen or more priests and followers but not the man you describe," replied Jasper.

Finn smiled. "Well, perhaps this thing is ended. It is doubtful whether there actually is a deity by the name of Kalanisha. Just ask and anything will be yours."

"We need little," explained Silmar. "But there is a cave up in the hills up the valley. Outside it you will find two trees. In between them is buried a stash of treasure. Use it for this village to grow and expand. Strengthen your laws and defences. We have kept a little of it for ourselves but the vast majority of it is still there. The cave is an entrance to the Shadow World. We have to go back in there but after we do, it may be a good idea to seal up the passage and perhaps the cave too."

Finn agreed to do this. The group decided that they would have a day's rest and continue with their journey at first light next morning. Jiutarô's new companion encouraged much attention with the children of the village. Sushi rather enjoyed the petting and delighted them by flying over their heads and making noises. Some of the mothers were not quite so keen though. It did look ferocious with those rows of small sharp teeth and that tail looked positively dangerous.

Later that afternoon, while Jiutarô was standing by the village gates, Sushi took herself off for a flight. She came back after a few hours and, although exhausted from her flight, she chattered excitedly to Jiutarô. He fed her some strips of raw goat meat and she settled happily around his shoulders. Within two minutes she was fast asleep and purring gently. Jiutarô was now very concerned, but not for Sushi.

CHAPTER 20

"**W**ELL, SPEAK!" demanded the warrior curtly. "Where is he?" The man was black-skinned, very tall, heavily built and mounted on a great black stallion warhorse. He had a long, bushy, matted, black beard that hung down to the bottom of his chest. His black hair was also long and filthy. He was constantly scratching at his scalp and his grimy fingertips would occasionally come away with smears of blood on them. He was dressed in black furs and leather. He wore heavy riding boots that were much dilapidated. He carried only one weapon, a great pick. The handle of it was more than three feet in length and at one end was a large curved and pointed, black, steel horn sticking out at right angles and a full foot in length. Black feathers and strips of brown hide adorned the handle. It was said by the other warriors that the pieces of hide were taken off the bodies of those slain by the pick's owner.

"He issa dead anda de temple destroyed is, my Lord Saddiq. Alla his faithful issa destroyed him with." The mounted speaker was dressed in a dark red robe, similar to those worn by the clerics in the temple. He had a bald, tattooed head and was armed with a chipped and rusted shortsword.

The warrior dismounted and slapped his horse on the rump to encourage it to move aside. "The treasure?" he boomed. "Where is the fracking treasure?"

"Issa taken, my lord."

"TAKEN!" he roared. "I give your puny sect our protection! We even find you hostages to sacrifice, or eat, or whatever it is you do. I trust you with the care of my treasure. You live well from me!" The black horseman strode up and down, waving his arms in frustration. To his lieutenant at his side, he said, quietly "Kill him!"

The lieutenant signalled to a mounted archer and an arrow streaked into the cleric's chest, bursting his heart. The cleric fell from his horse onto the ground stone dead.

The other priests, all on foot, were now shuffling very nervously. The black leader pointed to one who began to quiver uncontrollably. "Who did this and where did they go?"

"My Lord! It-it is n-not known who did this b-b-but their tracks go to the vil – er – village of Dal – Dalcutta by the eastern end of the White Peaks."

"I know where Dalcutta is, idiot." He nodded to his lieutenant. Another arrow found its mark and another cleric lay dead.

He pointed to a third priest. A spreading wet stain showed on the front of this one's robe.

"How many were there?"

"Six, my lord."

"Six? Is that all? You live, for now! My Blade-Riders! Come! We ride to Dalcutta now! You so-called clerics shall ride with me and use your puny god to give me a victory this night! Death shall betide you all if your god or any one of you should fail me!"

The priest swayed and almost fainted.

The large band, forty riders at least, rode northwards, their huge leader to the forefront. They would get there just before dark. The spared priest recovered and wept with relief. His remaining companions kept their distance from him; he was a man marked for death. They rode after the band, struggling to breathe in the thick dust.

The robed men knew they had a problem; they were not priests. Well, some of them had been, once upon a time. But now they were followers of a cult that enjoyed the thrill of a sacrifice, the orgy that preceded it if there were women, or girls, or whatever took their fancy. They had no divine spells available to them. The few cult followers that were with them were ex-fighters of sorts who kept watch over the treasure. Many of them were once Saddiq's men but were now advanced in years or disabled through having taken part in one battle too many.

The band of fighters and priests did not know they were being watched.

Jiutarô rejoined his friends in the assembly hall. Most of them were dozing on straw mattresses. Billit was practising the phrases and nuances of spells from a small bound book he carried, wrapped in a silken cloth, in his pack. Taura was conversing quietly to her god; her hand tightly clutched one of her holy symbols, this being a polished wooden pendant with its design of a pair of spinning coins.

Silmar stirred and woke up as Jiutarô approached. He propped himself on one elbow and asked the Samurai if all was well. In halting words, the Samurai replied that he was worried because Sushi had flown back towards the cave and returned with important images.

"Red priests, horses go cave." Jiutarô still struggled to find the right words. "Sushi see. Many priests. Um –" He held up his hands with his fingers outstretched and then did it again. "Hey Silmar, that many, hai? How many?"

The elf smiled. "Hai, Jiutarô. That is twenty."

"Hai, twenty; I remember." Jiutarô smiled triumphantly while tapping the side of his head with his fingers. "Priests, aii, um, little swords; go big lake." He paused while searching for the words. "Big village, many man wait. Sushi make picture twenty, twenty, twenty. All come here. Leader black, ah, big black face-hair!" He used his hand to indicate a long beard.

"Ye gods! Døkkálfr? But with a beard? Nay, not a Døkkálfr. Not Darkling."

Jiutarô shook his head. "No Darkling; big black man, big black hair!" He indicated the head and beard again with exaggerated movements of his arms.

Silmar leapt from his blankets and reached for his weapons. "Tell Sushi, she is wonderful! Wake the others. We must alert the village. Sixty you say? Ye gods!" cried the elf.

The companions were all on their feet within heartbeats and Silmar rushed out of the door, closely followed by Jasper.

They discovered Finnucchi standing with a small group of men and women by a well in the village centre. The man saw their haste and walked over to meet them.

"You have need for speed?" the village leader asked. "There is concern in your eyes, Silmar! What is it?"

"Ho Finn, there ya are," called Jasper. "We may 'ave ended one problem but started another!" replied Jasper. "Tell, 'im, Silmar!"

"Jiutarô's cleret-wing dragon flew off towards the cave, saw a group of red-robed priests and followed them to a large river or lake at the foot of the mountains. There was a band of fighters not far from a large village. The gang was led by a huge black man. They are coming this way, about sixty of them!"

Finnucchi looked horrified. "Oh, my gods! The *Blade Riders*! We cannot manage this alone! What are we to do? It is too late to get help. Will you aid us? They will be here by dusk, before if they started a while ago."

Jasper took over. "Right! We 'ave two hours an' maybe, if they're riding 'ard, they'll be tired when they arrive so we must allow 'em no chance of rest. Get everyone 'ere who can fight, with all o' the weapons they own, but 'ide the women and children who cannot fight. You got just ten minutes. Go!"

The remainder of the companions waited in the village centre. They were fully armed and looked ready for battle. Between them they had carried all of Silmar's and Jiutarô's weapons while the pair had sped out to locate Finnucchi. They looked around the village perimeter.

"This wall is too weak," observed Falcon. "And the gates are thin. Difficult to defend against a small army." The huge barbarian shook his head in despair.

"But this is just a village," countered Taura. "They don't usually have to defend themselves against anything more than raiding goblins or kobolts."

The wall completely encircled the village, fortunately, and was constructed from thick wooden planks that were arranged upright on a sturdy framework. It was probably fifteen feet high with a rampart all the way round along which a guard, or number of guards, could walk. Although quite strong, a few good kicks from a warhorse might dislodge some of the planks. The gates, when opened, gave access just wide enough for a large wagon. They were very strong and were barred on the inside with two stout planks.

Villagers started to arrive in ones and twos at first but then in groups. Most of them were men, of all ages from fourteen to sixty. Remarkably, there were also a number of women including two tall, quite young ladies who carried bows and sheafs of arrows. They looked identical. Finn saw the quizzical expression on Silmar's face.

"These are the two Caspan sisters," Finnucchi explaines. "They are twins and the best archers in the Dalcutta region. No-one has bested them with a bow for five years. They practice every day! Just look at their broad shoulders! We have four other archers in the village too; they are arriving now."

"We shall have need of all of them this evening, Finn," said Silmar with a broad grin. "With me and Jiutarô, and the twins, perhaps we shall be able pick a few of the raiders off at the start."

Jasper took Finn's arm and quietly led him aside. They spoke together for a few minutes and then Jasper returned to the others while Finn, in turn, spoke to a handful of villagers.

Taura stood with her hands on her hips. "What was all that about," she asked. "Secrets, Jasper?"

"Nah, not secrets, just a little plan I've thought up. I'll tell you all 'bout it soon!"

Jasper and Silmar spoke with the villagers of their plans for the defences of the village. Very few villagers had been in the militia or had used weapons in anger. Apart from Finnucchi, only one other man had been an adventurer. He was a middle-aged muscular man who carried a broadsword and a heavy round shield. He was taking a few practice swings with his sword and seemed quite competent and confident.

It was agreed that the archers would be arranged with three on each side of the gates but were to keep their heads below the top of the rampart when the Blade Riders arrived. If the village was to show that it had archers, the enemy may decide to stay out of range. Billit and Taura would also join the archers. The villagers armed with swords, axes and other cutting or crushing weapons, would wait in two or three groups in the village. Altogether, there were armed fifty villagers, almost all of them menfolk, who were ready to fight. Finnucchi spoke to them all and encouraged them to fight to defend their families, their homes, their livelihoods and the village. The villagers responded with a rousing cheer.

Meanwhile, Taura arrived with about thirty women, the majority of whom were as determined as their men-folk to defend the village with their lives. Each of them carried a large wooden box and a cooking pot of burning coals taken from their own homes. These women were stationed around the village walls.

"What's all that about then?" asked Billit.

Jasper chuckled. "They got oil grenades! Yer gonna get a, er, demon-stray-shun in a little while. Wait and see!" He was very pleased with himself that he had been able to use a big word like that! Well, he would have admitted Finn had helped with it if anyone would have asked!

Finn introduced his wife Linette to the companions. She was a large, busty, pleasant lady with a permanent smile. "Show them, my sweet!" he stated, "the grenades that is, not your charms!"

A call went out to the villagers and they gathered to watch. From her box she took a bottle of liquid. Around the neck was tied a piece of cloth. She removed the cork and sloshed some of the liquid out of the bottle. Dipping the cloth into her pot of coals, she lit it then launched the bottle hard towards a rock. The bottle smashed and with a *whoomph!* there was an eruption of fire which totally engulfed the rock. The blast of heat was felt by almost everyone in the village. Any person caught in it would be incinerated. A loud cheer went up.

The sun was now starting to dip behind the hills to the west and Finn told the villagers to make ready. Within a few minutes the village was quiet. Just the barking of a couple of dogs and the calling of crows broke the silence.

Finn ordered the gates to be closed and barred.

The village waited.

"Who are you and what is your business?" Finnucchi used the officious tone that the gateman had used when the companions had first arrived at the village early that morning.

"You don't know who I am?" came the reply in a deep, booming tone. Coarse laughter came from his riders. "I am severely disappointed. You soon will. I am the Lord Saddiq." The speaker indicated himself with a grand flourish. He then indicated behind him. "These are my Blade Riders. We are hungry and thirsty. You will open the gates and let me and my men in so we can feast, rest and, ah, enjoy ourselves."

"I cannot do that. It is late. We do not have enough food, ale or room for you all in my village."

"I know for a fact that you are a wealthy village; my men have told me this. Your Cleric of Diette, one Orban Hilger, came to me and was one of my own trusted priests, that is until he fell off his horse today." There were guffaws of laughter from his men. "He said how your villagers wanted for nothing."

"We had a hard winter," responded Finn. "Now we live frugally."

"I tire of these games. I wish to speak with your leader." The voice was uncouth and adamant.

"I represent the leader," Finnucchi replied. "You may converse with me."

"Very well then, I shall get to the point. You have something of mine." Finnucchi laughed. "And what is that? Have you lost something?"

"Don't play games with me! I already told you that. You know what I seek." Finnucchi grinned and pointed to Silmar who was standing beside Finn.

"Trinkets? Copper coins?" Silmar called. "I have seen them but they are not here, they were not worth taking so we left them underneath the bodies to burn."

"Ah! So, it was you and your villagers who destroyed that temple," roared Saddiq. "I care not a whit for those that died in it. But you lie, there was a treasure. I left it there for safekeeping. So, it is mine by right, you see? You have it. Let me in right now or I shall shatter the gates, burn your homes, take your women and girls for my own amusement and later for the amusement of my men, and slaughter everyone else here."

A small cheer came from his riders but a glare from Saddiq silenced them.

This time Jasper responded. "There was no treasure in that tunnel, just trinkets an' copper, an' very fat priests with expensive gowns, perfumes and silk clothes. Speak to those who kept it for you."

Saddiq considered those words for a moment, then spun his horse away and, with his lieutenants, rode over to the priests.

Silmar was impressed. "Good words, Jasper. He will be furious! I think some heads will hit the ground. That was a neat little line!"

The exchange between Saddiq and the priests couldn't be heard at the village walls but soon, they heard some shouting and screaming and those on the ramparts reported a commotion and a flurry of whirling swords.

Saddiq returned with three lieutenants each bearing two blood-soaked shaven heads. Six more priests had lost their lives.

"Now I *know* you lie; the priests would have confessed to me in their terror and fear of me. You *do* have my treasure and I have come to get it back. You have to the count of fifty to open the gates and let me in."

His men were milling around on their horses, taunting and shouting obscenities at Finnucchi, and they were very close to the village gates.

Finnucchi turned slightly and called "Now!"

The eight archers simultaneously leapt to their feet from behind the ramparts and began pouring arrows into the throng of warriors below. The blade riders were caught by surprise in the trap. Not one arrow hit Saddiq but twelve of his men went down in the first few seconds. Only two of them were still moving, one of them screaming. A few crossbow bolts were returned but only one came close to finding its target; it glanced off Finnucchi's helmet and into a thatched roof beyond. By the time the horsemen had ridden out of range, they had lost another eight, two of whom limped away with arrow wounds while two more screamed in agony in addition to the first two on the ground. A loud cheer erupted from the village at the sight of Saddiq having lost a quarter of his men. Of the remaining red-robed priests, there was no sign. They were either hiding or had made good their escape from the tyrant while he was under attack from the archers.

Saddiq threw his head back, roared in anger and strode towards the village followed a few paces behind, by his remaining forty men. They were all on foot now and held their shields in front of them. At his command, they rushed towards the gate.

Finn gave another command. "Now!"

At once, twenty women, stooping low on the ramparts, simultaneously rose to their feet and hurled their bottles of oil towards the fighters below. Every bottle had a burning rag tied to it and all were uncorked to enable them to smash. Most of the bottles shattered on the road below and flames engulfed many of the men. Even those that did not smash had the oil pouring from them so they soon burst into flame anyway and could not be thrown back. Screams of anguish sounded and a few burning bodies staggered about soon to collapse on the ground. The archers found a few easy targets and after a couple of minutes only Saddiq and about twenty of his men were left to fight. His clothing was smouldering, smoke streaming from his mass of hair and his beard. He frantically brushed at his smoking hair and roared with anger once again.

He knew he had allowed himself to become complacent with the result that the attack on the village had gone disastrously badly for him. He now did not have the strength of force he considered necessary to retrieve his treasure. At a word from him, they backed off again out of range using whatever cover they could, even each other, and didn't stop until they were almost two hundred yards away. Meanwhile, at least eight wounded men were scattered in front of the village walls screaming in agony.

He hadn't moved as his men backed away. "I shall return for my treasure!" he roared. "Send me your best fighter for a duel. I shall show you what a real warrior can do. If he bests me, my Blade Riders will leave, for now! If I win, I take your women and girls for my pleasure and the village is mine. You see, I am a fair man." He stood there with his hands on his hips with an expression of arrogance and confidence and then casually strode out of bowshot.

Silmar called Jiutarô and asked him, "Can you get him with an arrow from here? It is a long way, probably three hundred paces, and it is getting dark."

Jiutarô nodded slowly. "Hai! I try. I go down fight him! He slow; see eyes, show moves early."

Silmar shook his head slowly. "Nay, I think not, Jiutarô. Now is not the time for his games. You cannot trust him, he may hold you hostage to exchange you for the treasure. He's not so stupid really. He knows he can't now beat us by force. It is time to finish this."

Jiutarô shrugged and studied each arrow in turn before selecting the one most suitable; he looked along the shaft, at the arrow-head and at its fletchings. He then fitted it to his bowstring. Both of the female twin archers argued as to whether or not the shot could possibly hit the target at this distance, especially with the failing light.

The Samurai smiled at them, dropped a little dust from his fingers to measure the breeze and lifted his bow. "From here? Pah! Easy! Watch!"

He used the traditional Samurai method of bringing the arrow back past his right ear and sighting along it. Adjusting for the distance, air movement and the difference in height between himself on the ramparts and his target, he loosed the arrow. It flew too fast for it to be seen in the evening gloom. He immediately nocked another arrow.

Nothing happened for about five heartbeats. The remaining light was just sufficient for the defenders on the ramparts to see Saddiq fall backwards. The gates of the village were flung open and the armed defenders yelled and shrieked as they charged towards the few remaining *Blade Riders*. It was a long way and by the time the villagers reached the point at which they hoped to do battle, the riders had mounted their horses and ridden off hard.

Saddiq lay dead with an arrow through his left eye. Jiutarô later insisted he had been aiming at his right eye! The Samurai was hailed a hero! The two young lady archers certainly thought so; they showed their appreciation for some hours that evening. Sushi enjoyed the affection of all three of them but later, she flew off and didn't return until soon after dawn. Jiutarô had been awake for a couple of hours fretting for the claret-wing dragon.

The news from Sushi was that the remaining riders had ridden eastwards. They wouldn't be coming back, that was certain. Sushi spent the day playing with the children of the village. She learned to use her tail to hit a ball to the children. It was just as well she was occupied because Jiutarô was very busy with his two new friends. All day! He did check on her from time to time though – she *was* very important to him!

The companions decided to spend the rest of the day in the village resting. They would return to the entrance to the Shadow World, with some of the villagers, that evening.

CHAPTER 21

T HEY RE-ENTERED the mines through the destroyed Temple of
Kalanisha. Billit's *fire-blast* had virtually rendered the bodies of the
so-called priests and their followers to ashes. The walls were blackened
and all signs of what the chamber had once been were obliterated. Even
Billit was surprised at the way in which the destruction had been so total.
Silmar looked over at Taura but, apart from a small smile, her face was
expressionless. The elf shook his head and decided to say nothing.

The villagers had assured them that would do as much as they could
to destroy the entrance to the cavern and, if they could, would attempt to
seal the cave as well. Many of the villagers had escorted the companions and
Sushi had flown over to ensure that the area and the cave were deserted.
A wagon and horses had been brought along to take the treasure back to
the village and two men set about digging it up while others looked on.
The shock on their faces and the stunned silence that came with it as they
removed the bloodstained robes from the precious items was a sight that
the companions would remember and talk about for years after. There were
no long goodbyes, except for Jiutarô and his two young ladies. The village
would prosper and grow; that was a certainty.

The companions were back in the dreaded tunnels, well rested and fed
but still not feeling as if they were sufficiently prepared for what terrors
might come. The sound of rocks and boulders being pushed into the stairway
from above was very loud in the tunnels. Now there was no going back.

"That's the way of it down 'ere," said Jasper. "You'll never feel that yer
ready fer this shit-'ole!"

There was no natural glow from fungus down here at this time. They
used their light-tubes to show them the way now. Sushi was not settled in
the Shadow World and she gripped Jiutarô's shoulder with her talons until

he was sore. After a couple of hours, she did relax a little, her little body and tail were tightly wrapped around his neck and shoulders. The floor was now flat but quite dusty and some tracks were visible in the beams from the light tubes. Many of them seemed to be of small rodents but from time to time, Falcon, who walked in the lead, noticed larger footprints.

"Stop!" the barbarian whispered. He went down onto his haunches and studied the ground in front of him. "Look at this," he murmured. His fingers pointed to a footprint, or rather a boot-print.

The others craned their necks to look. "This looks fresh, the edges are sharp an' it's smaller than human," responded Jasper. "It's that choddin' Darkling, bet yer life on that!"

"That is why we here," growled Falcon. Although he rarely spoke, his fear and loathing of the Døkkálfr gave him a reason to speak out. "We here to kill the bastard Darkling!"

"Kill him? You take 'is head off and I'll shit down his neck!" grunted Billit.

Taura gave a mock expression of horror. The depth of loathing by the group had not receded even though they had had no contact with the Darkling for a couple of days or more. None of them had forgotten the victims that they had encountered on their way from Westron Seaport to Northwald City and beyond, and then on to the entrance to the Shadow World.

"We make careful," said Jiutarô. "He, ah, waiting. Sushi say to me if smell. Aii, she good ears, hear, um, mouse piss fifty steps!"

They all laughed so much that Jasper had to get them to quieten down.

"Yer still all a bunch o' childish fools," he mumbled. "Prob'ly a good thing Sushi's with us though! Let's be off again. I'll lead for a bit."

Taura remained very close to Falcon while in the Shadow World even though their own fear of being down in the mines was not as great as it had been. They stopped to rest, eat and drink after some hours. Once again, they decided to try and move in the dark so that their skills at doing this wouldn't be lost. Billit's silken cord, as before, was loosely tied between Jiutarô, Taura and Falcon. They came upon small areas of a dull glow from the fungus, but only occasionally. They set off once again and, although the pace was slower, they felt a little safer.

At one point, Sushi gave a hiss and the group stopped and crouched down. Her claws dug into Jiutarô's shoulder and he imagined the word *beast* in his mind. He whispered this to his companions. In the darkness, their other senses sharpened, particularly their hearing. Only Billit could hear a faint and fast snuffling sound. Soon, it was accompanied by a skittering sound of little footsteps.

Lightson!" said Silmar. "Three; two; one; on!" The beams were uncovered, their brightness momentarily blinded them all. There was a squeak and a creature resembling a large rat bounded off into the darkness.

"What was that?" asked Taura, a hint of panic in her voice.

"Dunno! A sort o' rodent I think," replied Jasper. "I only seen it as it buggered off down the tunnel! Keep going, it won't get ya! If it does, it won't eat much of ya! Heeheehee!"

He continued to snigger as his own joke for the next few minutes. The light-tubes were covered up and, after a short while they were on their way again. They would hear the sounds of snuffling and skittering many times during their walk along the tunnel. After a while they began to ignore them. They walked mostly without using their light-tubes, unless the tunnels narrowed, twisted and turned or there were obstacles. They put all their trust in Billit and Jasper even though their dark-vision was limited. Silmar could see virtually nothing when he strained with his dark-vision.

The Shadow World did not seem to vary much in width and height along this section. It was ten to twelve feet in width and six to ten feet in height and quite straight, as far as they could tell. It caused more of a problem for Falcon who, without the use of their light-tubes, had to march with his hand in front of his head. There were few obstacles and no crevasses across the path but the marks of picks and other tooling was evident along its entire length. It was as if the way had been kept clear through regular use. Every time they uncovered the light-tubes they could clearly see the tracks of a pair of boots, small in size, in the dust and fine rubble.

Occasional caverns were evident on each side of the tunnel and they investigated a few of these. Only rarely were there signs of them having been mined but that would have happened long ago. They saw rusted mining tools, wheeled trolleys, tatters of clothing and perished leather belts and pouches. No weapons of any sort were apparent and no coins or items of value. Jasper recommended that they should rest, eat and sleep in one of the caverns. They set up a sentry roster.

Fortunately, there was no disturbance of any sort during their rest period. The following 'day' they continued along the tunnel, in total darkness mostly. The mine was getting wider now; about twenty feet across in some places with concave pillars supporting the roof and the disturbing knowledge that there was a massive amount of rock above them.

At one stop, Sushi gave a loud hiss which made them all stop instantly. By now, they trusted her instincts completely. Jiutarô once again felt a word in his mind; this time it was *people*! He whispered this to his friends.

They all moved across to either side of the tunnel and crouched down. They could hear voices coming towards them – they were the voices of dwarves! They could hear their own heartbeats thudding inside their chests. Nerves were jangling in each of them.

Jasper whispered, "Grey Dwarves! Foul. Lots! Be silent! Get lights ready!"

Probably only Silmar, Jasper and Billit had any idea of what, or who, the Grey Dwarves were. They were known to inhabit the deep tunnels and mines of the lands but not necessarily just the Shadow World itself. They did, however, send the occasional hunting or reconnaissance party along the tunnels of the Shadow World and were known to be ferocious killers who would slaughter the unwary traveller in the subterranean tunnels without mercy.

Jasper, Silmar and Billit were understandably nervous; they knew that if it came to a fight, it would be hard and bitter, and they would very likely sustain casualties. It would all depend on just how many Grey Dwarves there were. At this time, none of them could tell.

The voices were getting closer and the sound of their heavy boots was now much louder on the dusty, rocky floor.

Fifteen? thought Jasper. *Twenty? About that.*

The tunnel just ahead of them had a slight bend which would be of an advantage to the waiting companions. They were barely breathing now. Jiutarô could feel Sushi's claws digging into his shoulder and the pain made him wince; he did not cry out though.

Taura felt a dusty irritation well up in her throat. It was all she could do to resist the need to cough.

The footsteps and voices were now coming around the curve and would soon be only paces from them.

"*Lightson!*" gasped Jasper. The companions immediately closed their eyes, shielding them as the lights erupted from the leather torches as the covers were removed.

All the hells of the Void broke loose. The Grey Dwarves, who had all been using their dark-vision, were caught in the startling glare of the light tubes. All were blinded and were grasping and fumbling for their weapons amid oaths and gasps. The companions, however, were already armed, prepared and, apart from a momentary blindness, could see everything clearly. The dwarves had two prisoners; Chthonic gnomes. Each was securely and painstakingly tied, hand and foot, to a pole that was being carried by a pair of Grey Dwarves, one at each end. The blinded dwarves dropped the poles and the gasping grunts that followed indicated that the gnomes were still alive.

Jiutarô, without Sushi on his shoulder, charged forward with his sword held high. With him were Jasper, Falcon and Silmar. They all waded into the group of Grey Dwarves with blades and weapons whirling.

The Samurai caught two Grey Dwarves with one sweep of his katana and both fell heavily to the floor. The mighty barbarian crushed the head, complete with its helmet, of another which also crashed to the ground. Silmar kicked one in the stomach, thrust his shortsword through the throat of a second and then returned to the first to finish off the first. He was too late, this Grey Dwarf, although slightly blinded, swung a hand-axe and tried to embed it in Silmar's left thigh; fortunately for the elf it was the back of the blade that caught him. Even so, Silmar grunted, lurched against the tunnel wall, pushed himself off it and swung his weapon to open up the dwarf's chest. Falcon was roaring and swinging his massive warhammer catching many a Grey Dwarf. With Jiutarô swinging his katana with practised and efficient moves, blood sprayed about the tunnel as more fell and would not rise again.

Taura brought her staff down heavily onto the helmet of one and judging by the deep dent the damage to its wearer was fatal. Jiutarô leapt over three bodies and swung his sword in a horizontal sweep that passed straight through the midriff of a Grey Dwarf. The two separated sections splattered to the floor spraying more blood, this time over the supine figures of the two captive gnomes.

The surviving Grey Dwarves were starting to recover their sight and now were fighting back. Two of them, seeing that the elf appeared wounded, came at him from two sides. The hair of one of them though, burst into flames as fiery magical darts hammered into him. Within seconds, his head was a mass of fire and he screamed and reeled along the passage.

He fell shrieking to the ground as the flames overwhelmed his head and upper body.

One Grey Dwarf was fighting off an attack from Sushi. She was far too quick for him and her tail whipped with a *snap* as the barb embedded itself in the side of his neck. Screaming, he went down immediately and shuddered in his painful death throes. With flapping wings and a blur of movement, she spun away to find another prey.

Billit had three Grey Dwarves circling about him and for a time seemed vulnerable. Taura, however, waded in with her staff, swinging it with all her weight behind it. Its iron-shod tip caught one Grey Dwarf on the side of his iron helmet, denting it so badly that its wearer spun sideways and crashed onto the tunnel floor, probably unconscious. She moved her hands to the centre of the staff and made it whirl faster than the eye could follow. One tip of it crashed down onto the Grey Dwarf's helm just as Sushi's razor-sharp claws raked the face and eyes.

Silmar risked a quick glance about him, in the dim light he could see Jasper laying unmoving on the tunnel floor. He pushed through the swirling melee.

Billit however, was still under attack from the third dwarf and had blood streaming into his eyes from an injury to his forehead. Just as Taura turned her staff towards this dwarf he began to chant a magical spell. Suddenly, a long, dark dagger buried itself in the Dark Dwarf's back and he fell stiffly, face down to the ground.

Silmar meanwhile, was down on one knee with blood pouring from his nose. He persistently jabbed with his sword to keep an attacker at bay but it would only be a matter of time before his attempts would fail. Another Grey Dwarf, seeing the elf in difficulty, yelled in triumph and joined in the melee.

Jiutarô was besieged on all sides by three Grey Dwarves and his katana was scoring hits with each swing, but they were now keeping out of range of his blade. As he swung one way, so a dwarf would charge in from the other side with axe and shortsword. He had been hit two or three times. He was getting wise to this tactic, nonetheless. He feinted to the left and as he turned his body to the right an attacker came in. The Samurai continued his circular swing and brought his blade back around to take the head from its shoulders. With the same swing, this time powerfully executing the fearsome *butterfly* stroke, he took one, then another attacker, obliquely across both of their chests and stomachs.

Two Grey Dwarves remained to threaten Silmar and they were not about to give up the fight; it was not in their nature to do so. They knew they would be given no quarter; no mercy.

"Someone help Silmar!" cried a voice. It was Taura.

She commenced battle with one of the dwarves and stunned him with a swing from her staff as he was about to launch a frenzied attack on Silmar. The elf had backed against the tunnel wall and was kneeling on the ground with his lower face covered in blood. Jiutarô leapt into action and, his katana dripping blood from his previous encounters, swung it two-handed vertically upwards and removed an arm from one of the two dwarves. The Samurai reversed his swing and cleaved the stricken dwarf's head in two. Silmar's remaining adversary made the mistake of glancing over at his collaborator. This was just the opportunity that the elf needed to thrust his sword under the dwarf's left armpit and into his heart.

The fight was over. There were body parts, dead Grey Dwarves and blood everywhere. The walls and floor were running with it and most of the group had been injured.

Billit sat on the floor cursing. "I couldn't do no magic," he moaned. "Face bloody 'urts! I couldn't concentrate on me spells. Sorry."

Silmar was half sitting against the tunnel wall with his leg stretched out in front of him and wiping blood from his chin with his sleeve. Jiutarô had a bloody wound to his right hip and right arm and blood oozing from a deep scratch on his chest; he was also sitting on the floor. Falcon seemed unharmed apart from a graze to his left cheek; he apparently received this when he collided with the tunnel wall during the battle.

Jasper stirred and tried to rise from the floor. He fell again. He had a small dent in his helmet and was looking very dazed. He sat down on the ground and took his helmet off, rubbed his head and swooned. Sushi had received a stab wound on her back leg causing her to lick at the dark blood that welled from it. Whining, she dragged herself over to Jiutarô who held his hand to the injury to try to stop the bleeding.

Taura was the only one who was completely unharmed, she was desperately exhausted. "So many injuries!" she wailed. "Oh, Neilea give me strength! They are all injured!" She knew she wouldn't be able to treat them all.

Falcon advised that she treat Silmar first. "He will quickly die if you do not and then see to Nib—"

"Drop your weapons!" a thin, high-pitched voice commanded. "If you want to live, do as we tell you."

In the glow of the light tubes, a line of gnomes stretched across the width of the tunnel. They were garbed and heavily armed as if for war.

"Wait!" the, voice commanded again. "We shall help you! Do not fear us! We shall help!"

After a pause in which the companions looked at each other, Taura gestured and called out to them in a despondent wail. "Come, help! Please!"

The gnome leader barked a command. A handful of gnomes rushed over and started attending to the injured, rummaging in their packs for materials, potions and salves. Two cloaked figures pushed through the throng of gnomes and arcane glows lit up the tunnel. Unlike Billit, who had wispy red hair, all of these gnomes were completely bald apart from short, sparse, white beards. With a cry, four of them rushed over to where the two captive gnomes were still trussed up on the poles and started cutting them free. They seemed unharmed apart from bruises and small cuts. Once they had wrapped the worst of the injuries to the companions, the leader came across and stated that they would escort the party to a place of refuge close by.

Billit was by now unconscious and had to be carried; Jasper was concussed and was barely aware of what was going on; he mumbled incoherently. Jiutarô was able to walk and he carried the whining Sushi in his arms. Falcon helped Silmar to walk because of his loss of blood. This battle had left most of them severely battered and with numerous combat wounds.

The gnomes gathered up the various weapons and equipment that the party had dropped and took them a few hundred yards back along the tunnel in the direction that the group had come from and then stopped in front of the tunnel wall.

"Behold, the haven of the Chthonic peoples," stated the leader.

"What?" exclaimed Taura. "I see nothing here!"

"Of course, a good camouflage will hide a city, will it not?"

With the Chthonic Gnomes posted ensuring they were not being overlooked, the leader uttered a series of gnomish words and waved his hand in an arc across the wall. A section of rock the size of a small, narrow doorway seemed to dissolve and an entrance to a tunnel appeared before them. The gnomes silently filed in through the entrance and Falcon squeezed in behind them while supporting Silmar; the Barbarian was almost bent double as he went in through the opening but was able to stand almost upright once inside.

The entry was closed behind them and they were led, or taken, along a lengthy, straight passage. Silmar was starting to regain consciousness and was groaning with the pain of his injuries, old and new. Billit was also coming to and tried to sit up on the makeshift stretcher made from two staffs and a cape. His face was still covered in drying blood and he wasn't able to see through it.

"I'm blind, ohhh, I cannot see!" be moaned, more in dread. He was told assertively to keep still.

The march continued for what seemed like an hour, but which was probably considerably less, when the passage opened up into a dimly lit hallway. The leader called out *"Teaccasia"* and a number of Chthonic gnomes appeared through one of the many arches cut into the walls of the hall.

"Take them to the healing caverns!" called the leader.

The companions were led and taken away and the gnomes disappeared through other arches. Once more, the hall was silent.

"We are the Chthonic gnomes. I see you travel with one of our kinsmen from a surface realm. Although he is distantly related to our tribe, he is not known to us. We see he is a mage! Interesting! Is he useful to your party? Gnomish mages rarely aspire to much more than simple conjurers in our domain!"

Taura and Falcon were resting on straw palliasses laid out on the floor in a rocky chamber separated from the others. They had been left there when their comrades were taken elsewhere for treatment. A single candle guttered in a dish. Taura had slept, she did not know for how long. Falcon, because of his size, was on two beds. He had dozed fitfully. They were both awakened by the gnome leader coming into their chamber. He carried an oil lamp that gave a little extra light.

Without preamble, he continued "Tell me of your mage."

Taura swung off the bed and struggled to her feet. Although not particularly tall, she stood a foot and a half over the gnome. "He is a bold, courageous and valuable member of the party and is a powerful wizard," She spoke with a firm voice. "Well, he will be one day; of that I have little doubt. He studies constantly when we have a peaceful rest."

Although of small stature, the Chthonic gnome leader had a presence that indicated a position of influence in his tribe. He nodded and moved over to a wooden bench and sat down.

"The elf carries an item of power," he continued. "One of us has felt its influence and believes it to be evil. I do not believe you or your mage are evil, nor perhaps, are those others with whom you travel. I wish to know what this item is that you have with you and whether it poses any danger to us in our haven." His statement was neither a question nor a command. But Taura felt that she was being given no option but to speak of it.

She took a deep breath and exhaled slowly. "You are right," she replied nodding her head. "It is a holy artefact that has been made wholly evil. But we are not. We are taking it somewhere to destroy its evil. We have been given a task by a Priest of Haeman, one Halorun Tann, and must see it through."

The gnome snapped his head up sharply. "Halorun Tann! Hmm, that name is well known to me. I shall consult my Assembly and discuss this. Very well, for now I shall ask no further questions of this and we shall continue to provide your group with aid and succour where we can."

Taura persisted. "But the task itself is beset by evil. We are hunting a foul creature that desires the artefact. At the same time, he hunts us, or rather he hunts Silmar, the elf, seeking revenge as well as the artefact."

"You speak of the Døkkálfr." It was a statement, not a question.

"You know of him?"

"We have been tracking him for a couple surface-days. He is two days ahead of you although he waits and listens from time to time. I expect therefore, he indeed waits for you. We have disabled many traps that he has left."

"But but we have seen nothing!" gasped Taura.

The gnome chuckled. "Nay, we do things properly down here! We have been tracking you since Kalanisha. You destroyed an evil which has endured there for thirty years! That is impressive! We left it for it posed us no threat. You have much power and inner strength. Halorun Tann was right to entrust this quest to you."

"So why did you not destroye the Darkling?" asked Falcon.

"Because we do not know whether he is the herald of a greater force that is to follow. Or there may be those who await his coming. Either way, we may create a difficulty for ourselves if we intercede now. We are content to watch and wait and avoid the risk."

"He has no following army and travels alone," stated Taura. "He killed many innocent victims to force us into following him. He may well be meeting others down here. But I think that is pure conjecture."

"It certainly won't be the Grey Dwarves, although there will be a fearful anger when they come searching for whomsoever carried out the destruction of their patrol. Another worthy battle your group has fought! The Grey Dwarves will think nothing of killing the Døkkálfr. Perhaps we shall leave sign that their deaths were caused by the Døkkálfr. The Grey Dwarves have no regard for one of his kin. No, I believe the Døkkálfr most likely intends to meet up with the Grullien, the Shade Gnomes, our bitterest enemy, rather than the Grey Dwarves! He will give them promises of treasures and slaves to work their silver mines. If I do point the finger of suspicion at the Døkkálfr, this stretch of the tunnel will be far too dangerous for you to travel. We shall guide you by a parallel path."

"Where are the Grullien?" asked the barbarian.

"They are at the extreme end of this mine."

Taura continued. "The Shadow World mines are huge, far bigger than I ever imagined they could be!"

"Do you really believe that this is all of the Shadow World? If so, you are mistaken. There are many tunnels linking mines, chasms, underground rivers and even cities to the Shadow World, and they spread like a spider's web throughout the lands of Amæus. Far, far away is the mighty Døkkálfar city of Myrkheim. But even that can be reached from the mine tunnel you have travelled without ever having to go back up to the surface. You have met and destroyed those so-called priests in a temple; you have destroyed a small Grey Dwarf hunting party. Døkkálfar are rare in this area and the one you seek is the first I have known during my lifetime."

Taura looked across at Falcon but his eyes were looking down at his feet. "When we have adequately recovered, we shall have an urgency to continue our task," she explained. "I would assume that our quarry is far ahead of us by now. Can you warn us of what we can expect on the way ahead?"

"There is far more than just a Døkkálfr down here," the Gnome continued. "*He* will be in as much danger from threats as you are, probably more so because he is alone. I warn you however, to beware! Think about this carefully. I shall leave you to rest once again. Food and drink will be brought to you soon and I shall have news of your friends, oh, and of the captives you freed! You have done extraordinarily well and have our immense gratitude."

Taura watched as the gnome leader, she still did not know his name, left the chamber and she settled down to sleep. Falcon had already descended into a deep slumber. Food and drink arrived some time later. She was surprised to see that there were nuts, berries and meat on the tray as well as hunks of bread and warmed honey. She woke the barbarian and together they ate the meal. She then spent a long period of time in praying to her god, The Lady Neilea, for guidance and good fortune in what lay ahead. She fervently hoped that The Lady could still hear her prayers and entreaties despite the vast amount of rock that was above her. After a while she was rewarded with a wave of warmth – although this may have been her imagination brought on by fatigue.

Falcon and Taura may have slept for many hours for she was stiff about her hips and shoulders when she awoke, but they both felt somewhat refreshed. Surprisingly, her head was on his shoulder and his arm was around her with his hand clasping her bottom. Although another meal had been left for then, along with water to wash with and cloths to dry themselves, they had no idea how long they had been left in the cavern.

Within an hour a young gnome politely coughed by their doorway and asked for them to accompany him. He led them down a long passage and into a large chamber. There, sitting on low benches, were Jasper, Silmar, Billit and Jiutarô. Sushi was sitting up on a pile of cushions looking very playful and, as Taura and Falcon came over to embrace their friends, the little dragon chittered and purred happily. All of them looked fairly well recovered from their wounds although bandages were wrapped around heads and arms; it was obvious that Chthonic gnome healers had used considerable healing skills.

Sitting on a bench on a raised dais in front of the companions were five gnomes. They were dressed in their normal costumes of leather hose and boots and canvas jerkins; but each also wore a fine gown.

The stern-faced leader was clearly a gnome of dignity and influence; he sat in the centre of the group and the others had risen to their feet as he came over to sit. He began the discussion.

"It is time for introductions." His voice was gruff but not unpleasant. "I am the Lord Cephod, the leader of this community. This is our mining area and we are able to do this without being detected by other species and races that live down here. Oh, do not misunderstand me; our presence is known of. Both the Grey Dwarves and the Grullien are aware that we are here, somewhere. The biggest threat to us is from the Grey Dwarves, we have lost some of our people to them, both as captives for ransom or killed in battles.

"You see, they are greedy for that which we mine – crystal-silver, valuable and harder even than elven steel, and rubies of immense purity. They had only just caught my son and his guard. On my right here is Cephal. He was the one caught and trussed up like a lizard for the spit!" Cephod had spoken with a raised voice and was clearly angered with his son who sat there with a dejected and embarrassed expression. "If your group hadn't come along when you did, the rescue party would not have been there in time. For that alone you have my immense gratitude and that of the community otherwise we should not have allowed you into our haven, despite your predicament. You see, my son had talked his two personal guards into stepping out into the main tunnel and within moments they had blundered into the Grey Dwarves. One guard was able to escape and warn me but these two were taken hostage. It would have cost us dearly to get them back and may well have compromised our secrecy here."

Lord Cephod briefly paused while he drank from a small pewter cup. "We Chthonic gnomes have a trade arrangement with certain communities on the surface above. We have our own access to the surface and, through some acquaintances of ours, have trading posts in towns as far away as Northwald City on the Landsdrop Coast, Gash and Nasteed in Shordrun. Here we have wagons and horses to take our wares to cities."

At this Jasper interjected. "Pardon me, my Lord Cephod. We have recently been to the village of Dalcutta. They are now growing and would be delighted to have a trading post there, I am certain!"

"Hmm, we shall look into this as a future opportunity," said Cephod, looking at the gnome seated on the far right. This gnome nodded but remained silent. "This is Merwian, who manages the mining operation and the trading businesses. He is also my Master at Arms and takes responsibility for the safety and security of our community.

"Here on my right is Trefannwe, she is our healer and Priestess of Clambarhan, the God of learning, artifice and invention, and wielder of the great warhammer: *Craftmaster!*"

Both Cephod and Trefannwe bowed slightly. Taura, taking the hint, also bowed her head in respect in response to mention of her deity. "We also have a mage in our haven and that is Cerianath. I understand that he would like to speak afterwards with you, er, Billit, who we welcome into our haven as a brother. I do not believe Billit to be your real name but we shall leave that for later. It is always a pleasure to greet one of our kinfolk. But, although we rarely open our halls to peaceful travellers in the tunnels, you are all welcome here.

He took another mouthful from his cup. "I and my Assembly gathered before you, have expressed concern over that which the elf carries. But before you satisfy our curiosity, as I sincerely hope that you will, I should like you all to introduce yourselves. We keep a journal of our history in this community here. On the rare occasion that we gather with other clans of Chthonic gnomes, we tell stories of our exploits and occurrences. I think this will one day become a magnificent story for us to tell. Perhaps the Priestess of Neilea would like to begin. Please, go on."

The adventurers looked at each other and Taura rose to her feet to begin her introduction. "Erm, well, I am Taura Windwalker and I come from Casparsport in Lopastor. I was one of six daughters and the youngest. I also had two brothers. I was studious when my sisters were playing games so my mother encouraged me to study in the Temple of Neilea in Casparsport. It is a city of much vice and gambling so Neilea has many followers there, the temple is one of the biggest in the city. So, there I stayed for nine years. But I saw nothing of the world and listened long to the stories told by visiting adventurers when they stopped by for a blessing on their way to the gambling house. That was the fee I charged them you see – instead of a silver piece, I asked them for their stories. That is why I am here today; I want to see the lands and do some good. I have no regrets about my decision."

"No doubt you are now collecting stories of your own, young Priestess of the Lady of Magic and Serendipity," said Trefannwe, bowing once again. "I hope you shall tell us some of them before you leave."

Taura smiled. "It will be my pleasure, my lady!"

"And such courtesy too!"

Taura sat down, relieved that her story was over. Cephod glanced across to the companions.

"Er, me next Lord Cephod?" began Billit, rising to his feet. "Obviously, this name is only an epithet that some humans gave me because they couldn't get their lazy tongues round me real name! I'm Niebillettin, originally from a mining community in them Brash Mount'ns to the east of Triosande. We *rock-jumpers*, as the 'umans name us, like you are Chthonic Gnomes, well, we've traded there for centuries. If I'm not mistaken, I wouldn't be surprised if your tribe was originally from that area too, M'Lord."

Cephod frowned briefly and nodded. "You are quite correct, Niebillettin. This community was set up two centuries ago, when my forefathers decided that the Chthonic gnomes were becoming too numerous to be able to support themselves in one place. Then, of course, the goblins and ogres flooded into north Cascant and the whole tribe was driven out. Continue."

Billit shuffled his feet, twisting the cord around his waist between his fingers. "Well, I was the only child of Af-Niebillettin but I, too, was studious. I didn't wanta be, oh no! Not at first. I wanted to get out with the lads and fight and play games. But my father goes and decides I should study. Oh, lucky, lucky me, I thought! By the time I was eleven winters old I could read! Well, that was it! Off I was sent to the College Tower o' Magic in Norovir. Hah, a tower! It was three stories of a badly built wooden structure run by Evialannais, a fat, drunken ex-battle-wizard who, it was said, had been asked to leave the Royal Palace o' King Barsani Dar-Cascan VII in Norovir by none other than the Royal Magician, Barganisseroi, hisself. Oh Aye. The royal family, with many o' the Corps of Foresters, the elite soldiers o' Cascant, are in exile in the west while Barganisseroi and the Corps o' Battle-Wizards defend the south o' Cascant from Norovir. Anyway, me and the two other trainees virtually 'ad to teach ourselves from magic books because Evialannais couldn't keep off the rough wine and was considered too unreliable as a teacher. He 'ad taught me the basics, mind you, but the rest I taught myself by spending hours and hours with his old books o' spells and his alchemicals that I, um, borrowed when he slept. I knew I was doing well when I blew the front door off his library! He was livid; he thought I was trying to burn down his tower!"

The Assembly did not give any indication that they were amused by Billit's story.

Consequently, Billit's smile dropped away. "Aye, well, it was time for me to go when I reckoned I knew more than 'e could teach me, so I got a ride on a mule train. I went from one mule train to another until I ended up in the *Ship's Prow* at Westron Seaport!"

Puzzlement appeared on the faces of the Council. "Oh, that's an inn in Westron Seaport!" explained Billit. "So, anyway, here am I, too, with this sorry-looking bunch!"

"You tell an interesting and amusing story, mage Niebillettin," said Cephod. "I should like to discuss more with you, perhaps later, alone!"

The Chthonic Gnomes from the surface, known as *rock-dwellers*, were ever the storytellers. They would go into great detail of their stories of bravery and exploits with enthusiasm and with much waving of arms and falling about to emphasise or demonstrate a point. It was as if the retelling of great events would make a little folk appear larger. But here in the roots of the mountains, the Chthonic gnomes did not seem well disposed to hearing one of their own tell a humorous tale. Everything about them was sullen and withdrawn. Not once had a member of the council given the faintest glimmer of a smile.

Silmar started to speak but the wave of a hand from Cephod silenced him. "I would like your story to be the last to be told, warrior-elf. I should like to hear of the giant human."

"You want that I speak now, Lord?" offered Falcon.

Falcon was not used to speaking more than a few words at any one time. The Universal tongue was not his first language and he did struggle with it at times. But, taking a deep breath, he began to speak, slowly at first. The group of adventurers listened avidly because he had told them nothing of his background so far.

"I am Falcon-Hawk Makkadan from Livuria. I travelled far, for two winters. The Wytch Queen and her wytches banished me, their magic taking away my, er, my war-rage. I killed wytch's champion in a challenge. They do not forgive that. They will hunt me if I return but here in the western realms, I am far from their reach."

"So there is some truth in the legend that your warriors are *ragers?*" enquired Merwian, the master at arms.

"Ragers, aye. But not me! Not now." Falcon looked sullen. "Not even with Livuri *fire-berry* wine! But now, I am on my *wanderlust.*"

Once again, puzzled frowns showed on the faces of the council members.

"Explain," said Cephod.

"Wanderlust, I travel to see Amæus. I meet new friends here and now we travel and fight together!"

"Perhaps your rage is better left beyond your reach!" responded Cephod. "It is said to be uncontrollable, as much a risk to your friends as it is to your enemies. Do not look for something that may well occur naturally in time of great need."

Falcon dropped his face dejectedly as if in silent repose but then a faint smile spread across his face, beneath his beard. His sadness was plain to see, however, so Cephod said no more to the Barbarian. He turned instead to Jasper.

"I should like to hear your story; surface dwarves have ever been friends to the Chthonic gnomes and are trusted here. There is something about you that stirs old memories from within me. Have you been here before? I know not your name."

"Hrrrm, yes! I'm known as Jasper but me real name is Harval Cleaverblade. Soon after me an' mah brother, Ralmon, first passed through yer realm, 'is arm was taken from 'im in battle. Aye, many years ago, with this 'ere elf's father, Faramar Galadhal, the *Spirit Panther* as 'e was known to 'is friends an' enemies alike."

At this, Silmar's eyebrows rose in surprise – he had not heard this before!

"It was 'e what saved me brother's life but could not save the arm!" exclaimed Jasper.

"The Spirit Panther indeed!" exclaimed Cephod. "A name I remember well, we were there when the enemy was vanquished! He was unconscious; his shattered arm lay twisted beneath him. He must have lost all but a cupful of blood by the time Faramar applied wadding to his wound and tied a cord around to stop the flow. This undoubtedly kept death at arm's length, if you excuse the term; I apologise if you consider it to be in bad taste. But it was our sister, Trefannwe, who asked Clambarhan to intervene and save the life of one of the two dwarven heroes who were prepared to sacrifice their all for the fight."

Jasper's jaw dropped with surprise. "M-My lady! I didn't know of this!" he stammered. "B-Blessings on you and, er, an' to the Lord Clambarhan."

He prostrated himself at the feet of the Priestess but she placed her hand on his shoulder saying "Rise Harval Cleaverblade, friend of the Chthonic gnomes, be thou not at my feet."

The dwarf rose and returned alongside his friends. He muttered, "Mah brother 'as taken the name Half Harval 'cos of 'avin' just the one arm." For the first time a slight smile quickly manifested itself on the face of Cephod. But, just as quickly, it faded.

The gnome lord continued. "Clearly, you are still campaigning. Have you not retired from this life? What life have you given yourself now?"

"Well, aye! I got this tavern in Nor'wald City. The priest Halorun Tann pays me a visit every once in a while. Half Harval's got a tavern as well, but in Westron Seaport. He calls it the Ship's Prow 'cos it's near the docks and it keeps 'im comfortable, if yer knows what I mean. I met this sorry bunch of adventurers when they called at me place with a barrel of bloodwine from me brother. And that's 'ow we got into this mess in the first place!"

"A sorry bunch?" gasped Cephod. "Nay. It seems to me that they have achieved more than would be expected even for an experienced group such as yourselves."

"Well, er, actually it's our first campaign!" exclaimed Taura.

Now it was Cephod's turn to display surprise on his stern face. "What? Impossible! Such a small and very inexperienced band of warriors! I salute you all! You certainly have achieved much."

Merwian, the Master at Arms, Trefannwe, Priestess of Clambarhan, and the mage Cerianath similarly looked at each other and at Cephod. Lord Cephod's son, Cephal, who had been sullen and quiet during the story-telling, looked surprised at the group of adventurers sitting on the benches before him.

"I wish to hear more from your companions. I see someone from the race of men that I have no knowledge of. The features I do not recognise, the garb is strange but he carries himself with a self-assuredness and dignity the like of which I have never seen before, even in the race of men. Something tells me that he is a warrior from a far-off land. Your little companion is very attached to you. A cleret-wing dragon, I believe."

Sushi had been wrapped around Jiutarô's shoulder throughout most of their time in the haven. She raised her head as the eyes of the Assembly turned towards her and Jiutarô. The Samurai, however, looked with some incomprehension.

At this, Trefannwe rose to her feet and looked straight into the eyes of Jiutarô. She signalled with her right hand for him to approach and he stood before her. Standing on the dais, she was able to reach towards him and she placed her right hand on the side of his head. Sushi's claws tightened on his shoulders momentarily and she gave a little hiss but a quick look from the mage seemed to settle her. The Samurai stood rock still and did not flinch nor even blink his eye. She maintained that link for many moments and then she let her hand fall away.

"Nay, Lord," spoke the mage. Her expression was one of sadness. "I can let it be known that he comes not from any land on Amæus but from across the skies; a world amongst the stars; a land in turmoil as those in power exploit those who serve. I read it in the sadness and confusion that surrounds him. One of forty-seven is he. Return he shall, to face his doom. Each of that number shall share the doom of his comrades. Know that his honour shall have its rewards. Search him not for answers to those puzzles and doubts that he himself will not understand. His courage and loyalty are without question."

The members of the party looked at their comrade with puzzlement but theirs was nothing compared to that of the Samurai. A period of silence followed and Trefannwe said no more as she returned to her seat. Her words had been confusing to him and none understood all that she had said.

Cephod broke the silence. "No doubt all will become clear in time," he stated. "The elf has much to tell us about himself and in particular the burden he carries. I have spoken of it and the evil it is imbued with, but evil is not in the group that escorts it. Please tell us more, elf Silmar Galadhal, son of Faramar, the Spirit Panther."

Silmar took a deep breath. He had been turning his story over and over in his mind, fully aware that he would have to explain in detail everything that had happened. Once he started talking however, the story flowed easily from his lips. He recounted his early years as a patrol leader, how he had started his journey, his arrival in Westron Seaport and meeting with his new companions. He carefully told of his first encounter with the Døkkálfr assassin and the discovery of the artefact on the dying Priest of Clambarhan. He explained how Halorun Tann had given them much advice and prepared them for their quest.

Cephod interrupted continuously, asking for clarification or more details. At times, Trefannwe also asked him to repeat or explain further some of the details. A full hour passed in the telling and retelling of Silmar's story. At the end of it, Cephod refused the offer to examine the artefact.

"It is not necessary for me to see that which is evil, I have no doubt that it is there. I can feel its influence as can we all, none more than Trefannwe. We shall now take the time for you to rest, eat and sleep. You shall be returned to the quarters where you slept and recovered earlier. In some hours we shall escort you by some paths that are known only to us. Once we come close to the main tunnel, with your agreement and for your and our safety, we shall blindfold you so that you will be unable to disclose our secret ways even though you may be compelled, physically or magically, to do so. Are you in agreement?"

The companions looked at each other and all nodded their agreement.

"Good, then let it be so. Niebillettin, I request that you remain with the Assembly here for a while. I wish to speak with you further."

Trefannwe added "We have known that none of you are evil from the start."

To her surprise, Taura replied "Yes, I am aware that you cast a *Discern Evil Intent* across us. I felt it and also did the same to you! Did you not know?"

"You are a cunning young human, Taura Windwalker. I felt it not! I trust that the response you felt was to your satisfaction. Accept my apologies, please. I was acting in the best interests of my community. I hope you understand. A thing of evil would normally be carried by a person of similar evil, do you not agree?"

Taura nodded and said "Apologies are not necessary, Holy Mother Artificer. But I do offer mine in return. I would have done the same to ensure our safety. If you are happy, we shall speak no more of it and remain as friends in the eyes of our deities."

The two priestesses bowed and parted. Two Chthonic Gnome warriors escorted the party to their quarters.

Apart from Cephal, who sat at the end of the dais, the Gnome Lord and Billit were alone in the meeting hall.

"By birth, you are a Rock-Dweller, a Chthonic Gnome. How long is it since you were in the darkness with your kinfolk, cousin Niebillettin?"

"Not since childhood have I been below the surface, lord."

"Are you not aware of your innate capabilities commensurate with your race, then?"

"I don't understand, Lord. I am strong, fast and seem to be able to hide behind a pebble, an advantage for being small of stature. I feel confident and not to out-of-place or frightened in the Shadow World. I have some skills as a mage and these are growing quite well since I started on this campaign. But if that is what you mean as innate capabilities, I am no different to any other Rock-Dweller, I think."

"You are indeed a mage of swiftly developing powers, according to Trefannwe. As a priestess, she herself has powers beyond my understanding but she also has a gift of far-sight. She can look into the distant past or the future merely by a touch on the person and applying her mind's strength. That is how she knew of your strange warrior. As both sage and priestess she is both wise and powerful. But she is not a mage. The far-sight power could well be yours in years to come, she tells me. She says it is not a god-given power nor is it magically learned but rather a skill that comes from exercising the mind as one might train one's muscles to develop physical fitness. By Clambarhan, she can implant thoughts into the mind of others! She can even move objects by the power of thought. Who then, cousin, do you consider as being your most hated foe?"

The sudden change in direction in Cephod's conversation caught Billit unawares for a few moments, having been so wrapped up in the apparent skills of Trefannwe. "Ah, that's simple," he said, "anyone who is a threat to me or my comrades at that particular time. But if I must select a race or species then it would probably be Dökkálfar. They're the evillest of all those we have met so far."

"And what of those you have never met, or perhaps are yet to meet?"

"It's strange really my Lord, but there is somethin' that sends a shiver down my spine when I hear them mentioned. I don't understand why. I've never encountered 'em but heard 'em mentioned a couple o' times over the last few days. It may just be something I remember from many years ago."

The Lord Cephod had been sitting upright in his chair and now he leaned forward towards the mage. "Tell me who it is."

Billit scratched at a drying scab in the sparse hair on his chin. He looked at the piece that had lodged under his fingernail and flicked it away. "There are a couple really," he said slowly. "Kobolts, because their threat is understated, and although they are very small they have such great numbers that they can overwhelm you. And those damned Grullien! The Shade-Gnomes. When I think of 'em, I imagine a foul smell in my nostrils and a rasping voice yet I am certain I haven't seen 'em during my lifetime."

"It is not so strange that you should mention them. The enmity that exists between the Chthonic gnomes and the Grullien has been so for countless generations. Ever have they sought to destroy us or take captive our people for food, trade or slavery. Yes, they are known to eat their captives as do the Grey Dwarves. Ever have we sought to destroy them, our most deadly of foes. They are not so intelligent, but they are cunning. We are miners and can move from one place to another in our own tunnels in complete secrecy. We hear and see much that occurs in this Shadow World. You have dark-vision, cousin, do you not?"

"Er, aye. I do, Lord. I can see quite a long way but it's not very clear, a bit fuzzy-like. The dwarf and the elf, now, they can really see well. At least, that's what they tell me. But they are different 'cos the elf needs a bit 'o light but not so the dwarf."

"Good, but you have been too long on the surface, cousin. For clear dark-vision you would need to spend your life in these tunnels. But you have made your choices in life and you must accept the consequences. As a mage, you have knowledge of spells that you have had to learn and relearn no doubt. Would it surprise you to know that you also have other magical abilities that you have no need to learn? Magic that comes naturally to you when in the darkness of the tunnels?"

Billit looked dazed. "What? Really? Nay!" He shook his head doubtfully. "What are they? How do I start 'em up? What can they do? Can I blast my enemies asunder?"

Cephod chuckled. "Calm cousin. It may be better for another to explain." The Lord Cephod closed his eyes for a moment and then opened them again. A few heartbeats later a distortion in the air appeared as if it were a large bubble in water. Through it stepped Cerianath and he stood before them. The distortion disappeared. Billit blanched at the sight.

"Merely a portal from my chamber to this Assembly chamber, cousin Niebillettin," explained Cerianath. "You summoned me, my Lord?"

"Thank you for your promptness, Cerianath. I wish you to explain to our cousin the innate abilities of magic that he has, in addition to those he acquired. Surprisingly, or perhaps not, he has no knowledge of this."

"By your command, my Lord. It should be no surprise that you have no knowledge of these gnomish abilities, Niebillettin. Long have you been estranged from your kinfolk. Who, then, would school you and encourage you? There are simple abilities which, after much patience, come naturally to a mature Chthonic Gnome. I can spend some time with you, if you and your friends can spare that time, to instruct you in these ways. There are two skills. Use them wisely. You can use them with your other magical abilities without detriment. The effect of these skills is only temporary when cast on the target. Depending on your power with these, the effects will last longer the better practised you are. *Black blindness* is one. Casting this will cause a black sphere to appear in the line of vision so that the victim cannot see before him. *Hazed sight* is the other. The receiver cannot clearly see friend from foe and this confusion will either cause him to attack any who stand before him, should he be of a ruthless nature, or force him to withdraw from battle. Use them both wisely. I shall council you with the use of these. Being a mage, you should quickly learn these, I am sure."

The expression on Billit's face clearly showed his astonishment at having learned of these new powers.

"There is one more," Cerianath continued, "however, that you will always find useful. It is a *Hide from sight* spell."

Cephod spoke next. "This spell we use constantly should we be in the main tunnel of the Shadow World." Looking towards Cephal, his son, he added, "Foolish indeed is the gnome who does not use this ability to protect himself. But perhaps I am unfair. In this case, my son still achieves maturity and the innate magical powers still develop within him. Take no notice of a concerned father, my son; I was sure that you were lost. My heart soars to see you returned to me."

At this last remark, the morose expression finally lifted from the young gnome and he rose to his feet, bowed to his father and left the Assembly chamber.

"What is this *Hide from sight* spell, Lord?" asked Billit.

"You are probably aware that we have the advantage of being able to move with stealth and can be difficult to observe, let alone catch! Did you not yourself say that you can hide behind a pebble? Well, the *Hide from sight* spell will allow you to pass unseen and not be detected by any magical charm. It will hide you from the cunning eyes of a mage of any power less than that of a demi-god. Consider the potential, cousin."

Cephod rose to his feet and addressed Cerianath. "Take our cousin and school him in the new arts, Lord. Advise him in the best way for him to free his mind to release the new powers. I shall now speak with the elf warrior, meanwhile allowing the remainder of our guests to rest and gather their strength for they have more tests to overcome. One of these causes me grave concern – even with our numbers, we dread to walk that path and avoid it completely." With that, he was gone.

Cerianath motioned to Billit and said, "Follow me!" With a flick of his wrist and a muffled word, another portal appeared before him. He stepped into it and was gone from view. With a nervous sigh, Billit followed.

Silmar was led by a gnome messenger along a short passageway and into an austere chamber. Cephod and Trefannwe sat on two simple chairs and gestured for him to be seated on a somewhat larger wooden bench.

The two gnomes exchange a brief glance at each other before Cephod looked at Silmar directly in the eye. Trefannwe sat with her eyes closed and her hands clasped in front of her face.

"Have you brought it here with you?" he asked curtly and without preamble.

"I have," the elf replied. "It is in my pack."

There was silence for a considerable time until Trefannwe opened her eyes suddenly and took a deep breath in.

"It is an aberration!" she cried out. "A travesty. How can its presence be tolerable, Lord?"

"Undoubtedly, it cannot be," the gnome lord stated brusquely. "What can you tell us about its provenance, elf warrior?"

Silmar explained in much detail about how he had taken the artefact from the dying cleric of Clambarhan and that Halorun Tann had informed him that the dagger was of unique religious significance to the Church of Clamberhan. It had been stolen by the followers of Adelenis, corrupted by them and then taken back by the cleric carrying it who had eventually been slain by the very Døkkálfr that now skulked in the mine tunnels.

"We intend to return it by the long road east to Carrick Cliffs in Kamambia and the Temple of Clambarhan so that it can be restored once again. We are all resolved to do this no matter what the risks will be. We have come far and we have much, much further to go."

"No matter how that foul thing makes you feel?" interjected Trefannwe.

Silmar paused before answering. "Aye, but it has been of some benefit to me, somewhat surprisingly. You must understand that, by its nature, it knows when an evil presence draws close at hand and, in some strange way that is unexplainable to me, it seems to attract them to me. It is that influence that affects me badly in such a way that also warns me to the approaching danger. By misfortune, that warning manifests itself by a wave of nauseous, and occasionally painful, reaction. At other times it gives out a coldness which produces frost inside and outside of my pack. I do bear the artefact with fortitude, though. The burden, as I call it, is inside a box resting in a bed of lead powder otherwise the reaction would be much worse, I am told."

The discussion concluded soon afterwards. Silmar was invited to join the Assembly to discuss the threat and influence of the artefact. In his opinion, the debate went around in circles without reaching a conclusion. The Lord Cephod spoke for the Assembly when he stated that the companions would be escorted away from the Haven City of the Chthonic Gnomes as soon as they were sufficiently recovered.

"Where do you think he is?" A sleepy-eyed Taura was starting to show concern for their little friend Billit. They had been led back to the chamber where they had continued to recover from their wounds and had eaten and drunk. They had been advised to get what sleep they could to complete their recovery and prepare for their remaining journey.

Like all the other chambers and the tunnels, the floor, walls and ceilings were smoothly carved into the rock and there was little sign of the tooling marks that had originally fashioned them.

More hours passed and there was still no sign of Billit. Silmar had been whisked away some time ago for an audience with Lord Cephod. He had taken his backpack containing the burden with him. Falcon had risen from his bed and, with his head held low, was now pacing back and forth across the dimply-lit chamber. A gemstone set high into the wall seemed to give off the dim light. Falcon resumed sitting on his two straw palliasses. The height of the room had made it impossible for him to stand upright. Taura also sat on his palliasses, leaning against the barbarian as he placed his arm protectively around her shoulders. His fingers soon strayed down to her breast and she made no effort to remove it.

Jiutarô was sleeping with his arm over his head to block out the rumbling snores coming from a deeply sleeping Jasper. It was unusual for the dwarf to snore but he often did so only when in a safe environment. Sushi slept beside the Samurai.

"He probably talks with his long-lost kin," replied the Barbarian. "We are well treated so I am sure he is too. Do not worry about him. But should one of our hosts come in, I shall ask."

More time passed and eventually a Gnome messenger entered the room, he made a sound as if clearing is throat and the party slowly awoke.

"Have you lost this?" he eventually asked as the group climbed to their feet. Into the archway stepped Billit, his little face smiling broadly.

"Up, you lazybones all," Billit exclaimed. "We are going soon. Eat, drink and then off on our travels once again."

Behind him, next to the messenger, stood Silmar, a dour look on his face. Despite questions from the others as to what he had been doing, he remained non-committal, giving just a few short phrases. He looked irritated so they gave him some space.

They spent a little time checking their packs and weapons. Billit stood grasping something close to his chest. It appeared to be a book.

"Look at this," he proudly boasted. "He gave it to me! It is priceless and he gave it to me! Cerianath!"

"A book!" said Jiutarô. "Just book."

"Nay, not just a book! It is a magical spell-book. It contains spells that are more powerful and 'e says they will be within my skills soon. I read some and I think I may be able to do some of 'em. Others I can't get my head around." He carefully wrapped the book in a cloak and placed it in his pack.

Once again, they were taken to the Assembly chamber where Lord Cephod and the rest of the Assembly were standing.

"The time has come for you to take your leave of our haven city," he said. "We have benefited from your being here as much as we hope you have. We now have another trade opportunity and you have regained much of your fitness and your strength and resolve to face your next difficulties. You shall be led through the tunnels of our haven, as aforesaid, we must ask that you wear blindfolds, and we shall lead you out into the Shadow World. You shall be led a short way still wearing blindfolds, but these will then be removed. You will be quite safe. We shall leave shortly but there is something else we need to do. Merwian?"

"My Lord," replied the Master-at-Arms and he passed to Cephod a small linen bag.

"The council wishes you to accept these as a token of our friendship. As we are not likely to meet within the tunnels of this haven again, we would like to present you with small gifts that will enable you to keep in your memories the friendships we have made this day. There is one for each of you." To each he presented a carved and polished ruby. Although the size of a pigeon's egg, each gem was crafted into the shape of an apple. Its surface was perfectly round and smooth.

Each of the adventurers gazed at the gems with wonder.

"My Lord," exclaimed Silmar. "This gift shall be treasured. The story of its presentation to me shall be told and retold and never forgotten. I am honoured. I am sure I speak similarly for my friends too."

Each member of the group nodded and spoke in agreement. Jiutarô looked confused but Billit explained to him.

Trefannwe reached out towards Taura. "Take these, Lady of Neilea." In her hands she held three glass phials. "A dark poison may afflict some of you. If so, these will be needed. You will know when. Take also this sack – it is quite heavy. Within are items belonging to Grey Dwarves. These will aid you at the right time. You will know that time."

Jasper reached over and took the large, heavy-looking sack, opened it and looked inside. "There's a helm, a hand-axe, some arrows and two swords, one of which is broken. He looked puzzled and gave a questioning look to the soothsayer. She said nothing more. Falcon took up the sack and swung it over his shoulder.

Cephod turned to them all and said, "It is now time to leave."

CHAPTER 22

T HEY STOOD together once again in the Shadow World mine tunnel. The Chthonic Gnomes had removed the blindfolds and without a single word had melted into the darkness. No sound from them was heard, not even the scurry of their small feet.

After a long moment, Taura nervously reached around her in the pitch darkness. She could hear her own heartbeats hammering in her chest. Her hand collided with clothing.

"It is I, Taura," murmured Jiutarô.

She whispered into the darkness. "We are back. It is almost as if it didn't happen at all."

There was a wave of relief as she heard Jasper's reply. "It did, we're all together, I 'ope so, anyway! Are we all 'ere?" Softly spoken responses from each of them confirmed that they were all together once again.

Surprisingly, each of them quickly grew accustomed to the darkness. They could make out pebbles and rocks that littered the floor. There was a vestige of light they recognised as being from fungus and mould that aided Silmar with his dark-vision.

"I believe we are quite safe here for the moment," he whispered confidently.

The passage was very wide here, probably just enough for the five of them to walk in line abreast. Large rocks, the size of a crouching man and smaller, were scattered about on the floor. Pieces of wood, cloth and leather, all in various stages of decay were also strewn about. A rusting helm, too small for a human or elven head, lay by a boulder. There was no sign of its original wearer.

Taura kicked it gently; it clattered across the floor and its chin-guard fell off it.

"Oo was that?" growled Jasper.

"Sorry," Taura squeaked.

"That was choddin' stupid," he hissed. "It might 'ave been joined to a trap an' the sound of it can carry for miles along 'ere. Don't do it again! Lead us on, elf!"

They had been walking for what seemed a few hours and they agreed to stop for a while to take a little water and food in the darkness. They then continued on for another considerable length of time.

They passed many openings on either side which had been hewn through the rock long ago. These were generally narrow.

The dwarf grabs Silmar as he is about to enter one of these openings. "We 'ave been choddin' stooped," he hasped. "That bastard could be in any one o' these openings, ready to attack us or somethin'. We bin goin' past 'em an' even goin' in some of 'em. Stoopid!"

"Gods, you're right," Silmar whispered. "We must take more care. If we use one to rest in, we need to check it properly. We need to rest, some of us need sleep."

They trudged past some openings. One however, appeared in the wall to their left; it was both wide and tall enough for them all to enter side-by-side in pairs should they have felt the need to, but it was full of rusting mining tools, handcarts, old crates and detritus. Rather than look through it all they decided to continue on. The main tunnel however, started to narrow considerably from then on until it was no more than two paces across. It bent sharply to the left and suddenly came to a great chasm across the floor. It must have been at least thirty feet across. There was no bridge or means to cross it and no ledge to climb around. The walls to each side were smooth and sheer and the bottom could not be seen even by the members of the group blessed with dark-vision. The continuing tunnel could be seen stretching on from the far side of the chasm.

"Tunnel on side," gasped Jiutarô. "Small it is."

"We need some light, I think," Taura hinted.

"Lightson," warned Silmar. "Three; two; one. Now!"

Three beams of light cut through the gloom. In the dim light, Jiutarô had seen the black opening of a tunnel to the right side, half-hidden behind large boulders.

"How did you see that, Jiutarô?" asked Silmar.

"Feel air."

"We can't cross the gulf," said Jasper under his breath. "No other choice. 'Ow about you lead, elf? Then if there's a nasty accident we won't lose nobody important. Heh heh!"

The dwarf always managed to make the title *elf* sound like an insult. Silmar was learning quickly to ignore the taunt.

The narrow tunnel led off to the right and they followed it with the light beams scanning the floor and walls. The beams flitted across the ugly, pale faces of Grullien, the dreaded Shade Gnomes.

"Where are they, those godsdamned the pale-skins!"

The Døkkálfr assassin had plodded for a long time and there had been no sight or sound of his quarry. He knew noise could carry a long way through these mines but he had heard nothing. He was worried that they had given up the chase and had gained the surface once again. He couldn't let that happen. He must have that artefact, it would be his neck on the altar and his blood running into the vessels otherwise.

He was now deciding whether to backtrack the way he had come but the difficulties that would present would be immense. The leg-wound from the arrow a few days ago had been serious and he had not enough healing concoction to treat the burn after he had used most of it on the arrow wound, to little benefit. He had resorted to using a needle and thread to do his own repair to his leg and the stitches pulled as he walked. Still the wound bled but, for now, it was not life-threatening.

He had found a niche in the tunnel and had taken some badly needed rest. He hoped the sound of their approach would arouse him if he lapsed into a deeper sleep than he intended.

Sometime later, he awoke to the sound of shouts and what seemed to be a battle. He knew from experience that any noise of battle being fought in tunnels and mines would sound much worse, or closer, than it actually was. It was possible that some members of the following group of surface rats were meeting their doom, after all, they were few in number. They had started the journey a human cleric, a human warrior of some sort, a gnome and the bastard Ljósálfr, the pale elf he had sworn to kill slowly and painfully. But they seemed to have picked up some extra help on the way, a huge human and a dwarf!

He waited.

The sound of the battle continued but after a while grew less and less. Then there was silence. Had an enemy defeated them all? He just needed to get back there to observe. He rose to his feet and left his niche. Quietly limping back up the tunnel, he approached the source of the noise. Godsdamn! He could see no bodies of his prey or any other beings. Not a single one of them had perished out here. He cautiously and silently turned off the main passageway while listening to the muted conversation of his enemies. They were discussing destroying something! Were none of them defeated? It seemed he was underestimating this enemy! He had left many traps but none had worked. He had tried to ambush them but he had been the one to be injured.

They get stronger while I get weaker. I'll have him though! Soon! In the deep city! Hah! My brothers-in-arms will be there waiting for me.

The Døkkálfr turned away and limped back along the passage and into the main tunnel. He had gone no more than a hundred paces when he heard a hiss. A sequence of clicks followed and he made some clicks of his own.

"Brother! Are you *The One?*"

"It is I," he responded.

"Long have we waited. Too long. *Her* patience wears thin. Two of us there are here. Four more wait in the city beyond and four again at the surface. Do you have it?"

"I do not!"

"What? Your life will be forfeit, brother, if you do not present it. Where is it?"

"Do not presume that you may castigate me, you low-born scum! Listen to what I have to say and bite back your tongue."

The Døkkálfr assassin briefly told of his difficulties and of the group that pursued him through the mine tunnels. He explained how he had left traps and danger in his wake and he said how the group still survived to follow him still.

"We shall proceed direct to the City of Shade then," stated one of the other two Dökkálfar. The assassin hid his displeasure at being told what to do by these underlings. A thin blade between the ribs would silence that one's attitude soon enough if he wasn't more humble.

The second Døkkálfr however, was more respectful. "Perhaps we could spring our own trap, or ambush. Not far ahead, but beyond the razor-rocks, is a great pillared hall. Were we to spread ourselves across the hall, we may be able to have better success and turn our, er, problem into a triumph?"

That idea was much more to the liking of the assassin. He nodded his head in quiet acquiescence.

The trio marched on in the darkness in total silence for many hours. Eventually they came across a change in the tunnel floor. The flat surface abruptly changed into razor-edged rocks that protruded upwards and were difficult to walk across.

"She anticipated the need," one of the assassins whispered, "and furnished us with these gifts."

The two Darkling had arrived suitably prepared. A potion was administered to each of them and, although encumbered with weapons and packs, they were nevertheless soon able to rise off the floor and float above the surface of the tunnel. Using their hands to guide their weightless bodies over the razor-sharp rocks and against the walls and ceiling, they made their way to the far end of the obstacle, a distance of about two hundred paces. It was a long time before the effect of the potions wore off but it was not instantaneous when it happened and they gently sank to the smooth floor.

Will the fools behind me be so well prepared? mused the assassin. *I doubt it.*

"Look at this boot-print!" indicated Silmar. "It's his for sure."

The fight with the six Grullien had been short. They were bald-headed and their eyes large and dark. Their mouths were wide and their teeth pointed, including their abnormally long canines. They wore armour of thick, rigid leather on their chests and backs and were armed with short-swords and picks with long, sharp spikes. Billit destroyed two with a *Storm-Bolt* spell that lanced a white hot shaft at his foe, and Jiutarô sliced through the chest of one with his katana. Meanwhile, Jasper pummelled another with his war-hammer, smashing his skull. Silmar and Jasper engaged the remaining two in a bitter melee, these Grullien proving to be relentless in their ferocity. Taura used her staff to batter Jasper's foe on the back of its neck and was rewarded with the sound of breaking bones. She finished it off with a thrust of the staff onto it bald head. Jasper and Silmar joined forces to slay the last Dark Gnome. The companions stood back to survey their handiwork.

"Nasty little buggers, weren't they?" observed Jasper. "Wouldn't want ter meet loads o' them."

Leaving the bodies of six Grullien behind them, the group studied a boot-print they had seen in the dust.

"It's him, isn't it?" Taura whispered.

Falcon shrugged. Silmar hissed, "Probably."

They marched on and from time to time had used the beams from their light-tubes to find their way. In this way, they saw much more sign of ancient occupation of the mine tunnels. There were remains of wooden boxes, pieces of rusting armour and helms, broken shields and weapons too. There were the complete skeletons of humans and dwarves, as well as of others that were not so easily identified. In some cases, the bones were scattered about is if more recent travelling groups had callously kicked them about.

Jasper even picked up one or two copper coins that had been caught by chance in the light-beams. They were coated with the green patina of age. He rubbed one vigorously with his thumb and studied their surfaces. The ancient designs embossed upon them were unknown to him. As an innkeeper, he was familiar with coins from many of the kingdoms on Amæus, or Amæhome as it was more commonly known, but the coins he held were very old from long-forgotten empires. Some of these he pocketed; they would still have some value. If not, he would mount them on the beams of his tavern in Nor'wald City.

The tunnel became quite narrow at one point, being no wider than would allow two people to walk tightly side-by-side. After a while though, it widened slightly but Billit, who was now leading them, pulled them up.

"'Ow in the seven 'ells of the Void do we go on from here?" he asked quietly. His whisper sounded loud in the narrow confines of the tunnel.

Ahead of then the floor was carpeted with upright razor-sharp stones.

Jasper murmured, "This is choddin' bad. The floor 'as gone an' these rocks is damned sharp. We won't easily be able ter walk across 'ere. My legs is too short an' so is yours, Billit"

"We will have no choice. We'll need to go on. How far does it go?" asked Silmar.

"Sushi look?" asked Jiutarô.

The cleret-wing dragon purred and perched on his shoulder. "Look for me?" whispered Jiutarô in his own language, knowing she would understand his thoughts. "Nuts and fruit for you? Fly, friend!"

The little creature launched herself away and Jiutarô closed his eyes. Within a few dozen heartbeats, Sushi was back. She returned to her favourite spot on Jiutarô's shoulders and twittered in his ear.

"I see Sushi eyes," he explained.

The meaning was unclear at first. Then Billit laughed gently. "'E means that what Sushi sees, 'e can see through his eyes."

"He's sorta mentioned this afore, din't 'e?" murmured Jasper. "But I weren't sure what 'e meant. A 'andy trick, that one."

"Aye," replied Silmar. "'Tis true for I have heard it mentioned by our loremasters. It takes a while and the two of them must be closely-bonded for it to happen but, when the cleret-wing dragon allows it, she can enable her human partner see images through her eyes."

"Rocks, um, two-hundred walks, er, walks?"

"Paces?" asked Falcon.

"Hai, paces. Hai!" The Samurai was feeding the promised nuts and dried fruit to Sushi who nibbled them delicately.

Forgetting to keep his voice low, Jasper growled, "That's a choddin' long choddin' way! I been 'ere before and they weren't 'ere then! What do we choddin' do about it? Some o' yer longshanks can walk through it but not me 'n' the gnome."

"Shhh!" hissed Silmar.

Billit leapt about excitedly. "Hey! I might 'ave an answer to that," he murmured. "Wait a bit, let me think."

"We ain't got all choddin' day!"

Ignoring the good-natured jibe, the little gnome continued. "A couple o' you big ones can take all the packs across an' come back for me an' Jasper. What d'yer think, eh?"

"Can you not try a magical spell," asked Taura. "You must know something suitable."

"Dunno one like that," the gnome admitted. "Might be something in my new book but I can't go into that here. It would take too long."

"I shall carry them both," Falcon volunteered.

His last passenger was not such a straightforward task. Jasper was deceptively heavy. By the time Falcon had carried the dwarf across to the smooth floor of the passage, his short goatskin leggings were badly torn from scraping the jagged rocks, he had many gashes and deep scratches on his legs and arms from the jagged rocks of the floor. Taura spent a long time with him, longer than was really necessary, attending the worst of his injuries as best she could and then curled up in his arms.

They agreed that they should rest, eat and sleep. Taura felt a strong need to converse with her God and Falcon badly needed sleep.

Silmar couldn't help but wonder how the Darkling managed to cross the razor-rocks, if he indeed had done so.

In the darkness, the Darkling waited. The ambush was set. It was fool-proof. *We shall finish these fools and put to an end whatever quest they thought they were on. And that damned Ljósálfar! He's mine! He shall know pain before he dies at my hands! He will wish for death.*

From their vantage points, each of the assassin's companions, using their well-developed dark-vision, they could clearly see the archway through which the group would enter. Unlike the light-loving Ljósálfar, the Døkkálfar needed no faint vestige of light-source in order to see in the darkness. Generations of Døkkálfar beyond reckoning had dwelt in the dark, low places of Amæus and their vision had developed such that differences in temperature of every material, be it rock, wood or flesh, enabled their shapes to be clearly defined.

The assassin had refused the offer of one of his two companions to rush the short distance to the City of Shade to bring the four brothers-in-arms to the assassin's aid.

The two Døkkálfar warriors sat apart from each other with their light-crossbows and throwing-knives at the ready. The assassin waited to one side, away from his companions with his sword and daggers loosened in their scabbards. He reflected on the wisdom of declining that offer. The surface scum had proven themselves to be tenacious, having survived his numerous attempts to entrap them.

CHAPTER 23

THE COMPANIONS had rested on the floor of the tunnel, Falcon was sleeping and Taura was deep in meditation. Jasper reckoned that some hours had passed but sleep did not come to him. Silmar, Falcon, Jasper and Jiutarô had taken turns in keeping watch over the sleeping group. The elf stood in silence, his eyes straining to see the merest speck of light in the deep blackness for without it he had no dark-vision. His keen hearing detected no sounds at all from the darkness ahead of them but, of course, this was no guarantee of safety. So many lessons had been learned during their perilous journey in the mines of the Shadow World. Danger might have come from almost anything that walked, flew, slithered, burrowed or ate its way through the mines. It wasn't just from Døkkálfar, the Grey Elves, the Grullien, or even from undead that were rumoured to infest areas of the deep. The very walls of the tunnel seemed almost alive with hazard and even death. They could be under scrutiny now, from eyes unseen. But there was good here too. For many years disparate races had endured the Shadow World and they had adapted to survive in its hazardous and treacherous darkness.

The elf had roused Billit first and the gnome was now huddled beneath a blanket, with a light tube, studying and learning new spells. This was a necessary activity because this mage, like any other magic user, could not cast a spell unless he or she had taken the time to study the vocal nuances and gestures required so that the spell, when cast, would be successful. Only sorcerers had a natural ability to hurl spells without practice.

After a while, Silmar roused the rest of the party. Water was getting very low. They had perhaps the equivalent of a wineskin's worth between them. It would not last a day's march. It had been a long time since they had come across a source of drinkable, clear, flowing water.

Within a few moments, they were walking again without light beams. Jasper led this time, with Silmar to one side and slightly behind him. They moved in the pitch darkness and, anxious that the floor might be hazardous, were all linked with lengths of rope; but the going was miserably slow.

The dwarf was confident, however. "I think this tunnel is getting wider," he whispered. "Can we risk some light, do you think?"

Although he was whispering, all of the group could hear him more clearly than was comfortable.

"I think so," replied Silmar. "Move to the sides of the tunnel just in case. Ready? *Lightson!* Three; two; one. Now!"

Three beams of light lanced out before them from the leather tubes in Jasper's, Silmar's and Taura's hands. They squinted their eyes for a few moments until they became accustomed to the brightness and could see the tunnel stretch out ahead and behind them. It curved to the right within a few dozen paces and the floor and walls seemed smooth and solid. With surprise, they noticed that the floor was littered with crumbling bones, decaying cloth and leather, and rusting armour and weapons. In anger tinged with frustration Jasper kicked at a helmet and out of it rolled a dwarf skull.

Taura recoiled in horror into Falcon's protective arms. "You told me not too –" she began to admonish him.

"It's a Grey Dwarf helm so I don't care! Old battle, long ago. *Lightsoff!* Move quietly now," mumbled the dwarf angrily and the beams were extinguished. The darkness closed around them and the group of friends felt vulnerable once more.

They moved forward, using the tunnel wall on their right-hand side as a guide.

Nerves were jangling.

❧ ❧

Where are they? The assassin was getting very impatient. He badly needed to relieve himself despite not having drunk water for a very long time. His mouth was dry and his head ached from dehydration. Damn, he should have taken some water off one of the other two but he felt, in his arrogance, that this would have shown a flaw on his part.

Have they found another route? How can they? There is no other way, I am certain of it.

He could hear the faint rustlings coming from his two companions and a muted cough.

Damned undisciplined fools!

There was a faint *clink!* as a Darkling blade gently struck a rock and a shuffle as the malefactor shifted position.

I shall skin them if they have alerted the surface rats!

Both Silmar and Jasper stopped and stiffened at the sound. A faint chitter came from Sushi and her claws dug gently into Jiutarô's shoulder.

"Metal!" breathed the elf into the dwarf's ear.

"Døkkálfr?" replied the elf.

"Aye, gotta be."

Silmar gathered the group around him. "Døkkálfr ahead, maybe. Total silence now. Billit, can you make magical light?"

"Aye!"

"Immediate?"

"'Ow 'bout this? I can make ready the *Radiance* spell 'n' hold it 'til you say *Lightson!*"

"Good. Ready everyone?"

Each of them reached instinctively for their weapons, slowly withdrawing them to avoid any scraping sound. They crept forward at a snail's pace in silence, still using the wall as a guide and taking care not to scuff the ground. Unfortunately, this was made almost impossible due to the scattering of old armour and bones.

There was a whistling sound. Falcon grunted and the party stopped.

"Lightson!" murmured Silmar.

A small ball of light appeared in Billit's hand and momentarily, the group was illuminated. He flung it forwards and it hovered above the scene. They saw two Darklings, one to the left, the other to the right, huddled behind pillars of hewn rock. *Two of 'em?*

Silmar heard rather than saw the light crossbows in the hands of the pair of Døkkálfar warriors as bolts were released almost by instinct rather than aimed purposefully. *They've hit Falcon! But, which one is the assassin?*

But the giant Barbarian was on his feet, apparently unhurt. He had been hit – a bolt jutted out from his left hip. Seeing the pair of Darklings, he charged. But not straight at the Darklings; he collided with the pillar itself and struck it hard with his right shoulder. Some debris fell from the top of the pillar as it moved, grating against the ceiling. He pushed again with all his strength and more movement was evident as one of the great stone sections slid a little to one side. With an ear-splitting yell, the barbarian took his great war-hammer and struck the displaced stone with all of his might. It shattered to small pieces. The top sections of the pillar crashed down, followed by massive boulders from the roof of the chamber. The two Døkkálfar squinted upwards in the glare in horror. One of them leapt to the side but the other had no chance to escape as the rocks struck him and crushed him to pulp.

Billit and Jiutarô rushed forward looking for an enemy but all they saw was Falcon falling, retching and twitching, to his knees. Jiutarô dropped beside the warrior just as the man fell to his side. There was no sign of the claret-wing dragon. He looked over and saw Silmar circling the Døkkálfr that had survived the rock fall, each wielding a drawn sword. Neither was making any attempt to open with an attack.

Taura moved around to find a better target, her lips moved as she chanted a prayer. There was no sign of the Darkling assassin. He had not been one of those either crushed under the rocks or in melee with Silmar.

With a lunge, Silmar drove the point of his rapier at the Darkling's chest. The dark elf avoided the attack by a whisker's width and countered with a swing at Silmar's neck.

The elf was ready for this and deflected the attack with the cross-guard of his weapon. Instead of replying with another swing or lunge from his blade, Silmar kicked out with his foot, connecting it with the Døkkálfr's kneecap. The Døkkálfr flinched with pain but did not cry out. There was a flash of movement and the Døkkálfr dropped to the ground with Sushi's tail wrapped about his head. The little dragon had released the stricken Døkkálfr by the time he hit the ground and she glided back towards Jiutarô. The Døkkálfr was clearly dying, albeit slowly and in acute agony, while twitching and clutching at his neck. He expired almost immediately.

"You have something I want, white elf!"

The voice was harsh and bitter. Silmar looked to his left. The Døkkálfr assassin stood just behind Taura, his scimitar across her throat and his hand clutching a handful of her hair. A trickle of blood ran down her neck where the blade had made contact. Her staff clattered to the ground.

"Give it to me immediately, now! No counting to three or any other dramatic action to give you time."

Silmar knew he had no time to bluff or try to rescue the Priestess.

Suddenly, Taura disappeared from sight! The Darkling's face showed surprise, but that expression turned to shock as he looked down to where a small dagger jutted out from his right thigh.

With a grunt, the Darkling took hold of the dagger, pulled it out from the muscle of his thigh and threw it at Silmar.

The elf easily dodged it.

A smiling Taura was standing right behind him. "What did he do with my dagger?" she asked.

Billit's conjured light began to fade. Under cover of the deepening darkness the assassin staggered behind pillars and rubble and was gone!

"Damn, he's gone. What did you do, Taura?" asked Silmar.

"Ah, well, that was easy. I could say I let myself get captured by him on purpose but that would be a small lie and Neilea would not be happy with me. He was behind me before I knew it, but I managed to draw my dagger and stab him in the leg. But then something else happened and I changed places somehow."

"That was me doing a *Secret Jump* spell on you, girlie," called Billit. "I was looking at that one when after I got woke up earlier! I didn't think I could do it yet! Taura, come and 'ave a look at this Barbarian, will you? I think he got poisoned by this bolt."

"Falcon!" she cried and rushed to his side.

Sushi sat atop the Barbarian's prone form and licked at his face but then took off from his chest. Almost immediately she gave a shrill cry and settled back down onto the ground next to him. Falcon was lying there with two small crossbow bolts sticking out the side of his chest next to his left armpit. Silmar listened carefully to the Barbarian's breathing. It was very shallow indeed.

Then Billit called out excitedly. "Falcon is still breathing. It might be venom. What did my cousin the gnome Sage say about venom?"

"I have it!" replied Taura. With a little rummaging inside a small pack on her belt, she held aloft the three glass phials.

Billit held out his hand. "Trickle some down Falcon's thro—"

"I know what to do," replied Taura sharply.

Within a while, Falcon's breathing began to improve.

The Priestess of Neilea went over to Billit and kissed him on top of his head. "I'm sorry," she said. "I was very worried. He has been saved from a probable painful death."

"It's alright," the gnome replied. "I do understand, missie."

Taura looked pensive. "How did she know?" she pondered. "The Chthonic Gnome soothsayer, I mean."

Silmar smiled. "Amazing, isn't it?" he replied. "She's a sage, how can the likes of us explain this?"

Taura looked doubtful. "Whatever. I expect Falcon will be asleep for a long time while the poison leaves his body."

"We are now stuck between Grey Dwarves on one side and the Døkkálfr on the other," said Silmar. "I don't know where the Grullien are but they are probably ahead of us somewhere. May the god's help us if a force of either one of them comes this way. The Grullien patrol around the tunnels looking for slaves from Chthonic Gnomes and Grey Dwarves."

"What do they use slaves for?" Falcon asked.

"Aye, yer right about the Grullien bein' ahead of us," admitted Jasper. "They use 'em to dig their mines fer the silver that they crave. That bastard Darkling may've gone off to the Grulliens. That light spell of Billit's was ideal; it really blinded those Darkling. We may be able to use that against the Grullien too. Should imagine they don't like bright light either. The Chthonic Gnomes say you can smell their City of Shade long afore you get there. Real bad too! Trouble is that we 'ave to go through the Grullien city to get to the end o' this tunnel."

It was a long time before Falcon woke up. For what seemed like ages, he was drenched in sweat but eventually he shivered. He had thrashed about for a while suffering from nightmares. When he did awaken, he was still cold.

Taura walked over to Silmar and whispered something in his ear. The elf nodded and spoke quietly to the others. They went a few paces down the passage, leaving Taura alone with a recovering Falcon.

In the dark, Taura slipped beneath the blanket and cuddled Falcon in her arms to give him the warmth of her body. She gasped as his coldness touched her warmth for, under blankets, he was naked, and soon after so was she. Long after, when both of them were warm, he awakened fully.

"What do you think they are up to?" whispered an exhausted Jasper.

"Use your imagination," laughed Silmar, also quietly. "I'll keep watch for a while. You and Sushi next, Jiutarô?"

"Hai! You wake me. *Domo arrigato!* Um, thank of you."

A smiling Silmar stood guard in silence, thinking of a very beautiful young human lady in Westron Seaport, not for the first time, either. He was fully aware of the warnings his father had given him over the years. For an elf to have a relationship with a human there would be consequences to consider. These could be bitter-sweet; wonderfully joyous and then tragic. The human partner would grow old and die while the elf would still be relatively young. Offspring would, of course, be half-elven but while their features would show the signs of both races, their traits would favour only one and, should that be human which was most likely, the day would come when the elven parent would be the one to bury their partner and, eventually, their own offspring. Many elves had found this hard to bear in the past. Silmar was resolved to take this in his stride and see what would happen.

Sometime later the companions were roused and they moved on, again in silence. Nothing was said to either Falcon or Taura.

They continued walking for a few hours. For the most of it, there was some dim light emanating once again from the mould-growth on the smooth walls of the tunnel. There was a smell of dampness now, which they had not really perceived before. Having tried the water which had settled in pools in some places, it was found to be bitter and undrinkable; they now had almost none to share and were urgently looking to fill up their empty water-skins.

After trekking for another hour in silence, Billit gave a sniff and said "Choddin' reeks down 'ere now, like something crawled 'ere an' died!"

It was a powerful, pungent, smell of decaying matter.

"Silence!" whispered Silmar. "Hide!"

There was insufficient cover; nowhere for them all to hide. Billit seemed to disappear from Silmar's dark-vision. Within a few heartbeats, they could clearly hear the sounds of shuffling & rattling.

It was too late. Before them, in the dim light from the mould on the walls, they could see Shade Gnomes, the dreaded, cruel, Grullien; probably almost twenty of them not thirty paces away from the group of adventurers and every one of them armed and ready to fight. They spotted the companions straight away.

There was a moment of surprise, silence, disbelief.

Inevitably, accompanied by much yelling, the war-band of Grullien moved to engage the companions. Each of them suddenly felt a warm glow envelop their bodies. *Very strange*, thought the elf as he reached for one of his blades. In the other hand, he held the leather tube, its cap was loose enough to be flicked off with his thumb.

"Ready light-tubes," Jasper yelled at the top of his voice. "*Lightson*, NOW!"

Three beams of light streaked into the Grullien and with roars and gasps, many of them surged about blindly. A couple of them dropped their short-swords; they clattered to the rock floor as they raised their fists to their eyes.

The Shade Gnomes were horrible to look upon being virtually identical to the six they had vanquished earlier. Arrows streaked repeatedly from both Jiutarô and Silmar and immediately three Grullien fell to the floor. Two writhed in pain. Billit reappeared to the right side of the tunnel with a blindingly white glow on his hand and he yelled "Hit the Floor!"

They needed no further prompting and, as one, they dived head-first to the ground. There was a very loud *Whoomph! A Fire-Blast* cast by the little mage into the tightly-packed cluster and immolated many of the Grullien. The companions felt the heat from the blast as it seared across the backs of their heads and necks. When they lifted their heads, the majority of the Grullien were dead. Billit leapt about in triumph, laughing at the top of his voice.

Jiutarô and Silmar were next to leap to their feet. The surviving ten or so Grullien were totally disorientated by the blast and it looked like all of them were suffering from effects from the heat and flame. Wisps of smoke curled up from the clothing and armour of many of them, including that of the largest of the Shade-Gnomes who stamped forward shaking his barbed spear and yelling commans at the top of his voice. His face was badly seared by the flame but it did little to reduce his ferocity. On the contrary, he screeched his commands to the surviving Grullien and they gathered around him. He pushed them aside.

Arrows from Jiutarô & Silmar continued to streak into the remaining Grullien, including the leader, and two more of them fell. The leader, however, stumbled forward with two arrows protruding from his body but still, he did not fall.

A sing-song voice tore through the dimness – it was Billit again calling arcane phrases. A moment later, a very bright ball of light, centred itself on the Grullien leader; it lit up the tunnel. The surviving Grullien, now eight in all, were once again blinded for a few seconds. Even the companions blinked against the brightness of Billit's latest magical spell. This was all the time that Sushi needed to play her part in the battle. She darted forward and attacked the Grullien leader with her deadly tail sting and with bites from her needle-sharp teeth. The leader slumped to the floor with part of his throat torn out, his life-blood ebbing away and did not move again.

"Forward, my friends!" shouted Jasper. He, together with Silmar and Jiutarô, charged forward and took the fight, hand-to-hand, to the remaining Grullien. Swords, spears and an axe whirled in a confusion of movement in the now brightly lit tunnel. Jiutarô found himself besieged by two Grullien but a flurry of sword-swings cut through their weapons and despatched them before they could score a single strike with their barbed spears and short-swords.

The great Barbarian, who limped as he stepped between two Grullien, whirled his great warhammer with a single hand and both fell at his feet. With a curse, he immediately staggered to his knees in pain but using his warhammer as a crutch he slowly pulled himself up again. Taura rushed over to him.

The fight over and in less than two minutes all of the Grullien were dead and there were no injuries to the companions. Falcon still moved stiffly from his previous injuries and he examined one of the deep cuts that had torn its stitches. Taura was soon giving him attention.

"Was that warm feeling we had something to do with you, Taura?" asked Silmar.

"Aha, I asked Neilea to hold you all in her favour and give you all strength!" she replied. "I am pleased that you noticed it. I'm pleased she heard me in these tunnels."

"Well, that sure 'elped me, I was buzzin'," replied Jasper.

"What in the seven hells of the Void are we going to do with this little lot?" she asked. "If another force of Grullien stumble on these bodies, we may have a complete city of them after us."

"Wait a moment!" exclaimed Jasper. "Look! I got it! Trefanwe! She told us what to do! The dark dwarf weapons an' armour that she told us to bring. Drop 'em 'ere! Haha! It'll make it look like they done it."

"Hai!" exclaimed Jiutarô. "I have idea!"

He haltingly described a plan which, despite his language difficulties, seemed absurdly simple.

For a little while they looked at each other and one or two additional ideas were put forward. Although impractical, one idea led to another and then another.

"Lookit!" said Billit. "We need to work out 'ow to do it? Cerianath told me that I can move with a bit of invisibility. I thought I was just clever at 'iding and blendin' in but it looks like that is what it's all about with us gnomes. We're really good at doing it, that's all. So it makes sense if someone needs to go forward and yell swear-words at the toothy shits, then it's gotta be me! Well, 'ow far is it to their city?"

The others shrugged. "Won't be far off," pondered Silmar. "I don't believe they will have come far."

"I have these Grey Dwarf arrows," said Falcon. "They might be helpful. What is Grey Dwarf word for *run?*" suggested Falcon.

"I think their word for run will be *kra'kth!*" said Jasper.

"Krakth," echoed Billit.

"No, yer chod! Try it again. Krak'th! *KRAK'TH!*" The last word was almost a shout until Silmar shushed him.

"*Krrrak'th!*" tried Billit.

"Oh, shitty hells! That'll do, ya choddin' fool!"

"Look everyone," called Taura softly from a little way along the tunnel. "No wonder it smells so bad. There are all sorts of dead bodies dumped in this big chamber here. It's like a tomb. Ugh!"

Once more, the companions strode forward along the tunnel. The smell was intolerable for a while. They were totally silent now and, for once, even the young, giant Barbarian's footfalls were gentle.

The smell became slightly more bearable quite soon but the air remained stale - there was no ventilation. They had been walking for a little while and were aware of dull sounds of life ahead.

"We must be getting close to the city," whispered Silmar. "We need to find a hiding place."

They had noticed a few suitable places on the way, mainly small chambers and ledges. One ledge, however, caught Silmar's eye. A raised projection on the left side of the mine tunnel was at a height a little above Falcon's head and looked ideal. The elf nimbly leapt, caught the edge of the ledge and easily swung himself up.

"Come," he whispered. "I'll help you up."

Soon, all those except for Billit had climbed, or been hoisted, up onto the ledge and the elf jumped back down. In his hand he held two black arrows that had been taken from the Grey Dwarves. Silmar and Billit silently walked along the tunnel towards the City of Shade, the lair of the Grullien.

It was a while before Silmar returned alone to the ledge with his companions.

"Lightoff, now Billit!" hissed Silmar. "Crouch. Are those weapons ready!"

They could hear the faint sounds of voices and movement ahead. Once their eyes grew accustomed to the pitch darkness, they could both detect an increase in the light level ahead of them. It seemed to indicate that they were close to the centre of life, perhaps even the City of Shade itself. Silmar and Billit crept forward silently until a narrow opening allowed them to see the entry into the city. It was wide enough for three large men to walk side by side and as tall as a hill giant.

The pair could plainly see three Shade Gnomes, dreaded Grullien armed with barbed spears, short-swords and picks. They were standing guard a few paces beyond the opening. Flanking the arched doorway were two wide pillars and the entry itself was framed by a plain carved arch. The guards appeared to be taking little interest in the archway but were talking amongst themselves.

That is the nature of guards everywhere, thought Silmar, particularly when they would have been standing guard day after day for years or even decades.

Carefully, they inched a little closer to the entrance. Silmar wielded his bow and held in his right hand the two arrows taken from the Grey Dwarves earlier. The pair now had a slightly clearer view of the city. Although dimly lit, they could make out small, circular huts that appeared to be made of stone slabs. Each structure had a roughly hewn wooden door and an open window but there was no roof on any of them. It would hardly be necessary underground. The road from the tunnel led straight through the city but they were not able to see much further than a few hundred paces or so.

Silently, Silmar nodded to Billit who nodded back. The elf nocked an arrow, shorter than he was used to, into his bow, aimed it and released it. The second arrow quickly followed the first. There was a loud scream followed by an unintelligible word of alarm. With an evil-looking grin the elf nodded again at his companion.

The gnome mage winked back and shouted, at the top of his gravelly voice, a harsh *"Krrrak'th! Krrrak'th!"*

Then the pair took to their heels and bolted back down the tunnel.

They almost ran straight past their companions' hiding place, the ledge on their right-hand side of the tunnel. Jasper hissed "Here, you chods!"

Silmar hoisted the gnome up towards the ledge and Falcon lifted him the rest of the way. Before they had a chance to offer a lift to the elf, he had already nimbly climbed up unaided.

Nothing happened for a long time then gradually a noise cane from the direction of the Grullien city. It grew louder and louder.

They were coming in great numbers.

"Keep still," whispered the little gnome mage. "Wanna try something!" He mumbled and his hands weaved a series of complex moves. A faint blue glow flared and then died down. "Guess what, I think we are now invisible."

Perhaps sensing a magical field, the cleret-wing dragon nervously chattered. Jiutarô gently held his hand over her snout to calm her down. Within a few heartbeats a group of about a hundred Grullien, all of them heavily armed, rushed by along the tunnel, their feet clunking loudly on the rock floor and their voices screeching war chants.

"Hee hee! Now the fun begins!" whispered Billit as the tail-end of the army of Shade Gnomes passed by.

"Wait a while, some of them will come back in a bit," replied Jasper.

"They be mad," muttered Jiutarô.

"They will be more than a bit pissed off!" added Silmar.

"Oh, do shut up, you silly men!" hissed Taura.

"Er, I'm a gnome!"

"And I'm an elf!"

"Oh aye, an' I'm a choddin' dwarf! You mind who you is callin' men!" Taura was puzzled. "So what?"

"It's like this, human girlie! We're not men like human men!" replied the dwarf with a chuckle.

"Well, you're all males!" she whispered forcefully. "It's the same thing! So just shut up!"

"Hmmmph!" the three non-human males all went, in unison.

After a long period of silence, they heard a commotion along the tunnel. There were high-pitched shouts of alarm and anger.

"Ooh, them find bodies!" hissed Jiutarô.

A while later, five Shade Dwarves rushed by the hiding-place heading back towards the city.

This plan's developing very well, thought Jasper. "The big bunch of 'em will be along in a while," he whispered.

"Er, oh shit! Our hiding spell's worn off now," moaned Billit. "Couldn't hold it any longer. Not done it before. I'm quite, er, pleased with myself that I done it, though!"

"Can you do it again for when the main force comes along?" asked Silmar. "They might have mages with them, or priests. We must remain hidden."

"Well, aye. But I must 'ave time to prepare for it. I can't just turn on an *Invisibility Cloak* spell over six people and a miniature dragon like a, a water pump, you know!"

It must have been a full hour before the approach of a massive force of Grullien could be heard advancing from the city. Billit had just had enough time to prepare for, and cast, the *Invisibility Cloak* spell. So large was the force that it took almost an hour for it to march past.

The leading Grullien had been bristling with weaponry and their fury was deeply etched on their faces. In the lead had been larger and more heavily armed fighters of the species. These wore a variety of armour parts and wielded a collection of spears, swords and picks, and each of them held a round, battered shield. At the rear of the vanguard followed what seemed to be their battle-wizards or clerics. These were dressed in cloaks and each held a staff.

The main force though, was not so well protected. As they marched, their voices were raised in unintelligible war-chanting and the leaders were beating their shields with their spears in rhythm. More clerics or magic-users followed the tail of the army. As they passed, one of the cloaked Grullien paused momentarily, glancing up at the ledge upon which the companions were hiding. The Shade Gnome then looked away, seemingly satisfied.

The companions could now breathe a little easier.

Silmar puffed the air out of his lungs. "The city must have emptied itself of Grullien," he whispered.

"Hey, that was almost too easy!" whispered Billit. "I have to dismiss the invisibility now. I'm worn out!" With a single word and a brief flick of his hand, Billit dispelled the *Invisibility Cloak*. He was clearly shattered and running with sweat.

"It has served its purpose, Billit," replied Taura. "Well done. My heart was in my mouth when that mage, or whatever it was, looked up."

Suddenly, the beating and chanting stopped. The Shade Gnome army had reached the dead bodies. Suddenly there were new shouts of fury. "*Gabbrabba! Gabbrabba!*"

"Any idea what they are saying, Billit?" Silmar asked.

"Not sure," he replied. "Think it might mean kill, kill, or somethin'."

The sound of the army disappeared after quite a long time. The companions waited but there were no more shouts from the direction the Grullienn army had taken, nor any sounds from the direction of the city.

The group dropped off the ledge and carefully made their way towards the City of Shade.

They walked along the tunnel in complete darkness. There was a vestige of light here and there from little pockets of mould growth on the walls but to the humans, it was not enough to see by. The companions still needed to hold onto those blessed with dark vision. After a while the light grew. They were approaching the arched entrance to the city.

With weapons drawn, they inched towards the opening. At the arch, Jasper, Billit and Silmar, each using as much cover as they could, glanced in. Not ten paces away stood two Grullien guards. The bodies of the two killed earlier lay where they fell, each with a dark dwarf arrow protruding from their body. Twenty paces beyond them was a narrow bridge crossing what appeared to be a deep chasm. Two more guards stood on the bridge.

In a low voice, Silmar described what he could see to the others.

Judging by the waving of arms and coarse voices, the two guards were arguing over something.

The portal at which the three now stooped was at the top of a slope that gradually dropped as it crossed the bridge. From their vantage point, a little deeper in the tunnel, they could see across much of the city although, because of the dimness, it was difficult to see detail. Light throughout the city was provided by glowing globes placed atop poles across the city. Although termed a city, it covered little more than an area no larger than that of an average market township up on the surface, but the small, round structures were densely packed. These appeared to be constructed from stone blocks that were roughly laid in circular rows. The Grullien guarding the tunnel entrance and those at the bridge had yet to notice the companions, who, by now, were making little attempt at using the cover and darkness of the tunnel mouth.

The attention of the Shade Gnomes was centred on the few goings on across the city and they were gruffly babbling away in their own language. The city itself seemed almost deserted. There were very few Grullien about, except for a group in the city centre. There was no sign at all of the slaves that were reputed to be in the city.

"By the smaller gods!" whispered Jasper. "The city is nearly deserted but there's still too many fer us to fight."

"No, look!" breathed Taura. "Most of them are unarmed. Mind you, that group in the centre there look like they may have weapons. They're too far away for me to see. What do you think, Silmar?"

"There are about twenty of them and they *are* all armed," replied the elf. "One of them is huge, for a gnome; about the same size as you, Jasper."

"Eh? What you sayin'? I'm fat or somethin'? I'll 'ave you know –"

"Wait, there is another one though," continued Silmar. "He looks like a mage or something. That group. Maybe they're the females."

"Them guards are young, sort of children," whispered Billit as he peered through squinted eyes. "Look at how they 'old their weapons."

"We still won't manage 'em all on our own," whispered Jasper. "We could use an army; there may be more hidin' in the huts." He patted his war-axe. "C'mon, let's get out there an' see how it goes!" he growled. "Are you ready?"

They stepped out of the tunnel and made their way straight towards the two Grullienn guards. The Shade Gnomes turned and, with their mouths agape, dropped their weapons in terror as the strange shapes approached them. They fled shrieking across the bridge. The other two bridge guards saw the two approaching and did the same, this time taking their own weapons with them.

Laughing, the companions stopped at the bridge and looked across the city. They could see it all a little clearer now. It stood at a crossing where each road led to four tunnels that opened into the city. As with the entrance through which they had come, the other three portals were each flanked by two pillars that held a carved lintel. At the centre, where the four roads met, was an amphitheatre around which were rows of benches, roughly hewn from rock. Its surface, however, was polished smooth by countless years of use, or probably by Grullien artisans and their slaves. The chasm, across which the bridge spanned, stretched from one side of the city to the other. There was just the single bridge across it.

The area to the side of the chasm at which they had entered the city was narrow, probably no more than thirty paces at its widest place but it stretched two or three hundred paces each side. Amazingly, the rock roof over the city's cavern was not supported by pillar or any other means. The entire city was on the far side of the bridge, the area of which was divided into four quadrants by the four roads. The two closest quadrants to their left and right each had a large number of circular but roofless huts, each with its narrow doorway. It appeared that the two quadrants furthest away from them also just had the huts but there were also some significantly larger structures.

"Where are these slaves kept, do you reckon?" called Falcon.

"Behind – you look!" replied Jiutarô.

Sure enough, the cavern wall to the left of the tunnel entrance had dozens of cells hewn from the rock. Across these had been fitted crude, but strong, iron bars and doors. Grim faces peered at them through the bars.

"There is our army!" said Silmar.

"Then let's get the poor sods out!" growled Jasper.

"Look what I can see!" yelled Taura. She was rattling a gate, about five feet in height and three wide, that had bars too close even for them to stretch an arm through. She shone her light tube through the gaps. "This chamber is full of Grullien weapons and shields! It's locked, though, and I can't get in."

"Can't get these cells open to release the captives, either," called Billit. He had trotted over to one of the cells.

"Wait," called Silmar. He dropped his pack off his shoulders, opened it and rummaged inside. "I knew these would come in handy one day," he said with a grin. In his hand, he held up a number of long, thin keys on a ring.

"Lock picks!" exclaimed the dwarf. "You little devil, elf! Mah bruvver 'ad some once. Had to give 'em away 'cos 'e needed to 'ands to use 'em."

While Silmar started work on the crude locks, Falcon used his considerable strength to lift the gate of the weapon store right off its hinges. His muscles bulged with the strain but he also succeeded in tearing open the wound in his leg. With a screech of tearing metal, the gate came away and the store was open. He flung the gate to one side. By this time, the elf had opened the first cell and a dozen captives gingerly poked their heads out of the cell.

Silmar pulled open the cell door. "You are free, come out and take up arms against these Shade Gnomes!" he called. "It is time to avenge yourselves."

The captives were gaunt and clearly undernourished. They were also filthy and covered in body-waste. Looking into the cell, Billit noticed one figure hunched in a corner. He went inside and prodded the figure. It did not move. He prodded it again and the body toppled to the side. Leaning forward, the little mage knew that the figure would never move again. Taura looked at him and he shook his head.

Having opened the first cell, Silmar opened the other two very quickly. One cell had two dead inside, one of them having died some time previously. All the captives shuffled out of the cells and gathered together. The stink was overpowering.

Twenty-seven men and seven Chthonic Gnomes were offered arms and, although willing to fight, some would not be capable of battle such was their poor condition. Two Grey Dwarves stepped out from behind other captives. Jasper immediately readied his battleaxe but Falcon steadied his hand. The Grey Dwarves asked for weapons and swore a promise to Jasper that they would fight providing that they be allowed to leave afterwards. Their own condition was enough to show that they would not be too much of a threat to Jasper or anyone else if they reneged on their promise. The Chthonic gnomes looked at the armed Grey Dwarves with suspicion and contempt.

Suddenly, six well-armed Grullien stormed across the bridge. Nobody had seen them coming. Immediately the freed captives, under the command of one of them, rushed to meet them. Weeks and months of captivity, slavery and mistreatment had built up dormant ferocity in them which exploded in a whirl of frantic fury. The Shade Gnomes were quickly and thoroughly despatched by the freed slaves but at a cost. By the end of the fight, two men and a gnome lay dead. The weapons wielded by the dead Grullien were of a better quality than many of those that some of the freed captives held. Some of the rusty spears and swords were cast aside to be replaced by the better ones.

A shout came from further along the cavern wall. Arms reached out from behind another cell door that had been concealed around a slight corner. Silmar rushed across. After some effort Silmar finally opened the last cell and was astonished to find twenty stronger and fitter captives. These were clearly recent additions to the slave numbers. They were mainly human, a few Gnomes. Most were offered weapons.

A large number of Grullien, most of them armed, stood a hundred paces back from the far side of the bridge. They could clearly see that their captives were now freed and armed and they were becoming extremely agitated. A group of Grullien was still standing together in the amphitheatre a few hundred paces away.

"I think we are ready to confront them," called Silmar. "We are not after wiping them out or harming their females and young. We seek Døkkálfar, Darkling!"

"Darkling?" called an ex-captive, spitting the word as if it was vitriol. He was the one who had led the others in the fight against the six guards. "We saw damned Darkling here earlier; about eight or ten of them. They mocked and taunted us and encouraged the Shade Gnomes to treat us badly. Many of us have been beaten on the orders of Darkling. One passed through a few hours ago. Not seen him before but he was in a fury. I wanna tell you that these bastard gnomes take the occasional captive away and eat them, we think, so I have no problem in wiping out the whole bloody lot of 'em."

Other voices were raised in anger against the Shade Gnomes. Silmar and Jasper silenced them.

"We want to leave these tunnels and you will want to come with us," Silmar called.

The two Grey Dwarves shook their heads and made to move away. "Grullien go to attack our community," said one. His voice was thickly accented as he struggled with the Universal tongue. "We go now help our kin. We want to find why they make war."

"Aye, go forth and fight your enemy," said Jasper who turned to wink at the others.

With that, the Grey Dwarves turned back and disappeared through the entrance to the tunnel.

Jasper grinned. "We're better off without 'em anyway!" he muttered. "All the less to worry 'bout."

"Down to the amphitheatre, then," called Silmar. "Do not attack the unarmed Grullien unless they attack you first. We do not attack unarmed, females and the young. If we do, we are as bad as they are."

As they filed across the bridge, they prepared to do battle with the large group of Shade Gnome warriors on the other side. However, these gnomes rushed back to take up a defence of the amphitheatre. The companions and their new forty-strong army made straight for the circle in the centre of the city. There was no longer and need for stealth and hiding. They marched along the road towards the central arena. Unarmed Grullien, presumably females and adolescents, although it was difficult to ascertain which, were standing away from the amphitheatre in between a cluster of huts. They backed away in terror as the group passed. A few armed individuals fled into the arena as the band approached.

Without warning, a group of about two dozen Grullien charged out from amongst the huts on the right. The group of captives unleashed their fury as the Shade Gnomes charged in amongst them.

The six companions also set to with their weapons and skills.

Although the captives fought hard, ages of captivity, mistreatment and malnourishment had weakened them dreadfully. Spears jabbed and blades clashed, the roadway becoming slick with blood and dismembered limbs and heads. Nine men and two Chthonic gnomes died almost immediately but the Grullien were quickly overwhelmed by the companions and the remaining freed captives. Not one was left alive, such was the ferocity of the revenge of the captives.

Silmar and Jasper, followed by their companions, led the remaining thirty-three men and four gnomes straight to the amphitheatre. As they arrived, the group of Grullien drew together in a tight group. Meanwhile, more bands of armed Grullien that had dared to resist the companions' small army either bolted, not to be seen again, or were quickly dealt with by the released captives.

There was a sound of marching feet on the rock floor as they approached. An individual marched before them. Arrayed behind him was a force of twenty Grullien guards, larger than those they had seen. By the look of the weapons and armour, they were the elite of the city. The shortest of them stood at about five feet tall, a full foot taller than the average Shade Gnome. One standing amid the group, however, was no warrior. He looked elderly, wore a long cloak of a shiny black material and carried a black staff upon which he leaned heavily. However, one individual standing alone before them was the Døkkálfr assassin. He was dressed fully in black although his straw-coloured hair looked incongruous across his shoulders.

CHAPTER 24

"**O**NCE AGAIN, we meet. You thought that you could evade me by colouring your hair, you white-eyed, surface rat Ljósálfr!" He spat on the road. "So, it was easy for me to get you to follow me instead of me hunting you. The outcome of either is clear. You have something that belongs to me, white elf. You will give it to me immediately."

"Come and take it if you dare!" replies Silmar. "I do not parley with a child-killer."

The Darkling chuckled drily. "Bah! Mere humans! What care I for them? And you? Oh, a simpleton, weak Ljósálfr!"

He nodded slightly. Without warning, a blast of hot energy erupted from the old Grullien's staff. Silmar was blown off his feet and lay on the floor with a singed chest. Amazingly, he staggered back onto his feet brushing off the singed tunic. The old mage looked amazed. So did Silmar, truth be told.

He repeated the spell. Once again, Silmar was blown backwards and once again, he regained his feet and his composure. This time though, his head was badly bleeding from a deep wound above his left ear, clearly from his fall. He was clearly quite dazed.

For a third time, the mage prepared to hurl the spell at Silmar. With a shout, Taura hurled a large fist-sized rock and caught the mage squarely on the nose. The old Grullien howled in agony, dropped his staff and fell to his knees.

"Thought he would hurl a blast of heat or something like that?" chuckled Billit. "No imagination, these Grullien! I just blocked it dead easy!" He strode over towards the Grullienn mage and kicked away the staff. "You are a very naughty Shade Gnome!" he added at the top of his voice. "Don't do it again!"

Taura knelt beside Silmar and tended his injury.

"So, the Ljósálfr is wounded," spat the Darkling. "And he has a pet to help make him feel better. Such a pity as I had hoped to do sport with him. Is there no-one to play sword-fighting with me? It is time now, for you to give me what is mine." He gave a signal and the twenty guards fanned out across the amphitheatre.

A figure stepped forwards from among the companions.

"I play sword with you," responded Jiutarô in a very calm voice. His dead-pan face, with its dark, slanting, slitted eyes, gave nothing away to the Darkling. "You black devil! You give *me* something. I *shall* receive your death!"

The Døkkálfr chuckled without mirth. "You? I think not. You may have a nice pair of pretty blades in your pretty sash and you may be quite good with that odd little bow, but with a sword? I doubt you even know which end to hold it! I shall teach you tricks with the sword for you to take with you to your grave!"

Hardly understanding a word the Darkling had said, Jiutarô withdrew his katana but, this time, without the usual exuberant and confident flourish. He grasped the hilt with both hands and with the blade extended over the top of his head towards the head, not the weapon, of his foe in the classic Samurai position of readiness. This gesture, of course, was totally lost on the Døkkálfr.

The Darkling immediately attacked with a flurry of circular swings. Jiutarô met each of these with apparent clumsiness and took a number of small steps back.

"Jiutarô!" cried Taura in desperation.

Encouraged, the grinning Darkling repeated his attack with greater ferocity behind each stroke. A swing to Jiutarô's right flank was quickly followed by another to his left. Each was again blocked but without a counter stroke.

The Darkling was now laughing but there was no humour in his amusement. "You are now just moments away from death. You use the sword like a novice! Hah!"

Another set of co-ordinated swings, with deft footwork and an obvious mastery for the blade was resisted by Jiutarô. This time though, Jiutarô was much faster with the blocks, meeting each stroke at the top of its swing and each thrust with fresh air. He turned aside as a perfectly executed lunge passed him by a hair's breadth.

For the first time, the Darkling's face showed the faintest concern. *He toys with me, this strange-looking swordsman. Have I underestimated him?*

The dark elf took a step back and he recomposed himself. His last attacks had been too uncoordinated, culminating in what he had hoped would be the killing stroke. The expression on the strange one's face had not changed. The dark assassin's breathing was deeper now because of the brutality of his opening attacks and he now wished he had been more cautious, more disciplined, more controlled.

Jiutarô turned his upper body to the right to stand sideways on to his enemy and he raised his katana horizontally at head height, the blade-tip still pointing at his foe's eyes. Puzzled by this apparent disregard for protecting the lower body, the Darkling made a sweeping attack to the Samurai's hip and belly. But the swing was in the opposite direction to that which a right-handed swordsman would naturally take and therefore lacked proper strength and control he might otherwise have had. Jiutarô countered easily with a block just below the Darkling's sword's guard. He followed it up with a swift kick to the Darkling's knee.

The Darkling stepped back sharply, his lips stretched into a grimace of pain.

Jiutarô locked his gaze on his opponent. His foe took on a wide stance with the sword held up and to the right. The assassin looked deeply into Jiutarô's eyes but the expressionless Samurai exhaled sharply and charged forward.

As he perfectly executed each attack, he screamed the name of each one. '*Shomen Uchi*'; '*Kiri Age*'; '*Migi Kesa Giri*'; '*Hidari Kesa Giri*'; many more besides. Years of dedicated, rigid training and experience, and the ancient code of *Bushido*, the way of the warrior, all but obliterated any creativity that his consciousness might have initiated.

His opponent barely managed to deflect or block each successive attack, dancing it seemed in a travesty of the deft footwork of the Samurai. He was almost unaware that he was now fencing defensively.

Jiutarô's attacks, meanwhile, were purely a means to gauge the proficiencies and limitations of his opponent. At this moment he was collecting information of the best way of killing the Darkling. In moments he knew he had discovered that weakness, the dropping of the shoulder that opened the Darkling to a finish. But the assassin stepped backwards out of danger and delivered an impulsive, audacious attack, his sword circling that Jiutarô barely managed to avoid.

There it was again – the dropping shoulder.

The Samurai's blade whipped faster than sight and dark blood welled from a cut to the assassin's forehead. A pull-stroke brought blood to the Darkling's right shoulder. A similar stroke made on the opposite side deeply bit into the left shoulder.

A look of panic crossed the Darkling's face and he launched a desperate swing towards Jiutarô's head.

Jiutarô's sword whirled faster than before as he achieved the pure state of *Bushido*, the way of the Samurai warrior. He easily deflected a weak attack, stepped forward and removed the Døkkálfr's head in a series of swings that were too fast for the onlookers to see. The headless body dropped to the ground and shuddered as the head bounced across the ground.

Jiutarô closed his eyes and dragged his mind, spirit and body back together, bringing himself back to the reality of the moment. He exhaled sharply, swung his katana in a circle to rid it of the dark blood and, with his customary flourish, re-sheathed his sword.

Silence descended on the gathering as the black-garbed body had fallen to the floor. It was many heartbeats before anyone moved or spoke. Suddenly, the remaining Grullien guards made ready with their weapons just as their mage regained his feet. As one, the companions and freed slaves brandished their weapons and stepped forwards. Faced with this, the guards flung down their weapons and gabbled away incoherently.

Jasper gestured to them with his arm and shouted "Go!" More quietly, he added "While you can, you bastards!"

The guards wasted no time in rushing out of the amphitheatre.

Nobody noticed as four other dark, lithe figures very quickly disappeared through an archway in the cavern walls at the top of a slope at the far side of the city.

"Your swordplay is amazing, Jiutarô," said Taura. "Unconventional, I must say."

"That murdering Døkkálfr swine has been defeated in great style," said a slightly dazed Silmar. "Hopefully, this is the end of the danger to us. All that is left is to get us all out of this place, out of the damned Shadow World, into the world above and off to the east."

"Aye," replied Jasper. "With thanks to our released captives fer their aid. Oh, an' we still need to fill up our waterskins. My mouth is as dry as a snake's boll– er, testicles!"

One of the captives pointed to a raised pool. "Over there," he said. "Good water."

Their *army* of thirty-three men and three Chthonic Gnomes offered to show the way back to the surface world. One of the men had stepped forward as a leader. "It's less than a day's march and the floor surface is good. But a big force of Grullien guards the way to the surface. It may be a tough fight."

The remaining Grullien guards and citizens were clustered in a single frightened cluster. They made no move to take up the discarded weapons but stood there with much spitting and hissing in a last act of bravado. But they merely cowered and whimpered with terror when the newly armed and freed captives made as if to step forward to attack them.

"We need some answers here," growled Jasper. "We need to get the bastards talking." He strode over to a Shade Gnome who, from the quality of his clothing, was clearly a leader. He grabbed hold of the terrified Grullien's collar. "Why was the Darkling 'ere? What was he doin'? Why did he wait?"

There was no answer from the terrified Grullien.

Jasper continued. "Was 'e meetin' someone? Who? Where are they?"

There was still no response.

"Perhaps they don't speak Universal," suggested Taura.

"Aye, he does," replied one of the freed captives. "That piece of sheep dung has spent a month threatening me and the men. He speaks it good."

"So you understand me, do you? Well answer me or I'll fillet you!" He pulled out his dagger and waved it in front of the Shade Gnome's face.

Questioning and threatening the Grullien leader had no response. The gnome jerked his head up and hissed in a sneering way, baring his filed teeth.

"So you refuse to talk, won't speak in Universal," growled Jasper who held his sleeve to his nose. "By the Gods, 'e stinks!"

"He pissed himself!" exclaimed Falcon.

Billit stepped forward. "Watch this!"

The little gnome mage mumbled, made a series of hand gestures and fired a streak of lightening onto a group of dead Grullien. A loud crack sounded, a metallic smell hung in the air. The bodies of the Grullien had jerked as if some vestige of life remained. The Shade Gnomes jumped in fear, as did some of the ex-captives.

"Yiz, human. I spik, I tell you," grated the leader in a guttural voice. "Dere izza more Darkling, four go 'way when you group attack zity. You not be zo brave iffa my, ah, war-band here iz!"

"Get on with it, shit-face!" growled Jasper.

"Darkling zeek zpezzal artfact, izza great power and, um, potenzee. Izza holy. One of you have. Bring-a small god, make her big god! Zhe zit by our god zide. Den all humanz die, all-a elvez zuffer and die, all 'Thonic Gnomes die. Darkling and-a they alliez on-a top world will be toolz of your deztruction!"

"Allies?" shouted an angry Silmar. "Who?"

But the Grullien, in particular their leader, were by now far too terrified and refused to answer any more questions.

Taura stepped in front of the group. "We must leave. The Grullien army will come back, if any left the battle alive! Which way is it?"

"Where is way out?" roared Falcon, completely startling the Grullien, the captives and the group alike.

The trembling leader pointed a shaking hand, indicating a doorway at the top of a slope behind a pair of pillars. His expression showed he would be glad to be rid of troublesome humans, elf and the 'powerful' gnome mage. The freed slaves agreed this was the entrance through which they were brought in as captives.

A call from the side of the city through which they had entered gathered their attention. For a second they thought perhaps the Grullien war-band had returned but, to their astonishment, a large force of Chthonic Gnomes was rushing across the city to the amphitheatre.

Within a couple of minutes the gnomes arrived, shaking their heads in wonderment.

"It is good that you are still here," the Lord Cephod gave a rare smile. "We have seen much of your progress after your visit to us. Your ruse has had a large effect in these mines. Know then that the battle has brought many losses to both the Grey Dwarves and the Grullien? But a large number of Grullien return now with their dead and wounded. Together, we would be enough to fight them but under the circumstances, Trefannwe tells me that it is the will of Clambarhan that we spare the Grullien. It is to maintain balance, she says. It is advisable that we all take our leave of this foul-smelling place. We shall return to our haven by using paths hidden to others. We rejoice that you have reunited us with some of our lost ones. We grieve for those who will not return but offer you our heartfelt thanks once again for what has been achieved at this time."

Trefannwe pushed back the hood of her cloak and bowed respectfully to Taura. "Take with you these ropes. You will need them."

She spoke no further words of advice. The band of Chthonic Gnomes turned and made their way back out of the city.

Jasper addressed the surviving Grullien. "You would do well to return to your homes. We have no wish to fight you or kill you. We shall leave now. Do not follow because we shall fight you and kill you. Our gnome's powerful magic will destroy you."

The Shade Gnomes made no move to comply so Jasper shrugged and led the group towards the tunnel entrance.

The companions, with their small army, made their way up the slope, out through the pillars and into the arched doorway, leaving behind them the City of Shade. They also left behind them the small and bewildered group of Grullien.

The Grullien picked up their fallen weapons and, with much spitting and hissing, shook them at the backs of the freed prisoners in a final act of bravado. This only served to raise laughs from the band. The Grullien looked at each other and towards the tunnel entrance at the other end of the city, wondering if their war-band would return but knowing that if they did not, or if only a few should return, the hard work of rebuilding their city would have to be done by themselves until they could capture more slaves. Should none or few of the war-band return to the city, the population would take generations to recover. What would happen then? How vulnerable they would be, forever at the mercy of those terrible, foul Grey Dwarves, even the cruel, mysterious 'Thonic Gnomes who, it was said, could walk through rock as if it were smoke with their strange and powerful magic.

One Shade Gnome, the apparent leader, pushed his way forward to address the few that stood there. The Grullien language was guttural and coarse to the ear of any other race. Few spoke the Universal tongue except sufficient to taunt and insult the slaves. "Did not some of the freed slaves threaten to return to kill the young and the females? Does this not show how barbaric the humans are? So, they make war on the defenceless? Why do they complain if we make war on their young and females? Check our females, our young. If they have been harmed the humans will pay!"

"How, you old fool?" replied another. "There are scarce enough of us to mount an attack on a wagon, let alone a village!"

"Our war-band will return, then shall we decide the future," shouted yet another.

"Calm yourselves, the defenceless are unharmed," spoke a female from a nearby hut. "We shall grow strong again."

Good fortune, the old seer would be right.

CHAPTER 25

W ITH JASPER and Silmar in the lead, the band progressed through the passage. Both the elf and the dwarf carried their light-tubes and searched about them for traps and obstacles. With so many in the group now, and with the Døkkálfar assassin killed, they had little fear of attack. The freed slaves were in high spirits and the chatter between them grew in intensity, becoming louder than the companions were comfortable with.

After a while, the mighty Falcon growled, "Be silent! We have met many foul beings in this tunnel and would rather not meet more! From now you whisper."

This had an immediate and long-lasting effect on the freed captives. Taura moved in closer to the Barbarian in admiration of his strength and confidence.

After an hour or so, an awful smell became overpowering. The companions looked inside some of the small chambers on either side of the tunnel and found putrid waste products from the Grullien thrown into pits and long-dead Grullien laid in heaps. Other caverns contained only a single body, but with armour & weapons. There was very little else of value.

"These must be kings or leaders, priests or high-ranking Grullien," surmised Silmar. Some weapons were taken from these bodies by the freed captives but what armour there was to be found was useless for the humans.

Once the group had passed the chambers, they came upon a large cavern where the roof was held aloft by many pillars. They decided to rest for a short while and took the opportunity to pass round the waterskins.

"I ain't very 'appy about things right now," said Jasper. "Been thinking. What if the Grullien war-band returns an' sets out after us? We got these farmers at our back an' things may turn out nasty. Mayhap they will follow us to avenge the trick we played on 'em or they could warn others who may in turn come along 'ere after us! We will be in the deep an' sticky cack!"

Silmar nodded in agreement. "We don't know what else is down here. They said something about Darkling and their allies. *We* may get out of the mines and feel safe. Some of these farmers may split away and make their way back to their farms or communities. The problem may not just be with the Grullien. What if the Grey Dwarves annihilated them and start looking for revenge? How can we stop them? The answer is simple – we can't!"

"Hai. Stop them easy!" replied Jiutarô. "Learn much talk. Block tunnel. Bring it fall down. Big rock fall!"

"Hey yes!" said Taura. "But how?"

"Well, if you want my suggestion," said Billit. "We could try to pull down part of tunnel to slow them up for a few days. But the problem is how?"

"The rope!" cried Falcon, then he laughed, his deep voice reverberating along the tunnels. "*That* was Trefannwe's idea. We use the rope and many arms to pull these pillars! By the gods! Magic will not work but muscle-power will. We have enough people and enough rope? Aye, because Chthonic Gnome sage said to take them! How did she know? Shall we pull down some pillars?"

"But we will need to pull down many of these pillars to make the tunnel blocked enough," said Silmar.

"Now, look," said Billit. "If you want a solution to this problem then think back to your childhood. Did any of you ever play the bones? You know, where you match up the ends and try to use up all your bones before your opponent?"

They all nodded but were still puzzled.

"Well then. What else did you do with the bones?"

They looked at each other still puzzled.

"Gods! You are all hopeless! Look. You stood 'em all up side by side…"

"And you pushed the end one to knock them all down!" finished Silmar. "That's what we can do to these pillars! One falls onto the next and knocks it down onto the third and so on! Hah!"

Billit, having a better understanding of the task, took charge. Three long lengths of rope were secures at points up the pillar that was furthest away from the doorway out of the chamber. The pillar appeared to be in four sections. The top was out of reach for the upper rope but Billit did not seem to think that mattered. He was sure that when pulled, the pillar would collide with the next nearest causing them to collapse in a direction towards the escape route. Hopefully, the roof of the chamber would crash to the floor, sealing this part of the Shadow World. The gnome arranged for men to take hold of the ropes, instructing them to release the ropes once the pillar started to collapse.

"Start running as soon as pillar starts to collapse! Start to pull!"

It too them quite a while and much tugging before the sections of the pillar started to show signs of movement. At first, dust floated down from the top, then pieces of rubble.

"Easy lads," called Billit. "Rest a bit."

The men dropped the rope and wiped the dust from their faces. This was not as easy as they had thought it might be.

"Once more then. Pull!"

This time, the men put everything into it. The top section didn't move but the next did. The lower three sections of the pillar started to slide and then lean outwards. One more pull and it began its fall.

"Run!" screamed Billit. "Run for your lives! Get outa here!"

The men didn't need telling twice. They started running as the first pillar crashed into the second. For a couple of heartbeats, nothing happened. Then the top section crashed down onto the pieces below it and the second pillar leaned towards the third. By this time all of the men had run out of the chamber into the tunnel and they all kept going.

Jiutarô stayed back to chivvy some stragglers and they too, raced for the archway.

"Run. Don't stop here! Run on!" screamed Billit as they funnelled into the tunnel.

They heard a deep rumbling and the ground beneath their feet trembled as massive amounts of rock fell downwards, not only in the chamber but along the tunnel behind them. Fortunately, the companions and their army were well clear of the falling rock.

There was a loud cheer as a cloud of dust poured along the tunnel. After what seemed a long time the crashing and rumbling ceased. There was so much dust that, even using the light-tubes, they could see very little. But there were no casualties. There was a lot of coughing and spluttering until the dust settled.

Silmar eventually found Billit and embraced him. "Well done, my friend. You did well."

Billit beamed with pride, especially when Taura kissed him on his forehead. Luckily, in the gloom nobody could see him blush.

Waterskins, now full, were passed around again and the group were soon on their way.

Except for one.

They had been walking in the tunnel, using the light-tubes, for a few hours when Silmar softly called "Stop! Stop!"

"What is it?" whispered Billit.

"Have you found somethin'?" breathed Jasper.

"Oh aye, by the gods!" gasped Silmar. "Boot prints, unless I'm much mistaken. Look! It's the damned Døkkálfar! There are many tracks here. There's Grullien, lots of them, look! Here's some human prints heading towards the Grullien city. Probably captives. One of these men here, hopefully. A few other prints I don't recognise. They are all quite old. But these boot prints are fresh and going in the same direction as us. There look! Some more. See how the edges are so sharp! There are more Døkkálfar out here somewhere. That Shade Gnome mentioned four of them."

Billit humphed. "I thought he was just bein' full o' shit," he said.

The men being led out by the companions were now visibly nervous. These were not soldiers, although some had been in the past, but in general they were farmers and young lads. A few of the older ones were ill with emaciation having been half-starved, beaten and badly treated for a long time. Although all were armed to some degree but few, perhaps six or eight at the most, had any experience with using weapons in anger. The adventurers knew that should battle occur, they would only be able to rely on limited support from the men.

The band moved forward in silence. From time to time, Silmar moved a short distance forward to examine the path ahead of them. The hours passed by and water was once again getting scarce. There had been no subterranean springs, waterfalls or pools from which to refill their waterskins. Some of the men were grumbling but a warning from Falcon kept them silent.

After a while one of them started to complain. "Hasn't yer got any water? I'm spitting feathers 'ere. We always had water back there with *them*!"

"Then choddin' well go back, idiot!" grated Jasper. "Else shut it and we'll find yer some soon."

The group walked on for another hour by which time there was no water left. Taura asked Silmar to stop the group. She stood at his shoulder for while and they spoke in silence. She then moved away and, with a light beam, looked at the path, the rocks and into cracks and pits.

"Found one!" she called.

Taura reached inside her tunic and brought out her sacred symbol of Neilea. Her hands weaved a complicated pattern around it, she called out a stream of complex words that no other could understand, and then she spat on the ground. The others slowly started to move towards her out of curiosity. As they approached, they could see a pit in the rock the size of a small barrel, slowly filling with water.

"Your drink!" she called angrily. "Use it sparingly. I cannot do this again; it taxes me too much."

The men eagerly crowded around it. Minutes later, using just their hands they had drunk a little each but there was still more than enough to fill three water-skins.

"Don't suppose you can magic up some bread!" one of the men called out.

"Don't push your luck!" replied Taura. "I am not a cook-house."

"Time to get out of this hell-hole!" whispered Silmar.

"Well, I like it here!" responded Jasper.

"You would, you contrary git!" retorted Billit.

The large group walked on with more confidence. It had been many hours since they had left the stinking Grullien city and they were now all hungry and tired. They had no idea of the time of day, or even of the day itself, nor even where they would be when they reached the surface world. They would not know what weather they could expect or whether there would be anyone waiting outside when they emerged. But every one of them was eager to step outside of the Shadow World no matter what awaited them.

The dwarf walked beside Silmar. "In all the excitement I forgot to ask. 'Ow's the burden? Have yer felt anythin' of it? I assume it's still there!"

"I can always feel its presence, Jasper. I feel the nasty taste of vomit in my mouth all the time. It's a bit like it's trying to remind me that it's still there.

I've not had any nausea or headaches since we confronted the Døkkálfr assassin and the Grullien so that's a good thing. At least I know if an evil *nasty* is close. I felt quite sick when the Døkkálfr was fighting against Jiutarô and, well, it was strange really. As soon as Jiutarô killed him the feeling went away and the Grullien were no real threat. So it has its uses really. I did check that the box was there a while ago, before the Grullien city and touching the box made me gag a bit. Oh, look out!"

The tunnel came to an abrupt stop. In front of them was a rock wall. There was no door or portal of any kind.

"Where do they go?" asked Jasper.

"They go up!" replied Silmar. "Where do you think they go?"

"Just choddin' askin'! No need for cheek! Mighta gone down. You goin' first, Falcon?"

The barbarian shuffled past Silmar and Jasper. "Aye."

The stairway, no more than steps cut into the rock, rose about sixty feet. There was much scuffling, and some moans and complaints, from behind as the large group in the middle of which the dwarf was chivvying the slower ones. "Keep the back ones moving, Juto," he called to the samurai. There was no reply from Jiutarô. None was expected.

At the top was a landing, about six feet wide and ten long, and in front of them was a circular boulder, rather like a very large grinding wheel, the width across it as great a man's outstretched arms. It had been rolled back to allow room for people to pass through the portal one at a time. However, in the space lay the body of a Grullien guard. It had evidently been killed by a single thrust of a narrow blade in the throat. Falcon stepped to the side to allow Silmar to see.

"Killed by Døkkálfar do you think?" asked Silmar.

"Could be," responded Falcon. The giant put his shoulder against the wheel and pushed it back a little further. He pulled the small body aside and tucked it into a corner, using his foot to cram it in.

Silmar bent down to examine the body, saying, "He hasn't been dead that long. The skin's cold, but then it would be anyway but it's still soft. They go all hard after a few hours. Watch out for Døkkálfar. Or for anything that might appear. I suppose there's no point in telling this lot to keep the noise down, is there?"

Behind him emerged the others, one at a time. It took quite a while for all the freed men to file out.

"There's five more bodies here," said Silmar softly. "They're all Grullien. There's been quite a fight but no other bodies. Better tell you that there's a lot more footprints here. Døkkálfar! Probably eight to ten of them. They kept horses in here too. There's dung and some oats somewhere, I can smell it. Be alert, they may still be around."

"I can smell it too, now you mention it," called Billit.

"Roll the stone back and close off the entrance," advised Jasper.

"We can't," replied one of the men. "You can only do it from the other side of the opening. It's behind this rock."

Falcon strode over to the stone and spat on his hands but, even with his great strength, he could move it no further than a hand's width. "Can you use magic?" he asked.

Billit gave him a har stare. "If only! What do you think I am, a battle-mage? It's far too 'eavy."

"Leave it, let's see where the cave entrance is," advised the dwarf.

The band made their way with Silmar and the group in the lead. The light grew slightly stronger and some distance ahead the mouth of the cave was clearly outlined.

Jasper had been walking amongst the freed captives. "Er, everyone, where's Ju-to?"

"Back there, isn't he?" replied Taura.

"Hey, Jiutarô!" Silmar called. He had to shout over the hubbub from down the steps.

"He's not here," cried Taura, with a tremor of panic in her voice. "Where can he be?"

"Shit!" exclaimed Jasper from below. "Shitty shit! He must 'ave bin in that big chamber when we brought it down. There's nothin' else for it. we choddin' well gotta go back and find him."

They called out for Jiutarô. They called Sushi, the little cleret-wing dragon. They waited for a few heartbeats. There was no response except for the echoes of their shouts from the long tunnel.

Their new friend, Yazama Jiutarô, the samurai sword-master, the strange man said by the gnome soothsayer to be from beyond the stars, lay beneath countless tons of rubble and boulders. One dust-covered hand poked out into the pitch darkness of the great cavern from between rocks and parts of a collapsed column. The skin was torn, a finger broken. The hand was unmoving.

The form of the little cleret-wing dragon lay close by, a ragged tear on the edge of one wing. It tried, unsuccessfully, to roll onto its feet called; she for her master with a cat-like mewling that turned into a pitiful wail of anguish.

WHAT NOW?

It seems Yazama Jiutarô, the intrepid samurai, is buried beneath countless tons of rock in the pitch darkness of the mines of the hazardous Shadow World. His little dragon, Sushi, would have sensed his thoughts had he survived but she, too, is trapped and believes herself alone. The tunnels are completely blocked and impenetrable from either direction. Even if the samurai lives, how can he possibly escape from beneath the rockfall and out of the tunnels? Can the companions do anything about it?

The answers will be found in Book 2 of **Far From Home**, now available.